"We are p   ,
   and v

The Herne said nothing, and for some long minutes they stood there, looking out at the moonlit landscape stretching out below them like a secret kingdom rendered in silverpoint. The only sound was the dogs cracking the bones of the hare as they continued to eat, unaware that their master's world had just become miraculously unbound.

The Sluagh collected the skeleton and the skull together and placed the parts back in the leather pack, then carefully rolled the flayed skin and held it in his hands.

"What will you do with him?" said the Herne.

"We will take him to the Scowles," said Badger Skull. "To the Shee. They will do what they can to restore his honour and put his parts to the long sleep."

"He was a Woodcock Crown," said the Sluagh.

"The Shee will mark his passing better than anyone," said the Sluagh. The Herne nodded.

"His house is north east of here?" he said. "This Mountfellon."

"The big ironstone mansion by Bowland's Gibbet, on the rising land before it drops to the fen country," said Badger Skull. "But he was not there. We were there, and if he had been too I would have killed him myself. He may be in London, he may be on the road between or he may have another rathole to hide in. Finding him will be a challenge for any hunter. You may have to sit and watch in the shadows. You may have to track him by his friends. But you are not just any hunter, brother. And that is why we came to you."

The Herne looked at the roll of cured skin for a long time. Then he hunkered down on his haunches next to the Sluagh.

"Tell me about this Mountfellon. Start at the beginning."

BY CHARLIE FLETCHER

The Oversight
The Paradox
The Remnant

THE STONEHEART TRILOGY

Stoneheart
Inkheart
Silvertongue

5/17

THE
REMNANT

CHARLIE
FLETCHER

www.orbitbooks.net

Copyright © 2017 by Man Sunday Ltd.
Excerpt from *Battlemage* copyright © 2015 by Stephen Aryan
Excerpt from *A Crown for Cold Silver* copyright © 2015 by Alex Marshall

Cover design by Lauren Panepinto
Cover illustration by Kirk Dou Ponce/DogEared Design
Cover copyright © 2017 by Hachette Book Group, Inc.

Orbit
Hachette Book Group
1290 Avenue of the Americas
New York, NY 10104
orbitbooks.net

Simultaneously published in Great Britain and in the U.S. by Orbit in 2017
First U.S. Edition: March 2017

Orbit is an imprint of Hachette Book Group.
The Orbit name and logo are trademarks of Little, Brown Book Group Limited.

The publisher is not responsible for websites (or their content) that are not owned by the publisher.

The Hachette Speakers Bureau provides a wide range of authors for speaking events. To find out more, go to www.hachettespeakersbureau.com or call (866) 376-6591.

Library of Congress Control Number: 2016960630

ISBNs: 978-0-316-27956-7 (trade paperback); 978-0-316-27958-1 (ebook)

Printed in the United States of America

LSC-C

10 9 8 7 6 5 4 3 2 1

For Jackmo and A-Girl from C-Dog
with all love, forever

DRAMATIS PERSONAE

THE OVERSIGHT

The Smith — *smith, ringmaker and counsellor*
Sara Falk — *keeper of the Safe House in Wellclose Square*
Mr. Sharp — *protector and sentinel*
Cook — *once a pirate*
Hodge the Terrier Man — *ratcatcher at the Tower of London, blinded*
Charlie Pyefinch — *apprentice ratcatcher*
Ida Laemmel — *huntress, mountaineer and member pro tem, from* Die Wachte *in Austria*
and
Emmet — *a man of clay*
Jed — *an Old English Terrier*
Archie — *a young Old English Terrier crossbreed*
The Raven — *an ancient bird*

IN LONDON

Francis Blackdyke, Viscount Mountfellon — *man of science turned supranaturalist*
The Citizen — *a sea-green incorruptible, thought dead*

A captive Sluagh — *an experimental subject*
A Green Man — *a similarly unfortunate captive*
Lemuel Bidgood — *magistrate and fount of local knowledge*
John Rogers Watkins — *owner of the steam-tug the* Monarch
William Ketch — *a Bedlam porter once a bibulous reprobate, now dry*
A whey-faced child — *a housebound invalid, given to watching the world from her window*
Ruby — *a rentable lovely with sharp eyes*

IN THE COUNTRYSIDE AND THEN LONDON

The Ghost of the Itch Ward — *formerly of the Andover Workhouse, real name unknown*
Amos Templebane — *adopted son of Issachar (mute but intelligent)*

THE TEMPLEBANES AND THEIR SERVANTS

Issachar Templebane Esq. — *lawyer and broker*
Coram Templebane — *adopted son, once a favourite, now much reduced*
Abchurch Templebane — *lustful adopted son, of considerable viciousness*
Garlickhythe Templebane — *adopted son, sharpshooter*
Vintry, Shadwell and assorted other Templebane sons — *adopted, variously talented, uniformly malevolent*
and
Dorcas — *a housemaid, accidentally beautiful and purposefully no coward*

ON THE CONTINENT OF NORTH AMERICA

Caitlin Sean ná Gaolaire — *a venatrix, from Skibbereen*
Lucy Harker — *a Glint and a lost girl, notionally her apprentice*
Obadiah Tittensor — *owner and master of* Lady of Nantasket, *out of Boston, Mass.*

IN PARIS

The red-faced man – *eminent merchant, fur trader, surprised*
Clothilde – *a biddable domestic*
The Wachman brothers – *Alps*

THE REMNANT

The Guardian – *first among equals in the Great Circle of The Remnant*
Prudence Tittensor – *wife of Obadiah, holder of secrets*
The bitch Shay – *a running dog of great accomplishments*
The dog Digger – *her offspring*
The Proctor – *an armed regulator*
Sister Lonnegan – *owner of an unbridled tongue*
F. Armbruster Esq. – *hunter, guide, trapper, prospector, mountain man*
Jon Magill Esq. – *the same*

IN THE HEBRIDES

A driver – *from Portree; owner of pony and trap, for hire*
Donald Ban MacCrimmon – *steward of Dunvegan Castle, not the piper his forefathers were*
Beira – *"Màthair nam Fitheach," very old lady living at the House at the End of the World*

RUTLANDSHIRE

A footman
Coachman Turner – *an unfortunate Phaeton*
The head gardener – *a poor man of fatally good intentions*

BETWEEN THE WORLDS

John Dee – *known as The Walker between the Worlds*
Two roundheads – *Mirror Wights, brothers*
A woodsman and a pussers mate – *Mirror Wights, unrelated*

BEYOND LAW AND LORE

The Herne – *a hunter, horned*
The Nose and the Sight Hound – *his bone dogs*
Badger Skull – *a Sluagh chieftain*
Hawk Skull – *a vengeful Sluagh*
Woodcock Crown – *an irreducible Sluagh*
The Shee – *wives to the Sluagh*

Geradeso wie unsere Leben aus dem Nichts entstehen
und im Nichts enden,
so sind alle Reisen ein Kreis.
Und ganz egal wie weit uns unsere Reise fuehrt—wir enden alle an unseren
Anfangen.

Just as our lives come from nothing
and end as nothing,
so all journeys are a circle.
And no matter how far the road takes us, we all end at our beginnings.

Carl Fleischl von Marxow

SNOW ON THE RIVER

In the end there is silence.

In the end she is in the water, but she cannot see the city.

In the end, at the very end, Sara Falk drowning in the Thames can see nothing but flame.

And failure.

And her hand, reaching, trying to catch the sky, trying to hold onto the air, trying to stop the growling river swallowing her too.

She is the last of the Last Hand.

She does not wonder if there will be another.

She does not wonder if one day The Smith will return and build anew.

Instead she wonders why the snow that is falling from the sky into the flaming river has come so early this year.

And she wonders when it will start to hurt.

And then she realises it already hurts. She realises it has always hurt. She realises it will never, ever stop hurting now, even if she alone survives this.

Because the others have not.

Because Sharp has not.

The Last Hand fallen. The Wildfire free.

No more hope.

No more heroes.

No more him.

FIRST PART

TRAVELLER'S TALES

Caelum non animum mutant qui trans mare currunt.

Those who run across the sea change the sky, not their soul.

Horace

On the Uncertain Mechanick of the Mirror'd World and its Illusory Potential

There are two ways in which the precise geometry of the mirror'd world may be accessed to effect a journey between widely separate physical locations: in the first, the traveller, equipp'd with both the ability and two parallel mirrors, steps through the surface of one looking-glass into the infinitely receding passageway afforded by the reflection of one upon the other, and then negotiates his way within that passage and all its attendant crossways. Wayfinding through the wilderness of mirrors is effected by a curious device of nested ivory balls known as the Coburg Ivories. Using this first method is fraught with danger and subject to too much unwonted jeopardy to be seriously considered, except in desperation. The second way allows for instantaneous transmission of the traveller between two looking-glasses that have in some manner been tuned one to the other, as a match'd pair of viols sustaining the same vibratory note: the traveller steps into one glass in—say—London and steps out of the twinn'd mirror in—again say—Leiden, as simply as striding through a doorway . . . The mechanicks of this are not known to me, but passage by the looking-glass is ever a perilous and unchancy thing, for there is nothing to be trusted about the mirror'd world. It is both snare and illusion. If this was not enough to discourage the putative mirror-walker, there are the added dangers of the Mirror Wights who reportedly haunt the world behind the glass, and though a man may travel the wilderness behind the world's surface, time does not travel with him at the same rate which is its own kind of peril . . .

From *The Great and Hidden History of the World* by the Rabbi Dr. Hayyim Samuel Falk (also known as the Ba'al Shem of London)

CHAPTER 1

FROM A DISTANT SHORE

"It smells different," said Lucy Harker, looking down at the bustling quayside from the temporarily elevated vantage point afforded by the top of the gangplank leading down from the deck of the *Lady of Nantasket*, newly berthed alongside Belcher's Wharf, Port of Boston.

"What does?" said Caitlin Sean ná Gaolaire, who had already reached the foot of the plank.

"America," said Lucy. "It smells . . . cleaner."

"Cleaner than the wide, wind-scoured Atlantic?" said Caitlin. "Sure but you're joking, aren't you?"

"Cleaner than London," said Lucy.

Caitlin filled her nostrils and considered the redolent mixture of smells as if noticing them for the first time.

"Less shite, more pine," she scowled, after a beat of reflection.

Lucy sighed. The fact was that the voyage across the Atlantic had not been an easy one for either of them: the *Lady of Nantasket* had been vexingly beset by contrary winds, and then something noisy and abrupt had happened to the steering gear which had necessitated a running repair that had added extra time and discomfort to the journey. More than that, relations between herself and Cait had changed markedly. Lucy was not sure what had happened, but it was as if the enforced proximity within the confines of the vessel had made Cait regret the generous last-minute impulse with which she had agreed take the younger girl on and act as her mentor. In her own case, Lucy disapproved of the way Cait had worked on the captain and used her considerable powers to charm him, though she was aware enough of her own heart to know that the disapproval was not a moral one, being built rather from resentment and jealousy.

"It just eases the way," Cait had said after Lucy had betrayed her feelings with an overly acid inquiry as to whether her notional tutor had enjoyed a recent visit to the bridge. "He's flattered by the attention, but he's a moral enough fellow, loves his wife too. Him liking me is just a means to our end. What I'm not happy with is you mooning about with a face like a slapped arse because I'm flirting harmlessly with the old feller. We had that conversation; we're not having it again. Now, have you washed my things?"

Washing Cait's clothes was part of Lucy's duties. When she had asked what laundry had to do with being trained as a venatrix, Cait had sharply told her it had nothing to do with the deeper arts necessary for survival as a supranatural huntress, but everything to do with obedience, and that obedience was a necessary pre-condition to instruction.

"If you can't bend yourself to do the simple things without bridling, you're not going to be worth anyone's while as a pupil," Cait had said. "And certainly not any of mine. I'm not trying to break your will, for it's a strong one and it'll serve you well one of these days: I'm just seeing if you've the heart to put it aside when you need to."

And maybe this was as much the problem as anything: her will. Becoming Cait's apprentice had seemed like a welcome way of staying with her, but the truth was that the reason Lucy had wanted to stay was more to do with the great ache she felt when she looked at her tutor than any real desire to spend the stated year as her pupil. Cait had been frank and open—painfully so—about identifying the crush that the younger girl had on her and explaining that it would pass and that even if it didn't, she was not disposed to return the affection in kind. What had not been properly assessed by either, on reflection, was whether Lucy was constitutionally able to take instruction.

She knew she was bad at this. She had been forced to survive on her own for most of her life, and was already resourceful and tough in her independence. She had enjoyed the unfamiliar companionship of The Oversight because she had come, despite herself, to like the other members of the Last Hand. But it was also in her nature to mistrust comfort as a softening snare and delusion, so as soon as she had noted this she had determined to leave, a decision only partially explained by her longing for Cait's company.

The reality of the deal they had made on the quayside in London was less congenial than either had imagined. Rather than bonding, Lucy saw they had drifted apart. From her perspective, Cait had not recovered her normal good humour following an initial week of the voyage that had seen them both badly beset by seasickness. Lucy had regained her appetite and vigour, but apart from the time when she found smiles and laughter for the captain, ocean-going appeared to have sucked all Cait's normal cheerfulness clean away.

It was a relief in more ways than one to escape the narrow confines of the ship and find herself on a gangplank that promised the new freedoms of a wider world so reassuringly beckoning at its far end.

She took another deep breath and scanned the milling scene spread out below her. She saw potential; she saw variety; she saw sights that were familiar, and others that had an indefinably foreign air to them.

She did not, however, see the pair of eyes watching her, eyes hidden in the shadows of an impressive brick and stone warehouse across the wharf.

On a normal day Prudence Tittensor had what she thought of as any passingly clever wife's natural abilities to manage her husband without recourse to her own somewhat more than natural faculties. And on any normal day she would have relied on them alone to dictate the style with which she welcomed him ashore after what must have been a long, cold voyage home to Boston, fighting the wind all the way across the sullen grey swells of the Atlantic.

She stood in the shade of the colonnade fronting the warehouse by

Belcher's Wharf, neatly folding the note she had just hurriedly written as she watched him move around the deck of the *Lady of Nantasket,* supervising the crew as they went through the well-drilled routines of berthing up and un-dogging the cargo hatches in preparation for imminent invasion by the stevedore gang waiting on the quayside below. She knew that in a moment—in fact as soon as she made herself visible to him—he would remember that his first mate knew every bit as much as he did about the matters in hand and was, in addition, a bachelor. Captain Tittensor would then, as ever, hand responsibility for ship and cargo over to him and become, for the next few hours at least, merely a land-bound spouse. And—on any normal day—Prudence Tittensor was not only expert in ensuring that he was a very happy and carnally satisfied land-bound spouse, but herself genuinely enjoyed the affectionate private warmth of their frequent reunions.

The sight of the two young women who had appeared on the gangplank had made her step sharply back into the depths of the warehouse colonnade and reassess her plans.

This had not been going to be a normal day from the get-go, since she was going to have to explain to her husband that the child they had adopted and brought home from London was gone, simultaneously finessing the moment of revelation by explaining that the reason for this was a happy one: nature had granted Prudence the miracle they had both long wished for, a miracle that she carried proudly before her in her expanding stomach. She had rehearsed the rationale behind her decision in passing the adopted infant on to a more deserving couple, and was confident in her ability to manipulate her husband's reaction.

What she had not been prepared for was the pair on the gangplank. She had seen them and immediately known both what they were and how much trouble they were bringing. She had stepped back into the shade and thought fast, then pulled a small pad of paper and a slender pencil from her bag and written three terse sentences.

The bitch at her side thumped her tail and made a low growling plea of barely controlled excitement.

"No, Shay," said Prudence. "No. You'll see him later."

She peeled a glove off her left hand, slid the note into it and folded it into an improvised envelope of sorts. She then handed it down to the dog, who gently took it in her mouth.

"This for the Proctor," she said. "And fast, girl."

Prudence then smoothed her hand over the growing bulge of her belly and stepped out of the shadows waving at her husband with a sunny smile that betrayed not a hint of her inner turmoil, her eyes resolutely ignoring the young strangers whose arrival had turned this into a decidedly abnormal day.

Lucy joined Cait at the foot of the gangplank and found she was expected to carry her mentor's bag as well as her own.

"Now," said Cait shortly, "let's be going. We've things to settle before we deal with the matter in hand."

"Do you think that's Mrs—?" began Lucy, observing the approaching figure of Prudence Tittensor, who was looking past them, up into the beaming face of her husband, who was leaning over the taffrail and waving enthusiastically back at her.

Cait gripped Lucy's arm with her free hand and squeezed it firmly.

"Don't look," she said calmly. "We've time enough for her later, once we've found out when the next ship sails home."

The plan was simple and well-rehearsed. Lucy ran it through her head as she followed Cait through the milling crowd towards the port office. Being both youthful and handsome, there was no shortage of importunate masculine offers to "help them with their bags," but Cait smiled and declined and never broke pace, and Lucy followed dutifully in her wake, trying to assume her mentor's easy air of knowing exactly where she was going in this town in which she had never before set foot. The plan was to find out the next sailing that could take them back to the other side of the ocean they had just crossed. Once this had been determined and passage booked, Cait intended to repossess the stolen infant at the last possible moment before the said sailing, and return it to the Factor and his wife at Skibbereen, from whose crib it had been stolen nearly a year ago now. The child had been taken by a changeling who Cait had tracked from County Cork to the City of London, a changeling Lucy had last seen imprisoned in the secret cells beneath the Sly House adjacent to the headquarters of The Oversight in Wellclose Square.

Captain Tittensor had been worked on by Cait on the voyage over to the extent that he believed it was his own idea that she should present herself at his home at the earliest opportunity in order that she might offer her services as a nurse to the adopted baby she had in fact determined to remove. The captain had given Cait his home address with the suggestion that she present herself for his wife's perusal at her earliest convenience, and had congratulated himself inwardly about the excellence of the plan. He liked all he saw of Cait and could not conceive of Mrs. Tittensor liking her a whit the less.

Caitlin Sean ná Gaolaire had none of Prudence Tittensor's qualms about using any supranatural faculties on the captain. But then she was a venatrix, a hunter sworn to rescue the child, come what may. And Lucy had noticed that Cait was—on dry land at last—both blithe and bonny but also utterly ruthless in the prosecution of anything she believed to be the right thing to do.

Within half an hour, they had found their way to the port office, and determined there was a ship sailing on the morning tide for Liverpool.

"So we leave in less than a day?" said Lucy, unable to keep surprise and disappointment out of her voice.

"Did you have other plans, missy?" said Cait, raising an eyebrow.

"Seems a shame not to see a little of this new country while we're here," said Lucy.

"We're not on a grand tour. We're on serious business," said Cait. "And I've found one place is pretty much like another, when you look closely."

"Would be nice to have a chance to look closely," mumbled Lucy as Cait led the way into an inn which the young man in the port office had recommended as being close, clean and cheap.

Cait turned and blocked the door.

"I'm no believer in Lady Luck, Lucy-girl, but when she smiles it's as well to smile back, bob a curtsey out of respect and take what she offers. It's an ugly thing we're to do here, because the captain's a decent enough man and likely has no knowledge that his babby's been stolen from another, so it's as well to do it fast, like pulling a tooth."

CHAPTER 2

HERNE THE HUNTER

Far to the north of London, close to the ancient heart of Britain, a Herne was on the hill, hunting by moonlight.

Like all Hernes, he pursued his prey with a brace of bone dogs, a Sight Hound and a Nose. The short-legged Nose was fifty yards lower on the slope, belly-down, snuffling along the curved edge of the ancient woods that ringed the bald upland like a tonsure. The tall Sight Hound stood beside the Herne, tense as a drawn bowstring, back legs quivering with anticipation, ready to explode into movement the moment the Nose flushed prey from the shadowy undergrowth below.

Though his face was a whorl of interlocking tattoos and he was sworn to the night, the Herne was both Sluagh-like and not-Sluagh: Hernes long ago removed themselves from the company of the Sluagh proper, disdaining to travel in their troops or to join their hosts at the ritual times of the year. They were no longer especially hostile to the Sluagh, to whom they were after all kin, but they chose to live solitary lives, alone with their bone dogs. The most startling visual difference to regular Sluagh was the deer antlers they strapped to their heads, the bases carefully chamfered to a thin, angled bevel and bound so securely in place that they appeared to sprout directly from the Hernes' own skulls.

The Herne on this moonlit hillside had short but vicious roe-deer antlers swept back from his head, each with three sharp points, which gave him a streamlined look, an impression confirmed when he ran along-side his Sight Hound, with whom he could almost keep pace.

The Sight Hound was a rangy lurcher with a lot of greyhound in its blood; small yellowing bones from different prey animals were tied along its back, bound into the long shaggy fur like an external spine, and it was on these ancient trophies that the Herne kept a steadying fingertip. The barrel-chested Nose snuffling below them had similar but shorter artic-ulated decoration along its backbone, but what looked regal on the lurcher looked more workmanlike on the Nose, which was a bastard cross between a badger-hound and a spaniel.

There was a sudden anticipatory beat of silence, like a hole in the world, and then something burst noisily from the tanglewood, followed by the baying Nose. The Herne lifted his fingertips from the plait of bones and the Sight Hound exploded into motion, heading for the fleeing creature with long, loping bounds which seemed to eat up the distance between it and the Nose in three heartbeats, and to hit the prey in a solid snarling thump in one heartbeat more.

The Nose barked excitedly, tail thrumming the grass as the Sight Hound shook the hare once, twice and dropped it dead. Both dogs turned to look back uphill at the Herne. The Sight Hound cocked his head; the Nose whined nervously.

The Herne had his back to them, looking at the crest of the hill.

"What do you want?" he said.

A lone figure stood on the skyline, clad in a long badger-pelt coat. He wore a badger skull in a circlet around his forehead, his face was heavily tattooed and a blade like a broken-backed sickle hung from his belt. He was unmistakably Sluagh.

"A hunter," said Badger Skull.

"What is the prey?" said the Herne.

"A daywalker," said the Sluagh. "Nothing dangerous. Just hard to get at, or we should have got him already."

"I do not hunt daywalkers," said Herne. "You know this."

The Sluagh walked down the slope towards him. The Herne snapped his fingers at the bone dogs who only now turned their attention to the hare they had caught, both tearing into the dead body with an unusual lack of competitiveness. They wrenched it apart and each lay with their own half, side by side, eating companionably.

"Fine dogs," said the Sluagh.

"They do not hunt daywalkers either," said the Herne.

The Sluagh squatted on his haunches and looked at the feeding dogs. He carried a large leather bag high on his shoulders like a pack.

"There is a man called Mountfellon, who splits his time between London and a house to the north east of here," said the Sluagh after a while. "He committed an outrage on one of us."

"Is this not rightly a case, then, for The Oversight?" said the Herne, who did not choose to squat next to him. "They are sworn to protect the two worlds from each other, and here is a daywalker harming—"

"The Oversight itself is all but dead and gone," spat Badger Skull. "You know it failed to protect us long ago and its writ no longer runs further than the inner bounds of London, and hardly there even, for—"

"The Oversight is most dangerous when most reduced," interrupted the Herne. "There are many Pure now dead and gone who did not remember that."

The Sluagh spat on the grass.

"Sun rot The Oversight, brother. Their day is finally done. Besides. This was far from London."

"This is not for me."

"Look at this and tell me again that this is none of your concern," said the Sluagh. He opened the leather pouch and held it out to the Herne. The Herne took it and sniffed the contents, then turned it upside down.

A tangle of large bones fell onto the grass, followed by a human skull and what looked like a large ragged roll of parchment.

"I have seen skeletons before. What of it?" he said.

"Unwrap the bundle," said Badger Skull.

The Herne did so, unrolling the stiff parchment until it was clear it was not parchment but a skin, and what's more, a skin that had once covered a Sluagh. What began in impatience slowed down into a kind of reverence as he finished flattening out the hide and smoothed his hand over the distinctive tattoos that covered it. The whirl and tangle of black lines all came together in a giant tattoo of a woodcock's skull centred on what would have been the shoulder-blades, with the beak running down the cleft of the spine. The two large, hollow eye sockets seemed to gaze back at him in the moonlight as he stared at it.

"He skinned one of us."

He looked at the Sluagh. The Sluagh nodded.

"Captured, killed, flayed him either before or after, and boiled the flesh from his bones. This is not hunting for sport. This is hunting for justice. Someone must pay, like for like, Law and Lore," he said. "The Herne are sworn to help us when Pure blood has been spilled by daywalkers."

The Herne rubbed his face as if scrubbing sleep from it. He shook himself like one of his bone dogs and then nodded.

"Who told you I would do this? Who told you I was kin-sworn to these markings?"

"Woodcock Crown," said Badger Skull, his eyes on the bony Mohawk of sharp beaks running along the Herne's head, between the horns.

"So you sought me to claim kin," said the Herne.

"Affinity," said Badger Skull. "Not to me. I think you would sense one who had wronged one who bore your mark more strongly than any another."

"If this Mountfellon is gone into London, then I am as barred from him as you," said the Herne. "It is a useless hunt. London is ironbound and webbed with running water."

"Barred by iron? Iron like this?" said Badger Skull, his smile flashing white in the thicket of blue lines swirling across his face. He drew a knife from his belt and held it up to the night where it caught the moonbeams and flashed silver against the darkened sky. It was no ancient bronze blade like the ones normally carried by the Sluagh; instead it was a well-worn bread knife, but that was not what made the Herne gasp in surprise. What shocked the Herne, born generations deep in an instinctive fear of iron, was the fact that Badger Skull not only held the cursed metal, but then licked it without even wincing, without his tongue sizzling and blistering—without any effect at all.

"What is this?" said the Herne, his voice hoarse and strained with both the shock and the unfamiliar sensation of having to express surprise: the Herne was in his own way master of his hidden, solitary demesne. Badger Skull's actions had just shaken the very roots of that world.

"The Iron Prohibition that was laid on us aeons past is broken," said Badger Skull. "I broke it."

He threw the knife to the Herne. Instinctively he stepped away and let it bounce on the grass.

"You can pick it up, and no harm will come to you," said Badger Skull. "If you can't then I withdraw my request, for you are clearly no kin and time has indeed sundered out ancient common bond. But if you can hold it, then the good I have done touches us both, because the prohibition no longer lies heavy on you either, being thus provenly Sluagh-kin. And all I ask, if this is so, is that you repay me by finding this Mountfellon and a way to have at him."

The Herne bent slowly and skated his hand in the air just above the blade, as if feeling for warmth or some malignant fizzing in the air around it. He looked up at the watching Sluagh.

"What have you done?" he said hoarsely.

"Touch it," said Badger Skull.

The Herne paused, then decisively laid his fingertips on the blade. He kept them there, then picked it up, sniffed at it and then, as the Sluagh had done, licked it.

"You spoke truth. There is no longer any ill in it for us," he said in wonderment. And he held the knife out to the Sluagh.

"Keep it," said Badger Skull. "I stole it from the inn at the bottom of the valley. I can steal another whenever I like. Daywalkers' houses are open to me now; their iron locks and bolts and horseshoes are no hindrance any more. We are putting the world back to rights, and we will have our place in it."

The Herne said nothing, and for some long minutes they stood there, looking out at the moonlit landscape stretching out below them like a secret kingdom rendered in silverpoint. The only sound was the dogs cracking the bones of the hare as they continued to eat, unaware that their master's world had just become miraculously unbound.

The Sluagh collected the skeleton and the skull together and placed the parts back in the leather pack, then carefully rolled the flayed skin and held it in his hands.

"What will you do with him?" said the Herne.

"We will take him to the Scowles," said Badger Skull. "To the Shee. They will do what they can to restore his honour and put his parts to the long sleep."

"He was a Woodcock Crown," said the Herne.

"The Shee will mark his passing better than anyone," said the Sluagh. The Herne nodded.

"His house is north east of here?" he said. "This Mountfellon."

"The big ironstone mansion by Bowland's Gibbet, on the rising land before it drops to the fen country," said Badger Skull. "But he was not there. We were there, and if he had been too I would have killed him myself. He may be in London, he may be on the road between or he may have another rathole to hide in. Finding him will be a challenge for any hunter. You may have to sit and watch in the shadows. You may have to track him by his friends. But you are not just any hunter, brother. And that is why we came to you."

The Herne looked at the roll of cured skin for a long time. Then he hunkered down on his haunches next to the Sluagh.

"Tell me about this Mountfellon. Start at the beginning."

CHAPTER 3

THE BLOODY HOMECOMING

On hearing that the Sluagh had committed an atrocity within his most private and hitherto invulnerable *sanctum sanctorum*, Francis Blackdyke, Viscount Mountfellon, had returned to Gallstaine Hall with a speed that had half killed his horses and broken the pelvis of his unfortunate coachman. Mountfellon had sat in the back of the speeding conveyance seething with anger and outrage. His mind, always agile, leapt from imagined horror to imagined horror, each worse than the other. He had bound his home and his study with bands of iron. It was inconceivable that any supernatural creatures who were, every reputable source agreed, repelled by iron should have gained entry. In fact, as a man of science he had seen empiric evidence of the phenomenon in the experimental chambers The Citizen had created beneath the house on Chandos Place. He had seen how a captive Sluagh's flesh had almost seemed to boil as it tried to avoid the application of the hated metal in the form of a horseshoe bought in expressly for the purpose.

It was also a horseshoe that had led to the injury to the coachman, who had dared to slow the coach on the high road since, as he shouted down to the noble lord, he thought the lead horse had thrown a fore-shoe and that they would need to stop in the next village to have it replaced. Mountfellon had been fuming about the reported fact that some of his highly prized specimens had been desecrated and removed, and the coachman's solicitude for the dumb animals under his charge was the straw that broke his master's hold on rationality. Instead of answering, Mountfellon had simply torn open the door of the carriage while it was still in motion, hauled himself up onto the driver's box and, without a word had grabbed the unfortunate Phaeton by the Belcher handkerchief around his neck and hurled him clean off the seat and into the road. The very large and surprised man tumbled through the air in a particularly ungainly fashion, his double-caped box-coat flapping and all four limbs flailing with all the unhandsome gracelessness of a hurled turkey. The shriek of pain that he emitted as he hit the hardtop and fractured himself was lost behind the noble lord who did not once deign to look back as he whipped the horses into a breakneck gallop and thundered towards Rutlandshire with all the reckless speed of a modern Jehu.

His arrival at Gallstaine was accompanied by much wailing and gnashing of teeth as those servants who had dared to remain and wait for the anticipated storm of recrimination bore the brunt of his rage, an anger unabated by the fact that those who had let the Sluagh and their mute companion into the building had had the sense to leave without notice and look for safer employment elsewhere. The only footman who had been a witness to the intrusion and who remained had had his mind turned so completely by what he had seen and been forced to do that he was quite comprehensively bestraught, useful for nothing more than sitting in a dim-lit corner of the stable and dribbling into a tin cup that one of the horse-boys had been kind enough to give him for the purpose.

Mountfellon looked at him in disgust on arrival and then went up to his collections. He came straight back down and thrashed the unfortunate lunatic until he broke the whip, and would have done more had not he injured his own shoulder with the fury of his onslaught.

He then staggered back up into the main house and took a more detailed but no less wide-eyed appraisal of the comprehensive outrage visited on his meticulously arranged collections: previously the cathedral-like immensity of his great hall had been an ordered space, held in a kind of muffled aspic, the furniture covered in drop cloths, the chandeliers above bagged neatly against the unnecessary accretion of dust, the marble floor kept shiny by regular sweeping. Now the great staircase that swung up to the first floor was scattered with shards and debris, glass, insects and bone fragments giving a clue to the likely state of the long corridor of specimen cabinets beyond.

"Didn't like to clear up afore you got here, Milord," mumbled the remaining sane footman who had not been present on the night in question. "In case we damaged some of the insects and . . ."

Mountfellon backhanded him so hard the blood from his burst nose spattered across the marble as he landed in a shocked pile against the balustrades. The few servants who had gathered at what they had deemed a safe distance back in the hall hurriedly reassessed their estimate and faded even further back into the shadows.

Mountfellon walked carefully up the stairs, quivering with outrage at what each new step brought into view. The long corridor leading to what had once been a ballroom but had long since been converted into his study had been a source of immeasurable pride to him. It had been physical evidence of the rational precision with which his mind had achieved a complete understanding of comparative anatomy. Walking between the cabinets had provided a representative taxonomy of living organisms ranging in size from meticulously pinned flies and beetles to the flensed and bleached skeletons of the great apes, human and even suprahuman animals at the other end. All the specimens had been neatly displayed in carefully considered order, pinned and pegged out in pleasing patterns with painstakingly labelled precision. None of that remained: in its place was chaos and confusion, a mess more akin to the aftermath of a frenzied riot in a madhouse. The front of each cabinet had been smashed, and the contents within methodically stripped and tipped out onto the floor. He gave up trying to avoid treading on any of the once-prized specimens and crunched his way onward, slipping and sliding over the drift of glass shards which shaled the marble floor. If he had not known as an inevitable law of physics that running would lead to him falling, he would have sprinted towards the ironbound doors hanging so treacherously open at the far end. The corridor, he felt, was prologue: the true horror of his violation lay beyond those doors. The skeletons of the great apes were unmolested, though the vitrines behind which they stood were as broken as all of them. Beyond them, the final two skeletons were missing. The Sluagh one had had the flayed and cured skin pinned out on the wall behind it to display the totality of the tattoos that covered it. He imagined the Sluagh had taken them.

The fate of the human skeleton from the specimen cabinet was revealed once he entered the iron-gridded immensity of his study. At first he was shocked by the lack of broken glass, the absence of any real mess. He had thought his great cliff of irreplaceable books would be tumbled and perhaps torn or burnt, yet there they were, as he had left them. The great oak dining table still stood foursquare where he had left it, untipped and still containing the unmolested neatness of the piles of paper he surrounded himself with. The greater shock was of course the absence, the thing not there.

The great long case that had contained the Sluagh's Banner was gone from its place against the wall. Just above it, the Sluagh had pinned the human skeleton, driving a dagger that normally did duty as a letter opener on the table through one of the eye sockets, deep into the plaster beyond. It hung slightly lopsided, and held something in its teeth. He reached out and pulled it. It was a letter, or rather an envelope. It was the envelope in which Templebane had sent the note summoning him to London for his first failed attempt on The Oversight and the Safe House, the ruse that had hinged on the French girl that The Citizen had provided as bait, the glint. The Sluagh had outlined the seal on the letter in what looked like blood. The central motif, impressed into the wax, was another skull and the reminder "AS I AM, YOU WILL BE."

There was no doubt in his mind. It was more than a message.

It was a promise.

Mountfellon crumpled the paper and kept a grip on it. Then he went to the desk and sat there, breathing heavily, reaching for self-control and the power to engage his rational mind, the great tool of which he was normally so proud and in control.

"Think," he hissed between clamped teeth. "Think now . . . how did this happen . . . ?"

The banner had been a thing of power, or if not an actual power he could measure empirically, it was thought to be so by the Sluagh, and belief and sentiment were compelling in equally strong but less measurable ways. Its value to him had been in its antiquity, its associations and crucially its usefulness as a bargaining counter with which to make the Sluagh do his bidding. He was shocked to find they had managed to pierce his two lines of protection, the ironbound room within the ironstone house, and the stream he had had diverted and split as it flowed through his parkland so that the house was guarded by what was in effect a flowing moat. It was inconceivable that the Sluagh had overcome both the prohibition represented by cold iron and that of running water. And yet the box the banner had been rolled in was itself iron. And they had carried it away.

"So," he fumed. "*A posteriori* reasoning says iron is no longer toxic to them."

The thought gave him a shudder of anxiety, immediately and rigorously suppressed.

"But the water," he said, rising. "But the water."

He crossed to the floor-to-ceiling shutters and unshackled the pins with which the iron straps that held them closed were fastened. Metal shrieked against unlubricated metal as he pulled them open. Dust motes swirled in the low evening sunlight thus allowed to enter the room, and he moved through it to stand at the window and look out. The view over the charming parkland thus revealed, bathed in the flattering golden glow of the dropping sun, did not calm him: instead it made him scowl and then, as he looked closer and checked that what he appeared to be seeing was real and not a trick of the light, he snarled and stormed back out of the room.

One side of the bifurcated stream was flowing merrily. The other was dry. As he forgot himself and began to run down the debris-strewn corridor, his feet flew from under him and he fell. He reached wildly for support and crashed into the cabinet with the great ape skeletons in it, destroying the display as he smashed through and landed awkwardly against the back wall. He sliced a hand on the glass littering the case bottom, and tore his coat. He pushed himself to his feet and shook his head, a terrible look of white fury sharpening his already hatchet-like features. He grasped the long thigh bone of a gorilla in his bloodied fist, hefting it like a club. And then, careful this time, he strode inexorably down the corridor looking for the head gardener.

The head gardener had one great advantage over all the other servants in that he was able to keep out of the line of fire by having an entirely legitimate reason not to be in the house itself. He had capitalised on this by deciding, should the furious noble lord come looking for him, to be found hard at work on a project that he felt would be approved of: he knew that Mountfellon was adamant that the streams which circled the hall should flow freely, and was sure that his exacting employer could not but approve when he found his gardener in the act of sedulously following those wishes. Thus far he was, in outline, correct. But the devil is in the details, and in this case the detail was the means by which the unfortunate horticulturalist had decided to ensure the channels remained unblocked by weed and silt. The intention was good; the execution fatally disastrous, for he had closed the sluice gate on the easternmost stream in order to dam the water and allow him and his boy to get down into the dry bed and take out the choking weed and the clogging silt, deepening the watercourse and speeding the future rate of flow. The gardener had initiated the project in order to curry favour with his irascible master. He expected, if not smiles, at least a grudging acknowledgement that he had been well served.

He was therefore particularly shocked when the evening sun was blotted out by the unmistakable silhouette of Mountfellon who seemed to be carrying some kind of cudgel, and the calm of the evening was broken by a low hiss that said:

"What the devil do you imagine you're doing, you old cretin?"

"Assuring the flow, Milord," said the old cretin with a note of understandable resentment at the title he had just been given. "Assuring the flow, as you like it."

Mountfellon jumped into the dry bed of the stream and stood much too close for the gardener's comfort.

"You do not assure the flow, you cunny-faced blockhead, by stopping it!"

"Milord, I had to . . ." began the gardener.

But the world never knew what it was he had had to do, because the noble lord lashed the gorilla's thigh bone into the side of his head with enough force that the skull shattered and he dropped into the slime and lay there, face down and twitching. Mountfellon watched until the twitching stopped, and then climbed out of the stream and walked back up to the point at which it split, where the culvert had been closed. He sighed and looked around for a servant to turn the great wheel that would open it again, but seeing none he gripped it himself and expended a further measure of his great frustration in wrenching it round and round until it was fully open and the dammed water freed to flow back into the dry bed of the stream.

The water found the body of the gardener and worried at it as it rose, loosening the grip of gravity and beginning to carry it downstream along with it.

Mountfellon didn't give it a second glance as he walked past it and strode back to the house.

As he entered the hall, he surprised the stable boy who was hurrying along the servants' corridor. The boy stopped and stared at him in shocked silence, too awestruck to step out of Mountfellon's way.

"What are you doing?" said Mountfellon.

"Beg pardon, sir, was looking for Mr. Turner, sir," gasped the stable boy. Turner was the coachman, and a great hero to the boy.

"Mr. Fucking Turner is walking home," said Mountfellon. And then as an afterthought: "If you want to be useful, go and get the gardener out of the stream. He's fallen and dashed his brains out, and I don't want him blocking the culvert."

And with that he pushed the boy aside and strode back to the desolation of his collection, determined to stay within his protective moat until he had worked out how to apply the same principal of retributive attack to those who had caused it: Sluagh, Oversight or both, he would destroy them.

CHAPTER 4

THE RUNNING DOG

The bitch Shay was a well-known sight on the Boston waterfront, being one of the parochial curiosities frequently shown off to visiting out-of-towners as she ran hither and yon, as often as not carrying something in her mouth. It was held to be a small marvel and a quaint source of local pride that the Tittensors had so cleverly trained the dog to scamper between their shipping office and the quayside carrying notes quite as effectively as if she were a regular messenger boy or carrier pigeon.

Some wharfside loafer had put the word about that the rangy hound was known to be a descendant of one of the two luckless canines executed for witchcraft alongside the twenty human victims variously hanged or pressed to death during the puritan frenzy of persecution that had taken place just up the coast in Salem a century and a half ago. This detail of the dog's pedigree, whether true or not, only added to the lustre that accompanied her reputation as a neighbourhood marvel: what was undeniable was not only that Shay was faster than any two-legged runner, having the blood of Irish Wolfhounds in her tangled ancestry but, being a mongrel, was smarter than any three pure-bred dogs put together.

Her passage, carried out at a fast lope through the crowded harbour and the adjacent streets, was not therefore particularly remarked upon by anyone who saw it.

And no one took any notice of the fact the shaggy dog arrived at the shipping office and kept right on going, accelerating as the crowds thinned out, heading for the heart of the city.

CHAPTER 5

OF FIRE AND MIRRORS

The Citizen was now the sole tenant of the house on Chandos Place, his erstwhile host and collaborator the Viscount Mountfellon having hurled himself homewards to Rutlandshire as soon as he had heard of the outrages visited on his precious collections at Gallstaine Hall, and taking the only servant with him. The lack of a servant was the only irritation, and it had begun to occur to him with increasing regularity that he should equip himself with a helpmeet loyal to himself alone. There were mundane things he needed done which he would much rather have someone else occupy themselves with, while he kept his physical and mental energies focused on his own important work. He needed, he secretly acknowledged to himself, some kind of general factotum.

The ancient Frenchman did not mind the solitude itself, and had enjoyed the opportunity it had given him to sanction Coram Templebane to go ahead with what must have been a final fatal blow against The Oversight. The satisfaction he felt at that did not, however, ease his growing worry that Dee, his associate within the mirror'd world, had not found him the Alps, breath-stealers who he had thought he had cunningly put in place a long time ago, and whose ministrations he now needed.

So he was gratified when he heard the sound of a small bell tinkling within the mirror's cabinet set into the wall of his basement study. He was looking at the two caged inmates of his laboratory when the noise distracted him, and he dropped the curtain on the alcove, hiding the tiled laboratory that was—even he had to admit to himself—beginning to look more like an abattoir than a place of rational experimentation, since he did not have the energy or inclination to use a mop and bucket to remedy the situation. He walked stiffly up the two steps back into the body of his study proper.

Skirting the paper and book-strewn desk and table, he unlatched the door of the cabinet, grimacing as the catch stuck, as it always did. It was not a device with the fine glasswork and smooth mechanism of a true Murano cabinet, but it performed the same essential purpose. He tugged the door open and stepped back as a tall, stooped figure with a goat's beard and hawk's eyes stepped into the room, emerging from the mirror within.

"Dee," he said.

"Citizen," said John Dee, his head dipping infinitesimally.

"You have found my breath-stealers?" said The Citizen.

"I have, and more than that I have mapped a safe and swift passage through the mirrors to them, which is something we did not previously possess," said Dee. "Thanks to this get-you-home."

He pulled an object from within his long coat. It was a complicated thing, like an extraordinarily large and elaborate baby's rattle, being a series of cunningly turned and pierced concentric ivory balls mounted on a handle of the same material.

"A Coburg Ivory," breathed The Citizen, almost as pleased with the device in Dee's hand as the confirmation that he would now have access to one of the creatures who were so instrumental in him extending the natural span of his years. He still smarted from the memory of the way The Oversight had killed his last one. It was in a forlornly desperate attempt to avail himself of some similar kind of supranatural energy that he had accelerated his experiments on the caged beings in the curtained laboratory annex to his study.

He had intubated both the ailing Green Man and the Sluagh and had been experimenting with their blood. He had given himself a series of transfusions according to the enlightened principals laid out by Blundell and Leacock who, he was forced to grudgingly admit, had achieved an infinitely more effective modus operandi than his countryman Jean-Baptiste Denis had ever managed. However, he had not noted any increase in his own vitality or resilience as a result of the efficient harvest and intake of new blood. The only measurable effect seemed to be in the donors, who grew weaker and paler, and in the case of the Sluagh, whose mind was already unbalanced due to the proximity of so much iron and his transport having taken him forcibly over so much flowing water, it had led to an almost complete descent into terminal lassitude and idiocy. The Green Man bore the physical effects better, but was permanently distressed at the confined nature of his incarceration, weeping and pleading so much that The Citizen had dosed him with laudanum and taken the opportunity afforded by his consequent insensibility to stitch his mouth together and insert a feeding tube via his nostril. It had been the only way to quiet the snarling creature, and The Citizen's work was after all too important to be disturbed by mere insensate noise.

But the truth remained that the transfusions were an act of desperation, and he was mightily relieved to know that he would soon have access to an Alp to revive him. He was vigorous enough at the moment, but he knew he would benefit from congress with one within the next two months, and begin to decline if it was not possible.

"I have better news than that," said Dee. "If I might prevail on you to step into the mirrors."

"I am not ready to leave quite yet," said The Citizen, stepping away from the proffered hand. "I have papers to pack, and baggage to assemble—"

Dee smiled and waved his hands.

"No, sir, I do not mean you should leave immediately; rather I mean that if you would step in and join me for a mere minute or two, I believe you will be both illuminated and deeply gratified by what I can now show and demonstrate."

The Citizen craned his head to look within the cabinet, as if able to see around the corner of the mirror.

"And can you guarantee my safety?" he said. "From Mirror Wights?"

"There are none close," said Dee. "For it is another pleasing attribute of these Ivories that there is a tell-tale flame that seems to illuminate within the smallest of the inner globes when they are close, and it will warn us in plenty of time should any be remotely in the vicinity."

The Citizen hesitated and looked around his chamber.

"If it is good news, could you not just tell it?" he said, licking his lips.

"Show is sometimes better than tell," said Dee. "I promise you will be safe, and I swear you will be gratified."

He handed The Citizen the Coburg Ivory.

"See. It will warn you if danger approaches, and we can just step back into this room and close the cabinet."

The Citizen twirled the Ivory slowly in his hands, and then nodded.

"Very well, but you will have to give me your arm, for I am not as sure-footed as I once was."

A minute later they had both stepped through one of the parallel mirrors in the cabinet and were standing inside a long and seemingly infinite corridor whose walls, roof and floor were uniformly mirrored, with the unsettling result that reflections of themselves were stretching away, seemingly for ever. The Citizen staggered a little, and Dee held his arm.

"I find the mirror'd world as disorientating as ever," The Citizen scowled. "What have you to show me?"

Dee took his arm and turned him around. Behind him the unbroken succession of reflections was not quite perfect. One of the mirrors was black.

"A Black Mirror," said The Citizen. "There is nothing new there—"

Dee smiled and shook his head with the air of a conjuror about to reveal the culmination of a very cleverly worked trick.

"The mirror'd world is broken," said Dee. "This we both know from painful experience. The reason I have not succeeded in mapping its many passages is not merely because the size changes constantly, perhaps as a consequence of mirrors in the outer world being newly made, or moved or broken. That was my mistake, thinking that this was the reason, but I now believe the mutability of the mirror'd realm is not the thing that stops us using it as we would."

"What is?" said The Citizen.

"These," said Dee, pointing. "The Black Mirrors. They have corroded a once perfect engine."

The Citizen shrugged his arm out of Dee's grip and stood in front of the obsidian face of the mirror in question. It reflected nothing at all back into the passage.

"But we believed the power of the mirror'd world came from the darkness beyond," he said. "Brahe and Fludd were quite assured on this point."

"Fludd was a fool and the only reason we give their writings credence is that they wrote them a long time ago. Antiquity does not guarantee authenticity."

"No," said The Citizen. "No, you are right, and perhaps we should be even more suspicious of the ancients when we are embarked on a quest to forge a new, modern means of control and power. Go on."

"The Black Mirrors are not a natural part of the mirror'd world," said Dee. "The ancients may or may not be right in saying the darkness beyond them has something to do with the power underlying the mechanism by which it works, but I think the Black Mirrors are like windows smashed by vandals. They do happen to show what lies behind, but they are an aberration and a sign of neglect. I have seen, as I have told you in the past, that they are caused by the spilling of blood. The blood is spilled almost exclusively by Mirror Wights who are, I know we both agree, parasites who have moved into the deserted realm to escape the grip of time. I have seen whole sections of passage blanked by the Black Mirrors, and the sense, the fluid vibration in the normal passages, is different on either side of them."

He turned and looked at The Citizen to make sure he was being understood.

"You do remember we found the passage in the surviving fragment of

Sacrobosco's *De speculatam cuniculis,* the one that described the mirror'd world as a great engine running by a species of occulted clockwork?" he said.

The Citizen shuddered as if in irritation at being taken for a dunce.

"Yes, yes. We disagreed on the translation of 'occulted,' but yes, broadly—what of it?"

"If we take his analogy, then the Black Mirrors are like broken teeth on the cogwheels—they cause the whole device to skip and run wrong. And certainly from my own explorations, in some places the entire system seems to have baulked and seized up, as if the great engine is jammed," said Dee. "That is why our attempts to find and then exploit a consistent series of shortcuts around the world have always failed: if the system functioned smoothly, if all the cogs were present and engaged, then travel would be as simple as stepping into a Murano Cabinet in Cheapside and stepping out again in Constantinople or Far Cathay a single pace later."

"Say you are right . . ."

"I am right," said Dee. "The device is broken . . ."

"I have not done what I have done, I have not survived the guillotine and wildly extended the natural span of years in order to give up," spat The Citizen.

"Nor I," said Dee. "Nor I. And nor need we—for I believe I have the cure-all. Which is to say, I know how what is broken can be mended. I know how to repair the Black Mirrors."

"How?" said The Citizen.

Dee drew a stub of candle from his pocket.

He snapped his wrist and it lit itself. "Observe. This is a candle I took from a man called Sharp who I found lost in the mirrors."

"A Wight?"

Dee snorted back a laugh.

"A member of The Oversight." He pointed to the Coburg Ivory still clutched in The Citizen's hand.

"At first I thought all I had to thank him for was this, the get-you-home, and in truth it has been a wondrous tool which has vastly extended my ability to explore. Indeed, it is because it helped me range wider and further that I have seen so many of these regions of the mirror'd world that are blighted and broken by the Black Mirrors. It is a thing of great precision and extraordinarily cunning artifice, and I would give an arm to have the understanding that those who made it must have had about the working of the mirrors. But in the end, it was a simple candle that gave me the clue we have been missing . . ."

He held the candle at arm's length.

"Watch the flame."

As he approached the Black Mirror, the flame began to flare brighter, but that was not the most striking thing, which was this: although the wilderness of mirrors in which they stood was a sterile place without the merest hint of a draught, the flame bent, as if being blown towards the Black Mirror.

"The darkness attracts the flame," breathed The Citizen. "Yes. I see. But we should have seen this phenomenon before!"

"No," said Dee. "The fault is not ours. A normal flame has no effect. The Oversight's candles are not normal. They are, as it were, self-kindling, each primed by its owner to carry a tiny spark of the thing they have always guarded most carefully. The Wildfire."

"I thought their great secret was the Discriminator," said The Citizen. "It was that which Mountfellon was sure was the Great Key."

"It is like The Smith to hide a secret inside another secret and then leave it more or less in plain sight," said Dee. "I am a fool for not having thought of it years ago. But watch close now, for this is the last of the three candles I had off the fool Sharp."

He held his hand even closer to the Black Mirror: the candle was vertical, but now the flame bent at a right angle and began to roar, as if being sucked towards the blackness. As it roared, the wax began to melt at an astonishing rate and then the flame leapt from his hand and splashed and lapped against the surface of the glass, filling it top to bottom, side to side. His fingers dripped with wax and the candle was soon gone. And then so too was the flame.

"*Merde*," breathed The Citizen, staring at himself in what had an instant before been a non-reflective Black Mirror but was now a looking-glass again. A terrible grin stretched across his face. "The flame mended the mirror . . ."

Dee nodded and matched his smile.

"And now we can mend all the mirrors, and our long-held hopes can be realised."

"But," said The Citizen, gripping his arm with a hand like a talon, "you say there are whole swathes of Black Mirrors breaking the flow. One mirror took your candle. From what you have told me there are not enough candles in London to do what you suggest. Are we not in the even more intolerable position of knowing the theoretical cure but not having enough medicine to effect it?"

"Oh, I am not going to go mirror to mirror, spending the rest of my days mending them candle by candle like some jobbing bricklayer repointing a wall," said Dee. "The candles are created by the Wildfire. The clue is in its name. It is the most destructive, voracious thing in the world. The Oversight and its predecessors have guarded it for millennia. When fragments have escaped, disaster has followed, such as the Great Fire of London, and only the wildest luck and the foolhardiest bravery contained that to London alone. There is a reason that the Wildfire is kept in the biggest city on the most powerful island in the world."

"The clue is in the word island, I perceive," said The Citizen with an awful twinkle in his eye.

"Precisely," said Dee. "If we were to release the Wildfire within the mirrors, it would roar through every nook and cranny of the great, broken machine, consuming everything in its way, restoring every Black Mirror to the newly silvered state of the one in front of you."

"Would we not be turning the mirror'd world into a maze of perpetual flame?" said The Citizen, his smile suddenly dropping off his face.

"I believe not," said Dee. "I believe the Black Mirrors would absorb it, but if I am wrong, there is a way to tame it again, as they did in the

Great Fire, for had there not been, London would still be burning, and the rest of Britain besides."

"And you know that way," said The Citizen.

"And I know that way," said Dee. "For I was there."

The Citizen's awful smile returned.

"Well. It would have the added bonus of incinerating the Mirror Wights. And since you say it is their propensity to shed blood that has led to the breaking of the machine, I cannot see that as any great loss."

"Indeed," said Dee. "It would be no more than pouring lamp oil down a rathole and setting it afire to cure an infestation."

"Well," said The Citizen. "Then all we have to do is destroy The Oversight, and take their Wildfire."

"And they have never been at such a low ebb," said Dee. "It is as if a benign providence positively wishes us to succeed as they fail so desperately."

"But where have they hidden the Wildfire?" said The Citizen. "Their house is destroyed, and it cannot be there."

"It will be in the river" said Dee, as if this was the most obvious and inevitable thing in the world. "Sealing it in a lead coffer and putting it beneath running water has always been their failsafe."

"And you are sure of this?"

"Did Mountfellon's first stratagem not fail when he tried to ambush them on the river as they were sinking caskets beneath the water?" said Dee. "They are not imaginative, and their options in dealing with the Wildfire are severely limited by its volatility. They will have had to move fast, and emergency measures do not allow for great sophistication. All we need to do is find someone to drag the river effectively for us."

"It is a very long river," began The Citizen. Dee snorted.

"With their numbers so severely reduced, they will not have had the resources to have taken it far, of that I am sure. And besides, the Templebanes have eyes and ears all over the city: I am assured their intelligence network will enable us to narrow the search area down considerably."

"You are so very sure of everything . . ." said The Citizen, still nursing a flicker of scepticism. Dee's answering smile was distinctly vulpine.

"You forget, dear Citizen. I know the ways of The Oversight. For was I not, in my sadly misspent youth, one of them?"

CHAPTER 6

UNDER THE HORNBEAM

Amos Templebane, in the service of his two fathers, had once worn a badge on a strap around his neck: it had proclaimed to the world, or at least that portion that was interested in the perplexingly silent state of the dark-skinned young bearer, that he was "mute but intelligent." Sometimes when wearing it, he had felt belittled like a dog wearing its owner's collar, but it had also given him a kind of status, or at least a sense of belonging, in that it parsed him for the strangers among whom he was bidden to go: it told that he was no mere simpleton; it explained that he could not speak; and it was evidence that he was connected to someone of substance, since the brass plaque was finely made and incised with handsome lettering. It did undoubtedly also evidence a kind of ownership as if he was, like the aforementioned dog, a domesticated pet bound to respond to commands in exchange for regular meals and a dry place to sleep.

The plaque and the explanatory rubric were long gone but even now, months later, he did not feel liberated. He had rebelled, walked free and ranged across the countryside, swearing to be his own man and live at liberty on his own wit and merit alone. He had almost immediately been assailed by a murderous tinker and had unfortunately killed him in self-defence. The fatality had not been intentional and his spirit had balked at the deed even though his rational mind had excused himself the manslaughter. So he had sworn a solemn vow that the homicidal tinker's blood would be the last he would ever shed or be responsible for shedding. It was the expression of an inner revulsion against all violence and a fervent, almost visceral desire to avoid it in future. It wasn't cowardice that prompted Amos to this, for he was resilient and brave; rather it was a general moral instinct mixed with a specific impulse to curb something largely unacknowledged within himself, for Amos knew he carried an inner power that needed to be ridden and limited, lest it itself become the rider and put the spurs to him. So Amos had committed himself to live a peaceful life of independent freedom.

But as Issachar Templebane had once said to a deputation of his "sons" when they had been pushed by the extreme cold to hesitantly express the wish for more sea-coal for the stove to keep the counting-house warm enough to work in, if wishes were horses then beggars would ride.

And now despite his best wishes and intentions, Amos was both literally and figuratively afoot on the muddy road to London, still somehow travelling with a woman whose passive tyranny over him was almost as insupportable as the nickname she had given him: the Bloody Boy. The name was all the more unbearable because it was demonstrably apposite: since so naïvely attempting to shun violence, he had been responsible for more death and self-slaughter than he could possibly have achieved had he taken the contrary course and embraced a career of violent mayhem. The memory of all that blood soaked his dreams, and the dark behind his eyelids was no refuge but a nest of shadows in which the gory scenes he had witnessed lurked, ready to disrupt his sleep and infect his nightmares. Even when awake, his head was no sanctuary into which he might retreat behind the protective veil of silence, since the disappointed and deranged companion he was somehow bound to shared his ability to converse without words.

The only benefit of the recent disasters and outrages that had been visited on them both by the band of Sluagh they had been forced to abet and then been abandoned by was that she, the erstwhile Ghost of the Itch Ward, had been so thwarted and betrayed in her own carefully laid plans that he had been able to slowly increase the privacy of his own mind. Her increased distraction allowed him the space to put in defensive foundations which she, if more alert, might well have been able to grub up before they bedded in enough to be built on. As it was, he had without instruction found a way to veil his inner thoughts from her: it was as if he had built a small redoubt into which he might retreat and find some privacy from the unwanted trespasser in his mind that she had become.

I know what you're doing. Her words came into his head unbidden as they sat under the twisted branches of a hornbeam that was still clinging to a few of its double-toothed leaves, now turned brown and lifeless.

Good for you.

You're keeping me out.

Am I?

"I don't care," she wheezed out loud, voice dry and scratchy as the noise of the dying leaves rattling in the mild evening breeze above them. "I don't care about anything except the one thing. I will do the one thing and then nothing matters."

I will walk with you to London. But I will not help with that one thing any more. Our ways will part.

"If you help me, I will give you a present," she said. "The loveliest of presents, really."

You have nothing I want.

"I have everything you want."

I want nothing.

"I can explain you to yourself," she said.

I know who I am.

"You do not know what you are. You do not know why you are different. You do not know there are others who are different, like you, like me."

In fact, Amos did know there were others like himself, or at least he had gleaned the fact of their existence from keeping his ears open in the service of the house of Templebane, his adopted family. He knew the Free Company for The Oversight of London was comprised of men and women who seemed to have unusual powers, powers that made their existence somehow insupportable to the interests of his fathers and to the actions of the Sluagh. The Sluagh had worked in concert with his fathers, and later had taken him prisoner and then used him: they were the main source of the blood-soaked dreams. They had opened his eyes to an alien darkness so inimical to human life that he felt just witnessing it had permanently befouled him. And the secret, the thing he was hiding from the Ghost behind the new barricades in his mind was that he was determined to contact The Oversight as soon as they got to London. Perhaps finding those who could fight the Sluagh could end the nightmares that were beginning to unravel his own hold on reality.

"I can teach you things," she said. "Stay with me until the end, and I will teach you the song of your own life. I will show you how to use the powers you have and those you do not yet know how to use."

He knew she was lying. When she lied, she spoke out loud, as if speaking in thought was too direct a means of communication to cloak falsehood.

I want nothing, he repeated. *From you or anyone.*

"Everybody wants something. Wanting and getting. That's the way the world runs, Bloody Boy. Wanting and getting and rutting and strutting, the world like a foul church with the powerful and the strong bestriding the brightly lit nave and the weak and the weary sent to the wall where there are benches over which the shadows may be drawn like a shroud so that none of the great men need see them as they wither and perish. But we all go to the wall in the end, Bloody Boy. The wall waits. The wall knows. And do you know what the wall says to me?"

Amos knew. It was the song and chorus of her obsession. It was the one thing.

Walls do not speak, he answered, trying to forestall the repetition of words that had become exhaustingly irritating to his ears.

"Oh, indeed they do," she said, a laugh coughing out of her mouth like a poor dying thing. "Oh, indeed they do, and if you were born a thing called a Glint instead of a Bloody Boy, you might hear them clear as that pheasant in the hedge across the road. Glints and things like that are what I can teach you about, show you the world you belong to—if you stay with me and help me do the one thing. My gift to you."

Behind the buttress he had thrown up in his mind, he did think that learning from her would pass the time on the road, and maybe give him useful knowledge, if he could separate the real from the imaginary raving. But he would not help her with her "one thing." But then again, he would not hinder her.

He stood up quietly. There was indeed a pheasant in the tangled hedgerow opposite, and he was hungry. If he moved slow and sharp, they would at least eat well before a cold sleep.

"You do know what the wall says, don't you?" she insisted, the unexpected gleam of her smile rather horrible in the failing light.

Quiet now. You will scare our supper.

Kill it, Bloody Boy. Kill it dead. Kill it like you-know-who.

He knew who.

Kill it like Mountfellon.

Her smile widened and got much worse.

For Mountfellon must die!

CHAPTER 7

THE PROCTOR

Once a room for a single night at the harbourside inn had been negotiated at a reasonable rate, and their bags left securely locked within, Lucy found herself back out in the streets of Boston, yet again trying to keep up with Cait's long-legged strides.

"Where are we——?" she began.

"You'll find that out when we get there," said Cait. "Now keep up and if it's conversation you're after, answer me this: what did you make of Mrs. Tittensor?"

"So that *was* her," said Lucy.

"Of course it was. Did you not see her earlier, with the dog?" said Cait.

"What dog?" said Lucy.

Cait shook her head in what Lucy was now conditioned to recognise as barely suppressed disbelief at her apprentice's lack of acuity.

"There was a dog," said Cait. "A big shaggy bitch that could take down a deer if it had a mind to."

"I didn't see it," said Lucy.

"Well, what did you see?" said Cait.

"She had lots of hair. She was well dressed. Um . . ." said Lucy.

"Lots of hair? Well dressed? Um?" said Cait, snorting in disgust. "That was your first impression?"

"I wasn't even sure that she was the captain's wife," said Lucy. Dry land had not returned Cait's joviality.

"You should have marked her before you did," said Cait. "I've told you, if you're to survive alone in the world then you never stop looking around, ever. And when you're arriving somewhere new, you sure as guns look twice as hard."

"When did you see her then?" said Lucy, aware she sounded truculent but not caring enough to hide it. She was proud of the fact that she had, until recently, survived well enough in the world without needing anyone's help, though it was true she had not prospered at much more than mere existence.

"When she saw us," said Cait. "She was by the warehouse on the right, with the pillars. And then she spied us and paused. Then she stepped back into the shadows."

"In that great bustle of people heaving to and fro, and at that distance you're telling me you saw all that?" said Lucy.

"Crowds aren't a problem, Lucy Harker, not once you know the way of them. They have rhythms and movement, like the tide. You want to hide, no better place to do so than in a crowd, but you have to go with the flow to do so, else you stand out like a salmon fighting its way upstream. See now, she was moving towards us, then she saw us and checked herself and stepped back to conceal herself and take a hidden keek at us. That's the odd movement I noticed."

"She hid herself?" said Lucy. "Why'd she do that?"

"Because she saw us," said Cait as if this was the most obvious thing in the world. "Or rather, she saw me. And wasn't I just saying a friendly goodbye to the captain as she did so?"

Lucy spooled her memory back to the top of the gangplank where they had given their fare-thee-wells and thank-yous to the captain, and he in turn had chuckled and handed Cait a slip of paper, holding her hand for what was in strict terms a beat or two too long as he joked about this being an "au revoir" rather than a "goodbye" as he made her promise not to forget to come and see him and his wife about a possible nursery-maid's position.

"Nothing untoward passed between you," she said.

Cait held up the piece of paper in question and waved it over her shoulder without breaking stride.

"But she saw *something* pass between us and, though I take no credit for it since it's just my mother's good colouring passed down to me by an accident of blood, to a wife no doubt used to wondering what her husband gets up to in foreign ports I look like trouble."

"So she was jealous?" said Lucy.

"I don't know. Maybe. She was something, that's for sure. And she sailed past us when we disembarked taking quite as much care to not look at us as we were taking not to look at her."

"Maybe she just didn't see us," said Lucy.

"People see me, Lucy," said Cait. "Men do. Women do. Wives especially do. At least people see me when I want them to. And unless you've been even denser than you like pretending to be, you'll have noticed they see you too. Faith, you're a handsome, strong-faced thing, like a little black thundercloud in a dress most of the time it's true, but men do still turn and look at you even if it's just to wonder what it'd take to make you smile."

Lucy didn't want to continue down this line of conversation, though she was secretly gratified to hear that Cait thought her handsome, so she just walked on, scanning the unfamiliar street and taking in as much of this new country as she could.

"You're not blushing now, are you?" said Cait without turning.

"No," said Lucy, immediately doing so.

"Controlling how you look is part of how to survive," said Cait. "It's how to stalk your prey too. You have to thin yourself down."

"Thin myself down?" said Lucy.

Cait sighed again, stopped and pulled her to the side of the house they were passing. They stood, protected from the flow of pedestrians and carts by the jutting steps of the house.

"Look at my face," said Cait. "Did you never play with paints as a child?"

"No," said Lucy, whose childhood memories were ragged and full of holes. "I mean, yes, paints, maybe . . ."

"Well, thinning yourself down is like adding water to your paints," said Cait. "You wash the colour down until that's all it is really: a thin wash. Like this. Look at me now and learn something."

Lucy was uncomfortable looking directly and openly into Cait's face, mainly because looking at it was something she actually did a great deal of, although she had spent a lot of time and effort perfecting the art of not being caught doing so.

She made herself look into the green eyes, the pale skin dusted with the lightest scrabble of freckles which had been positioned entirely perfectly in order to limn the contours of her cheekbones, features whose curves Lucy knew well from every angle as they swept up and away into the ordered disorderliness of Cait's thick red hair. And then her breath caught, not with the usual treacherous, empty pang behind her breastbone, but in surprise: Cait hadn't moved, nor had she appreciably changed her expression any major way, yet she had somehow . . . left. Which is to say Cait was still there as a physical presence, but she had somehow rendered herself drab and unexceptional, not merely by dousing the animating light in her eyes and slackening the muscles in her face but by some less obvious device, becoming dull where she had been radiant, and vague and watery where she had been remarkable and definite. She not only seemed altogether smaller and untenanted, but Lucy felt her eyes somehow wanting to slide off the lacklustre features and seek something more interesting to look at.

"How d'you do that?" she said.

Cait grinned, and it was like the lights coming back on in a deserted house.

"Practice," she said.

"Will you teach me?" said Lucy.

"Sure, and why would I not?" said Cait. "That was the deal, no? You just have to slacken your hold on the bits that control the outside of you and step a pace back inside yourself."

"Just?" said Lucy.

"I said it took practice," said Cait, stepping back out into the street. "Now keep up, and keep sharp."

Over the next few hours, Lucy became footsore and even more confused. Cait's progress through the tangle of streets seemed random at best, but by the time they ended up almost back where they had begun, they had acquired, variously, a half-pound of pork sausages from an Irish butcher on the back side of Beacon Hill and two small bottles, one labelled McMunn's Elixir of Opium, the other Mother's Gentle Laudanum Soporific. Cait had not explained either of these purchases, but had kept on admonishing Lucy to keep an eye out. Lucy didn't ask what for. She just looked for anything that looked wrong. She saw none of that, and instead rather liked what she saw of Boston, its bustle and energy—in fact everything about it—until they turned a corner and found themselves looking at a spreading shanty town which seemed to have been hurled carelessly across the lower slopes of Beacon Hill on the unpromising land penned between the sea and the saltmarsh beyond.

A group of drunken men came suddenly into view, having scrambled up the slope from the boggy ground below, and as they saw Cait they said something in a language that Lucy could not place let alone understand. The gist of what they said was, however, clear from the ribald laughter and the leers that they gave her.

Cait turned to look at them. Her gaze alone was steely enough to make some of them step back, but the drunker of the group just continued to comment about her, digging each other in the ribs and laughing, clearly feeling safe behind the impenetrability of their language. One of them stepped towards Cait and attempted to endear himself by reaching down, squeezing the front of his trousers and winking at her while grunting something that was—to Lucy—linguistically unfathomable but universally comprehensible.

Cait did not recoil. Instead she stepped towards the demonstrative suitor and let fly with a stream of invective in the self-same language that her admirer had used. He staggered backwards gurgling in shock and outrage, as if her words were a straight-arm to the throat, and then stumbled and fell ignominiously in the dust before any of his companions could catch him. They in turn all seemed to wilt and look shamefaced and suddenly uncomfortably sober as Cait turned the fusillade on them. By the time she finished her words had brought a dash of high colour to her own cheekbones.

"See, Lucy? It's what I said. One place is much like another. Here's a fine flowering of Irish manhood, except they wouldn't behave like that if they were still stood on their home sod in earshot of their mammies, who'd clip them around the earhole and send them to bed till they got over themselves. But hop them over the water and out of sight and they're strutting around, hooting like mad baboons with their winkles out."

They watched the men slink away back toward the shanties.

"And they say travel broadens the mind," said Cait. "Bad cess to them. Now, we'll have the meeting with the captain and spy out the land. I want to take the measure of this woman that spotted us. Something about her rattles my chains. And then once we know what the situation with the baby is, we'll be back after they sleep, give the dog a nice sausage with some of this soporific and then be away with the child and on the boat back to civilisation before anyone's any the wiser."

She seemed refreshed by having let fly at the Irishmen, and Lucy had to stretch her legs to keep up as she stepped out back towards the shore.

Two hours later, they had found the captain's house, and after waiting in the shadows between a pair of wind-bent jack pines until the appointed hour, they crossed to the house, which was a substantial three-storey clapboard building painted a buttery yellow and picked out in white trim. It had a steep pitched roof with a widow's walk and below it a covered porch that extended across the whole width of the building.

"Well," said Cait. "There's money in shipping, and there's no surprise."

She strode confidently up the steps and tugged the brass knob next to the door. There was the sound of wire scraping, and then a distant bell jangled deep in the house, triggering an explosion of barking much closer to the door. Lucy stepped back involuntarily.

"See," said Cait. "Told you there was a dog."

There was heavy footfall on the boards approaching the door, and then it opened to reveal a blaze of light from within.

The dog bounced forward and stood on the threshold, fur brindled at its neck, teeth bared.

Cait bent towards it.

"Arragh, stop that now. We mean no harm, do we, captain?"

She looked up at the black figure silhouetted by the gaslights. The man was taller and thinner than the captain.

"The captain's asleep," he said, and stepped forward so the porch light caught his features. His face was gaunt and pitted, and at some stage in his life his nose had clearly met something powerful going left while the rest of his head was going right, since it had been mashed sideways and mended thus, giving his face the look of something that had been badly folded before being put away.

"And whether you mean harm is something entirely open for debate."

He raised his right hand and pointed something at Cait. It was a long-barrelled pistol of a kind Lucy had never seen before.

"If you and your friend would step inside, I'd be much obliged."

Cait straightened slowly, her hand beginning to quietly flex towards the razor she kept holstered in a discreet pocket in the cuff of her dress.

The pistol in his hand made a definite metallic click as he thumbed back the hammer, making a sound like a trap being set. Cait stopped moving.

"And if you'd keep your hands away from your blades, then we won't be having to mop any bits of you off the Tittensors' nice clean porch."

Cait looked him in the eyes.

Lucy prepared to run, knowing her friend was going to work on his mind to fuddle him and buy them time enough to escape.

"And that won't work, missy," he said. "Not on me. I'm not some innocent lamb for the shearing, not like the captain."

"Who are you?" said Cait.

"Who don't signify," he said. "What I am is a Proctor."

Lucy thought she might have a chance if she threw herself sideways and jumped off the porch into the dark street beyond.

Cait reached back and gripped her arm as if she'd heard the girl's thoughts.

"No, Lucy," she said. "Look at him. Look at him properly. He's going to be fast. Fast as you. Fast as me. Maybe even as fast as Sharp."

The Proctor smiled and nodded his head slowly. It wasn't a cheering smile. And the gun barrel didn't waver as he raised it and pointed it at Cait's forehead.

"And I've five lead slugs in here even faster than that, ladies. This is the Paterson Colt revolving pistol. It'll make a hole about the size a navy bean going in, but it'll blow one the size of my fist coming out."

Cait and Lucy exchanged a look.

"Then I think we'll accept your kind invitation," said Cait.

"Good," said the man, stepping back and making room for them to enter.

"That'll be quieter, and whole lot less messy than the other way."

CHAPTER 8

THE LUSTS OF ABCHURCH TEMPLEBANE

Issachar Templebane had wreaked his revenge on The Oversight. On the one hand, it had been everything he hoped, in that he had destroyed their house beyond any chance of repair, but on the other hand it had also become the very thing he feared, in that some members had not only survived but had also probably identified him as the hidden hand that moved against them.

The reaction and retaliation had been shockingly immediate, for no sooner had the explosions taken place than he and his son Coram had come under retaliatory attack by, of all anomalous and hatefully unexpected things, a fusillade of crossbow bolts which had done for his erstwhile favourite son and nearly brought his own life to an abrupt and final full stop.

He had consequently and precipitously taken flight from London, closed up his counting-house and bunkered down at what was his family's ancient and ancestral bolthole in the country, far from the city. He was reasonably sure that The Oversight would not know of it, and even if they did, he was prepared. His sons, on the other hand, were not so sanguine about the enforced bucolic retreat.

Abchurch Templebane, for example, cursed with over-protuberant eyes and an almost complete absence of chin, did not like the enforced exile from London that had followed the destruction of The Oversight's premises on Wellclose Square. He didn't like the countryside one bit and wholeheartedly mistrusted the smells, the wildlife, the absence of crowds, the fresh air, the open spaces, the oppressive greenery by day and the even more intolerable silence at night. He abhorred every single thing about it that was not London, bar three: of the three things he *did* like, the first was that the pain of the exile he was forced to endure was mitigated by the fact that the closest rival he had for supremacy among the other sons of Issachar Templebane had been removed by a crossbow bolt.

He assumed Coram was dead as mutton, since the betrousered hellion who had shot him and then had near as damn shot Issachar through the back wall of the retreating coach would undoubtedly have got him. Poor old Coram, knee blown to splinters, wouldn't have had a dog's chance. It was a notion that made him grin every time he thought about his rival brother, writhing on the ground, screaming at him for help as the coach separated them.

The second thing he liked about the country was the heavy horse pistol that Issachar had given him. He had never carried a gun in the city, they being noisy, cumbersome things and much less handy than a blade, such as the well-honed jack-knife that bumped along with him in his coat pocket wherever he went, or the leather sap, loaded with heavy lead shot, which he kept stuffed in his back trouser pocket, a thing he had carefully sewn himself. The gun, however, made a wonderfully loud noise, and the sense of power as it kicked in his hand was almost sexual. Issachar, ever parsimonious with anything that required the dispersal of cash money, was surprisingly liberal in his approach to powder and shot.

"Take the gun and practise, boy," he'd said as he handed it over. "Practise like the very devil, for devils indeed may be after me before things get back to normal, and you'd as well be able to knock 'em down before they get their hooks in us!"

So, much time was spent in the old orchard adjoining the even older house as Abchurch took it upon himself to drill the other brothers in the use of their own guns. He took pride in the fact that of them all, his was the biggest and the loudest, and though it might not have had the longer range of some of the others' weapons, there was no doubt that at close quarters the horse pistol had no rival in the damage it could inflict.

"Ain't a horse pistol," Abchurch would crow. "'S'a bloody elephant gun, cos I reckon I could kill one of the big grey bastards with one shot of this beauty."

And while they had great larks in the orchard, noisily obliterating flowerpots and bottles and anything they could think of as they competed for inanimate things to smash and perforate, he had a great and growing hunger to see what a full load of buckshot would do to flesh and bone. He had several attempts at birds in flight, which he merely succeeded in frightening, and one carefully aimed shot at an unwise rabbit that overshot the creature's long ears and blew an ugly hole in what had previously been a well-kept bit of lawn. It was a secret source of great irritation to him that the next youngest brother to him, Garlickhythe, was every bit the natural sharpshooter that Abchurch was not. He was very jealous of Garlickhythe's skill, but was cunning enough in the ways of inter-fraternal politics never to show a bit of it to anyone else.

The third thing he liked about the countryside was the maid who came and cleaned the kitchen, daughter of the normal caretakers. She was called Dorcas, and was not a bit as timid as the gazelle for which she had been named. She seemed in fact to be "froward and accommodating" according to the other brothers, who either did not understand the meaning of the first word or missed their grasp on the one they had been reaching for, since otherwise they were—as Issachar had pointed out when overhearing their gossip—branding her a positive oxymoron. The brothers had later debated as to what the father had meant and decided it must be that she was bovinely stupid. In fact, she was neither; just direct and unfussed by the sudden arrival of all the young men who had attended Issachar's appearance in the house. Since they did not sound or act like high-born gentlemen, she had decided to treat them with less deference than she might have had they spoken and acted better.

Abchurch had decided that, as notional principal among his companions, he should be the first to allow her to accommodate him, and had decided the best way to do this was to invite her to watch him fire his gun in the orchard. This treat was planned for the golden hour before dusk, and Abchurch had instructed his brethren to "hang the fuck off and leave me alone with the doxy" in order that he might have neither competition when displaying his marksmanship, nor witnesses should the young lady be as accommodating as he fondly imagined she might be.

His brothers had nodded and understood and been very biddable, which he took to be a sign of their acceptance of his position as *primus inter pares*. Ill-favoured he might have been, but Abchurch was vain enough to imagine what was evident to him was also obvious to others. Unfortunately, what was obvious to the others was only that he thought himself first among equals, and had, as a result "been coming it some." In the competitive self-levelling fraternal ecology that Issachar and the late-lamented Zebulon had set up, "coming it some" was a condition that inevitably led to "being cut down to size." And so when Abchurch stepped out into the glory of golden hour in the orchard, with the setting sun gilding the now bare branches of the fruit trees and sending long shadows across the soft grass, he was unaware that the young lady he was so proudly escorting was about to be treated to a succession of humiliating misfires, since his brethren had disobligingly doctored his ammunition.

This fact and the culprits behind it were revealed as a line of heads popped up over the orchard hedge after the sixth or seventh failure of his weapon, and a series of ribald voices rang mortifyingly across the evening stillness.

"What cheer, Abby? You shooting blanks, or you just going off half-cocked?"

"Half-cocked! That's the ticket!"

"Half cock? He wishes! Ain't even that—I seen it! Three-quarter of an inch shorter and you'd be calling him Fanny!"

The last voice was, to make things worse, clearly the voice of the hated marksman Garlickhythe. The laughter that followed his final sally was infectious, and Dorcas could not help but giggle.

The next thing she knew she was seeing stars and had tumbled back into the chilly waters of the thin rill which flowed through the meadow, roughly dividing it in half. She tried to get up but found Abchurch standing over her. He reached down and ripped the front of her bodice open, and then stepped back.

Dorcas was no coward. She let her dress gape open and laughed at him.

"Fill your eyes, you foul-breathed, chinless get! See what you'll never have. Because if you lay one hand on me, I've five brothers that will find you and bloody geld you with a blunt sickle."

He snarled and pointed the pistol at her.

"I'll give you something to laugh at, you cu—"

"ABCHURCH!"

His face jerked up to see Issachar storming over the grass towards him.

The line of heads along the hedge miraculously dropped out of sight and disappeared.

"Help her out of the stream, apologise profusely—profusely, I say—and then come find me," said the Day Father, turning on his heel. "I've an errand to be run back in London, and you just identified yourself as the lucky runner."

CHAPTER 9

AN UNEXPECTED DIVERSION

The man who called himself the Proctor led them straight through the house to the kitchen at the back. Lucy had the impression of a clean, well-ordered set of rooms with polished floors and plain wood furnishings, and then they pushed through a door to find Prudence Tittensor sitting waiting beside an iron range that for a moment reminded her of the much bigger one that was Cook's pride and joy back in London, far away on the other side of the ocean. And then she focused on the waiting woman, and not one but two dogs sitting beside her, and all thoughts of cosy familiarity fled from her head.

The two remarkable things about the captain's wife were firstly that she was dressed for the road in a bombazine cloak which made her look like a squat crow that had just perched by the fire, and the second was that she held two pairs of manacles in her hands.

Cait stood staring at her.

"I'll not be wearing those, thank you very much," she said with an air of calm finality.

Mrs. Tittensor looked at the man in the doorway behind them.

"You'll do what the Proctor tells you to do."

Cait sniffed and looked at the woman as the dog Shay padded in between Lucy and herself. The two other dogs, who looked younger, sat up and watched alertly.

"Should have bought more sausages," said Cait.

The two sitting dogs growled, low and threatening.

"Digger, Robber. Be still," said Mrs. Tittensor.

The larger dog lowered itself onto its haunches. Lucy watched it sit and gaze at them both, its liquid brown eyes strangely impassive.

"You sent that dog for this Proctor creature," said Cait. "At the harbour."

"What I did or do is no matter of yours," said Mrs. Tittensor.

"No, no, missus, you'd be about as wrong as you could be there. What you've done is precisely my business," said Cait, turning her head to look at Lucy. "You get what she is, right?"

"They're both . . ." began Lucy.

"Exactly," said Cait. "She's some kind of animal shifter, like Hodge."

"And you're *fiagaí*," spat Mrs. Tittensor. "Venatrix or some such, here without let or licence."

"I need no licence," said Cait. "I cut my own way."

"That may be how things are in the old country," said Mrs. Tittensor. "You'll find it isn't how we do things here."

"Ah," said Cait, as if something was beginning to make sense, though Lucy had no clue as to what that might be. "And how pray do you do things here in this fine new country you have?"

"We like things regular," said the Proctor. "That is to say, regulated."

"And here was I believing all the brave talk back home about this being the land of liberty," said Cait.

"Plenty of liberty to go round here," said the Proctor. "Regulating things is how we keep it so."

"Well, you'll pardon the freedom of my language, but it sounds to me like you're talking out of both sides of your arse," said Cait.

"Just put your wrists out, ladies," sighed the Proctor. "Time enough for talking once we get there."

"Oh, and where's that?" said Cait, keeping her arms at her sides.

"Out to Marblehead way," said the Proctor. "The Guardian's going to want to see you."

Cait turned to look at him without flinching at the blued steel still pointing unwaveringly at her face.

"Do you mean us harm?" she said.

"No," he said. "Which is to say, not yet, perhaps. But that would be contingent."

"On our behaviour?" she said.

"That and what the Guardian makes of you," he replied.

Cait closed her eyes as if doing a complicated calculation in her head, then she opened them and nodded decisively.

"Right. Here's the thing of it: I'll come with you, give you my parole for the journey, be meek as a lamb. But I'll not wear shackles. Try and make me, we'll find out if you're really faster than I am. Likely you may be, but I'd rather try it than wear any man's iron, and there's the end of it."

He looked at them both.

"They're dangerous," said Mrs. Tittensor, voice shrill with barely repressed tension. "You should do your job. You should—"

The Proctor's face ticked slightly, almost imperceptibly, but Lucy caught it and read the suppressed moment of irritation. This was a man who did not like to be told what to do. He took a deep breath and then clearly bit back what he was about to say, instead letting out a long hiss of air.

"Your blades," he said, nodding at Cait. "Shuck 'em and any weapons the Glint there's carrying on the table now. Do that and I'll take your parole for good behaviour until we get to the Mansion."

Cait tossed a couple of razors on the table and reached under her dress for the thin knife she wore in a boot sheath.

"Hear that, Lucy-girl? He knows you're a Glint and we're going to a Mansion, no less."

The Proctor tilted his head at Lucy.

"Your word stand for her?"

"It does," said Cait. "Isn't that right, Lucy Harker?"

Lucy saw the warning look in Cait's eyes, swallowed what she wanted to say and nodded.

"She armed?" he said.

"I never thought it polite to ask," said Cait. "But the world being what it is, she'd be a fool as a woman if she wasn't."

Lucy reached under her jacket and slid out the slender dagger she wore in a horizontal sheath sewn into the waistband of her dress.

She put it next to Cait's weapons.

The eyes on either side of the heroically broken nose looked into hers, without blinking.

"More'n one way to be a fool," he said.

Lucy sighed and reached into the wrist of her gloves. She had begun carrying a small cutthroat razor there in direct imitation of Cait's habit, and found her face colouring at having to expose what now seemed a callow and revealing instance of hero worship.

She was surprised to see Cait grin in approval.

"Nice to see you're learning something at least," she said. "Nine times out of ten razors get the job done better than a knife. Hope for you yet."

There was a carriage waiting at the back of the house, with two matched bays which looked more like hunters than draught horses, and a coachman who was too muffled against the evening chill to register as anything more than a hunched shape in the gloom.

He seemed entirely unsurprised to see two women led out at gunpoint and ushered into the carriage. Mrs. Tittensor and the dog Shay followed, and by the time the door was closed the space inside was more than crammed. Cait and Lucy sat beside each other, and the Proctor and the captain's wife sat facing them, with the dog sitting at attention on the floor between them, her eyes locked on the two parolees.

As soon as the door clicked shut, the carriage lurched into movement. There was a certain amount of rocking and pitching as the driver negotiated the close-built streets of the neighbourhood, but in five minutes they had descended to the coast road and the horses opened out into a brisk trot that made the going smoother.

Through all this, Lucy noted the Proctor's gun and the dog's eyes had remained steadily unmoving, aimed directly at them as if mounted on gimbals.

On the right side of the road they could see a full moon reflected on a fretful sea, the offshore wind deckling the disordered remains of the long Atlantic rollers as they surged ever landward, broken into choppy fragments of their former oceanic grandeur by the protective jumble of barrier islands visible further out in Massachusetts Bay.

Initially the moonlit seascape was visible through the palisade of masts, spars and cranes which lined the working shore of the bay, but after a while the wharfs and boatyards and warehouses thinned out and the view was unobstructed.

Lucy felt a lurch in her stomach at the thought that all she knew of the world was hidden far beyond that distant horizon. She turned and looked out of the other window. On that side there was no water, no sea, just a few lit windows in the houses dotted along the rising slope of land. The heavier darkness hunched and waiting beyond those lights made her stomach lurch again. And she was surprised to find it was not a wholly unpleasant feeling: it was excitement, excitement mixed with trepidation certainly, but mainly what she was feeling was the thrill rather than the fear of the unknown.

"I like your dog," said Cait, leaning back in her seat, as if this was all a fine lark.

"She doesn't like you," said Mrs. Tittensor. "One wrong move and she'll take your face off."

"That's what I like about her," said Cait with a smile. "What I like about any dog: loyalty."

"She'll have your throat out," said Mrs. Tittensor. "You stay where you are now."

"You've a very gory turn of phrase, Mrs. Tittensor, sure you have," said Cait. She shifted to smile at the man with the gun. "Is she normally like this, Mr. Proctor?"

"I'm just a Proctor. My given name doesn't signify," he said.

"Well I'm Caitlin Sean ná Gaolaire, and this is my apprentice, Lucy

Harker," said Cait. "And you'll no doubt be interested to know why we've come all this long way over the bounding main, seeing as how you like things nice and 'regulated' in this brave new world of yours?"

She smiled at Mrs. Tittensor. Lucy realised she was trying to unsettle the woman. "She'll be less interested, but maybe a little more concerned, because she knows fine well. Isn't that right, Mrs. Tittensor? Do you think the gentleman with the revolving pistol here'd be quite so solicitous of you if he knew the truth of it?"

Mrs. Tittensor gave her a look that would have curdled milk.

"Save it for the Guardian," said the Proctor. "This ain't the time."

"She stole a babby . . ." began Cait.

"Took it from a changeling bitch on the dockside in port o' London is what I heard," said the Proctor matter-of-factly. "Paid cash money too."

Cait sat back. She kept her face still, but Lucy knew she was surprised that the captain's wife's secret was known and openly spoken of.

"Like I said," scowled the Proctor. "Keep it for the Guardian."

"Where is the child?" said Cait.

Mrs. Tittensor didn't answer. Cait shrugged and closed her eyes as if the silence meant nothing and she had just decided to go to sleep. Lucy looked out at the moonlit sea. The sky was not so clear now as clouds had begun to roll in overhead. She stared at the view until a squall blew a sharp spatter of raindrops against the carriage windows, and then she watched the water runnelling down the glass until she too slept.

CHAPTER 10

FOR WANT OF A TWELVE-INCH BASTARD

Despite the Ghost's thwarted vengeance dictating the need to make all speed with their journey to London, they were sorely delayed on the road. Will-power alone, however manic, was no match for the crippling ague with which she was assailed on the day after the conversation beneath the hornbeam.

It had been a bright morning, and the early sunshine had been a welcome addition of warmth to limbs stiff with cold from a night spent beneath a ruinous old barn that had been abandoned to the rats, rats whose bold scuttlings to and fro had made the night one of broken sleep and worse dreams than usual when that sleep did come.

She had spent the morning talking, telling him about the tension between the worlds of the natural and the supranatural. He knew she had decided to turn tutor, as it were, as a means of binding him to her. He listened attentively despite her motives, for the plan of things that she sketched was in parts surprising and in other parts conformed to what he had picked up and assembled for himself both from his personal experiences and from eavesdropping on the edges of conversations held by his "brothers" and the two fathers. He had always hidden his ability to hear others' thoughts from them all out of a well-honed instinct for self-preservation: it had enabled him to overhear not only what was said quietly or on the other side of unguarded keyholes, but also what remained unsaid and merely thought. Initially he had been worried the Templebanes would punish him for what was, to them, a freakish ability. Later, once he had learned of how they connived with strangely abled confederates like the Sluagh, he wondered if he might gain preferment within the purposely competitive pecking order of the sons by letting the fathers avail themselves of his facility, since it would make him the perfect spy and tattle-tale. He dismissed the impulse after a couple of hours' consideration: the reasons were several but the main one was that he simply didn't trust them. He was scared of them, certainly, but his obedience was a practical thing, not a matter of loyalty. He had watched his brothers fight and betray each other to inch up the greasy pole of preferment. He had stood apart in his silence and known, he now realised, that this was not for him, because one day he would walk away.

The Ghost had begun to tell him about The Oversight, which piqued his interest, but she had spoken in a meandering and disjointed way, weaving their history in with stories of other esoteric pursuers of different truths: she spoke of London's past, of alchemists and natural philosophers, of Kabbalists and Rosicrucians and fine upstanding members of the Royal Society, whatever that was, clever but foolish men who had turned occult scientists to attempt to understand the supranatural so they might control it. At some point in the early afternoon, she had begun to ramble in her speech and seemed to be weaving her own family history into the lesson, for it became clear she had had a father who was one of these "clever fools" who travelled as a kind of itinerant tutor to other great men, passing on supposed truths about a world he knew less of than they thought, at a price far above any practical worth.

"He was a charlatan," she said. "A very intelligent one, and a charlatan by default rather than by commission. I loved him, but once I realised what I was, what I could do and that he could not do it, I saw him for what he was. The tragedy was that he believed he was a wise man; he believed he had knowledge. So, an honest charlatan, my father, peering into the shadows and seeing less than he imagined he saw, and saying he saw more than he did. And yet he appeared to know enough to earn his living at it, and I was young and foolish enough to think myself the gentleman's daughter he raised me to be. Spend enough time in a pigsty, you become hoggish, they say. Spend enough time in the households of great men, a similar varnish adheres to you. I thought I was safe, clever and loved even . . . and then—"

And then she coughed, stumbled and pitched forward into the road, as if poleaxed by an invisible assailant.

They had been far from any buildings, and Amos had carried her to the side of the road and wrapped her in the one blanket they shared, a thin thing filched from a washing line two counties ago. Her face had gone alarmingly white and the blueness of her lips made him convinced she was finally dying. He had smelled woodsmoke and heard voices on the other side of the wood, but when he had found them he'd been dismayed to find no human habitation beyond the temporary lean-tos of a gang of charcoal burners.

The charcoal burners were borderline outcasts, as charcoal burners always have been, haunting the woodland like soot-stained wraiths, reeking of smoke and tar as they tended their carefully constructed conical kilns, but as is the case with most groups living a liminal existence, they were accepting of others clearly wracked by misfortune. They made space for the Ghost by the fire, and they quickly used their billhooks and axes to make a temporary shelter for her to lie in and sleep. Amos indicated by sign language that he would help them work, but they shook their heads, went about their arcane trade as if only someone trained to it could understand how to stack the logs in concentric circles, or pile the wet earth and boughs around it to make the distinctive flattened beehive shape of the kilns. Half of them were involved in construction, and the rest chopped trees.

The oldest men, clearly the masters, moved least but endlessly monitored the colour of the woodsmoke emerging from the top of the kilns to ensure the heat was constant, day and night, poking holes in the clay walls when they felt more air was needed to aid the combustion, slapping patches of wet mud over the same openings when they wished to smoor the fires.

Amos and the Ghost stayed with the charcoal burners for several days as she seemed to flutter like a moth along the thin line dividing life from death. Amos was finally allowed to work for their keep, helping to tend the camp-fire and carry the finished charcoal out of the woods to a prearranged point on the road, where a carter awaited to take the product of their toils away to market.

Although Amos was keen to get to London, he couldn't abandon the Ghost, not because he felt deep loyalty to the woman who had betrayed him, but because he thought she was dying. The thought came to him that it would be a very cold and terrible thing to die alone, and so he remained, not as a friend, but simply as one who knew her. He also understood that the thought was a strange one, and probably came from a weakness within him: there really was no particular benefit to him for acting in a kind way, and he was sure she would have even now betrayed him again in an instant if by doing so she might have ensured that Mountfellon would die as a result.

He was musing on this late one night, sitting on a recently cut stump a little way from the camp, leaning against the long handle of a felling axe whose head was buried in the circle of wood, which made an impromptu backrest. He had removed himself from the immediate vicinity of the others because he wanted some quiet in which to ponder what to do if the Ghost didn't die. He was far enough from the camp not to hear the low hubbub of everybody's thoughts, but close enough to see the golden light dancing among the remaining tree trunks, and the contrasting white light of the moon broken into pieces by the dark tracery of branches overhead. Someone was playing a mournful fiddle tune on the other side of the camp, and the wind was getting up enough to make him think of going back to the meagre warmth of the fire and the comforting smell of the woodsmoke which now permeated all of his clothes.

Something gently touched his neck.

"What is this?" said a quiet, ruined voice.

He looked down. One of the distinctive broken-backed bronze blades carried by the Sluagh had been hooked around his neck from behind. He swallowed and turned slowly. He was unsurprised to find a face full of interwoven tattoos looking at him with interest. This Sluagh looked older than any of the others Amos had seen. His head was shaven in a tonsure like a monk's. The bald dome of his head was decorated with a tattoo of a hawk, and the hair that ringed it was interwoven with a circlet of falcons' skulls which made a strange bony wreath that clattered as he moved. The cruelly curved beaks were dyed black and were surprisingly small in comparison with the bulge of the birds' skulls with their giant eye-sockets that stared blankly back at him.

The hawk-skull Sluagh ran his fingertip around Amos's neck, tracing the thin and barely visible line where he himself had once been marked.

"White Tattoo," said Hawk Skull. He laughed quietly. "You're the boy Badger Skull used."

Amos nodded.

"And yet you are scared of me. I don't think you like me. I don't think you are truly our friend."

Amos shrugged.

What do you want?

"Ah," said the Sluagh. "You can talk like that can you?"

What do you want?

"I've been wanting to see you again," said the Sluagh, and he stepped closer, his smile widening and emitting a foul-smelling gout of breath as he chuckled nastily into Amos's face. "For old time's sake, you know . . ."

I've never seen you before.

"I have seen you before, boy. And that's what interests me. When you came to see Mountfellon. Not recently, but earlier. The first time. See, when Badger Skull told of how he had used a boy who could not speak to break into Mountfellon's house and take the flag for us, I thought it was you. Do you know we hunted you the night you came to Gallstaine in the rain, myself and two brothers? We were going to take you from

Mountfellon's coach after he changed horses at the inn before Hertingfordbury, but you must have heard us and ran away. We nearly had you too, but you jumped into the canal, and running water saved you. Do you remember that? Thwarting us, balking me, nearly drowning?"

Amos remembered the night, and he remembered seeing shadows in a field beyond the inn suddenly move and resolve into three Sluagh on horseback. At the time, it had been one of the most frightening things he had seen in his life, though since then he had seen and done much worse. Still, the memory of that fear ran through him like a cold shudder. He remembered hearing them make their plans, and he remembered sneaking into the stable and picking up a twelve-inch bastard file for protection and then running for his life, pelting blindly into the dark, leg muscles burning with the effort as he tried to sprint away across ploughed fields with clay-clogged boots which dragged like cannonballs.

He shook his head.

Wasn't me.

There was something in the way Hawk Skull had spoken, something gleeful and knowing that made him lie. And more than that, made him wish he had the protective security of that heavy iron file in his hand.

"It was you," said the Sluagh, stepping even closer, the curve of his sickle blade holding Amos close to him. "And I told Badger Skull and he said he didn't believe me, but I told him you was in league with Mountfellon afore he found you, because you carried a name we know, because you was a Templebane, and Templebanes is nigh as bad as Mountfellon is. And so, if you were in league with Mountfellon from before, why then, you might be useful to us in working against him or the two brothers in London, eh?"

He shook his head as if trying to dislodge a bad memory.

"Anyway, Badger Skull has a liking for you so he said he didn't believe it because if you had such bad blood in you he'd have felt it. But he's young, is Badger Skull, and so he's soft. So I come to find you and bring you back. Because even if you can't help, you can be punished,"

For what?

"Mountfellon's crimes. He skinned some of us for his collection. We'll have the skinning of him for that, by and by, but till then maybe we could start with you."

Amos wished he had that file, any file, any weapon in fact. He felt the blade prick the side of his neck and steeled himself not to look towards the axe in the stump.

It wasn't me.

"Oh, it was you, boy," said Hawk Skull, tugging Amos towards him so they were almost nose to nose, so close that Amos could feel the hotness of his breath against his face.

"It was most certainly you, certain as moon follows sun it was you," he repeated, his free hand pointing to his circlet of falcon skulls. "Eyes like a hawk I have, boy, and memory like a brock."

He sniffed.

"And you smelled just like that."

Like what?

"Like you're going to piss yourself with fear."

You're wrong.

Amos shivered and looked downwards.

I have pissed myself. And you too . . . I'm sorry—

The Sluagh's eyes looked down, and he stepped back instinctively.

Amos slapped the curved blade to one side with his left hand and at the same time grabbed a handful of the falcon-skull tonsure. He felt the sting as two of the sharp little beaks pierced the palm of his hand, but he gripped even harder as he yanked the Sluagh's head down into the up-swinging pile-driver of his knee. Things jarred and went crunch and the Sluagh gagged and choked, as if winded. He fell backwards into the undergrowth on the other side of the stump.

Amos looked at the axe handle he had been leaning against, sticking out of the wood like a sundial.

The old Sluagh had not got to be so old by being slow or weak or lacking in resilience. He shook his head angrily, sending blood from his ruined nose to the right and to the left. And then looked up at

Amos on the other side of the stump with a look of coldest, murderous fury.

He gripped his blade and leapt at him, teeth bared in a snarl.

Something broke inside Amos.

It was a sharp feeling, like a strap snapping in two.

He didn't run away.

He'd decided to stop running a while ago.

He leapt right back towards the Sluagh, jerked the axe out of the stump and swung straight down.

As he did so, he had enough time to notice that he seemed to be moving fast while everything, including the approaching Sluagh, was moving oddly slowly.

The blade chopped through the Sluagh's head with such force that it chunked into the open face of the stump between them, pinning him to it like a bug. Amos stumbled back and watched in a kind of horror-struck relief as the circle of newly cut wood, white in the moonlight an instant before, went dark with the lifeblood of the Sluagh.

It had happened quickly and without loud noises, and so no alarm was raised in the camp below. Amos's eyes swung away from the fires and scanned the shadows in the depths of the surrounding wood. He jerked the axe free and held it ready, sure that at any moment those same shadows would move and reveal a horde of other avenging Sluagh. He was so focused on watching that the gush of blood that spattered him from the split head went completely unnoticed.

As he watched, he felt the thumping of his heart and heard his breath returning to normal. But most of all, he felt the looseness within his chest. That thing that had felt like a strap breaking had done something to him. And he was not sure that it was a bad thing. Indeed, he felt it had been the thing breaking that had somehow enabled him to move so fast that the Sluagh had appeared to slow himself down in a kind of pantomime physical joke that would have been funny had the punchline not been an axe through a falcon tattoo and a tree stump stained red with gore.

He felt the blood now cold and wet on his clothes in the light breeze. He was, once again, the Bloody Boy.

But the shadows remained still. And after a long while, he forced himself to take hold of the Sluagh and drag him through the wood until he found a scrape where the charcoal burners had dug out some clay, and then he tumbled the body into the shallow pool of water which had gathered in the bottom and threw some mud and branches over it, and then he allowed himself to step quietly back towards the camp, still clutching the axe.

It was time to move, Ghost or no Ghost.

She was, to his great shock, standing by the fire. She looked at him with no corresponding surprise in her own eyes.

"There was a Sluagh," she said.

How did you know?

She shrugged as if it was nothing.

"Something in the wind. Or I dreamt it. Or I saw it."

There was. It's gone.

She looked at his blood-soaked clothes.

"You'll need to steal another shirt," she said. "We can do that on the road to London."

She had obviously decided not to die quite yet.

SECOND PART

THE RETURNED

This visible world is a trace of the invisible one,
and the former follows the latter like a shadow.

Algazelus

On the Unkindness of Ravens

Ravens are wholly unlike other birds, which is why the old Book of St. Albans calls a group of them "Ane vnkyndennys of rauynnys," in that they are unkind, as in not the same, rather than unkind meaning malevolent . . . and it is not possible to think of any bird that has a closer sympathy with the human, and the history of The Oversight has always been closely entwined with the ravens they both protect and share duty with. Further, it is said that The Oversight itself is overwatched by one particular Raven among ravens, an uncannily long-lived bird that remembers everything it has ever seen, and has the unsettling knack of being in two or even all places at any time. Moreover, the Raven has always had strong supranatural associations as a proven mediator between life and death . . . from this stems the potency of the Raven as war token or shield-bird . . . Ragnar Loðbrók sacked Paris beneath a banner known as "Reafan," emblazoned with the fell bird . . . the flag was so powerful that if it blew in the wind, victory would follow, but if it hung flat and unmoving then he would be defeated . . . the last great Viking, Harald Hardrada, killed by the doomed English king Harold at Stamford Bridge, died beneath his own raven banner "Landeyðan," which fell with him and now is lost, though some say it is buried beneath the White Tower . . . Friedrich Barbarossa sleeps beneath the Kyffhäuser in Thuringia along with his knights, guarded by ravens who circle the mountain continuously, waiting for the day when they cease their avian vigil and he will rise and save Germany again . . . just as King Arthur is said, in some medieval materials that make up the Matter of Britain, to lie sleeping beneath a raven shield, hidden in a chamber under a hill, also guarded by ravens where he waits until Britain's need is direst . . .

From *The Great and Hidden History of the World* by the Rabbi Dr. Hayyim Samuel Falk (also known as the Ba'al Shem of London)

CHAPTER II

EVERY HOMECOMING A BETRAYAL

A dusting of unseasonably early snow had arrived in London just ahead of Sara Falk and Mr. Sharp's return from Paris, where they had endured both a long ordeal in the mirror'd world and then an escape from the catacombs beneath the city which had involved nearly drowning in a bottle dungeon and witnessing a catalogue of horrors that had exhausted them both.

The destruction of the Safe House, its reduction to the rubble-strewn wasteland at the bottom of Wellclose Square was almost the last blow, and if Charlie Pyefinch and a cohort named Ida, previously unknown to them, had not found them at the peak of their distress, Sara felt she might have easily lost her mind for a moment. As it was, the two new younger members of The Oversight had reassured them that at least the others survived, and brought Hodge's familiar dog cart to convey them with all speed to the temporary new headquarters at The Smith's Folley out on the Isle of Dogs.

The scrape of snow was already melting beneath the wheels of the cart as they bumped out of the square, leaving the desolate scene behind them.

Sara looked at Sharp, who was white-faced with exhaustion and what she knew was rigidly suppressed worry and guilt. The protection of the Safe House was his especial concern, a duty he had taken upon himself a long time ago, that and the responsibility for her specific protection.

She knew the catastrophic destruction of their home was hitting him hard. She put her hand on his knee.

"Bedrock and bone," she said. "That's enough for us to build on, no matter how desperate the news is."

He nodded. Sara turned and tapped Charlie on the shoulder.

"Right," she said. "Tell me what happened—everything. There is not a moment to waste."

Charlie grimaced and shot a glance at Ida as if asking for help; she just shrugged.

"I don't how to tell it," he said. "I mean, I don't know how to tell you everything. All at once. In the right order, like . . ."

"I expect we can wait until we get to The Smith's," said Sharp, looking at Sara with concern. To him, her face looked as tight as a drum, and her jaw muscles were clearly visible, clenching and unclenching beneath the taut skin. "Let The Smith tell it."

"Well. Er . . ." said Charlie.

"Er?" said Sara.

"There's no Smith. Not there. He's gone north."

"Why?"

Charlie looked at Ida for support.

"So much to tell," she said. "Maybe Charlie is right: can you wait till Cook and Hodge can do it? They will say it better, I think."

"Yes," said Charlie. "There's just so much been going on . . ."

"Start with what happened to the house," snapped Sara. "Sorry. Start with what happened to my home."

"Ida can tell you best," said Charlie, ignoring the look of betrayal the girl shot him. "No, seriously, Ide. You saw it all. Me'n Hodge didn't see the beginning. Not like you did."

He turned to Sharp and Sara.

"If Ida here hadn't been on her way to see us, if she hadn't been sitting in the square, well, you wouldn't have just lost the Safe House: we'd have lost Cook too, no question. It was Ida who saw it all happening and got into the house to warn her so they could get out in time."

"I was just in the right place," said Ida, looking embarrassed.

"If you saved Cook, then you are my friend for life, Miss Laemmel," said Sara.

"Trousers," grinned Ida. "Cook calls me Trousers."

"Because she wears them," said Charlie.

"But you can call me Ida," said the girl.

"Ida. Please tell me how my house was destroyed," said Sara. "It will help me to start somewhere, to get a grip on a lifeline, for I fear that I feel my world is in danger of unravelling . . ."

Ida nodded.

"So. I was, like Charlie says, sitting in the square. It was early and I had just come from the docks. I had news for you, as I said, from my colleagues in *Die Wachte*, news about a breath-stealer and a letter we had found about their activities in London, but I can tell you about that later. So. Again: I was waiting for it to be a reasonable time to knock on your door, and I was also just looking around, getting my bearings, so to speak. I saw the sugar factory at the top of the square, and I saw this man, a young man whose eyes were wrong, and before I could make up my mind why they were wrong he rolled these little round metal balls with fuses— what is the word, Charlie?"

"Grenadoes," said Charlie.

"He rolled these grenadoes like a man playing skittleballs, and they went in through the big open door of the factory and— Oh wait, sorry, there was another man just before, a big man who had stopped his horse cart at the bottom of the square right outside your house, and then he left it and walked away until he got to the corner and then he ran, and that's when I saw the cart was loaded with *Lampenöl*. Do you say, er, lamp oil, *ja*? Anyway barrels of it, and that's when I looked back at the factory and saw the grenado-bombs being rolled in and then they exploded and I saw the giant vats of boiling sugar tip and crack and then there was rivers of burning treacle running downhill towards the house and, um—"

"And that's when she chased down the bomber and shot him," said Charlie, taking an evident vicarious pride in his friend's prowess.

"Shot?" said Sharp. "With a gun?"

"Crossbow," said Ida. "I am a hunter. The bomber was getting into a waiting carriage around the corner. I shot him and broke his knee. He fell in the street and then the carriage whipped away and left him."

"She had a crack at the carriage too," said Charlie. "Two bolts in the back of it, then she legged it for the Safe House and got in just before the fire did, and warned Emmet and Cook and they got out through the tunnels to the Sly House after the burning sugar exploded the lamp oil and the front of the house went in. Least Cook and Ida did. Emmet brought the roof of the tunnel down on top of himself and stopped the fire getting them."

"And Emmet . . . ?" said Sharp, and stopped, either surprised to find he had gripped Sara's arm without meaning to, or because the question had got stuck in his throat, which he now cleared with a gruff cough. "What happened to Emmet?"

Sara placed her hand on top of his without looking at him. She was both aware of how close the bond between Sharp and the mute clay man had been, and how he would not wish to be observed reacting to what sounded like it was going to be very bad news.

"He's all right," said Charlie with an unexpected smile. Sharp felt Sara give his hand the merest hint of pressure before letting go. "No, Smith had us dig him out from the blocked tunnel once the ruins had cooled off above. Took five days. Me, Hodge, The Smith, even Cook and Ida pitched in. All his clothes burned off him, but he's right as a trivet. Takes more than hellfire and a house landing on him to kill a golem is what Cook said. And that's what the burning sugar looked like, right enough, like hell had opened and the rivers of flame come flooding out . . ."

"And what of the Wildfire?" said Sara.

"Cook saved it and got it away," said Charlie. "Smith said if Ida had funked going into the house barely one step ahead of the flames, and if Emmet hadn't done a Samson and brought the house down around his own ears—why, half of London would have gone up most likely."

"Smith was exaggerating," said Ida, looking away, the tops of her ears pinking with embarrassment.

Charlie turned and grinned at Sharp and Sara.

"Ida don't funk much," he said. "She's a terror."

Sharp and Sara looked at the dark-haired girl.

"It seems the list of things we owe you is getting longer by the minute," said Sara.

"Nobody owes me anything," said Ida. "Any of you would have done what I did."

"Not me," said Charlie. "Not without second thoughts, and by the time I'd have had them, it would have been too late. It was that close . . ."

"Who was in the carriage?" said Sara. "The one you shot at?"

"Issachar Templebane," said Charlie. "Ida got back out on the street and tried to follow it."

"Templebane," said Sara. "I should have shot him when I could . . ."

"That's not what you are, Sara," said Sharp. "That's not what we are sworn to."

"This is my failure," said Sara, pulling her hand away from his. "I should have dealt with him before I . . . before I went into the mirrors."

"Well, since through them you found me without a minute to spare, I cannot be entirely unconflicted in my view on that," said Sharp. "And if blame is to be put, I think my claim takes precedence, since it was I who went into the mirrors in the first place."

"You were trying to save me," said Sara, her voice strangely bleak.

Charlie thought he had never seen such a terrible expression on anyone's face as the one he saw on hers as she looked away at the buildings passing on either side. It was like she was being torn in half. It was unbearable to see. So was the look on Sharp's face as he watched the back of Sara's head, now turned away from him, gazing sightlessly out of the window. Charlie felt as though he was in the wrong place, as if Ida and he were witnessing something too intimate and private. He nudged Ida.

"Go on," he said. "Tell them what happened when you went after the carriage."

Words, any words were better than the uncomfortable silence hanging between Sharp and Sara.

"It was long gone," said Ida. "So was the fellow I wounded, but he was hit hard and left a good blood trail and so I followed."

"She found him in the sewer," said Charlie. "The new one they've been digging up west."

"He shouldn't have gone in there," said Ida. "Not underground in the excrement. He lost too much blood and he got human filth and who knows what all over himself. So. The wound went bad and the hospital had to cut his leg off above the knee."

"I'd have cut it off at the neck," said Sharp.

"Well, he lost his head the other way," said Charlie. "Fever and infection and the surgery sent him clear round the bend. He don't make much sense, but what sense he did make made him a Templebane, Coram by name, one of the sons of Issachar."

"And we have him?" said Sara.

"We did. We don't now, but we know fine where he is. Smith had him in the cells in the Sly House and then he put him in Bedlam. He ain't coming out any time soon is Coram Templebane. He's got his own special keeper too: a bloke called Ketch that Cook says you put a judgement on, Mr. Sharp."

"Bill Ketch," said Sharp. "I enjoined him to muteness until the May flowers bloomed, and then swore him to service at the Bedlam since he had sealed Lucy Harker's mouth with pitch and hessian and brought her to us in a sack. He had been worked on by the Sluagh . . ."

There was more silence. Sara appeared not to have been listening. The carriage bucked and clattered as it went over the narrow wooden bridge which crossed the thin but deep cut of water known as the Gut that divided the rest of London from the Isle of Dogs.

"Well, there may be a symmetry in that," said Sharp. "Templebane was mixed up in it somehow too. Ketch was a sot, with a wet brain easily worked on. There was no especial malice in him. He's as decent a jailer as we could provide, if this Coram is to be suffered to live. Better than he deser— What?"

Sara had suddenly lunged across him in order to look out of the window on his side, her normally lithe body now stiff and taut.

She stared open-mouthed as she looked backwards at something they had just passed, something unbelievable beyond the two wheel-tracks they had left in the thin dusting of snow that remained on the narrow bridge, protected from the melting sun by the shadow of the tall warehouse close by.

"Sara?" he said, his hand touching her back. The contact broke whatever spell was keeping her still and quivering and like a hunting dog on point. She slammed back into her seat and rapped the ceiling.

"Stop!" she said. "STOP!"

Before the carriage had fully halted, she had opened the door and jumped to the ground, landing with a great splash in a deep puddle-filled rut and not paying the least attention to it as she stared back at three figures standing in the deep shadows of the warehouse on the other side of the bridge. Sharp leapt after her, and Ida and Charlie were right on his heels.

"Charlie Pyefinch," said Sara, turning to him in a gesture so fast he would have sworn that the long braid of her prematurely white hair cracked like a whip as she did so. "How many knives are you carrying?"

"Ah," said Ida.

"They're not doing any harm," said Charlie.

"They're Sluagh!" said Sara. "In my city. I've never seen them so bold."

"Or in such numbers," said Sharp. "Charlie, give her what knives you have."

"No," said Ida.

"No?" said Sharp. "Miss Laemmel, these are Sluagh!"

"They just want to talk," said Charlie.

"They're leaning on the railing," said Sara. "Jack, look at them."

Her voice had a stutter in it.

"They're just waiting for The Smith," said Charlie. "They've been there every night for a week, and in the day they do that: lurk in the shadows."

Sharp had stepped closer to the bridge and was peering at the unmoving figures, two of whom were leaning on a section of railing, the other sitting casually on it, leg dangling idly like any wharfside loafer.

"They're sitting on the railing," he said, looking back at Sara. "You're right. The iron railing."

Sara and he looked at Charlie and Ida.

"They're not . . ." began Charlie. "That's to say . . . well, it's one of the things I reckoned the others could explain better . . ."

"They are no longer scared or bound by iron," said Ida.

"The Iron Prohibition . . .?" said Sara.

"Broken," said Charlie.

"But they still won't cross running water," said Ida. "So we have that."

Sara's face now matched her hair. Charlie thought she looked as tintless as a calotype, her black oiled-silk riding habit making her seem like a monochrome figure erroneously added to a coloured picture.

"How did this happen?" she breathed.

"Dunno," said Charlie, painfully aware that this was not a suitable answer to such a momentous question. He looked at Ida for support.

"This is what Wayland Smith went to see," she said.

"The flag," said Sharp. "But they cannot have found the flag. It's safe; it's always been safe on—"

"—the island in the island," said Sara. "Two rings of running water protect it from any Sluagh, even if they found out where it was."

"Well that's where he's gone," said Charlie. "And now you know as much about that bit of the story as I do."

CHAPTER 12

NORTH BY STEAM

The Smith had indeed gone north to find out if his suspicions about why the Sluagh were no longer prohibited by iron were well-founded.

The first time he had made this journey, it had taken a great deal of time, tough horses ridden hard, a sworn company of battle-hardened followers, several weeks and a lot of fighting. That first time he had arrived at his destination, the island-within-the island, his great hammer was still bloody at his side and an equally well-used broadsword was strapped to the furs across his back.

Time had moved on but he was still here, he thought. He still carried the hammer, but now it was in a long leather travelling bag. And where he and his companions had once struggled up from the south through snowdrifts and raiding parties, he made the present journey sitting uncomfortably inactive in a carriage pulled northwards by the rhythmically puffing engine of a coal-fired locomotive, his only companion a stranger with a vaguely nautical air who was fast asleep in the corner of the bench-seat opposite, using a tarpaulin jacket as a blanket against the chill. If the hardy men and women who had accompanied that first journey had seen and heard the train he now rode as it passed in the night, they would like as not have thought all the old stories about dragons were true. And now they themselves were an old story, the corrosive passage of time having rusted their heroism from sharp-edged history to a blurry myth no one really remembered anyway. This, he decided, was one thing wrong with the easy modern passage from place to place: the absence of physical effort left too much time for thinking useless thoughts. And a man with his past had far too many things to remember.

It was not the first time he had travelled by train, but he was still surprised and somewhat exhilarated by the speed and the smoothness of the passage. He spent most of the journey watching the country slide past the window at his side. As it did so he was struck both by how much had changed and by how much remained of the landscape he had known for such an unnaturally long span of years. The journey took him through the now familiar countryside of tall hedgerows and copses and fields, past low-lying water meadows and the high woodland marching in step along the rolling hills above them. He recognised this Britain, had seen it hacked out from open heath and wilderness and marshalled into the particoloured patchwork of greens and browns it now was. He'd ridden over the land before the most ancient blackthorn hedge had been planted, and the wide rivers he now crossed so effortlessly on ingeniously built viaducts he had once forded on blown horses, soaked to the cruppers.

"How have I lived so long?" he mused, thinking the thought he had trained himself to avoid dwelling on. "And to what purpose if the Iron Prohibition is broken? If the old ravenous power of the dark is behind it, how do we stop it?"

The stranger asleep on the seat opposite shifted in his sleep and, as his jacket slipped, The Smith saw his assessment of him as a sailor was further corroborated by the florid Union Jack and fouled anchor inscribed on a meaty forearm.

The Smith had once been a tattooed man, both like and unlike the Sluagh, in the time before the Sluagh were even Sluagh. He had leached the darkness out of himself in an act of furious vengeful will-power, and sworn his life to the light, but there was so much darkness in the world that keeping it at bay and stopping the mark of it returning to blight his skin and his heart had required a binding woven as tightly into the Sluagh's flag as the Iron Prohibition itself. Indeed, the binding to the light and the Prohibition interlocked and bound each other in place, keeping the equilibrium. It was he who had fought the battles which led to the Iron Prohibition being imposed, and it was he who had bound it there with more than oaths. And now he was travelling an old road to see why the ancient things that should have remained interlaced had begun to unravel. He needed to examine the flag.

The industrial midlands shocked him, not so much because of the sprawling factories and mills or the forests of belching chimneys, of which he had seen plenty in London, but because they had sprung up in what seemed to him to be an instant, when compared to the long span of his memory. Jerry-built slums stretched in all directions from the industrial buildings like a ramshackle infection bent on blighting the outlying countryside. He thought it looked like radiating blood poison in the moment when it begins to visibly blacken the veins which criss-cross the previously unblemished skin of the dying patient. The land between Birmingham and Manchester seemed to have become ulcerated as a result of mouldering beneath a permanent pall of smoke. North of Manchester, the countryside reasserted itself, wilder now than it had been, higher fells and more open moorland, dry-stone walls taking the place of the hedgerows as a means to mark the divisions in the landscape.

He watched it all and tried to stay seeing it in the now, and not through the lens of memory. He was travelling to confront present danger and the past was only relevant if it contained clues as to how to succeed in the future. Sometimes the weight of accreted remembrance felt as if he had the world tied around his neck like a millstone and he just needed every ounce of energy to stay afloat.

He arrived in Glasgow at night and decided he needed to stretch his cramped limbs after so much sitting, and so walked from the station down to the wharf on the Broomielaw on the north side of the Clyde. Having slept everywhere and anywhere over the years, he thought little of spending the night on a bench beneath the open sheds beside the passenger steamers, and was thus the first aboard when the Skye Steam

Packet, the *Superb*, began embarking customers at 5.30 the following morning.

Once again, steam power afforded him a faster and infinitely more comfortable passage north than his first journey: he breakfasted well as the boat churned down the Clyde and turned right into the inner sea-lane leading to the Hebrides. He sat outside for most of the journey, relishing the clean, cold air, and the Highlands passing on one side and the islands on the other. They emerged from the Sound of Mull and rounded the desolate headland at Ardnamurchan, where there was a flurry of interest from his fellow passengers who all congregated on the starboard rail to point and comment on the building work occurring on the wild west-ernmost point of land. He understood it was the foundations of a new lighthouse being erected by an enterprising Mr. Stevenson, apparently a great builder of such things. When he turned to the empty rail on the port side, he saw the open waste of the Atlantic stretching to America and he thought of Lucy Harker and the Irish girl, and wondered if they had got there and what their fates might be. He wondered if Lucy was looking back across the same sea, thinking about The Oversight and what she had left behind. He had developed a gruff fondness for the awkward girl, and though he had taken pains not to share the thought with anyone but Cook, he had been more than sad when she decided to leave them and find her own way in the world. He had taken her under his wing and shared more of his deep past with her than he did with most. It wasn't that he felt she owed him loyalty because of that. It was the simpler, less definable thing of just having begun to like her, perhaps because she clearly had so much trouble liking herself.

Cook said Lucy had a romantic liking of her own for the venatrix Cait, a thing that would make her unhappy, since the tall Irish girl did not share her inclinations. He hoped she had found fulfilment elsewhere. He hoped she was forging a new and happier path wherever she was across that grey expanse of constantly shifting water.

The boat was not very full, and he remained undisturbed for the main part of the journey. Most of the passengers spoke in the Gaelic, and he felt a strange thrill of recognition and something like nostalgia as he heard it again, for it was an echo in his head and a reminder of earlier times, when even the English language wasn't formed as it was now. When he'd first come north, he and his band of fighters had not spoken a language that his present companions in The Oversight would understand. Riding over open land before the oldest hedgerows had been made was one thing; outliving a language really made you feel old. He smiled at the thought and just for a moment felt a deep pang of sadness that he had no one to share the wry observation with.

The boat passed the night at Tarbert due to an unscheduled stop requested by the engineer who suspected a bearing was about to give way. He worked through the night to repair it, and the boat completed the journey by reaching Portree mid-morning on the next day. The Smith had stood on deck and watched the towering scenery on both sides slide past as the *Superb* churned doggedly northwards between the island and the mainland, turning westwards at Kyle of Lochalsh where the view opened out to reveal a vista which included the contrasting mountain ranges of the Red Hills and the Black Cuillin: the sunlight caught the granite on the former, giving them a rosy glow, which along with their more rounded shape afforded them a friendlier feel than the aggressive jumble of sharp peaks, deep gullies and cavernously shadowed corries cut into the dark basalt and gabbro of the Black Cuillin beyond. The Red Hills reflected the sun, thought The Smith, whereas the Black Cuillin seems to swallow the light. And then the *Superb* rounded the small island of Scalpay where an immobile herd of sheep stood at the water's edge and watched, unmoved by the spectacle as the boat entered the Sound of Raasay and found, as if by accident, the small harbour town of Portree at the base of the hidden inlet that was its ultimate destination.

CHAPTER 13

WIGHTS

The mirror'd world did seem untenanted and sterile to the uninitiated. And even the few who were used to negotiating their way through the seemingly endless maze could become careless of the fact that every mirror held the possibility that other eyes were staring back at you through the veneer of your own reflection.

Once The Citizen had been convinced of the sense of Dee's plan, he had returned briefly to his quarters to assemble a minimum of necessary luggage, and then had allowed Dee to lead him back through the mirror. Dee had led The Citizen away from the looking-glass from which they had stepped out of London and the known environs of the house on Chandos Place with great care and attention but he had been so concerned with following the clicks of the get-me-home that he had not once looked behind him.

And so he missed something.

The thing that Dee missed, just as he turned the first corner and failed to check behind him, were the Mirror Wights.

First one head dropped, as it were, out of the looking-glass ceiling a couple of hundred yards beyond the place Dee and The Citizen had entered the mirrors. It had a long sailor's pigtail, which was the first thing to appear, then a round face, shockingly white as all Wights were, with staring black eyes like jet pebbles. It peered after the departing group, and then smiled as they turned out of view, revealing similarly black teeth.

It rolled itself out of the ceiling, uncurling like a monkey and landing quietly on bare feet. It wore a sailor's jacket and short wide-legged trousers, all bleached to a uniform white that was almost as complete as his skin. He beckoned behind him, waving unseen companions on with a flat-brimmed hat.

As he scuttled soundlessly towards the spot that Dee had emerged from three more pale figures stepped from the mirrors and clanked towards him. They were not sailors, but two were soldiers, Roundheads of the era of Cromwell's army from the look of them, pale figures from whom every last bit of normal pigment had too been leached by the mirrors: they wore breastplates and swords and wore heavy soled boots. The other was a murderous-looking man with a spade-like beard bleached as white as the rest of him.

The one who still wore a helmet arrived at the sailor first.

"Sure this is it?" he said, holding his eye close to the mirror.

The sailor nodded.

"No doubt. They smelled of blood, and I'm thinking it come from in there."

"Well then, brother, who wants to go first?" said the unhelmeted one.

The sailor stood up between them.

"Me," he said. "It's always me, innit?"

And without further pause he checked the mirror for himself, and then, drawing a nasty-looking dirk from his belt, stepped through it and into The Citizen's study and laboratory.

The others waited, swords drawn on either side of the mirror. And then, after a long pause of almost a minute, the sailor's head reappeared.

His mouth was leaking a tiny bead of bright red, and when he smiled his teeth were slick with something not saliva.

"Oh, lads," he said. "We are lucky, lucky bastards and no mistake. I never seen such a lovely thing. Come on in."

The others stepped through the mirrors and found themselves in the dark room. The sailor grinned from ear to ear and led them into the tiled laboratory area behind the curtain.

"Feast your eyes, lovelies, and then drink your fill," he giggled.

He was pointing at two cages. In one a depleted-looking Sluagh lay on the floor, and the other held a nearly naked man with green skin and fear-crazed eyes. Both were chained in position, and each had been arranged so that one arm was strapped clear of the cage, with a cannula emerging from the wrist.

"Why, brothers," he said, pointing at the arrangement. "It is as if the departed gentlemen have left these packages here for us, for look, they even have blessed straws inserted into their veins, so we can drain as much or as little as we need quite as if we were in our former lives and availing ourselves of a barrel with a spigot."

"Fuck me," grinned the helmeted soldier, unbuckling his chinstrap. "It's Christmas."

"I know," giggled the sailor. "But don't drain 'em, mind, and make sure you turn the little tap on them tubes so they don't leak, 'cos from what luggage they was carrying them as just left here ain't coming back in a hurry. So tomorrow can be Christmas too, and the day after and all the ones beyond."

The Green Man saw them approaching and screamed, a sound of pure terror.

"We should gag this monkey," said the sailor. "He'll only draw attention to himself, and that won't do at all."

CHAPTER 14

THE GUARDIAN

The journey from Boston to Marblehead had taken just over an hour. Cait had nudged Lucy awake as the horses slowed to a walk. They were in another built-up township, bordering the water. She could smell the tang of the sea, and woodsmoke and the smell of fish drying on racks on the stony beach beside the roadway.

They turned up a slight rise and approached a handsome three-storey mansion built in the Georgian style, with a shallow, columned porch whose triangular portico echoed the much larger one on the roof above. Two oil lamps burned either side of the main door, the lights of which reflected off the glass panes in the generous astragal windows that flanked them.

"Now that's some house," said Cait.

"Lee's Mansion," said the Proctor. "Least it was. It's a banking house now. Or the half of it is."

The carriage halted level with the door, which swung open as if on cue.

"Jeremiah Lee was once the richest man in America," said the Proctor.

Cait stepped out of the door and onto the steps. She ran her hands across the wooden façade of the house.

"Couldn't afford stone though," she said. "Just mixed sand in the paint to fake out the wood and make it look like honest ashlar."

"Sorry it don't meet with your approval," he said.

"Well," said Cait. "What's the point of America if it tries to look like somewhere else?"

"I've always admired the effect. It's ingenious," said the Proctor, ushering Lucy out of the carriage.

"Ah," said Cait looking studiedly unimpressed. "Yes, I spent much of the voyage over being told that about you."

"About who?" said Prudence Tittensor, emerging with her dog.

"New Englanders," said Cait. "Proud of their ingenuity."

"You have something against New Englanders?" said the Proctor.

"Well," Cait sniffed. "I'd have thought the old England was mischief enough for one world without the need for a new one."

Lucy followed her as she walked up into the dark hallway within. At first she thought there was no one there, and all she saw, by the light of one meagre candle on a table by the far wall, was hint of fine panelling, an expanse of rich red turkey carpet and a wide staircase with barley-twist bannisters sweeping up to the floors above.

Then the shadows moved and she realised there were people standing along the walls, waiting for them. The shortest of these figures retrieved the candle from the table and approached them. She was an old lady in a plain, pale grey dress the colour of sun-bleached driftwood. She wore a matching woollen shawl drawn around her narrow shoulders, and her hair and her eyes were precisely the same hue as the rest of her clothing.

"If you'd follow me," she said, her voice surprisingly strong as she turned and led the way to a door behind the stairs. They did not have time to take in much about the other figures who stepped away from the walls and followed behind them, other than the general impression that they were of both sexes and all ages.

The grey lady, who Lucy took to be some kind of housekeeper, led them through a pair of rooms, unlocking doors as she went from a ring of keys attached to her belt on a long silver chain. The rooms were also lined in wood panelling and seemed handsome, if sparsely decorated. Then their guide pushed a section of panelling aside and led the way down a narrow set of hidden stairs which brought them to the largest room so far.

The door that opened into the room was wide and heavy. It had five locks on it and in the centre carried a sigil which looked like nothing so much as a child's stick-drawing of a horned man. Despite its simplicity, Lucy found it strangely ominous, but had little time to ponder why this was so as the old lady pushed it open and beckoned them in.

Whatever Lucy had been expecting, it had not been this. Other than plain unpainted tongue-and-groove lining and a brick hearth in which a welcoming fire was crackling, the four walls were entirely lacking in ornament.

The floor was bare wood, unpolished but well scrubbed, and a wide circle of plain wooden chairs was arranged around what was clearly a meeting room.

The only other piece of furniture was an ornate mirrored closet in the far corner of the room, a design Lucy recognised immediately, having seen the Murano Cabinet in the Safe House in London. The familiar object in the unfamiliar surroundings was both unsettling and something to think about when she had time: right now there were more pressing novelties to compute, not least of which were the many pairs of eyes scrutinising her.

Many of the chairs were already occupied with a haphazard collection of seemingly ordinary men and women who appeared to have nothing else in common other than their shared location and a fascination with the two newcomers.

The most palpable and unnerving thing about the assembly convening around them was that they clearly all had "abilities." The kick of the supranatural was strong and all-encompassing, a tang so thick that Lucy felt she could smell it coming off them in waves. Yet despite the fact she was in a confined space with more people who shared her kind of abilities than she had ever been in her life, it was a peculiarly lifeless and undynamic feeling, especially when she compared it to the exhilarating crackle that had always been in the room when she had sat with

The Smith and Cook and Hodge and Charlie Pyefinch. Contrasting the feeling generated by this score or more of people with the five of them, she was surprised to find that it felt like constraint, not dynamic potential.

"Say nothing," said Cait quietly as they were shown to two adjoining seats facing the fire. Lucy nodded.

"Rings and watch fobs," added Cait and looked away.

Lucy kept her face disinterested as she let her eyes drift over what seemed curiously like a congregation shuffling into position as the remaining figures entered the room and began filling up the rest of the chairs. She saw that the men who were sufficiently genteel or affluent enough to wear watch chains all had similarly shaped pendants dangling from them. Those who seemed more of the artisan or working class in their dress wore rings. The women wore smaller rings.

Seated as they were, directly facing the blazing fire, Lucy and Cait had the distinct disadvantage of not being able to really see the faces of those opposite them, while also being unable to keep track of those to either side. Instead they were both conscious of the light and heat playing on their own faces which were clearly the object of universal scrutiny by the stony visages ranged around them.

The Proctor sat down next to them, and Lucy lowered her eyes and looked sideways, trying to discern the design on the fob of his watch chain while ignoring the pistol he kept pointed at her waist.

"My, but that's a splendid old fireback," said Cait, stepping meaningfully on Lucy's foot as she did so.

"Came with the house," said the old lady, who was the last to sit, taking a seat just to one side of the blaze.

Lucy looked into the grate and tried to make out the design cast in relief on the iron slab behind the flames. It was a shield of some sort, and though she could not make out what was on it because of the intervening fire, she saw, with a jolt of recognition, that a lion and a unicorn reared up on either side, as if supporting it.

"Now," said the old lady, who suddenly didn't look so little, or so much old as timeless. "I'm the Guardian. There's no need to be gallied; all are welcome in this circle."

"Gallied?" said Cait. "I don't know what that means."

"Means frightened or confused," grunted the Proctor. "Everybody knows that."

"Not where I come from," said Cait.

"And where *do* you come from?" said one of the women sitting to their left, her voice betraying a recognisably Irish flavour.

"Skibbereen," said Cait.

"You've the sound of it," said the woman. "Mayhap you should have stayed there."

"Sister Lonnegan," said the Guardian sharply.

The room went silent except for the crackling of the logs in the grate.

"Good," said the old lady. "Now we shall have a few minutes of silence. I should explain to our two guests that this is common practice with us. It enables us to tidy our thoughts and calm our tempers for any deliberations to come."

There was a clearing of throats and a general shuffling of bodies as those around them settled in their seats and lowered their heads, preparing to be still. It all had the unwelcome air, for Lucy at least, of a religious meeting. It reminded her of the convent she had been imprisoned in as a child. She did not bow her head. Neither did Cait.

As the silence progressed, Lucy made use of it to examine the bowed heads around her. It was, as she'd first thought, a varied selection of ages and sexes, but there were none as young as she, or even Cait, and they all seemed to have chosen their clothing with an eye to excluding as much colour as possible from it. Greys, blacks and the most lifeless browns clearly constituted the acceptable range of the palette. The only exceptions to this were two men sitting on the left-hand quarter of the circle. They could not have looked more different to the rest of the group or in fact to each other, one being tall and the other short, the taller having a thick head of steel grey hair, his neighbour with a high forehead presently swathed in a bandage which dipped lopsidedly over his left ear. The taller man wore a long and travel-stained buckskin coat with long fringes on the hems and arms which gave a kind of extra ragged and somewhat wild aspect to his appearance, especially when contrasted with the bright red waistcoat he sported underneath. The shorter also wore a buckskin coat of a darker hue and less flamboyantly fringed, and sported trousers that were, given the uniform drabness of every other leg in the room, shocking in the violence of the yellow and green check of which they had been woven. Both also wore well-worn riding boots. Other than the contrasting splashes of colour that they added to the room, Lucy noticed them because they alone, among the rest of the group, seemed to be observing everything with a controlled amusement rather than a sense of solemnity. They carried themselves differently to the others, as if they were comfortably of the majority, yet simultaneously also observing it from the outside. The shorter one caught Lucy looking at him and winked good-naturedly at her. She found the cheeriness strangely unsettling given the circumstances, and looked away.

The silence seemed to drag on so long that it turned from the simple absence of sound into an actual presence, with a stifling quality all of its own. Lucy squirmed in her seat and wanted to shout. Instead she bunched her hands inside her gloves and bit her lip. Out of the corner of her eye, she saw Cait nod in approval.

And then finally the old lady opened her eyes and spoke.

"So, ladies, what are you?"

"*Fiagaí*, you'd call me," said Cait. "And she's a Glint that I have the training of."

"And you've come here to take the child from Prudence Tittensor," said the grey lady. "Just like that?"

"Yes," said Cait. "Just like that."

"By what authority?" said a man sitting to their right.

"I need no more authority than doing what's right," said Cait. "The child was stolen from the Factor and his wife at Skibbereen. I've sworn to return it."

"Your oath has no currency, and you have no authority," said the

Irishwoman who had spoken earlier, her voice sharp and hostile. "That's not how we do things here."

"We cannot help you anyway, sister," shrugged the old lady, her voice gentler. "The child is gone."

Cait leaned forward in her seat.

"Gone, you say?"

"Nor can we allow you to work . . . unregulated," said the Guardian.

"Where's the baby?" said Cait.

"The child is in good hands, and safe. And far, far from here by now," said Prudence Tittensor, who had taken a seat close by the old lady.

"You'll be wanting to explain that one for me," said Cait. Lucy noted a deepening edge to her voice, a dark undertone that she had not heard before.

"I did take the child from the woman in London," said the captain's wife, head cocked defiantly. "We'd wanted a child for so long but none had found any purchase within me. And yes, I knew she was a changeling, the woman that was selling her, but they being notoriously careless of the lives of the ones they steal, I thought the child would at least be safer with me than her. To my mind, had I not been there, the changeling was as like to just decide to ditch it somewhere, like off the end of an empty dock."

"Oh, so it was a charitable act?" said Cait in a voice that said it was anything but charitable.

"No," said the old woman, reaching a hand out to stop Prudence Tittensor from replying. "It was a desperate act, and a mistake. But Sister Tittensor is one of us. When she became pregnant, when this new child found that purchase in her womb that had been so repeatedly denied to its stillborn predecessors, she told us what she had done and what she wished to do to make amends. And so we came to an arrangement."

"And what arrangement was that?" said Cait.

"There was a young couple from just across the bay here. Name of Graves. Fisherman families on both sides for three generations," sighed the Guardian. "The wife had lost a child in a butcher's shambles of a birth, and in consequence of that misfortune was not able to have another. It was a family beset with misfortune. It was decided in this circle that the child should be given to them."

"Now if we're concerning ourselves with authority, that is something you had not a whit of by which to do as you've done," said Cait, her eyes locked on Mrs. Tittensor's face. "None at all, and see now there's another family to be hurt when I take the child home to its true parents."

"You'll not be doing anything of the sort," said one of the men sitting to their right. "We can't be having every wash-ashore running wild and thinking themselves free to do as they please. We have order here. We have a balance."

"You'll do nothing the circle does not approve of," said the Guardian before Cait could reply. "Brother Lee there is right. We order things differently here. We cannot have anarchy. It was decided a long time ago that whatever balance between natural and supranatural pre-existed among the natives of this land before the arrival of the first settlers should be maintained."

"And how's that going?" said Cait, looking around the room. "For I only see white faces and no red men or women in your precious circle."

"Imperfectly," said the Guardian, "but it is not for want of honest effort on our part."

"Who are you?" said Lucy. She had to speak. She was feeling claustrophobic and powerless. Everything about their situation was making her feel itchy and uncomfortable.

"I said I'd do the talking," said Cait, shooting her a look of irritation.

"We are The Remnant," said the Guardian.

"Remnant of what?" said Lucy.

"The Oversight," said Cait. "Now hold your tongue, girl, for the adults are talking."

The words and the look that they came with stung Lucy like a lash.

"The Oversight of London, yes," said the Guardian.

"But how can you be a remnant?" said Lucy, ignoring Cait. "I mean, isn't there still an Oversight . . ."

"We are The Remnant of the true Free Company that was destroyed in the Catastrophe of 1661," said the Guardian. "The Great Fire of London. What they were charged with, the burden of patrolling and balancing the margin between the natural and the supranatural, we are sworn to do here in this newer territory."

"Wait . . . you think The Oversight was destroyed by the Great Fire of London?" said Lucy.

Cait mashed her heel into her toes.

"No," said the Guardian. "It was the other way round: London was all but destroyed by The Oversight."

"What?" said Lucy.

"The Oversight were disordered, poorly regulated and they lost control of the Wildfire and nearly obliterated the very thing they were sworn to protect," said the Guardian.

"But—" said Lucy.

"Another word and I'll slap you so hard you won't talk for a week," said Cait. And her face said she meant it. Lucy's face couldn't have flushed redder if she had hit her; outrage sent hot itchiness prickling all over her. She felt her fingers, almost working without conscious thought, peeling her gloves off. Even though the fire kept the room warm, her skin immediately felt cooler as the leather slipped off and her hands came in contact with the outer air.

"There was a schism among the surviving members of the Free Company. We, or rather our forebears, have been here ever since. Governor Winthrop of Connecticut brought us over. A great man," explained the Guardian, smiling at Lucy. "My great-grandfather, as it happens. As great a man as John Dee in his way. He brought us here, and we ordered ourselves anew, as you see, a community of equals—"

"Yes, well, begging your pardon, but what I see is a bushel of folk who should know better—seeing as how they know the truth of things— brothering and sistering each other and aping a prayer meeting like a cart-load of Quakers," said Cait.

"Our forebears saw much virtue in the habits of their friends who had faith," said the Guardian. "We benefit from their habits of calm and self-regulation without sharing their credulity and religious belief."

"Well, this is lovely, but I didn't just cross the ocean for a history lesson," said Cait.

"You are impatient," said the Guardian.

"I told you. I want to know where the child is."

Cait scanned the room; no one looked away from her gaze, nor did anyone speak.

"What?" she said. "Sure now, but I thought we did the silent bit already. Where is this fisherman?"

"Gone," said the Guardian.

"Gone where?" said Cait.

"It doesn't matter," said the Guardian. "The circle came to a decision."

"I don't accept that, no matter how often you say it," said Cait. "I have a prior duty."

The old lady shrugged and spread her hands wide.

"Sorry, child. But you have no standing on these shores. We do not allow free agents here who act alone. History and sorely won experience has taught us that disaster lies in that direction."

"And just because you set yourselves up as in charge, you think you can forbid anyone else in the same line of work from—" began Cait.

"You are not in the same line of work," said the Guardian. "You have told us you work alone. You are condemned out of your own mouth. People in our line of work are those belonging to other groups like ours, working under sworn charters. We are not unsympathetic to foreign requests: we have co-responding relationships with groups like *Die Wachte* or the Paladin. We even maintained cordial relations with the rump of the old Oversight in London until a generation ago when they suffered a further disaster, after which communication became intermittent and then stopped entirely. But we will not, we are sworn not to allow free agency. That way anarchy lies. The old Oversight all but destroyed London with too much freedom. And we will not countenance that kind of destructive entropy. This is a land of boundless opportunities: the potential for unlimited abuse is equally present. Just as these new United States are bound by a rational, written constitution instead of the old unwritten tyranny of monarchy, so did our forebears in The Remnant decide we would bind ourselves with firm, good rules for the good of all. Freedom through regulation is our watchword."

"Freedom through regulation?" snorted Cait. "Joining two opposite things together may sound clever to you and your brothers and sisters here, but you know what it sounds like to me? Sounds like this pious old bastard with a farm next to my brother's at Killahangal who was a great one for beating his poor wife like a drum, then telling her he loved her. Sounds just about as convincing as that."

"It would sound like that to you, being unreconstucted *fiagai*," said the Guardian with her well-armoured smile of seemingly imperturbable gentleness. Lucy could see that the more she smiled, the more irritated Cait became. "The process of regulation would open your mind to the sense and rightness of our chosen path. There is a strength in being part of a circle that vastly exceeds solitary, arbitrary action. And what shape is smoother and more perfect than a circle?" She waved a hand at the ring of chairs. "Regulation is not a bad thing. It is not something to be feared. We would encourage you to perhaps embrace it. We would make you welcome here."

Cait's jaw worked, but she said nothing. Lucy, watching her, became aware that the general colourlessness of the Guardian and her companions was matched by a muffling effect that seemed to be sapping the energy out of the room. She saw Cait was struggling against something, like a candle being deprived of oxygen. And now that she saw it happening to Cait, Lucy realised it was tugging at her too. The circle was pulling at them. Maybe it was just the effect of being surrounded by such an unusually large concentration of gifted people, but it was a sapping, dampening sensation that she had not felt before. She had always heard the voice of her own mind, clear as a bell, different to the world outside. Now it was as if there were a chorus of other voices becoming ever louder, threatening to drown her out. Lucy did not know if it was conscious assault on her individuality and her will, but she certainly felt the tidal pull in the room.

It was not malicious danger, for most of the faces were neutral or smiling with a similar impenetrable kindness to the Guardian's, but it was danger nonetheless. And realising the peril, she saw that Cait was going to do something, like a guttering flame which flares brightly the moment before it fails. Even as the thought was occurring to her, she saw that she held the key to this dilemma, that in fact it was easy and obvious, and that had she not been deadened by the atmosphere in the room she should have acted on it already. Of course Cait's sharp words had further muddled her thinking. She shook her head as if to clear it of the cloying tangle of thoughts and then, as she opened her mouth to speak, it was too late and Cait had taken the first step, standing so abruptly that her chair fell backwards and clattered on the floorboards.

"Now this is what's going to happen—" she began.

"Sit down," snapped Lucy, thinking fast and standing as she did so.

Cait turned on her as if slapped, heat flushing her cheeks.

"Lucy Harker—"

"Sit!" said Lucy.

Their eyes were locked on each other's, but even so Lucy could feel the multiplied force of every other eye in the room boring into her.

Cait sat down. Lucy turned on the Guardian.

"Tell us now. Where is the child?"

The Proctor reached for her arm and tried to pull her back into her seat with a derisory snort.

"Girl, we aren't going to help the *fiagaí*; we're certainly not going to help her novice—"

Lucy let him pull her halfway back into the seat as others around him joined in his chuckles.

And then she went fast-but-slow, squirming and twisting—

—and then there was a gasp and a kicking over of chairs as half the room seemed also to leap at her, also fast-but-slow—

—and then they stopped dead.

Because she had twisted the revolver from his grip and now had the barrel pressed to the side of his head.

There was a man lying on the floor with a burst nose, and Cait was grimacing and blowing on her knuckles, and Lucy realised that the man clutching his nose was—extraordinarily—laughing, and had clearly been fast enough to have been about to stop Lucy had not Cait, in her turn, stopped him.

And then Cait herself froze as something went click behind her ear, and her eyes swivelled sideways to find the shorter man with the kind eyes had a pistol of his own, whose muzzle was lost in the unruly disorder of her hair.

Lucy swallowed.

The Proctor scowled up at her along the length of the gun barrel.

"Easy on the trigger, if you please. It's a light one, and I do like my head attached to my neck," he said. "You're faster than I credited."

"Everyone stay still and listen to me," said Lucy.

"And why should we do that?"

"Because Law and Lore command it," snapped Lucy.

"Who are you to talk of Law and Lore?

Lucy held her bared hand out in an unwavering fist. The ring on her finger caught the light from the fire and reflected the blaze back at the watchers.

"We are The Oversight," said Lucy, repeating the formula she had learned at The Smith's side. And as she said them, words she had never thought to say in earnest, she felt buoyed up, part of something bigger than herself. Just for an instant, she felt as if The Smith stood at her side, and not just The Smith, but Cook and Hodge and her friend Charlie Pyefinch. It was a fleeting sensation, but she stood taller because of it. "We are The Oversight. And by your own words, you are bound to assist us."

"May I?" said the man with the bloodied nose. "On my word, no foolery and no piking, but I'd just like a close look at that ring of yours."

Lucy looked into his face. It was weather-beaten, a traveller's face, much like the faces of the sailors she had been surrounded by on the voyage across the Atlantic, but on closer inspection it was much younger than the prematurely grey hair that surrounded it. The eyes were clear and direct, but it was not this that led her to nod and allow him to step closer. It was that there was something in his demeanour that felt reassuringly familiar.

He stepped closer and looked at the ring on her finger. Then, to her surprise he reached into the depths of his coat and produced a folding magnifying glass which he opened and used to peer even more closely at it.

"Yep," he said, and it appeared to Lucy that he was only speaking to the man holding the gun to Cait's head. "It's good, Jon."

The kind-eyed man nodded, uncocked the gun and stepped back.

"My apologies," he said to Cait. "I was just trying to calm things down."

"What do you mean it's good?" said the Proctor, still held at bay by his own gun and clearly liking it less and less with each passing moment.

"It's a Smith's ring," said the grey-haired man, only now seeming to notice his bleeding nose as he disappeared the magnifying glass and produced a large red bandana handkerchief in its place, which he used to staunch the flow.

"The devil it is," said Sister Lonnegan.

"If Armbruster says it's something, that's what it is," said the man called Jon. "Anything he don't know about metals or smithing just isn't worth the knowing of."

"Then I think we should all take a breath and sit down," said the Guardian. And she bowed slightly in the general direction of Cait and Lucy. "For it appears things are not what they seemed to be, and it may be we do owe you assistance rather than . . . regulation."

There was a grumble of dissent from some of the figures in the room, but the Guardian swept the crowd with a stern look, and everyone returned to their seats.

"Lucy—" said Cait.

"I know," said Lucy. "But you weren't getting anywhere."

She took a step away from the Proctor and aimed the gun at the floor. Now things were calm, she spared a moment of thought as to the horrible tug she had felt while she held it to his head. A gun was different to a blade. A blade did not urge you to use it in the way this pistol had: it was as if it had one purpose, a potentiality just like the chemical explosion pent up and waiting to happen in the close confines of the chambered round. Knives never felt like they wanted to bite. They were just metal, sharp metal no doubt, but neutral, as useful for eating or slicing or whittling as anything else. Perhaps they were neutral because they could be used for so many different things. The gun was not neutral. In her hands, it had felt like it wanted to fire: the potential stored in that explosive charge was a dark pull, very much like the thrilling urge to take that one extra step when standing on the edge of a high cliff. Just that one step. Just that extra pressure on the trigger. Just one small pace. Just one tiny click. And then the whole equation of life would change—

"Would you take this?" she said, holding it out to the Proctor.

He stared at her.

"Now you're . . . just giving it back?" he said.

"I only needed to get everyone's attention," she said.

"Still. Put a gun to a man's head, then just hand it back? That's a dangerous play, young lady. A man might bear a grudge . . ."

"You haven't killed anyone with it," said Lucy.

"Have I not?" he said.

"I'm a Glint, remember? I'd have felt it," she said. "So if you've been able to resist it so far, I think you won't start now."

He gingerly took it from her unresisting fingers. She felt a thrill of relief mixed with a surprisingly strong tang of regret. The power banked up in the thing was palpable to her. But only now that she no longer held it did she realise what a dangerous thing she had done in grabbing it from his hands: if the weapon had been used to take life, she might well have glinted, and if she had been caught in the grip of the moment as the past slammed into her and disabled her senses and motion as it always did, then she would have been totally at the mercy of the circle, and she and Cait might well have been in a worse state than the one in which they now found themselves.

The Guardian was observing her across the width of the room, pale grey eyes seeming to bore into her head and see her thoughts.

"Firearms and glinting don't sit well together," she said, leaning back in her chair. "Next time you do it, you'll want to keep the gloves on."

Lucy shivered and avoided Cait's glare as she carefully sat back down in her chair.

"There won't be a next time," she said. "I don't like guns."

Even to her own ears it sounded like a lie.

CHAPTER 15

HOME AND NOT HOME

The reunion at The Folley was a double-edged thing all round: Cook and Hodge were dumbfounded, delighted and distressed in equal measure by the sudden appearance of Sharp and Sara: they were overjoyed to see them yet worried by the spectacle of physical depletion that they presented; pale, drawn, enervated and almost translucent with fatigue. Cook, who was never knowingly lost for words, was rendered quite speechless with joy and made up for it by hugging them both repeatedly and then disappearing into the storeroom where a thunderous cacophony of nose-blowing and handkerchief work took place. Hodge took his turn in embracing them both, while Jed darted between their legs, tail threshing and barking happily.

"You need rest and physic," he said to Sharp, holding him at arm's length as if his ruined eyes could see.

Sharp's hands reached towards the well-healed wounds on his old friend's face, and then paused.

"Your eyes," he said.

"Ah now, old Jed don't mind me sharing his," said Hodge. "Besides, I'm getting some blurry vision out of this one, like looking through a piece of dirty ice. Other one's a goner, though."

"I'm so sorry. I should have been with you all," said Sharp.

Sharp was not a demonstrative man, and the audible catch in his throat was a sign of precisely how reduced his normal vitality had become after his ordeal.

"Well, we saw 'em off well enough," said Hodge gruffly. "And Cook got to play pirate again, so not a complete waste of time, eh?"

Cook had salvaged a very few things from the wreck of her domain and set up a new kitchen in The Smith's workshop itself—the tiny kitchen he normally satisfied himself with having been condemned as being no bigger than a water closet with no room to swing a cat, nor even contain a table that would accommodate the five members of the Last Hand. So somehow the already jumbled order-within-disorder of the workshop had been re-arranged to incorporate a working kitchen, the actual kitchen having been relegated to the status of storeroom (in which Cook was now wiping tears from her eyes with a tablecloth-sized red and white spotted handkerchief).

Seeing the huge, well-remembered kettle from the Safe House on the red coals of the forge, sporting new dents and dings but evidently care-fully repaired and burnished to a fine coppery sheen as it bubbled away like a baby hippopotamus, was enough to bring the prick of rigorously suppressed tears to Sara's eyes. And here lay the paradoxical poignancy of the reunion for the returnees: the Safe House was gone, but here was home; here was hearth; here was warmth and safety and the society of friends and the closest they had to blood kin. And yet it was not so, since the juxtaposition of well-known things in such a strange setting only emphasised the abrupt change in their world, and made it seem all the more irreversible. The joy of return was undercut with the strange pain of well-loved, familiar things in an unfamiliar setting.

Cook emerged, red-eyed and smiling, brandishing a basket of eggs and a leg of York ham encased in golden breadcrumbs, which she plumped on the table and from which she immediately began to carve thick, pale pink slices of meat.

"Now," she said. "Sit down close to the fire, and we shall get some victuals in you both. Trousers? Make the tea."

Making the tea was one of the things that Cook prized above all duties, being of the firm conviction that no one could do it as well as she, except possibly Hodge. That Ida was being trusted with such an honoured responsibility spoke volumes about how high the Austrian girl had risen in her estimation.

"Right," said Sara, allowing Sharp to help her into the chair closest to the fire. "And now please tell us everything, from the beginning."

"Food and drink first," said Cook. "For it's not news to be taken on an empty stomach and you both look so wretchedly sharp-set and pale you might as well be made of parchment."

"No. Everything, now," said Sara. "Before . . ."

"Before what?" said Hodge. "Before it's too late?"

He spat into the fire.

"It's already too late." He waved his arm around the forge. "This is what too late looks like, Sara. Doesn't mean we're out. Just means we're down. And if we're to get back on our feet, Cook's right. You need food and drink and rest. A lot of rest. You both look like the very life's been sucked out of you."

"It's just the mirrors," said Sara, thinking of the pale, bleached-out Mirror Wights. "They leech the colour from you."

"And the vitality," said Sharp, nodding at Cook. "Food and talk at the same time then, if you please . . ."

"You were away so long I had—we had thought you were both lost," sniffed Cook, turning to the fire and pulling a frying pan closer in over the flames.

"Time is different in the mirrors," said Sharp. "It's elastic. But not consistent. A day can seem like a minute, and then suddenly a minute seems to have lasted a week."

"Wouldn't catch me going into the mirrors," said Hodge.

"Where is Emmet?" said Sharp, looking around the forge.

"Smith set him to guard the Wildfire," said Hodge.

"Where is the Wildfire?" said Sara.

Cook harrumphed and riddled the coals beneath the frying pan, making the slices of ham sizzle and emit the most delicious of smells.

"Smith sealed it back inside the lead casket and sunk it in the river again," she said. "Seemed like the safest course in the circumstances."

"Safe under flowing water," said Hodge. "No mischief will come to it unless the Thames dries up, and that ain't going to happen, not with the wet weather we been having."

"And Emmet?" repeated Sharp. Alone perhaps amongst the rest of The Oversight, he had an especial affinity for the golem. Where others saw the giant clay man as some sort of automaton, Sharp had always felt calmer in his presence, and had enjoyed the long periods of silent companionship he felt they shared. There was little in his life that was tranquil and he was, by at least half of his nature, pulled towards a violence of action with which the remaining part was uncomfortable. Emmet had been, by his very stoic stillness, a means by which Sharp could balance himself and find repose. More than that, he claimed that if you slowed yourself to the golem's pace, you were able to notice things about Emmet which hinted at thought rather than mere obedience within the empty shell of his being. None of the others had time or inclination to test this, but it was a belief Sharp held firmly to.

"He's with it," said Hodge, head down over his terrier who was allowing him to run his hands through his broken fur, looking for the ticks the dog picked up as he ran rabbiting through the high grass around The Folley.

"With it?" said Sharp.

"Underwater, sat on it. Don't look at me like that," said Cook. "Emmet doesn't need air."

"How long?" said Sharp.

"Couple of months," said Hodge.

Sharp shook his head angrily.

"He's not a machine."

Hodge shrugged and continued checking Jed for ticks with even more apparent concentration. Even though he was blind, he was clearly uncomfortable with having to meet Sharp's gaze on this point.

"Smith says he's as good as, nigh enough for make-do," he said.

"Smith's wrong," said Sharp.

"Well, you'd best tell him when you see him."

"I will," said Sharp. "There must be another way. It's inhumane for you all to have—"

Cook spun from the fire, face reddened with more than the heat of the flames.

"You weren't here. Sara wasn't here. With Lucy Harker taking off with the Irish girl and going gallivanting all the way to America, we didn't have a Hand, or we wouldn't have if Trousers over there hadn't turned up in the nick of time. Without that bit of luck EVERYTHING would have gone for a ball of chalk anyway—"

"I'm just saying—" said Sharp.

"Just sit down and stop saying and eat this," thundered Cook. "We are all but ended here, Jack Sharp!"

She smacked a plate of eggs and ham in front of him, and then slid the other more gently in front of Sara. She leaned back against the anvil by the fire and took a deep calming breath. It didn't work.

"You two need to realise something and realise it now: we are clinging on by the very tips of our fingernails to the edge of an abyss that is crumbling away right beneath our grip. And I don't like the idea of that poor creature sitting alone and blind under that bloody beast of a river, but if The Smith says it's the safest thing, we have to do it. We had to make things safe." She took a second deep breath, then blew her nose again. "And you weren't here."

"And we weren't here," said Sara, putting a weary arm out and pulling Sharp back down into his chair. "We weren't here, but we are now. So. I want to know everything else that has happened, for we have clearly been away longer than we thought we had been, and then we will tell you what we in turn have found out."

"What have you found out?" said Hodge.

"About the Disaster," said Sharp.

"It's not going to make you feel any better than you are going to make us feel with your news," said Sara. "But we have found out what happened and who was responsible. We'll tell you, we'll eat and then I need to sleep and so does Jack, and then when we wake we will all roll up our sleeves and start putting things to rights."

She looked at her mug of tea.

"No fine china here, Sara," said Cook. "That's all smashed to buggery under the old house. It's Smith's crockery we're doing with, and a tin cup holds tea just as well as anything else."

"It's not the cup," said Sara, "it's the tea."

"Same as it ever was," said Cook.

"And you're the same as you ever were," said Sara. "Have you put something in it?"

"What do you mean?" said Cook, doing a very good job of looking innocent and affronted.

"I mean, did your box of medicines survive the fire?" said Sara.

"Yes," said Cook. "But on my honour, I haven't dosed the tea."

"Because it would be very like you to see us so reduced and deduce we needed a little help with our resting, wouldn't it?" said Sara. "It's not like you haven't done it before . . ."

"It would be very like me," said Cook, and she reached over and took the tea from Sara and drank half of it in one mighty gulp, and then for good measure she cut a wedge of ham and ate it, giving Sara a look that said "See?."

"But it wouldn't be like me to take my own medicine and put three of us to sleep at the same time now, would it? Not with our numbers so depleted. Mind, if you can't sleep, you tell me and I've just the powder for that."

Sara held her eyes for a beat, then nodded and drank.

"That's good," she said. "Hot and bitter, just as it should be."

She looked at the plate in front of her and allowed herself to inhale.

"And that smells good too."

She cut a piece of ham and ate it.

"My grandfather would roll in his grave if he saw me eating this," she said.

"Your grandfather didn't know what he was missing. And he was notoriously inconsistent in the superstitions and beliefs he adhered to himself," said Cook. "Don't think he'd begrudge you a decent breakfast in the circumstances. Now, tell us what you need to."

Sharp and Sara took it in turns to tell of their adventures behind the mirrors, both so caught up in the story and in devouring the breakfast that neither noticed Cook pouring a powder into her own tea cup and swallowing it with a quick grimace.

When the story reached the point where Sara told of having glinted the mass drowning of the members of The Oversight as they fell into the trap laid for them by The Citizen, Cook shook, reached over and took her hand.

"Are you sure, Sara?" said Cook. "All of them?"

"I counted their bones," said Sharp. "And it took their rings."

He laid the handkerchief bundle he had brought all the way from the hellhole beneath Paris and untied it. A tumble of gold rings, set with incised bloodstones, spilled across the scrubbed deal tabletop.

Jed stood on his back legs so that Hodge could see the pile. He was silent, as was Cook.

"Eighty-five," said Sharp. "As many as went into the mirrors. Tally them up if you don't believe me. Trapped and drowned."

"I saw my mother die," said Sara. "I saw her die making sure that none of us ever got lured into that same trap. I glinted and saw The Citizen make some ritual pact with the outer darkness. He sacrificed a Sluagh to do it. And we know that those who have been washed in that darkness on the other side do not die on this side, or at least do not die as others do. So we will put things back in order, and then we will find this enemy who I believe must still walk and work against us behind the scenery, and then we will destroy him.

"How will we do that?" said Hodge.

"First we will sleep on it. Then we will go amongst our enemies and smite them hip and thigh," yawned Sara.

"We'll find them and kill them," said Sharp.

"Turn executioners?" said Hodge.

"But Law and Lore," began Cook, "they should be brought before The Smith's court and without The Smith . . ."

"Law and Lore can only be executed if we remain," said Sara, visibly fighting the tide of sleep trying to suck her into insensibility. "First we must survive. I have seen the face of the darkness and it has seen me. We can flinch and fail, or fight and flourish, for I fear the bloody time is upon us."

Hodge shook his head.

"If the danger is so great, we must scatter, gather new members and rebuild."

"If the danger is so great, we cannot scatter," said Sara. "We cannot desert our posts. We must make a stand."

"I agree," said Sharp.

"A last stand is a glorious thing until it's over," said Cook. "Then it's just a defeat, same as any other."

Sharp opened his mouth to object, then found himself taken over by a yawn.

"No one needs a dead hero," said Cook, and as she spoke she pointed at Ida and Charlie. "And you two better take this in too, because you're young and too foolhardy for your own good."

She turned back to Sharp and Sara who were both clearly struggling to stay awake.

"Dead heroes are off the job. And the job never dies. So the hero, the real hero is the one who endures, who keeps at it even when they're losing. Heroism isn't a grand gesture: it's grinding, unacknowledged commitment and endurance. Heroism's doing the boring stuff that needs getting done. Even if it means walking away from a fight they're doomed to lose so they can fight another day, when they might win. You want the other kind of hero, all puffed up and shiny, go to the music hall or a parade."

"Cook's right," said Hodge. "With The Smith gone north, we haven't even had a full hand."

"If Lucy Harker had stayed," began Sara, shaking herself free from another yawn.

"Lucy Harker was never going to stay," said Hodge.

"You do not know that."

"I know her destiny lies elsewhere," said Cook. "Not apart from ours, but away from it."

"How can you know that?" said Sara.

"Because she said so," said Cook. "And we make our own destiny. That's what freedom is, Sara. That's what we fight for."

Sara's head was bobbing as if she was drunk but desperately trying to stay alert.

"We fight for others' freedom. We are different. We are sworn and bound by an oath. We stand by our word," said Sara.

And then Sharp caught her as her head bobbed forward and she slumped against the table, fast asleep.

"Thing about oaths, Sara-girl, is you got to know when to break them," said Cook.

"You did dose her tea then," said Sharp. "You lied."

"Not her tea. The ham," said Cook. "And not so much a lie as a bluff."

"Was a lie really," said Charlie. "Not a bluff."

"A bluff is a lie. Stands to reason the other way round must be true too," said Cook. "And don't talk back. And given her state, a bluff is better than a bloody battle; there's no way she would have taken the medicine and the rest she needs without fighting. She's never known when to slow down. Just runs and runs until she hits a wall. And then she takes ten times longer to get back to normal than if she just paced herself and rested like a normal person."

"Sara Falk a normal person?" said Hodge with a snort. "Wish you good fortune with that."

"And my ham?" said Sharp, again fighting a yawn.

"Your tea," said Cook. "Half what I gave her. You always heal faster."

He stared at her, then nodded.

"You're right," he said. "She would have fought you like a catamount. And she is spent. As am I."

He turned to Charlie and Ida.

"Please carry her to a bedroom upstairs. I fear I cannot trust myself not to drop her."

"Room at the end of passage," said Cook.

"I can sleep in the stable," said Sharp.

"You will sleep in The Smith's bed and do as you're told," said Cook. "Ida, take his arm and make sure he doesn't take a tumble on the stairs. Charlie can manage Sara on his own."

She watched as they left the room, then began clearing the plates off the table.

"She called him Jack," said Hodge, raising an eyebrow at her. "She hasn't called him Jack since they were little nippers."

Cook grunted non-committally and turned back to the fire.

"I'm just saying," he said. "This'd be about the worst time for that sort of thing."

"It's always the worst time for that sort of thing," said Cook. "Take it from someone who's had the glory days that Trousers and Charlie there hopefully still have before them: the fragility's all part of the joy and the sadness of it."

CHAPTER 16

ARMBRUSTER AND MAGILL

After it had been confirmed that Lucy's ring was the genuine article, the circle had broken into small groups, presumably to discuss the new turn of events and its implications. Lucy and Cait were asked to sit and wait.

Cait stared into the fire and said nothing to Lucy, which was ominous.

The Guardian left the room with a knot of people which included Mrs. Tittensor and the two travellers in the fringed buckskin jackets who had validated the ring, Armbruster and the one he'd called Jon, who had smilingly introduced himself as Magill before absenting himself.

The Proctor went to a table in the far corner of the room which was laden with jugs and glasses, and came back with a glass for each of them.

"You'll be tired and thirsty after all this," he said. "Have a drink. It'll refresh you."

Lucy watched him drink from his glass. His eyes caught hers. He stopped drinking and held his glass out to her.

"Here, swap if you think it's a trick. But on my word, we're past that now. It's refreshment pure and simple."

Lucy was thirsty, but she was still Lucy, and so she accepted his glass and swapped it with her own.

The drink was sweet and sharp, with a decided bite to it. She couldn't decide if it was strangely delicious or mildly disgusting.

"Switchel," said the Proctor. "Don't you have it back in the old world?"

"What is it?" said Lucy.

"Water with vinegar and sweetened up with plenty of longlick," he said. "And a goodly amount of ginger for the kick. Refreshing, ain't it?"

"Longlick?" said Lucy.

"Molasses," he said.

She finished the glass and nodded.

"Thank you," she said.

Cait held her glass as if she'd forgotten it was in her hand, eyes still anywhere in the room except the bit that had Lucy in it.

Lucy was about to encourage her to try the drink when the door opened and the Guardian led the others back in. The circle reconvened, and she smoothed her dress before addressing Lucy and Cait.

"Please make yourselves comfortable, for we have talking to do," she said. "We are agreed that you have authority to operate here, and a right—a customary right—to our help."

"Right—" began Cait.

"Not you," said Mrs. Lonnegan. She pointed her finger at Lucy. "Her."

Cait opened her mouth again. And then closed it.

"Sister Lonnegan is correct. You will have to stay and be regulated to our ways and satisfaction," said the Guardian. "Unless the official representative of The Oversight, as a recognised entity, takes responsibility for your actions. And you in turn take an oath to be governed by her."

Magill said something low that only Armbruster heard and smiled at.

"Mr. Magill thinks we are too concerned with rules and strictures," said the Guardian. "Is that right, Mr. Armbruster?"

"Yes, ma'am," said Armbruster. "That's about the size of it."

"Mean no offence," said Magill. "It's just a matter of taste, though I see your hearts are in the right place and you likely mean well enough."

"It's just that we do things a little more rough and ready out in the territories," said Armbruster. "I'll allow we aren't used to all this sitting and talking and circling round things."

"Not used to roofs either, come to say," said Magill. "We spend more time under the sky than indoors, as you know. Hope you'll pardon our rough ways."

The Guardian swung her grey eyes towards Lucy.

"Do you mind their rough ways?" she said.

"Me? No. At least . . . I don't know the gentlemen well enough to know," said Lucy. "Why ask me?"

"Because we've undertook to take you west with us, if you want it," said Magill. "If you're set on following the baby you come so far to find, that is.

"Of course, you'll have to control your friend," said Armbruster, still dabbing at his nose. "She's got a punch like a mule kick and a fist like a pine knot, and I've taken to liking my nose the way it's always been."

"I should explain," said the Guardian. "You two ladies are not the only visitors to our circle this evening. Brother Armbruster and Brother Magill have come here from the very edges of the Great American Desert to make us aware of things they have found which concern us all. They are not part of our circle as such, being affiliated to the newer Western Remnant which presently bases itself in the proud river city of St. Louis."

"You have more than one Remnant?" said Lucy. She was aware that Cait was being unusually silent.

"We have a greater circle of which this small, and if I might say it without pride, original circle is both progenitor and part."

"So. The fisherman Graves and his wife. They went west?" said Cait.

"Far west, and kept right on going," said the Guardian. "Truly I do not know where, for the place they have set their feet towards is unmapped territory outwith the bounds of these United States, on the other side of the Great American Desert, up and over the Stoney Mountains, way beyond the Continental Divide."

"Why'd a fisherman go so far from the sea?" said Cait. "This sounds like a story that doesn't have a lot of sense in it."

"It has sense and a lot of sorrow," said the Guardian. "You've not been here long enough to taste the atmosphere hereabouts, but sadness came with the great gale a year ago. We've been cod fishers here for more than two hundred years. You'll have smelled the drying fish as you came along the shore, no doubt. Anyway, cod fishers we've been—"

"To the devil with the cod: tell me about the child," said Cait. "Why'd they take the child from here and go inland?"

"I'm getting there," said the Guardian. "Shortest route's not always the best one. So, cod fishers we've been here, and none more so than the Graves family. They've been casting nets out at the Grand Banks off of Newfoundland for generations. Seawise men with salt for blood. September last but one there was a blow out on the Banks with winds like no one ever seen before, nor like to see again. Waves like running mountains they said, those that came back. Eleven boats went under the sea-green shroud in one day, that was sixty-six men and boys now lying fathoms deep and gone for ever. Samuel Graves watched his father and his wife's father, three of his brothers and two of hers just eaten by the sea in about as many seconds as it takes to tell it. He was saved by luck and brought home to shore a hollowed-out thing. Worse, his wife was pregnant, but the news of all her family gone, for her mother died young—why, it puts her into such a decline that two days later she falls down the stairs and loses the baby, as I told you."

"And that's when this Tittensor woman comes to you with her sad story about a stolen baby she doesn't need because she's carrying one of her own making," said Cait.

"It wasn't like that," said Prudence Tittensor, her hand spread protectively over the great curve of her stomach. "I'm not a bad person."

"Sam and Hetty Graves were broken by the sea," said the Guardian. "They heard talk of the great wagonway opening up to the west and decided on a new start. They sold their house, their father's chattels and headed for St. Louis with a plan to turn farmer, as far from the hungry Atlantic as they could."

"So they weren't running away to hide with their stolen baby?" said Cait, not bothering to hide the disbelief and the disgust in her voice. "Well, that's convenient, is it not?"

"It's the truth," said the Guardian. "They heard talk of the new road, the Oregon Trail, and decided to venture all on an inland voyage and stake all on a new voyage on the Willamette."

"You'll never find them," said Prudence Tittensor, and then she held up a hand to stop Cait interjecting. "I don't say it with any pleasure. But it's the truth. There's a tide of humanity starting to head west, and they're lost in it."

"It's true, ma'am," said Armbruster. "It's a big country out there and you could spend a lifetime trailing a man and never find him."

Cait stared around the room. She looked absolutely exhausted by the news.

"Lucy," she said. "I thank you for your help, but I think we must part now. You may go where you will, but I have no choice."

Lucy knew she meant she was going west. There was an implacable look in her eye. More than that, Lucy knew that something had broken between them. It had broken at the precise moment when she had disobeyed Cait and told her to sit down. It had happened when she showed the ring.

"I have told you twice now, we cannot let you operate alone," said the Guardian. "The Glint claims assistance by right of her ring. The Oversight we can help. A *fiagaí*? We cannot allow that, now you have come to my notice."

"Truth is, you think about it with your head on straight, you really don't want to be going west," said Armbruster, cutting through the Guardian's dogged repetition. "I mean, if you're set on it, we'll take you, but it's no place for a woman on her own."

"We've had letters from those as took the trail last year," said the Guardian. "They say the going's hard as hickory and you suffer like a thole pin."

"She won't be on her own," said Lucy. "I'm going too."

She knew she was going to mourn this later on, but right now she was just trying to stay in a game whose rules and boundaries she only vaguely understood. And there was something else, something to do with the lost baby. Something she'd had a lot of time to think on on the voyage over.

"The devil you are," said Cait. "We'll part friends, but we're done with, you and I. I've no need of a pupil that can't do what I say. That was the rule we set."

"So your rules are fine, but theirs should be bent?" said Lucy. "They're going to keep you here and do whatever this regulating is for a year, and then how much chance do you think you have of finding your needle in a haystack?"

"In a thousand haystacks," said the man called Magill. "And the timing's all wrong: three weeks to St. Louis and that's just the jumping-off point. If they've gone all the way to the Willamette Valley like they planned, you could be six months or a lifetime getting there. By which I mean there's plenty ways you could die out there on the trail. And you got no reason to think they might not have changed their plans and headed south to California—hell, maybe they took the Salt Lake cut-off and turned Mormon!"

"People do change their plans on the trail," said Armbruster. "It's a long slog under big skies, and it saps the soul if things don't go right, which of course they don't."

"I'll be going," said Cait. "I'm bound to it. Lucy Harker, you're not coming."

"I am," said Lucy.

"Listen," said Cait. "I know you want to come and we both know why and this isn't the place to say it, but we've talked about this, so let it lay, eh?"

She underlined her words with a very direct look. Lucy suddenly wanted to hit her. Cait shook her head.

"No, girl, I've no use for a pupil who won't do what she's told, and there's an end to it. And as a free agent, you have no cause to—"

"I have every cause," said Lucy, and what surprised her more than the vehemence with which she found herself speaking was that she meant it. "Do you know what it's like to be stolen as a child? Do you know what it's like to have big holes in your memory where you can't remember your true parents? Do you know what it's like to never quite belong anywhere and not know why that is, other than suspecting it's because someone took you away from where you were meant to be?"

"No," said Cait. "But . . ."

"No buts," said Lucy. "I do. And I think we should stop arguing and find that baby so it doesn't, right?"

Cait stared at her, and there was something in her eyes that Lucy had never seen before: Cait looked surprised.

"Well," said Cait after a beat. "Fair dos."

"But how will you know them?" said the Guardian. "You have no way of recognising them . . ."

Cait nodded at Prudence Tittensor.

"She knows them. She can tell me."

The captain's wife lurched to her feet, one hand clutching her belly, the other steadying herself on the back of her chair.

"You're mad!"

Cait nodded.

"Sure but there's every chance of that."

Armbruster held out his hand and eased Mrs. Tittensor back down into her chair. She winced and held her belly as she sat.

"This woman's in no shape for the road," he said, "let alone a journey beyond where there's two thousand miles or more where there never was a road at all . . ."

Magill nodded.

"I don't need her," said Cait. "Not the whole shebang anyway. I just need her eyes."

"You'll not be taking anyone's eyes, you hellion!" spat Mrs. Lonnegan, leaning over stabbing a long bony finger right in her face. Cait didn't blink or flinch.

"It'll stand to you to take your finger out of my face, missus," she said calmly. "Or I'm just as like to snap it off and use it to plug your hole."

"Sister Lonnegan," said the Guardian.

The angry woman sat back and withdrew her fingers.

"That's the shot," said Cait, turning to look at the Guardian. "I'm talking about the dog."

"What?" said Mrs. Tittensor, making to rise from her seat again. Armbruster gently caught her arm and restrained her.

"Your one here's a sharer, is she not?" said Cait, jerking a thumb at the pregnant woman. "Holds herself in an animal's brain? That big shaggy dog of hers, Shay, she rides alongside as it were, sees through its eyes, talks to its thoughts even? Amn't I right?"

Mrs. Tittensor was staring in outrage at the Guardian.

"I've had Shay since she was a pup," she quivered.

"Sure, and I'd bring her back," said Cait.

"You might not come back yourself," said Magill. He reddened slightly as if aware that all the attention in the room had suddenly refocused on him. "Which is, on the long trail, nothing's certain."

Cait looked at Mrs. Tittensor.

"You want to come instead of your dog?"

"No," she said. And then she sat back and nodded slowly. "No, I think it wouldn't suit me even if I wasn't carrying a child. I get itchy if I can't see the sea. I can't see an inland voyage suiting me one bit."

"So—" began Cait.

"But I have a better idea," said Mrs. Tittensor, smiling for the first time. "Your plan's not a bad one, but I won't send Shay with you either."

Before Cait could object again, she went on.

"We can make a deal. I will let you have one of her pups; you saw them earlier. Take one of them. It can be my eyes as well as Shay, and either of them has more stamina, being younger."

Cait looked at Lucy.

"Well, seems we're going west, Lucy Harker. Looks like you're going to get your sightseeing after all. And a puppy, can you believe it? You should be smiling."

Lucy looked back at her.

"And you should say thank you."

CHAPTER 17

THE COMING STORM

Amos and the Ghost finally entered London like almost everybody else, which is to say they arrived unnoticed and unremarked and were immediately stirred into the great stew of people milling through the city, all of whom were much too concerned with themselves to remark on two new ingredients as they quietly added themselves to the pot.

They would certainly have been remarked on had they arrived in the ragged and filthy state in which they had left the charcoal burners' camp, but whatever had snapped within Amos and allowed him to move in the new way he instinctively called fast-but-slow had a very useful side-effect, which was that he could now hunt with extraordinary success, catching rabbits by hand even, so that they ate better than they had before, and, less admirably, he became a better thief as a result of his enhanced abilities. Something made him leave things in exchange when he could, and he didn't steal from those who clearly had very little. But he entered London wearing a decent enough overcoat which he had lifted from a coat-hook on which he had left a brace of pheasants and a hare, and the Ghost wore a patched but clean cambric dress whose faded print contained tumbles of rosebuds several shades brighter than her cheeks, and a warm shawl he had taken from a clothes-line which he left garlanded with five freshly killed rabbits in exchange. The boots he now wore were the best he had ever owned and he had left nothing for them because he had stood in the shadows of a barn and watched their previous owner, a stupendously drunk farmer, thrashing his horse and then his wife when she came to remonstrate with him. She had escaped and the farmer had pitched forward into the hay, vomited and instantly fallen asleep, snoring so stertorously that he didn't notice when Amos had relieved him of his footwear and left him face down in his own mess.

So while they did not enter the metropolis in any very great style, they did look clean enough to escape comment and were, within an instant, merely part of the background. The only significant aspect their arrival was that it was attended by the noise of thunder and distant flashes of lightning as a storm rolled in from the east, as if to meet them.

They entered together but still in two minds: Amos was determined to find The Oversight; the Ghost was determined to find Mountfellon.

A bare hour and a half earlier they had stood in the open countryside at the top of Stamford Hill, at the rural junction between Hangar Lane and Seven Sisters Road, looking across the hedgerows and fields at the distant brooding mass of the city below. There was still a remnant of yesterday's light snowfall on the fields around them, but the day was not as cold and it held the promise of rain rather than snow in the air. The incoming storm was at this point just a dark smudge on the horizon to their left. The New Reservoir reflected the dull morning light just beneath them and the winding course of the New River traced a looping path from it into the great sprawl of the metropolis beneath. It made a silvered thread, linking the last of the clean green fields with the endless scrabble of wet slate roofs and smoking chimneypots spreading back up into the open landscape like brick-built fungi blooming along the course of the old high roads.

To one who had spent so many months walking away from it across the forgiving wind-cleansed bounty of the shires, the ruinous sprawl of the city skulking beneath the pall of smoke looked terrible, like a great surly beast growling beneath its own fug.

And it felt like home.

"Mountfellon must die," said the Ghost.

The repetition is superfluous.

"He is somewhere down there in that tangle of streets. I know where, if he has not shifted his lair in the long years since I knew him. I know where, and you will help me get in. Perhaps you will kill him for me, though I would much rather do it myself. Revenge may be a dish best served cold, but cold dishes may have hot sauces to them and I would like to feel the warmth of his blood at the end," she said.

I have brought you here but I will have no part in what comes next.

"That is not our deal," she said.

We have no deal.

"The Oversight will not give you what you want," she said. "Everything I have told you of them should have alerted you to that fact."

You do not know what I want.

"Revenge. Justice. Power. You're a man. Take your pick. That's what you all feed on."

Again. You do not know what I want. And you do not know what The Oversight will be able to do for me. Nor do I, it is true. But I think they can help me. I think at least they can protect me from the Sluagh, if anyone can.

"The Oversight is an illusion. It cannot even help its own. It was a fine idea but a busted flush."

My fathers feared it.

"Your fathers resented it because it was an obstacle to their commerce. Templebanes have been traders in fear and rumour and what they call 'dark intelligence' since they came out of the stinking fens that bore them and turned from witchfinders to brokers and lawyers. They have no powers to speak of, only that of arcane knowledge and the means of parleying with those who walk in the shadows, those who might be bribed or placated enough to help the Templebanes and those whose interest they represent."

He stared at her in shock. He had until this moment not had any hint that she knew about the house of Templebane.

You know of the Templebanes?

"As I know about The Oversight. You should believe me, Bloody Boy. This game has been going on for many lifetimes."

Just because you know of the Templebanes does not mean you are right about The Oversight.

"But I am right and I do know. I know they are done. They cannot protect their own; they could not protect them even when I was young. It is because of their weakness as much as Mountfellon's perfidy that I lost what I had. Their day is done."

It is not, his thoughts sounded desperate even to his own inner ear.

"Done as yesterday's breakfast kipper," she cackled. "My, I would like to eat a kipper again . . ."

How do you know? About The Oversight?

She turned.

"Because I was one of them, Bloody Boy, and you—if I had still the ring I once bore—would do as I say because I could make Lore and Law command it!"

For a moment she did look commanding and strangely, defiantly magnificent, holding her fist towards him as if it bore the imagined ring of authority. And then, without moving, almost by a trick of the light, she seemed to collapse and look old and tired and broken again.

"But my rings are stolen, and I would not wear the bloodstone even if I had it. I broke it when I foreswore the damned Oversight and went away. Law and Lore did me no good, giving me neither justice nor vengeance on the one who wronged me, and those days when I was foolish enough to believe in them are winnowed and as gone with the wind as my own dear lost children."

The lost child or children (she was always perplexingly inconsistent in how she told this part of her history) was the thing that had ultimately driven her mad, he knew. He had heard enough fragments of her past as they had walked the long miles together to be able to make a more or less coherent patchwork of her history by joining up the pieces that recurred with the most consistency. She had been wronged by an admirer whom she had loved and trusted; she had not been able to satisfy her need for revenge, and had fled far away from London, somewhere she had thought herself safe with her child (or children), and then one day agents of the great man who had been searching for her took her away from them. Sometimes she said she had been experimented on like an animal; sometimes she said she had been repatriated and immured in the Andover poorhouse in the expectation that she would die shortly after. The children (or child) were lost for ever, as were her wits. The only thing that had not died was her desire for vengeance, the only thing that had kept her alive.

"Gone and gone with the wind," she repeated with a sigh. "Like my doomed and departed darlings."

A minute later, with nothing resolved between them, they were also gone, walking out of the countryside into the first layers of the metropolis.

As they walked, Amos thought about her latest revelations behind the buttress he had built in his mind: was she lying? She was, he was certain, a liar. Why had she saved this revelation about The Oversight until now, this last moment? She never said anything that was not in some way manipulative. And even the things she did not say were artful, it seemed, else why would she have hidden her more detailed knowledge of the Templebanes? Could she really be what she now claimed: a lapsed member of The Oversight? A fallen initiate?

He trudged on beside her, his head full of this, determined that the only safe thing was to stick to his plan of going to The Oversight and laying all that had happened and all he knew at their feet and then seeking their protection. And yet, and yet . . . he kept looping back to the new question of the Ghost and her latest revelations. It itched in his brain, because he could not work out if she was manipulating him by feeding him carefully edited titbits, find if that were the case, what she was trying to achieve by doing so. Avenging herself on Mountfellon was her one aim, but he could not see how she imagined the information she was rationing him with would change his mind about being an accessory to the planned vengeance.

And then, as they entered the warren of streets of the old city proper, the heavens opened and rain as heavy as he had ever seen began to pound the cobblestones around them and introspection stopped and the search for shelter took over completely.

The rain seemed not to fall as much as to be being hurled with a spiteful ferocity from the dark clouds overhead. It hit the cobbles so hard it bounced, sending six inches of spray back up into the air, soaking their lower legs even as they hunched their heads into improvised hoods made by coat and shawl respectively. Within less than a minute, the roofs overhead had filled the guttering with too great a volume of rain for the downpipes to drain, and sheets of water began to fall into the street around them, rendering passage along the slick pavements as perilous as walking under a cataract. The drains clogged, the sewers revolted, and five minutes into the inundation the city seemed to be drowning.

Shopkeepers rushed out and pulled their goods inside their premises, while those with awnings wound them away, depriving the passing pedestrians of their shelter, not out of malice but in order that the canopies did not founder under the weight of the biblical torrent pounding in from above.

Amos and the Ghost took refuge with a crowd of similarly soaked refugees beneath the one remaining protective covering of a greengrocer whose winding gear had conveniently—for them but not him—jammed. They stood and miserably watched as the proprietor and his wife attempted to save the bellying canvas from splitting under the volume of water it contained by poking at it with broomsticks to channel the water off the side before the weight of it split the material. It was unfortunate they were standing beneath the seam running down the centre of the awning, because it was there that the rip happened as weatherworn stitching gave up the struggle and drenched them quite as comprehensively as if they had decided to take a shower beneath one of the aforementioned waterfalls.

The force of the falling water actually knocked the Ghost off her feet and she went sprawling into a barrel of apples. Amos caught her arm and was alarmed to see a streak of blood on her temple.

"I'm fine," she said, shaking off his hand. He watched the red blood thin and pink in the falling rain. He looked around. The street was all too familiar. He was one junction away from the house of Templebane, the scene of all his past miseries. But he knew that just beyond it was a closed alley with a gate which he had the knack of opening by jiggling it in a certain way. It was the empty premises of a cartwright who had gone bankrupt. Amos had used it as a private means of getting in and out of the Templebane establishment when he wished not to be seen by his brothers or the fathers. It was sure shelter from this deluge, and he knew it would be, as ever, empty, because in truth the Templebane fathers—who already owned the untenanted building on the other side of their house, and for the very same reason—had bought the deeds from the bankrupt man "in order that no damned neighbours should know our business by doing no more than leaning on a party wall with a bloody tumbler at their ears." Thus the two empty premises on either side of the house of Templebane were a perpetual no man's land, a secret *cordon sanitaire*, and in this case, a place of refuge. He pulled his coat up over his head like a hood and steered the Ghost into the street.

I know where we can shelter, but you must not draw attention to us, for it is an empty dwelling but right close by my father's house.

CHAPTER 18

THE ISLAND WITHIN THE ISLAND

On arriving at the small neat harbour at Portree on Skye, The Smith had disembarked at the stone quay and walked past the white-painted houses which lined the harbour, feeling an urgency that had been somehow increased by contemplation of the light being drawn into the dark basalt peaks beyond the town. He had made inquiries at the low-built inn at the end of the main street, and within ten minutes had engaged a man with a pony and trap to drive him to his destination.

Just under an hour later, he was standing on a stone bridge, new to him but already old in the memories of the present inhabitants of the island, looking down at the vertiginous drop into the gully between the rocks below where a stream had cut both sides of a small islet beyond, and where the water flowed on down to the sea and into the west.

"Ancient burial ground, that is," said the driver, who was chewing on his pipe.

The Smith looked away to the other side of the bridge, where the ruins of a low-built blackhouse was falling slowly apart, breaking itself back down into the landscape, the roof gone, the rocks that had been its walls beginning to tumble to the ground from which they had been gathered. Stone bramble and willowherb had taken residence in the room-space within the walls, and a single elder had rooted in one wall-end and was slowly splitting it apart.

The Smith's face hardened. He turned back to the driver.

"You're tired, I think," he said. "You'll have a sleep until I return."

"Well, it is true that I am tired," said the driver, who until that very moment had been under the impression that he was brimming with vigour and ready for anything, and he yawned and sat back in his seat and began to snore.

The Smith stepped off the road and dropped down the steep slope beside the bridge, moving fast, but taking care not to slip as he descended. He emerged from the shadow of the stonework and forded the right-hand stream with little worry about getting wet, so that he arrived on the boat-shaped island with his trousers soaked to the thigh. He ducked beneath a bent rowan tree and found himself facing a grassy enclosure on the surface of which lay a series of rudely carved stones, like ancient grave markers. Some were incised with runic markings; others bore rough-hewn effigies of knights with pointed helms and swords held in their crossed hands. He strode over these and found a longer stone, almost buried below the wild grass. This stone was undecorated. He knelt and felt the edges of the thing; he shook his head. If anything had been listening, it would have heard him suck his teeth in disappointment. As it was, the pair of eyes watching him was too far away to hear, but they saw him shake his head, brace his muscles and then lift the edge of the stone. Teeth gritted, he held it ajar with one hand while he retrieved a candle from his coat, snapped his wrist to light it and held it in the hole, peering into what was clearly a deep space below.

He winced slightly, as if stung, and something in his face died as he looked in the hole, and then he scowled with an unaccustomed sourness, his face stuck halfway between dread and disappointment.

He extinguished the candle, stepped away and let the stone drop back into place with a dull thud. He stood very still for nearly fifteen minutes, as if absorbing what he had—or in this case had not—seen as he rubbed the small of his back, trying to ease the twinge which had made him flinch at his discovery. Then he smacked the dirt off his hands by clapping them together and strode away without looking back. He crossed the stream again, and climbed the wet rocks leading steeply up to the road with less care than he had descended them.

The driver woke to find The Smith had remounted the trap and was pointing at the ruined blackhouse.

"The family that lived there. Do you know them?"

"Ho yes," said the driver, rubbing sleep from his eyes. "Ho yes, and how would I not? A very famous family on the island they were too. MacCrimmon they are called, and great ones for the *Pìobaireachd* they were, yes indeed. Pipers you would call them in the English."

"And where might I find them?" said The Smith.

"Oh, gone, gone away now, to be sure. Red Donald went away, and Black John—why, he was the last of the hereditary pipers, you see. No, no there's none of them left, no pipers and the family gone. Except for the one chap, that would be Donald Ban, the fair-haired one. But he has no children Donald Ban, so the family is all but departed, which is a sad thing, they having been such ones as they were, yes indeed."

"And where can I find this Donald Ban?" said The Smith.

"Oh, just where he always is. At the castle. He is the steward there, though he does not play the pipes as his forefathers did, more's the shame of it."

"Take me there," said The Smith.

As they drove the driver expressed disappointment on The Smith's behalf that the MacLeod himself had just left the island to visit his fine architect in Edinburgh, since he was sure that his lordship would have been delighted to welcome the English gentleman to his castle, in particular to show him around the new marvellous improvements that were being erected around it.

The Smith explained he was only interested in finding the MacCrimmon and the conversation petered out until they drew in sight of the castle itself, which was a suitably impressive and angular imposition on the softer curves of the surrounding landscape, perched atop an imposing block of columnar basalt that rose ten yards or so above the encircling waters of Loch Dunvegan: it appeared both impregnable but also severely under attack, the illusion of beleaguerment being given by the scaffolding which encircled the façades of the old stone fortifications like so many siege towers.

"Stonemasons brought all the way from Glasgow," said the driver, shaking his head in wonder. "He's no mind for expense these days, has the MacLeod."

The Smith left the driver and made his way to the castle, crossing the narrow bridge on foot. He walked purposefully, and those he met were quick to take him to the steward, compelled by the authoritative direct-ness of his manner and something fierce in his eyes that persuaded them that this visitor was on an errand that brooked no delay. A stonemason's boy took him to the master of works who recommended him to a passing house servant who took him inside the castle, where an elderly retainer who appeared to have the undemanding duty of sitting smoking a pipe outside the main door passed him to a red-cheeked maid who was scrub-bing the stone flags within the hall, and she finally took him to the steward, Donald Ban MacCrimmon.

Donald Ban was a pale, sandy-faced man whose watery eyes seemed happiest either when examining the floor or looking at an indeterminate patch of air just to one side of whoever he was addressing. This gave him an evasive manner that was at odds with his mode of speech, which was very precise in the way of the natural Gaelic speaker forced to express himself in a language of which he had a punctilious technical mastery but no great affection. His "j" was chopped out like a "ch" so that "just" became "chust" and he lingered on the "s" sound at the end of words so that, for example, "was" became "wass," and thus all his sentences contained their own hiss of barely restrained discontent. He also smelled strongly of spirits. All in all, his demeanour was sullen and truculent even when The Smith had caught his eye and worked on him to ensure his compliance.

He met The Smith in the main hall, and once the cursory pleasantries of greeting had been done with, the traveller wasted no time in asking why the flag was no longer interred on the island-within-the-island.

Normally the abrupt question would have surprised MacCrimmon, but he was in the thrall of The Smith's thunderous gaze, and so he did not think to wonder why this stranger was asking such a question, nor how he knew to ask it of him among all the other islanders. Instead he sniffed and examined the flagstone between their feet.

"It was not my doing. It was before my stewardship that it was brought to Dunvegan."

"Why was it brought?"

"I am thinking that they just thought it would be safer," he said with a shrug.

"Is Dunvegan an island in an island? For I just crossed a bridge over a dry ditch."

"Well. It is sometimes an island, when the tide is high, for the ditch fills with the sea. But better than an island, it is and always was a castle."

"No," said The Smith. "It is just a castle."

This imputation of inadequacy was offensive enough to the MacCrimmon's delicate sensibilities to drag his eyes from the wall just to the left of The Smith's head and make him stare in outrage into the wintry face in front of him.

"Sir. Dunvegan Castle is the home of the MacLeod, Lord of the Isles. It is not just any castle."

The Smith's hands flexed and clenched into hammer-like fists, which he then forced himself to unclench as he leaned closer, not allowing the MacCrimmon the release of looking away.

"If all that was needed to keep the flag safe was a castle, we, the people who entrusted it to your family would not have gone to the extremely perilous inconvenience of bringing it here. There were other fortified places further south that would have been much more convenient."

"It is safe," said MacCrimmon, mouth working as if trying not to swallow something unpleasant. "It is here in the strongroom."

"Then show me," said The Smith.

It did not seem to the steward that there was anything at all odd about the request from this southern-speaking stranger to open his master's strongroom, nor did it for a moment occur to him that he should do anything but comply.

In short order, he had led him down a flight of spiral stone stairs and had unlocked a thick ironbound door, studded with ancient nail heads. The strongroom was in the undercroft beneath the hall and was part armoury, part storeroom. MacCrimmon lit a lamp which smelled of fish oil and led The Smith to the furthest end of the room, where a long box lay against the walls.

He found another key on the heavy ring he carried and unlocked a rusting padlock on the long box, opening it with a deep squeal of complaint from the ungreased hinges. He nodded at the material-wrapped roll in the box.

"There you are, as you can see; there is no grounds for discontent," he said.

"This is it?" said The Smith, bending to carefully push aside the linen dust-cloth wrapping the inner roll of fabric.

"That is the Fairy Flag itself," said the MacCrimmon, a note of pride mixed with more than a little self-satisfaction colouring his voice.

The Smith ran his blunt fingertips over the exotic yellow material, sprigged with a carefully embroidered reddish/pink pattern. Then he stood, and cricked his neck to the left and right, as if working out a kink of irritation, before once more leaning into the MacCrimmon's face.

"Two things. There are no such things as fairies, nor have there ever been, and believe me when I tell you this, for I should know. Secondly, Donald Ban MacCrimmon, this is not the flag your family was charged to guard. This is— I don't know what it is. Silk. Foreign stuff. From the east."

"It's a thing of great power," spluttered Donald Ban.

"No," said The Smith. "It's something someone has swapped for a thing of great power."

Donald Ban stepped back, suddenly aware he was finding it unaccountably hard to breathe when standing close to this insistent and clearly angry stranger.

"It is not my fault," he said.

The Smith followed him as he backed up.

"It was entrusted to your family."

"It wasn't entrusted to me. I didn't ask for it. And I didn't do anything with it anyway. It was my father who took gold—"

"He sold it—?" said The Smith.

"I don't know what he did," gasped Donald Ban, finding his ability to back any further away was now hindered by the rough stone wall pressing into his shoulder-blades. "He told me a man came and took it. A man with authority. A man with a ring. He said our family's obligation was over. And the Macleod was paid a fine fee for the years of keeping it safe. And my father had some of it as a commission and went to try his luck with it in America before it crushed his heart and he returned a broken man. Why, it is that fee that has paid for all the improving works you see going on all around you . . ."

"What kind of ring?" hissed The Smith. Donald Ban wondered if The Smith was going to keep moving towards him until he pushed him through the wall, but The Smith stopped, nose to nose with him.

"Ach well, and but how would I be knowing that?" said the MacCrimmon. "I wasn't there. It was my father, you see. It was himself treated with the gentleman."

"I don't see why he would do that," said The Smith. "This was an ancient thing, entrusted to your family."

The Smith's eyes went far away for a moment, and his absence kindled a little spark of rebellion in Donald Ban, who certainly resented being pressed so close by this unwelcome and discomforting visitor.

"Well, whoever entrusted them maybe shouldn't have done it." He swallowed. "I say if you want a job done, do it yourself, and maybe they should have done the watching and the guarding and the keeping instead of getting other folk to do their work and never giving anything in return for it . . ."

The Smith's eyes returned from wherever they'd been and stared coldly at him. Donald Ban flinched and regretted his momentary forwardness.

"Do you play the pipes?"

"No, I don't play the cursed pipes," blinked Donald Ban.

"And did your forebears. All of them?"

"Yes indeed. They were the finest pipers in the world, generation on generation," said Donald Ban.

"And did your father?"

"Well. He did until he didn't."

"He stopped after the man took the flag box," The Smith said, nodding slowly as he stepped back.

The MacCrimmon looked up at him, a glimmer of interest in his eyes for the first time.

"And how would you be knowing that?"

"Because your family was given something for their guardianship of the real flag," said The Smith. "Something beyond price. Thank you for your time, Mr. MacCrimmon."

Donald Ban watched his back as he headed for the door. He dismissed a faint thought that he should escort the visitor from the premises, but something else told him such courtesies would only prolong his exposure to the uncomfortable presence of the hard-eyed Englishman, and that he had much better lock up the flag in its box and then secure the strongroom by which time the uncomfortable presence would hopefully have absented itself without the need for any more contact.

The Smith strode out of the castle without a backward glance, and everyone who encountered him on the way seemed to suddenly have other business and a strong disinclination to engage in any kind of greeting with what was now rather more of a storm-front than a mere person.

He picked a loose stone from the parapet of the bridge as he re-crossed it and paused to hurl it far into the water beyond the castle. He stood and watched it splash into the wind-chop, and remained like that for a full five minutes. Then he shook himself out of his reverie and jumped back up on the carriage, waking his driver.

"Back to Portree, if you please," said The Smith.

"So you'll be going south now, will you?" said the driver, snapping his reins on the back of the horse to gee it into motion.

"No," said The Smith, looking up at the louring clouds rolling in over the dark water of the sea loch below. "No, I fear I'll be going north."

CHAPTER 19

ARRIVAL

"Well," said The Citizen with an irritation born of great exhaustion at the long and seemingly endless walk through the mirrors. "We have arrived."

He and Dee stood beside the open door of an ornately mirrored cabinet. The room was a bedroom, with a fireplace and simple four-poster bed, from which hung thick curtains designed to keep the cold out. There was a very thin powdering of snow on the leaded windows, and the roof and wall opposite—which was all the view the window allowed—was similarly dusted in white.

"Colder than London," said The Citizen, turning to Dee.

Dee turned and took a tinderbox from the mantelpiece and bent to light the waiting fire.

"I will return as we agreed," he said. "There is no time to waste."

"No indeed," said The Citizen. "I shall recruit my energies and restart my experiments. If Mountfellon demurs, you may have more luck with the Templebanes, if any remain."

"I know how to play them off against each other, have no fear," said Dee. "We know how that tune goes of old."

The Citizen gripped his arm as he stood up and watched the well-laid fire crackle into life.

"Mountfellon has a will almost as terrible as my own. If he suspects we are using him as a tool to obtain what he himself desires, things may go badly astray. I cannot countenance that."

Dee looked at him coldly.

"You and I have each been on this trail for more than the span of a normal lifetime, have we not?"

The Citizen met his gaze and nodded, irritated. He had the surprised and uncomfortable look of a man not used to being stared down or treated as an equal.

"Mountfellon is a callow novice in this endeavour, for all he sees himself as a great and ruthless man. Our plan is calm and rational. His burning desire may be of use to us, but it will also be his downfall, for it enables us to mould him like a piece of molten glass. And in this case we shall, I think, use Templebane as the tongs with which to handle him and thus keep ourselves insulated and at arm's length. He will be useful to us. And then we shall take what he finds from him for our own use, and bid him a fine and possibly necessarily final farewell."

The Citizen nodded again.

"Yes, yes. Mountfellon a tool. To be betrayed at the right time. It is understood. All we need is the fire. The Wildfire is the thing. With the fire, all is possible; the world is ours to do with as we will and anything else is irrelevant and pointlessly lesser."

"You are preaching to the converted," said Dee, with a hint of tiredness. "Now, shall I announce you, call for a servant before I go?"

"No," said The Citizen. "I see no virtue in anyone witnessing the means of your departure."

"Indeed," said Dee. "Until I return then."

And he stepped into the cabinet, pulling the door closed behind him.

The Citizen waited a beat, and then opened the door again. It was empty. He smiled, closed it and sat down on the bed. He suddenly looked ancient and exhausted, as if he had been keeping up a façade for Dee, which he now was able to drop. He squinted at the room, taking in the dark wood panelling which ran around the perimeter at chest height, and the white plaster wall above. The decoration had not a hint of a woman's hand in it, but it was clean and handsome, if a little spartan.

He stood up and crossed to the door, which he locked, taking the key and pocketing it. Then, with a great deal of sighing and wheezing, he bent and removed his buckled shoes one after the other. He registered a mild, surprised disgust at the state of his stockings, which were soiled and foul-smelling with a pungency beyond that of being merely unwashed, reeking of something closer to real corporeal rot. He flung back the bedclothes with a snap of newly pressed linen, and buried his feet beneath the sheets and blankets and then lay back on the pillows, turned his face away from the light and began to snore.

Some hours later, when the shadows had moved across the room, there was a rattling at the door.

The Citizen stared at it with sleep-filmed eyes, for just a moment vulnerable as his consciousness swam back up from whatever stygian depths in which it had been sunk, and then he blinked and scowled.

"Shoes," he rasped to himself, swinging his legs stiffly back onto the bedside rug.

The rattling of the handle stopped and was replaced by an angry voice.

"*Hé, mais c'est quoi ces bêtises? Qui diable se trouve là-dedans? Qui est là?*"

The Citizen opened his mouth to reply but was hit by a racking series of coughs. He pulled the key from his waistcoat and unlocked the door to find himself looking up at a large, ursine man with a red face and a full beard which was quivering with shock and indignation.

"If you'd be so kind as to come in, sir," he smiled.

The red-faced man's eyes goggled at this decrepit old gentleman shrugging into his coat.

"Who the devil are you?" he choked. "And what the blazes are you doing in my house?"

The Citizen smoothed his coat and flicked an imaginary piece of dust from his sleeve before deigning to give him the most wintry of smiles as he pulled himself together and became something still and deadly.

"I am the man who has paid for this house."

"The devil you are! Are you mad?" said the man, turning to bellow down the stairs behind him. "*Jean-Marie! Baptiste! Venez ici immédiatement! Et apportez-moi une cravache!*"

"There is no need of a horsewhip," said The Citizen, and he pulled down the stock which normally encircled his neck displaying a clean silver line, like a tattoo that went all the way around, as clean and straight as a knife cut.

"I am the man who has paid for your eminence and your success. I am the Shareholder," said The Citizen.

"But, no . . . you are Sir Robert Spears?"

The man's eyes widened, his jaw dropped and then whatever he was trying to say got jumbled into a series of gulps and choking noises as he dropped to one knee and bowed his head. There was the noise of two pairs of boots thundering up the stairs behind him, and he turned his head and shouted urgently.

"*Non, non—oubliez tout ça. Retournez en bas, tout va bien.*"

The Citizen waved him to his feet.

"It was understood that I might appear at any moment, without notice, and that you would know me by the silver line around my neck," he said in French. "This should not be a surprise to you."

"But I have not had time to, er . . . prepare suitable chambers for you and your entourage."

"I have no entourage. I shall require a young, healthy maid, one without family here in the city," said The Citizen. "You will no doubt have one available immediately, since that is one of the ongoing stipulations of our agreement, no? Good. And have no fear, this room will do very well. The featherbed is more than acceptable."

"But—but this is my bedroom, sir!" protested the man.

"Not any more," said The Citizen. He pulled a sheet of paper from his baggage and handed it over.

"Everything on this list is to be brought up here as soon as possible. We will need all the rooms on this floor, in fact."

The man's eyes bulged as he perused the inventory, clearly both shocked at the peremptory nature of his eviction as much as the strange items he was being sent to acquire.

"Cages?" he said. "Scalpels . . . are you a surgeon, sir?"

The Citizen smiled indulgently.

"Do you like your tongue?"

"My tongue?" he said, confused.

"Your tongue, sir."

"Well, yes, sir."

"Then stop wagging it," said The Citizen. "The top two items on the list are to be here within the hour, as are the Wachman brothers."

"The Wachmans?" said the man.

"The Wachmans. I trust they are close by, as your reports have always indicated," said The Citizen, sudden steel in his voice.

"Yes, sir. But . . ."

The Citizen shook his head.

"Nothing has changed in your life, sir, except you now play host to the principal in your company, who is paying a visit. You will sleep elsewhere which should be no problem since the factory is a large one according to your reports and what I see of it out of this window. You tend to the business; I will attend to my researches and my new maid will convey my wishes if I am busy or indisposed. Is that clear?"

"Yes but I don't quite underst—" began the man.

"It is not important that you understand. Only that you obey. Have the boards, the weights, the maid and the brothers here within the hour or you can pack your traps and live on the street," said The Citizen. He saw a flicker of rebellion in the man's eyes and leant in to extinguish it with a hiss. "Oh yes, I can do that, monsieur. Read your contract. I have made you rich. I can make you a pauper in an instant."

The man swallowed, nodded and left the room.

The maid, when she appeared, was clearly greatly to The Citizen's liking. He walked around her, complimenting her on her fine, well-rounded figure, her firm muscles, the lustrous sheen of her thick hair, and the overall glow of healthy milk-fed vitality she exuded. She blushed at his compliments, her downy cheeks pinking prettily, and allowed that she had been raised on a farm close by the city. Her name was Clothilde. She was now an orphan.

He bade her stand by the fire and then took up the chair opposite her and explained that no impropriety was intended in what he was going to explain to her, nothing her dear departed parents might object to at any rate. He just wished to avail himself of her utility.

The word "utility" sent a small cloud of incomprehension across her biddable features, one that he dispelled with the warm sunny glow of the large gold coin he produced from his waistcoat pocket.

"The utility is something for which you will be well-rewarded, and as I said, nothing that you or a parent could possibly object to will be requested of you. Nothing," he continued, raising a finger to stall her. "Not even what I am going to ask you to do when the two gentlemen I have sent for arrive. It may be a momentarily distressing thing, but it will pass, and once done for the first time, you will see that it has no lasting negative consequences."

And then he told her what he wanted her to agree to. And she found she was suddenly sitting without having asked leave due the shock and directness of the request, and that the glass of liquor he had fetched from the flask in his baggage to recruit her somewhat overcome sensibilities was spreading a warmth and calmness through her which made it all seem much less terrible than she had at first thought.

The Wachman brothers were twins, hulking men in their thirties, blond-haired, stoop-shouldered, with mouths that seemed wider than the norm, like bullfrogs somehow, an amphibian effect accentuated by their unnaturally pallid skin and chins which disappeared into thick necks without any discernible delineation between the two.

They arrived in what was clearly now The Citizen's bedroom, each carrying a wide pine board, like a small tabletop. They looked dull-eyed at The Citizen as he pointed to the floor in front of the fire.

"There," he said. "We'll do it there. Where are the weights?"

They stared at Clothilde, who quailed a little at the nakedly evaluating nature of their gaze: she felt she was being weighed up as cold-bloodedly as any farm animal on market day, so lacking in human contact was the look.

"Won't need them," said the closest one to her. "Two of us, more than enough."

"*Sie müssen sie nicht töten,*" said The Citizen, "*oder alle Knochen brechen.*"

"We will break nothing," said the other. "We are gentle."

"*Ich möchte ihre Vitalität wieder und wieder zu nutzen.*"

"Yes, yes," the other brother replied. "Better to drink from a well many times than drain a bottle once and for all. We know what we are about and we know the best way to be it."

The Citizen nodded and beckoned Clothilde. The liquor he had provided had made the world a little fuzzy to her, not in a way that made her queasy or dizzy, but just as if everything that had previously had sharp edges was soft and unthreatening. He smiled, and the effect of the tincture made it a less wolfish smile than the one she had previously remarked. She smiled back.

He held out a small apothecary's measuring glass which he had taken from the bag with the flask and filled to the lowest mark etched on its side.

"This will help, Clothilde," he said. "There is nothing unseemly in what is asked of you; no indecency or impropriety. It is by way of a curative therapy, a medical remedy, if you will."

She took it, and though a submerged part of her baulked at the idea of taking it without question, the previous drink had made her biddable and quietly reckless, and she drank it in one. It too burned warmly as it went down her throat, but it stopped in the region of her chest and the heat seemed to tingle out in all directions from there, so that the warming effect appeared to soften her bones and make her very pleas-antly wobbly and pliable. She heard herself giggle, and wondered what was so funny. And then she saw the wall turn into the ceiling and was aware she had been gently lowered on to one of the pine boards in front of the fire.

The change of perspective struck her as whimsically odd rather than alarming, and she again heard her muted laughter as one of the frog-faced Germans placed a soft pillow behind her head and pulled a very hard sheet on top of her. She craned her head to look at the bedclothes to see how something could be so profoundly starched and ungiving, and then she saw why and tried to sit up.

It was already too late. As she raised her hands to push at the pine board which had been placed on top of her, she found that her arms were unaccountably heavy, and that she could not lift them from her sides.

And though she was enough in control of her rubbery bones to lash her head from side to side, the firm grip on her chin taken by the Alp kneeling at her side was enough to clamp her in shocked place as he lowered his gaping fishmouth over her own lips and nose, sealing around her face like a limpet as the other one climbed gently on top of the board and began to press the breath out of her.

Clothilde felt the air being forced from her lungs as if her chest was caught in a vice, inexorable pressure increasing steadily as reflex made her try desperately hard not to give up and exhale. Her will bent, her perception of the world softened and her body almost completely unresponsive and unable to defend herself, she still found the strength to struggle against giving up the last spark of what she was suddenly convinced would be her final breath.

At least, she thought, in a slow helpless panic, it would be the last breath and the inability to take another due to the compression on her lungs would do for her, but it then occurred to her that it might be a cracked rib spearing her heart, as the pressure increased, achieving a final, undrugged moment of resigned clarity—

—and then she choked and lost control of her airways and felt the Alp suck and suck and suck until her insides burned as if on fire with the acid pain of oxygen deprivation, and all she could hear was the pounding of her blood, and the world first went grey and then pinpointed down to black as her heart slowed and a horrible internal silence swept in and took her.

Clothilde did not see the Alp who had stolen her last breath rise and walk to the bed where The Citizen had reclined, propped on one elbow as he watched the procedure. She did not see him lie back and let the Alp lower its face onto his, and she did not hear the explosive hiss and the unusually long and drawn out groan as the Alp breathed her last inhalation deep back into The Citizen's lungs. She did not see The Citizen shudder and his fists clench. She did not see his parchment-pale skin pink and plump, his eyes brighten as the Alp rolled away and lay exhausted on the bed beside him. She did not see him sit up, delight and wonderment in a face suddenly younger, suddenly alive in a way that underlined how dead he had looked a minute or two before.

She did not hear his laughter pealing around the room, vigorous and celebratory.

And she did not feel the other Alp take a huge breath of its own as it stepped off the crushing board and knelt quickly beside her, clamping her nose shut with one hand while breathing deeply into her mouth at the same time.

Instead she felt the kick of her heart and heard the pounding of her blood again as her eyes fluttered back open and saw the Alp looking down at her, a concerned look in his eyes.

"Breathe, Miss Clothilde," he said matter-of-factly. "Don't move. Just breathe. You are safe; you are well. It is over."

And then The Citizen was leaning over her too, looking strangely different than she had remembered, but before she could quite pinpoint what it was that had come over the now not-quite-so old man, he had raised her head and poured another measure of something into her mouth, and this time it was cold and icy but also comforting in the way it radiated through her body and brought a gentle feeling of falling asleep beneath a snowfall that turned into a gentle rain of goose feathers that whited her world out and sent her peacefully into a deep and restorative sleep.

"That was well done," said The Citizen, looking at the Wachmans. "I have never felt so revived after a new breath. And I, you may know, have tasted the breath of a queen."

They looked at her on the floor.

"She has good, rustic vitality," said one.

"And we are very practised at this," said the other. "As I told you."

"As I have always paid your family to have you be," said The Citizen sharply. "And I have paid that commission for a very long time. Now carry her to the next room so that she can sleep. If I have dosed her correctly, she will not remember much of this, and nothing unpleasant when she awakes."

"Very humane of you, good sir," said the one of them lifting the head end of the board as they prepared to use it as a stretcher to take her away.

"I'm not interested in humanity," said The Citizen. "I just want her to keep letting you do this as often as we can, without damaging her."

"Then not much more than once a week or ten days," said the Alp. "She must recover fully."

"For now," said The Citizen. "For now anyway."

He stretched his arms wide and laughed as they bore Clothilde from the room.

"Gods, but I feel young again! I feel so young that one world alone does not feel enough to conquer!"

CHAPTER 20

THE KINGLESS COUNTING-HOUSE

The king was in his counting-house,
Counting out his money;
The queen was in the parlour,
Eating bread and honey.
The maid was in the garden,
Hanging out the clothes,
When down came a blackbird
And pecked off her nose.

Amos propelled the staggering Ghost through the pelting rain away from the burst awning which had so comprehensively soaked them and towards the gaunt building he knew waited for them just a little further down the street. And then as they approached it, on the other side of the road, he stopped dead and stared at something he had not anticipated in his wildest imaginings.

"What is it?" said the Ghost.

My father's house.

"But I thought we were not to draw attention to ourselves," she said. His face was slack with shock.

The building was shuttered and blank-eyed. The wide gateway which led to the inner courtyard and coach house was closed and the lantern below the discreet sign above the main door was shockingly unlit. It was shocking to Amos because in all his life he had never seen it extinguished. Indeed, it remaining alight was viewed as a symbolic talisman and proof of the truth of the Templebane brothers' promise so painstakingly picked out in gold leaf below the sign that read "Templebane & Templebane," the assertion that "We never sleep."

Amos, as the youngest of the adopted brothers, had been given the perilously heavy responsibility of keeping the reservoir of lamp oil which fuelled this hitherto unquenchable flame full: this office was given the highly humorous title of "The Wise Virgin," from the Parable of the Ten Wise and Foolish Virgins, and just as the foolish virgins had been subject to damnation for their lack of foresight in keeping their oil bottles full, so any son of Templebane who held this weighty office did so in permanent fear of the same sentence of paternal anathema, no doubt garnished with a sound thrashing. He had checked the oil reservoir on waking, at midday and at night, and every time he did so he cursed the fathers for not installing a modern gas globe in its place. If ever the reservoir had become too low, in the elastic opinion of his brothers, he had been thrashed anyway with a birch kept hanging in the counting-house for just such an occasion. So it had literally been drummed into him that this flame was eternal and inextinguishable.

And now it was out.

More than that, a pair of street sellers had set their stalls up in the space on the pavement normally kept clear for the coming and going of the carriage. This, as much as the absence of the everlasting flame in the lantern, told Amos that the house was certainly untenanted, for any opportunistic hawker who dared to block the ingress would have been pitched into the street by a gang of brothers sent expressly by the fathers, who had a particular distaste for what they called "wretched street Arabs clogging up our good frontage."

They have abandoned it.

He stared at her.

Why?

She looked up at him, hair rat-tailed with water, face white and shivering, and attempted something that might have been a shrug, or just a more intense shudder at the cold. Her thin lips didn't move, making a tight blue slash across her face as she kept her jaw clenched to control the chattering of her teeth.

How would I know? Where is this dry place? I do not feel well and my head hurts.

He led her across the street to the adjacent empty building where a forbidding gate emblazoned with three foot high lettering announced that "Ruck and Buchan, Master Carriage-Makers" had been the last lamented tenants. Looking around to make sure he was not being too obvious, he worked his trick on the pedestrian door that was let into the larger gate, and swung it open. The Ghost ducked under his arm, and he followed her in, carefully closing the door behind him.

They stood in the dry space beneath the archway, almost frozen in shock at the sudden absence of rain.

He stared around at the familiar vacancy. Nothing had changed. The workshop doors remained shut, the windows covered in newspaper. The works had been cleaned out by the brothers on the instructions of Zebulon and Issachar, who had wanted "no damn jumble and filth to attract rats."

He had been one of the working party what seemed like a lifetime ago, and it was while sweeping out the narrowest gap between the two establishments—an unpleasant job he had been forced into as the smallest brother—that he had made his discovery, the means by which he had his own private entry into the house of Templebane, an entry and an exit, of course, and one he used when he wished to absent himself unnoticed from the unpleasant bullying atmosphere that the fathers seemed to encourage.

He had discovered a door and a key.

The door was a slender one, half the width of a normal entrance, the relic of who knows what previous shape of the house; perhaps, from the traces left on the wall, leading into some kind of privy lean-to, before the premises of the bankrupt cartwright had even been built on the adjoining plot. He'd known the door from the inside, where it sat tight shut and unused in a back corridor of the Templebanes, between a store cupboard and the rack on which the brothers hung their winter coats. It was firmly locked, the key reputedly either lost in a previous century or kept jealously on the imposing key ring of one or other of the fathers.

He had found the other side of that door, and more than that, in sweeping he had discovered a loose cobble, a cobble so old that it was not stone but wood, and he had lifted it to find the keys, two identical ones, tied together with a length of twine that went to dust as soon as he picked it up. Any obedient son would of course have handed them to his elders.

Amos had not. He had left one key in place as an insurance against losing the other, and thus had, at a stroke, secured his own private back door to the house of Templebane, one he had taken great care in keeping secret. He stole lamp oil and greased the lock and the hinges of the half-door for weeks before daring to use it, terrified a squeak would betray him. The lock was surprisingly silent, but it took him a month of discreet hinge work to make the operation acceptably noiseless.

The spare key was still there under the wooden sett, greased and wrapped in a twist of new oilcloth as he had left it a seeming lifetime ago.

What are you doing?

Why be dry when we may be warm too? Stay there for a moment.

His heart raced as the lock creaked treacherously, and then he inched the door open, breath bitten back behind tightly gritted teeth. He heard no movement from within, only the sound of rain drumming on the roof, and slipped into the dimly lit back corridor. The row of hooks on which his brothers' coats normally hung was bare. Still, not trusting the strong sense of abandonment in the quiet house, he sat on the bench below and removed his boots. He tiptoed silently into the heart of the building, the counting-house, a barn-like space with two rows of high desks running down the middle and a pot-bellied stove standing cold and unlit between them. The roof above was broken by wide skylights which were thrumming noisily with the rain hitting them, and the lofty walls on either side were lined with cabinets, cubbyholes and ceiling-high bookcases crammed with ledgers and bulging bundles of dusty paper which overhung the shelf lips like bracket fungi.

At the far end of the counting-house was a raised half-glassed office somewhat like a steamship's wheelhouse, where one or other of the fathers was usually stationed, keeping an eye on the busy scene below. The office was now empty, its door hanging open. This in itself was almost as unprecedented as the extinguished eternal flame over the doorway.

For some reason, the words of a nursery rhyme began looping through Amos's head as he slipped silently up the twisting iron stair that led to the office, the one about the king being in his counting-house, counting up his money, the seemingly cheerful rhyme that began with singing a song of sixpence and ended up with a blackbird pecking off an innocent girl's nose. He peered into the heart of the counting-house: neither of the kings were there, nor was their money, and nor, from the dust, had they been for some considerable while.

The wardrobe-sized black metal safe at the back of the office stood with its double doors thrown wide: until this moment all Amos had ever seen of it was the outside of those doors with a phoenix-topped bronze medallion announcing it as "Milners Patent Fire and Thief Resistant HOLDFAST—Powderproof Lock." Now he could see the scarlet paint within, and the fact that it now held nothing, fast or otherwise.

They've done a flit, he thought.

Can I come in? asked the Ghost, her voice distant in his head.

One more minute.

He ran silently to the top of the house and worked his way down, room by room, ensuring that there really was no one left as a caretaker.

The shared rooms of the brothers were bare, beds left rucked and unmade, their clothes packed and gone. The only bed with clothes hanging by it was his own, and he felt a sting behind his nose as he looked at the threadbare fustian greatcoat, much mended and patched. It was a pitiable thing but it was dry and it was, in a way that made his nose sting with unwanted sentiment, his own. He reached for it and stopped dead in shock. In lifting it from the peg, he revealed something else he had never thought to see again, the seeing of which hit him like a cold slap, forcing his mind into a whirlwind of conjecture as to how it could have returned home without him.

It was the old brass plate, the one on a leather strap, lost in the head-long flight from the Sluagh when he had abandoned Mountfellon's coach. Its message was there, deeply incised and unmistakably his:

My Name is Amos Templebane and I am Mute but Intelligent.

He stared at it stupidly. It should by rights be mouldering in a field halfway between here and Rutlandshire. But there it was, in his hand. How had it got there? Who had brought it home? Why had someone taken the trouble to bring it up here and put it by his bed as if they knew he would one day return? It made no real sense, and the unreal sense it did hint at was one he was uncomfortable looking at, since it contained the idea that the Sluagh must have returned it to Zebulon or Issachar. It was an uncomfortable idea because that seemed to betoken a deeper involvement between the fathers and the Nightwalkers than he realised. And it reminded him that the Sluagh might well be abroad in the city in a way that had not been possible when he left it last. The Iron Prohibition had been lifted. Locks, horseshoes, railings and even blades would have no especial repellent power to ward them off any more. It might be that it was not only he and the Ghost who had crept back into the city. Maybe the Shadowgangers had preceded them, bringing their shadows with them.

He took the dry coat and a couple of blankets and the badge and continued on his swift reconnaissance. Two more floors of empty rooms strewn with the evidence of a swift abandonment, and then he was back on the ground floor. The kitchen stank faintly with the memory of long-rotted food, and the dishes left unwashed in the sinks similarly told the tale of a departure hurriedly made.

He grabbed a bucket of kindling and a scoop of coal and went back into the main floor of the counting-house. There was always the chance someone might come back unexpectedly, and from there it would be possible to hear the tell-tale bells on the front doors and gates, and so have time to effect a retreat unnoticed.

Come in, close the door behind you and go left. I'm lighting a fire.

It didn't take him long to get a roaring blaze thundering in the iron stove. He'd had long practice at it and the chimney always drew well. He left the Ghost on a bench drawn up close to it and went back to the kitchen to search for food while she changed out of her soaking clothes and hung them around the stove to dry. There was nothing edible in the store cupboards. Rats had got to the dry goods and everything else was spoiled with age. He took some tea and a kettle and put it on top of the stove to boil. The Ghost was wrapped in a blanket and staring at the red glow in the door of the stove, seemingly hypnotised by it.

He had been thinking, as he went through the cupboards in the kitchen, that this was a suitable punctuation point in their relationship, and more than that he had thought of a way to make the parting of their ways possible without the rancorous objections with which she was inevitably going to greet the proposal.

Seeing the badge again had reminded him of the last time he had used it, introducing himself to Mountfellon and delivering a letter to him.

The Ghost interrupted him by suddenly stiffening and turning a worried face towards him.

"You're sure they're gone?"

Yes.

"What if they come back?"

They might. But I think they're long gone.

He drew a finger along the desktop.

They've shuttered up and gone somewhere else.

"Have they done this before?"

No. The house of Templebane never closes. That's why there's a Day Father and a Night Father. But there's talk of other premises elsewhere.

"Where?"

Amos shrugged.

Was just a story some of the older brothers knew. Like a place where they came from. Before London.

She nodded and turned her face to the fire again, revelling in the warmth.

"We'll get warm and dry and then be on our way," she said. "I don't feel this is a very safe place to linger."

She had found an oversized pair of brass-handled scissors on one of the desks and clutched them like a dagger as she looked around the room.

He looked up at the storm hammering away at the glass overhead. It had not let up a bit. She put the shears down on the bench at her side and held her hands out to the fire.

"We can dry our clothes at least," she said, yawning grudgingly.

And we'll hear the doors unlocking before they do, so we can leave the way we came.

"What if they come in that way?"

You've never seen Issachar or Zebulon then. They are fat men. The door is too narrow.

He settled on one of the high stools and looked at the brass plaque he had brought down from his old bedroom.

"What's that?" she said sharply.

He showed her the badge and its broken strap.

Sluagh took it from me when I escaped from Mountfellon's carriage. If this hadn't snapped they'd have had me.

"And we might never have met," she smiled. "Fancy the sorrow in that. All the bloody fun we've had together."

Don't know how it found its way back here. It worries me.

"Templebanes deal in the shadows. Or maybe Mountfellon found it and sent it."

Why?

"Who knows? And who cares, Bloody Boy. It is your story, not mine."

And she bundled herself tighter in the blanket and lay back on the

bench, like a dog in front of the fire. He looked at her and felt the desire
to be free from her monomania like something he could taste in his mouth.
She was like a corrosion, a living rust that ate away at his sense of himself
the longer he remained at her side. He had even begun absentmindedly
thinking of himself as the Bloody Boy when he wasn't guarding against
it. He would not become the thing she prophesied, firstly because he did
not want to be responsible for seeing the shedding of any more blood
ever again, and secondly for a darker reason, one that he had only begun
to acknowledge to himself: there was something in him that knew he
was both good at and drawn to violence, despite what he clung to as his
better nature. The new facility he had discovered of moving very fast
while the world around him appeared to go slow made this worse. He
had felt something snap in him when the power had been released; he
now lived in fear of something else snapping within him and unleashing
that speed and violence without his conscious control, like a fox in a
henhouse. He did not want that. He wanted to be himself, not the corrupt,
corroded version that she seemed to be conjuring forth.

After this we part.

"No. We still have a common interest," she insisted, opening an eye
and staring at him. "You come with me to Chandos Place, you help me
find Mountfellon. Mountfellon must—"

*I know, I know. Mountfellon must die, and I am the Bloody Boy and all that
old song. But I tell you I will not be a part of it. I will go to The Oversight in
Wellclose Square.*

She spat on the floor.

"They will not help. They will not even open the door to you."

I will help you gain entrance to Mountfellon's house, but we must part.

This is the thing he had thought of, the means of effecting the desired
punctuation point to end the long sentence of their uncomfortable alliance. He had thought about this, and rediscovering his badge, and then
seeing the rows of desks with their inkwells and steel-nibbed scratch-pens,
had given him the idea. He had no love for Mountfellon, who had cut
his thumb open with a scalpel just to see his blood, and he had been

horrified at the collection of flayed things he kept at Gallstaine Hall. He even had a kind of sympathy for the hated Sluagh who had been convinced Mountfellon had experimented on some of their number before skinning them. And though he would not be the Ghost's weapon, he thought he might finally extricate himself from their association by opening a door for her. What she did once inside the door and close to Mountfellon was not his business. He would be shot of her.

I will write you a note in the name of my father Zebulon. It will say you have a particular message to deliver to his ears only.

She looked at him, head cocked on one side. And then she smiled her disturbing smile and stared at the stove, which was now roaring up the cast-iron chimney pipe and sending welcome waves of warmth into the room.

"That might do, Bloody Boy," she said. "That might do indeed, for it has been a worry for me that Mountfellon knows your face and might be on his guard. My face is so far withered from the bloom he once knew that there is no chance he will recognise me, not until I reveal myself in all my . . . my present loveliness."

She reached for the brass-handled scissors on the bench by her head and looked at them.

"These are lovely too, are they not, Bloody Boy?"

They are just shears.

"But do you not see why they are so lovely? I shall take them. I'm sure your fathers will not mind."

Amos was sure his fathers would mind, but just shrugged. She chuckled and held the shears out at arm's length, watching how the flames in the stove lit the steel blades. She yawned again and he, despite himself, caught the yawn and thought it might be nice to sleep for a while.

"Do you not see how . . . appropriate these lovely things are?"

He shrugged. He would write her note of introduction and then he would put his head down for a short nap, and hopefully when he woke the rain would have stopped, his clothes would be dry and he would have the energy to effect the parting of their ways. He would be at The

Oversight's premises within half an hour of the storm's end if he could possibly manage it.

Take them.

He dipped the pen, yawned again and began writing. He would keep it short and to the point, and he would make Zebulon's signature, which was the one he was most confident of imitating.

She spoke on, to the fire as much as him.

"You do not see. But he will, Francis will; he is a cultured man. Educated by the finest tutors that money could buy. Including my father. He and I shared that, if nothing else: a fine classical education."

He had never heard her call Mountfellon by his given name, and he hid that thought behind his buttress, wanting to see where this reverie led.

"What do you know of the Fates?"

Nothing.

The pen sputtered and spoiled his painstaking copperplate with blotches of ink. He scrumpled the paper and started on a fresh sheet.

"The old Greeks believed in many gods, but they believed even the most powerful of them were subject to the rule of destiny. And that rule was spun, measured and executed by Three Fates, three sisters: Clotho, one whose name escapes me and Atropos. Clotho spun the thread of a man's life. What's-her-name measured its length. And Atropos, the eldest and most implacable of the sisters, Atropos wielded the shears and cut the threads, bringing death as she did so. Do you know what Atropos means? In Greek? No, I suppose you don't. It means 'unturning.' Fate cannot be turned or avoided. And with these lovely shears I will be Atropos incarnate, and he will find my judgement and execution is equally inevitable."

She went on rambling about her vengeance and how sweet it should be, and he stopped concentrating on her words and, after three more false starts, finished a note to his satisfaction, and then when he had done so realised her voice had subsided and the only sound was the rain drubbing the skylights, softer now, but set in for a while. And he remembered how nice the idea of a nap was, and he put his head on his arms on top of the desk and thought he should probably stretch out on the floor on a blanket, closer to the fire. But he was footsore and tired, so he thought he might just sit like this for a moment, and then he did so and one moment rolled into another and the rain kept falling and the moments grew into an hour, and they both slept, and a small dribble leaked out of the side of his mouth and smudged the edge of his fairest copy . . .

He was lurched out of the warm darkness of sleep by a sharp click and the cold touch of metal at the nape of his neck.

Someone was standing at his back, casting a shadow over him. Someone who smelled of wet wool and sweat and a mouth full of at least one badly rotting tooth.

"Quiet now, young Amos Templebane, we don't want to wake your lady friend, do we?"

It was Abchurch. The sleep Amos had fallen into had been too deep a trap for him to have been able to hear the front door open, muffled as all sound was by the drumming of the rain on the skylights overhead.

Abchurch sniggered quietly.

"Course you don't ever really make noise, do you? But no fast moves or this goes bang and you go, well, you go everywhere, don'tcha? Now turn round, little brother, so I can watch you and your parrymoor here. She looks a bit old for larks . . . but any port in a storm, eh? And a boy like you is probably grateful for a bit of white meat even if it's old hen, ain'tcha?"

He eased back and allowed Amos to straighten up.

Abchurch had not got any lovelier in his absence. His face was a perfect blend of cruelty and weakness, only made even less appealing by prominent eyeballs and his woefully undershot chin. He reached out and pulled the paper Amos had been writing on closer so he could read it.

"Ho," he said. "A-counterfeiting are we? What's your game?"

And he giggled as he pointed at the carefully formed "Z" in the signature.

"Why, tell you what, if you're going to pretend to be someone you ain't, you chose the wrong father, cos old Zebulon, he's dead as mutton."

Amos couldn't hide his surprise at this news. The Night Father and the Day Father had bestrode his life as malign colossi, and the idea that they could actually die was so outrageous that he had not thought it possible.

"Ho yes, young Amos, 'e was drownded by The Oversight, baptised in the river and come up corpsified."

The Ghost had woken and was looking blearily at the new arrival.

"What ho! There she bumps!" he said cheerily, then pointed a warning finger at her without moving the gun from where it was aimed at Amos's face.

"No sharp moves from you either, Mother Hubbard, or I'll blow the soot off his face and we shall see what colour his insides are, hear me?"

He turned his attention back to Amos.

"Now where you been, cully?"

Amos shrugged.

"Must have been surprised to see the old place shut up and empty. Must have thought it was your lucky day. Sorry to spoil your little assignation. But just cos we ain't in residence don't make you cock of the walk. Fings 'ave 'appened while you've been off shilly-shallying: fings of considerable import. So Father Issachar, 'e decided that we should change premises and lie low a bit where retribution won't find us. 'E sent me back for some papers, but 'e'll be pleased as Punch when I bring home 'is little lost lamb too. 'E'll be very interested in what you and the old bitch there is up to, I'll be bound. Why, it's be like the return of the prodigal son, no doubt, 'cept this time I don't fink it'll be the fatted calf what feels the knife, no indeed. I 'spect it will be our own pet darkie facing the fire."

"Leave him alone."

His eyes flicked to the Ghost who was sitting up now and glaring at him in her most determinedly unhinged way.

"Come again?" he said.

"Leave him alone," she replied, voice unwavering. Abchurch snorted a laugh. She stood up. He stepped back on reflex, then flushed with anger.

"Or what, dearie?"

"Or he'll kill you," she said, stepping into the space he'd surrendered.

He bunched his fist and lashed out at her. She tumbled back into the bench and bounced untidily onto the floor.

"You can mash that noise, you old bitch, or you shall have another—"

Amos went fast-but-slow, despite himself, without thinking.

And less than a minute later he was stumbling out of the front door of the house, into the rain-slick street, hand over his mouth as if containing a powerful urge to vomit.

The deluge had stopped.

A cackle of the Ghost's humourless laughter followed him onto the pavement from the depths of the house he was hurrying away from.

"Blood cries out, Amos Templebane, blood cries out!"

He sidestepped the horse-drawn omnibus sluicing past on the half-flooded street and crossed to the pavement opposite, keeping on walking like a blank-eyed automaton. She emerged and followed him. He was still barefoot and he had a steel-tipped pen clenched in his right fist, like a dagger. East. She was carrying his boots and had draped the two blankets around her shoulders. She looked unnervingly bright-eyed and cheerful.

She took his arm, almost playfully, handed him his boots and looked at him as they walked.

"You're getting better at this," she said, reaching up and wiping something from his chin. "Scarcely any blood on you this time. I shall soon have to give you a new name."

CHAPTER 21

THE HOUSE AT THE END OF THE WORLD

The Smith had returned to Portree and found a new man willing to drive him in a trap to the small harbour at Uig. Here he had paid another man and his son to sail him across to the island of North Uist which lay stretched almost invisible beneath the clouds coming in from the north west. After a windblown, wave-buffeted crossing, he spent the night in the tacksman's square-built house overlooking the small harbour at Lochmaddy, where the initially surprised tacksman found, after looking deep into the stranger's eyes, that the Englishman was in truth no stranger at all, but an old family acquaintance who was of course expected, and most welcome to bed and board and the freshest fish to his supper that the island could provide.

On the morrow, The Smith thanked his host and borrowed a sturdy horse he was assured was sure-footed, being a recent cross between a large Norwegian Fjord and the smaller Eriskay pony, whose dappled silver coat it had inherited. He took the grey and turned it towards the winding track that led across the heather even further into the west.

Once more, it was a journey he had made before, but this landscape seemed scarcely changed from the first time he had crossed it, nor from any of the subsequent visits he had been obliged to make over the intervening chasm of years. The heather covered the interior of the island, hiding innumerable treacherous bogs and lochans, and he kept to the winding road that skirted the wayward swoops of the coastline instead. It was the long way to go round in terms of the ground covered, but it was, he knew, the shortest and surest means of arriving at his destination.

The island was low-lying with few significant hills or peaks, and so studded with inlets and small lochs that from the air he had been told—by one who could share the eyes of a bird—it seemed as much made of water as rock and looked more like lacework than firm ground. Because of this, the coast road meandered seemingly without rhyme or reason. The few houses were all low and pleasing to the eye in the way that they seemed part of the land itself, with thick stone walls and deep-set doors beneath rounded mounds of heather thatch, held down against the wind by rope nets weighted with hanging stones. Some had windows, all had benches against the sunny side of the house close by the door and most had a territorially jealous sheep-dog that would run and bark at them as they passed. The horse was steady and didn't shy, perhaps knowing the barking and growling was mostly for showing teeth and not a prelude to using them.

As the day progressed, the houses became fewer and spaced further apart. He turned off the main track and headed on to a deserted peninsular, skirting a hill and climbing a little as he did so until he found the whole wide Atlantic spread away into the distance before him, with only a single black house tucked into the lee of the hill above the patch of machair, where the dark heather gave way to the softer green grass of the sea lawn and a small hidden bay beyond it.

It looked deserted, but he knew he was expected.

The ravens had begun circling him at a discreet distance ever since he had left the more cultivated and peopled flat part of the island known as Middlequarter, about four miles back. He dismounted and unsaddled the horse, leading it to a small burn beside the house, where it dropped its head and drank deeply.

"You can unbridle it too; it won't wander," said a voice from the other side of the building.

He unbuckled the leather straps and patted the grey.

"Thank you," he said into the horse's ear.

"Acht, he won't understand your foreign English," said the voice. "That's a good island horse. Only speaks honest Gaelic . . ."

The Smith walked past the rounded end of the building and saw the back of an old woman sitting on a rock at the top of a small round hummock which made a natural terrace in front of the black house. Her long white hair whipped like a pennant in the light breeze and she seemed too engrossed in watching the featureless seascape below to turn and greet him. She was surrounded by ravens: more than thirty of the dark birds ranged around her pale figure like a bodyguard. And in contrast to her, they were all facing him, black eyes locked on his every move.

"Glory of the day to you," he said.

The old woman turned to look at him out of eyes that seemed still to be sharp despite being clouded with age. Her face was as much of a contrast as her hair was to the ravens: it was aged, tough and weather-beaten, but there was a concentration of lines radiating from the corner of her eyes which somehow spoke of a lifetime of smiling and laughing.

"Glory of the day to you too, Wayland."

The pair of eyes which had followed him since he left London dropped out of the sky as the Raven joined the battalion of what were clearly her blood-kin.

The woman levered herself off the rock and walked towards him with a lopsided gait which bent her to the left as she moved. She didn't pause as she passed him, but just clapped him companionably on the arm and went on into the house.

"Sit and rest your bones," she said, emerging with a horn beaker full of water, which she handed to him. He swigged half in one gulp and then the other in a second. He nodded his thanks.

"Sit," she said. "I'll get you another."

He lowered himself onto the well-worn bench and stretched his legs out, feeling the gentle breeze on his face to be as refreshing as the clear water he had just drunk.

She emerged and handed him the full beaker and eased herself carefully onto the bench at his side, leaning back on the sun-warmed stone of the house with a sigh.

"Your ride will have set tongues wagging from here to Berneray," she said. "We still don't see many strangers, and the island folk are sharp-eyed as ever."

"Do they never notice who you are?" he said.

"No," she said. "Of course not. They've forgotten who that was, long past. You, in London, do they?"

"No," he said. "But it's easy enough to go unnoticed in a crowd. Out here, in the open, the islanders so thin on the ground, must be harder."

"Oh no," she laughed easily. "I'm still no more than the old lady who stays at the westernmost point to them, the hag from *an taigh air iomall an t-saoghail*—the house at the end of the world."

"I'd still say it's harder to hide here than in a city," he said. "They'd notice things about you. Like you're always here, generation to generation."

"Oh well, as to that, I'm also the old lady who lives a long time and then goes away for a bit and then word comes that she's left her croft to her niece who comes back and carries on as before, until she too seems to their children to be an old lady who then one day leaves and another niece comes back, and so it goes on—"

"And they still never notice it's you again and again?"

"Acht, that's not the hard bit." She punched him good-naturedly on the arm again and gathered his cup as she stood. "The hard bit is remembering to make them see me getting older at the right pace, not as I really am. As I really always am—"

"I'd like to see that," he said.

"Would you now?" she said, raising an eyebrow in a very un-old-ladylike way. "And what would my neighbours think?"

He looked out at the empty moorland and machair, sweeping it with his eyes.

"What neighbours?"

"The ones who would be troubled if they were to see the snow leave my hair and my poor old back straighten, what would they think, the poor souls?"

He saw nothing moving in the landscape except for the birds on the beach and the flock of ravens on the rocks around them.

"I imagine they'd think you were a very beautiful woman, in the prime of your strength," he said, turning back to look at her.

She had gone, or rather she had stepped back into the door of the black house.

"Would they now?" she said, standing shielded from anyone's view but his own in the deep whitewashed embrasure made by the thick stone walls.

"Yes," he said, feeling an unaccustomed thickening in his throat. The old lady who stooped to one side and looked out from beneath a flag of white hair was gone, and in her place was a strong-looking woman somewhere between forty and fifty, with hair every bit as wild and sleekly black as the ravens around her door. The cloudy eyes were now clear and hazel-coloured and—at this moment—caught in something between a laugh and a challenge.

"There you are," he said. "*Màthair nam Fitheach*."

She smiled.

"I am always the Mother of Ravens," she said. "Just as you are always The Smith."

He found he was smiling back at her. It seemed as if he hadn't smiled in an eternity.

"I have travelled the length of Britain noticing how much has changed," he said. "You have no idea how it . . . how it is to see something, someone precisely as they were so long ago."

"And it's good to see you too," she said. "In the flesh. Though of course I have seen you with other eyes over the years."

He continued to look at her, taking in the forgotten but deep familiarity of her face until she waved her hand in front of it in a gesture of mild irritation, the sting of which was removed by the grin it came with.

"Are you pretending this isn't going to happen, Smith? The way you always do whenever we meet?"

"No," he said. "No, Beira, I am not. I am just thinking we are perhaps a little old for this."

Her laugh was deep and open—and then he was in the doorway too, then they were both lost inside the house and there was no thinking or talking for a long while, thought there was more laughter and some other mutedly joyful noises which only the ravens heard.

CHAPTER 22

OLD FRIENDS

Mr. Sharp woke from his deep sleep to find the light of a new day fighting a thick ceiling of storm-clouds over the city. The air was fresh and the gutters were still gurgling from a deluge he had clearly just slept through. He rolled out of The Smith's bed and was surprised to find his clothes were not where he had left them, tumbled on a chair, but were laid out clean and freshly ironed.

He could not find his boots so he descended the wooden stairs in his stockinged feet and entered the workshop-cum-kitchen to find them standing against the wall by the door.

"You'll be hungry?" said Ida, who was sitting cross-legged on a work-bench with her crossbow in pieces all around her.

"I slept all day," he said.

"And the rest. You missed a corker of a rainstorm and all, come down by the bucket-load it did," said Charlie Pyefinch, entering with a sodden-looking Archie trotting at his heels. "You been asleep a day and a night!"

"Cook's medicine," said Ida.

Sharp sat and pulled on his boots.

"Well, I feel better for it. Where is she?"

"Cook's sitting with Miss Falk," said Charlie.

Sharp's head came up.

"Why? Is she turned for the worse?"

"No," said Ida. "She's just sleeping. I think Cook just likes to sit with her. She was so happy to get her back. If you are hungry, there is tea in the pot and I can get you ham and bread?"

"I'll get it," said Charlie. "You've got oil all over your fingers."

"Good," said Ida. "One for me too then."

Sharp drank the tea and quickly made himself a sandwich. As he did so, he watched Charlie and Ida together and felt a pang of envy, both for their youth and their evident ease with each other.

Then he washed his mug and the plate he'd used and went into the back room of the workshop. He quickly unlocked a cupboard and selected a pair of knives which were identical to the ones stolen from him by Dee in the mirrors. He secured them in their accustomed places and walked back out into the workshop, feeling not only better than he had in an age, but properly dressed.

"Where is the Wildfire exactly?" he said.

"Lead chests are sunk just off the cut at Irongate Steps, between the Tower and St. Katherine's Dock," said Charlie.

"Please tell Cook and Sara if she wakes that that is where I have gone."

"I'll chum you," said Charlie, getting off the bench where he had been sitting with Ida. "Me and Hodge been doing turnabout at the Tower, and I should be getting over there soon anyway. I was just sitting out that downpour we had earlier."

So Charlie and Sharp set off and walked back west into the city, avoiding the deeper puddles and the overflowed drains with the young dog Archie ranging around them like an inquisitive scout, alertly sampling interesting smells and sights, but always looping back to check on them as he kept up his mobile patrol. The Sluagh were not visible at the bridge over the Gut, but the sun was high and the shadows they had been standing in were now gone.

"They're still watching," said Sharp, his hand inside his coat, close to the grip of his new knife.

"I know," said Charlie. "Feel it like an itch on the back of my neck, but I'll be damned if I can see where they are half the time."

Sharp smiled and clapped him on the shoulder.

"I have the self-same itch when being watched. I think we have a lot in common, young Charlie Pyefinch. Now tell me news of your parents. I haven't seen Rose and Barnaby in an age. Is he still telling tall tales?"

"Oh yes," said Charlie. "And making a good living at it at the fairs: you should hear him on the Battle of Waterloo—makes your hair stand on end and feel like you were there . . ."

And as they stretched their legs and kept a fast pace which each found easy to maintain, they talked, and by the time they reached the eastern edge of the Tower, Charlie found he had decided Mr. Sharp wasn't so forbidding and dry as he had thought, and Sharp had confirmed his opinion that his new young companion was definitely made of the right stuff and could see why Hodge had taken him on and honoured him with what was clearly, to anyone with half an eye, one of Jed's pups.

"Just down there," said Charlie, pointing over the line of pilings which ran up Irongate Steps, a steep-sided narrow cut leading down to the river with a treacherous-looking series of steps dropping down to the water. The tide was low and a small strand of mud and pebbles was exposed at the end as the river flowed greasily past beyond it.

"There's a couple of old mooring chains just round the corner," said Charlie, leaning out and pointing. "Out of sight from up here, anyway, the oldest one with all the green weed on it's the one you'll be wanting. You all right if I cut away and see Hodge now, Mr. Sharp?"

Sharp nodded, his eyes on the river, as if imagining what lay beneath the weight of water flowing inexorably past on its way to Gravesend and the cold North Sea beyond.

"My compliments to him, Charlie, and tell him I congratulate him on his choice of apprentice. I think the ravens will be in good hands for another generation."

He looked casually around to make sure nobody was close or interested enough to notice him, and then he slipped rapidly through the pilings and negotiated the slimy steps down to the river's edge.

Moments later, he emerged from the cut and turned right towards the forbidding mouth of the Tower's river gate, further down the bank, pebbles graunching against each other in the sandy mud beneath his boots. He found the weed-choked mooring chain Charlie had described, a massive, ancient thing he could well believe had been fixed to the embankment a hundred or more years past, and he drew his knife and tapped it against the metal, a series of raps and pauses that were the repeated secret knock by which he had formerly identified himself to the golem when he had used to return to the Safe House late at night, when Emmet's duties had merely been to act as gatekeeper and guard the door.

The signal was transmitted down the intervening links and on downwards beneath the water, following the chain all the way to the riverbed to where a large clay hand was patiently gripped around it. The tell-tale knock vibrated through the hand, whose owner, previously sitting immobile as a rock against one of The Smith's lead caskets partly submerged in the ooze at the bottom of the river, cocked his head and looked blindly up through the great weight of water.

Sharp sat on a discarded beam of wood which had at one stage probably been part of the jury-rigged buttressing holding back the walls of the cut before falling off. He watched the Thames pass by, and he waited.

Emmet hauled himself doggedly up the chain like a mountaineer in a gale, using it to brace himself against the pressure of dark water trying to sweep him away.

Sharp stood as the great clay head broke the surface; the golem simply walked out of the river and came and stood in front of him, the familiar hollow eyes looking down at him from either side of the heroically hooked nose. It was one of the peculiarities of the golem's construction that although he was a hollow clay statue, made in a perfect facsimile of a man in every respect, he had no eyes, so that the void within him was always apparent. But the unsettling lack was strangely offset by the fact that he still blinked as if he did have eyes. It was one of the things that Sharp felt made him much more than the automaton the others saw him as. In fact, he almost was sure that when he had been a young boy, Emmet had not blinked, but had begun to do so at some time in the intervening years, as if mimicking human behaviour: he again felt that this was evidence that the golem was much more sentient and capable of independent thought than was generally believed.

"Emmet," said Sharp. "I am so very pleased to see you."

Emmet stood and blinked at him. Sharp put out his hand. Emmet, after a pause, did the same, and the great clay hand folded gently but firmly around Sharp's, and they shook.

"Let us . . ." began Sharp. "Let us sit here a while. In the sun."

He squatted back down on the beam of wood. Emmet looked at him. And then he reached inside the dripping greatcoat in which he was clad and removed something which he carefully pulled onto his head, before lowering himself to sit beside Sharp, also facing the river.

"Ah," said Sharp. "You have a new hat."

Prior to the fire that had consumed it, Emmet had worn a tricorne hat, the relic of a bygone era. He now sported what had once been a coachman's hat, but prolonged immersion and storage within his coat had reduced it to a battered and lopsided ruin. Sharp was pleased that one of the others had gone to the trouble of finding it for the golem. He reached out.

"May I?"

He took the ruined hat and did what he could to straighten and re-block it into a more respectable shape, and then handed it back.

"Here."

Emmet looked at the hat, turning it in his hands. Then he placed it carefully back on his head and blinked at Sharp.

"I'm sorry you have to be beneath the water," said Sharp.

Emmet shrugged, or at least Sharp was sure he made the ghost of a shrug.

"We could just sit and enjoy the light," he said, pulling his coat tighter around him at the chill of the day.

Emmet blinked at him. Then he very slowly turned his face to the pale wintry sun and they sat together in companionable silence for a long time, as the river ground its relentless way past them. What Emmet thought of, if he thought, remained a secret: Sharp thought of duty and failure and the threats hanging over all their heads. He thought of Emmet's long confinement under the river and how he had no real idea how to shorten the golem's entombment, and then he turned from contemplation of the water and found he was looking at the ominous, barred river gate to the Tower, the one used to bring in those who were to be imprisoned for failing most wretchedly, those guilty of betrayal, and he thought how bitterly appropriate it was that they had sunk the Wildfire opposite Traitor's Gate.

He was still under a cloud of self-recrimination when he climbed back up the greasy river steps, having watched Emmet walk uncomplainingly back down the chain to take up his blind guard post at the bottom of the Thames.

If he had been less self-absorbed, he would probably have noticed the clearly rentable lady who spotted him as he slipped back through the pilings and onto the street.

"Why, Mr. Sharp! What cheer? Ain't seen you up Neptune Street nor round the square since your 'orrible fire. What you been doing down there? You given it all up and turned mudlark, 'ave you?"

He looked up and saw a smiling face with a little too much powder on it.

"Hello, Ruby," he said. "You are well, I trust?"

"Mustn't grumble," said Ruby. "But you look hipped and cold as a brass monkey's you-know-whats. I could warm you up a bit if you like?"

"Thank you, Ruby," he said, this being a familiar offer, as was his customary demurral. "You are very kind, but no thank you."

"Oh, I'm not just very kind, Mr. S," she said, winking. "I'm very good value. Ask anyone."

He smiled and bowed and walked on. And Ruby watched him until he turned the corner, and then her smile dropped and her brow crinkled as she tried to remember who it was that had offered cash money for any news of a sighting of Mr. Sharp or his companions. And then it cleared as she remembered, and she turned towards the pub where the man in question was usually to be found.

And ten minutes later she had coins in her hand, and the news of Sharp's return and the riverbank spot where he had been loitering was filtering through the complex and informal intelligence network of informers, scouts and tale-bearers so carefully nurtured by the Templebanes over the long years, and by which Issachar, even in exile, kept his eye on the city.

CHAPTER 23

THE DEATH OF HOPE

The blood-spattered memory of what he had done to Abchurch rode Amos so hard that he vomited three times on his dogged walk to Wellclose Square, though the third time was really just a painful dry retching into the edge of a giant pool of water caused by a blocked culvert outside the Garrick Subscription Theatre in Leman Street. Beneath a playbill advertising a revival of *When Claudia Stoops!*, he jack-knifed appropriately over the already filthy water and added a thin stream of stomach bile to the effluence below, his gut now being empty of anything remotely solid. Then he unthinkingly wiped his mouth with his sleeve, straightened and continued towards Wellclose Square.

The half-drowned city was putting itself back together after the unwonted assault of the thunderstorm, shopkeepers sweeping puddles from the pavement into the brimming gutters and backed-up drains that gurgled and roared as they overwhelmed the sewers and hidden streams beneath the streets. Amos, normally sharp and aware of his surroundings to an unnatural degree, barely noticed the torrents flowing along with him as he too headed downhill towards the river. He was still blank-eyed with shock, but he was driven onwards like a sleepwalker, his limbs powered by the conviction that only The Oversight could save him now: he hoped they would welcome him for the things he could tell them of his father's machinations, but he was aware that he in fact had little to say other than that he and his brothers were deputed to watch the Safe House on a continual rota, and that he believed his journey to Mountfellon was in some way connected with a plan of which he had known almost nothing. He was painfully aware that this was not a very strong introduction, and so was not going to lead with it, rather intending to tell them of the Sluagh and what he had witnessed and heard about them: this being a subject he did know a lot about. He had listened to the Ghost speak of The Oversight and their concerns, and based his hopes on her assertion that they were bound to help protect normal people from the depredations of the supranatural. Well, he thought, he might not be entirely normal, but he had certainly been most viciously depredated upon. Even as he finally stumbled into the top of Wellclose Square and, saw the familiar outline of the Danish church in the centre of it and the gold-pillared doorway of Wilton's Music Hall beyond, he could feel the itch of the white tattoo around his neck as strongly as if he was still under its *geas*, which was the word that Badger Skull had used, meaning curse of obligation. He raised his hand to scratch it, his mind almost dizzy with the relief of having made it to the very door of The Oversight's Safe House without further trauma, and then he stopped moving, fingers stalled a bare inch from his neck, the fiery itch of the departed tattoo forgotten.

The very door he had thought he had reached was not there. Neither was the wall it had stood in, nor the house to which it had given entrance; the plot where it had stood both in life and in his mind was a flattened rubble pile. The empty lot was like a tooth which had been abruptly snapped out of a known smile—wrong, painful and fundamentally unbelievable.

"What?" said the Ghost as she caught up with him. "Oh . . ."

And she saw it too. Amos felt he might break if she laughed. As she would laugh. As she always laughed at his setbacks and surprises. But she didn't: she stepped past him and also seemed dumbstruck by the enormity of the absence.

He looked around to his left, registering the pull of another void, something he must have seen with the edge of his eye, because he hadn't been looking at it, and there was another ruin where the Sugar Factory had been, although it was being actively rebuilt behind a new palisade of scaffolding. He had sat on the bench outside the building on many a cold night, smelling the seductive warm smell of caramelised sugar wafting from within. The bench was gone too.

What happened?

She shook her head slowly.

I don't know. But it was very final, I'd say.

The absence of any of the expected exultation in her voice made it much worse. The lacuna at the bottom of the square had not just taken his hope away, it had somehow removed her cheery malice. She hadn't looked at the factory. She was staring at the hole in the square's southern rampart as if trying to recreate what had stood there in her mind. But it would only ever exist in memory now, because where there had been a regular, foursquare façade and a solid, fortress-like building behind it was now an area of raked-over wreckage. Burned remnants of joists and floorboards had been thrown in a pile on the bottom, riverward boundary, like a giant's game of spillikins and someone had made a half-hearted attempt to salvage bricks by making a pile of them against the shared wall of the adjacent house. It looked like they'd just given up, for the stack was itself half tumbled down.

It was desolate, final and—for Amos—the complete death of hope. He felt it physically: he suddenly desperately needed to piss; his mouth was dry and tasted of stomach bile; and his leg began to shake uncontrollably. He stamped his foot to stop it, and stared around for something familiar to focus on.

And there he was—walking towards them, a bundle of important-looking papers under one arm, nose in the air as if sampling the new smells released by the rain-washed city and finding them rather splendid: the diminutive and visibly self-important figure of Magistrate Bidgood, one of the several local worthies whose comings and goings Amos and his brothers were tasked to keep an eye out for.

Amos nudged the Ghost and pointed at the approaching Bidgood with an infinitesimal lift of his chin.

This man. Ask him where they've gone.

You want me to speak to him?

I can't.

I haven't spoken out loud to anyone except you in years. Maybe decades. I lost count.

Please.

They've gone. You can see that.

Bidgood was only a couple of yards away now.

Please. Ask. I must know.

A pretty please?

A trace of her cheery malice resurfaced in the word "pretty."

What do you mean?

I mean deeds not words, Bloody Boy. What will you do for me if I ask?

Just please ask him. He's a magistrate. He'll know what happened. This is his parish . . .

The diminutive officer of the law sailed past without seeming to notice them. He was in fact looking at the sky and congratulating himself on both having missed the deluge and having had the forethought to direct his cook to make him a steak and oyster pie for his supper, to which he was now returning. He was very much in a humour for a steak and oyster pie. Amos nudged the Ghost more urgently. She looked at him with a calm, questioning eye that he found inexpressibly provoking, given the urgency of the situation.

And . . . ?

Amos jiggled from one foot to the other, pointing at the magistrate's back with exasperation.

And I, if they are truly gone . . . I'll come with you. To find Mountfellon!

And you will use your new skill, your wonderful speed?

Yes! No. No. Not to kill him.

The thought was suddenly awful in him that she might, given his sudden rudderless state be able to manipulate him to do the thing he had

forsworn. The thing he kept doing, no matter how endlessly he seemed
to be foreswearing it.

She cocked her head on one side, considering his proviso. He was sure
he would burst with frustration, and Bidgood was nearly at the corner
. . . and then she nodded.

What's his name, the strutting little man?

Bidgood. Lemuel Bidgood.

She strode after him, her voice like cut crystal, clear and commanding.

"Magistrate Bidgood, excuse me, sir, if you please."

Bidgood turned, conscious of the quality of the voice hailing him, a
patient smile forming on his lips as he did so, a smile ready at any moment
to grow into something even wider and more ingratiating. Amos could hear
the thought in the magistrate's head: he was initially surprised and excited
by the voice; he was sure he was being approached by some fine lady, a
personage of evident culture, wealth and distinction. As his eyes discovered
the waiting figure of the Ghost standing there, wrapped in a pair of blankets
draped over a distinctly well-worn dress, with matted grey hair that had
clearly been a stranger to any brush for a considerable passage of time,
Amos felt Bidgood's mind falter and panic as he attempted to readjust his
demeanour appropriately: he had thought to see a great lady, and now he
feared he was going to be "touched" for a few coppers by a beggarwoman.

"Er—" he squeaked.

The Ghost could obviously hear the same confusion within the magistrate's mind because she smiled and held up a hand that was, in the
circumstances, oddly gracious and commanding.

"No, sir, by your leave, I want nothing from you but some local
information. Would you be so kind as to tell me what happened to the
fine house and the occupants which were once situated in that derelict
lot over there at the bottom of the square?"

Bidgood relaxed, still confused by the mismatch between the gently
well-born voice and the villainously disreputable person from whom it
came. And then the thought hit him that it was odd that this woman
should be asking about this particular property—

"They were friends of mine, or rather, the family were friends of my youth, when I was not as you see me now," she said with a sad smile, tumbling a reply into his mind before the question of who or what she was had even really formed. Even in the extreme state of despair with which he was gripped, Amos couldn't help but admire her technique: there were advantages to hearing the thoughts of others that enabled one to direct conversations to one's own satisfaction, leaving unproductive and distracting lines of inquiry to die stillborn and unexamined. "It would mean so much to me to know what has occurred, and if they are well."

Bidgood relaxed. He guessed at a familiar, somewhat melodramatic but no less sad story for the woman's present plight: born to the purple, riches lost in her youth, a dissolute father perhaps, a rake, a gambler . . . Oh yes, he had seen the end of several such little morality plays acted out in front of him on the bench, and had seen some of the principal actors sent to the Old Marshalsea to languish in the cruel limbo of the debtor's wing which had only closed a couple of years before. Who knew, this lady might well be the sad victim of such a history. He looked up at the spire of the Danish Church and decided it behoved him to be charitable and answer her.

"Well then, I am sorry to tell you, sorry indeed to say that they are gone. I hope the news does not distress you." He indicated the building works going on at the top of the square. "There was an explosion in the old sugar manufactory that previously occupied the premises there, and it led to the house at the bottom of the square, due to gravity, being destroyed. Gravity, yes, gravity."

He cleared his throat. He was a man who enjoyed the sound of his own voice, and once started he often found himself saying more than he had intended. The fact that no one in his court had the authority to curtail his bent towards expansive peroration had fed this bad habit.

"Ah yes, fatal gravity and streams of burning treacle were the downfall of the house, you see, flowing like lava, downhill right past the very doors of Wilton's Music Hall here, all the way down to the house in question. Most unfortunately a cartful of kerosene barrels was hitched in front of the doomed building and this led to a terrible, which is to say devastating explosion. Devastating, yes, is the very word: all was lost, as you see, blown to smithereens . . ."

Ask about The Oversight.

He won't know about them as such.

Amos thought of the things he had witnessed in what he increasingly thought of as his previous life, the one spent fetching and carrying and spying; in the latter capacity, he had stood watch in the shadows on many nights, keeping a list of the comings and goings at the house for Issachar and Zebulon.

Ask about the white-haired young woman. Miss Falk.

"Thank you, kind sir," said the Ghost. "And do you happen to know what happened to a Miss Falk."

"Ah no," said Bidgood. "Miss Sara Falk, the jewess. No, she has not been seen for some considerable time. It is possible that she and her companions perished in the fire. It was a conflagration of an intensity, it was, an intensity strong enough to burn bones themselves, I believe. And the fall of the house: why, I witnessed that myself, though I missed the start of the fire. I had been called to the scene expressly once the alarm had been given. The fall of the house was a most considerable crash. A considerable one."

Ask about the others. Please.

"And her companions?" she said.

Bidgood felt a hungry rumble in his stomach and remembered the waiting steak and oyster pie, and decided that his charitable expenditure of conversation and information had reached the stage where it was coming between himself and the anticipated gastronomic delight.

"Er, I do not know who they were, but she did keep an irregular house; somewhat irregular, some might say . . . but anyway, they are gone and so must I be. Good day."

And with a tip of his hat he walked away supperwards, wondering as he went what it had been about the strangely commanding beggarwoman that had made him offer a salute instead of a ha'penny.

Amos slumped to the pavement, like a puppet with its strings cut. He did not notice or care that he was sitting in a puddle. This is what the death of hope felt like. Even when travelling by himself in the wide open, empty countryside, he had never felt so alone.

"Better come with me, Bloody Boy," said the Ghost, putting a hand on his shoulder that he felt too broken to resist. There was a kind of sadness in her voice, not the exulting tone he might have expected, which made the desolation in front of him cut all the deeper. "You thought I was exaggerating. Look at the ruin of the Safe House. It wasn't safe and now it isn't even a house. The Oversight it is dead and gone. I'm all the family you have now."

CHAPTER 24

THE SOUTERRAIN

The Smith and Beira were lying motionless and happily tangled on the box bed at the end of the one room inside the blackhouse, watching the sunrays turn gold on the smoke-tarred roof trees above them. It felt to The Smith, who never rested, that this was like a stolen moment suspended in time, so much so that as he dozed and woke and dozed again he could no longer tell if they had been here for minutes or hours, or even days. It was not an unpleasant sensation and he felt revived by it, and also strangely protected. It was as if they were a pair of flies caught in a tawny piece of amber and thus rendered unchanging and also incapable of any further action. And then she groaned happily and slowly stretched, rolled over and nudged him.

"Come on, old man, come sit with me outside and watch the sun dip."

"Are you not worried that your neighbours will see you?" he said.

"No," she smiled. "My ravens will see them before they come in sight. I was teasing you earlier."

"Teasing," he said, running the word around his mouth as if sampling an unfamiliar taste. "Is that what it was?"

"It was a ploy to get you to come inside," she said. "As you well knew. This is an old dance and we both know the steps by heart."

"Well, I like the dance, and the partner," he smiled back at her, sitting up and looking for his clothes. As he turned, she saw his back and involuntarily reached out and touched the small of it. Where the rest of his body was clear and unmarked, a swirl of ancient black tattoos was reaching up from his waist, as if filling in old track marks, the leading edges of the stains purple and yellow, like an intricate bruise, or infection of the blood. It was a noxious, diseased-looking thing.

"What?" he said.

"Nothing . . ." she said, her eyes leaving the stain and finding a bottle on a far shelf on the other side of the room.

"Oh, I know," he smiled again. "I felt a twinge back on the island-within-the-island. But it's nothing. You know it's nothing; you've seen it before. A little comes back when things falter, but as long as it's just a small bit like that, no bigger than your hand, I control it and it fades soon enough. You know that . . ."

"I know that," she said, and because he was turned away and her voice was unfaltering, he missed the stutter in her eyes. Her hand remained in the small of his back dwarfed by the black and corrupted swirl of tattoos spreading far beyond it, a thick trunk following his spine and then spreading ominously across his broad shoulders like the louring crown of a dark oak tree.

"Now let's have a drop of my *uisge* and enjoy the last of the light as it dies in the west," she said, slapping him on the back as she stepped off the bed and walked unselfconsciously naked to the shelf where she found a stone bottle from which she poured him a measure in a small horn cup and then one for herself. She picked up a blanket from the chair by the fire and wrapped herself in it as she returned and gave him the whisky with a nudge.

"This is the part of the old dance where you get sad because I'm not her, and I tell you she wouldn't begrudge you the little human warmth we just shared. And then you say nothing at all, just like you're doing now, and I say—"

He sipped the whisky and grimaced as it went down his throat, sending a warm fire into his belly.

"You say that without a little human warmth and softness I would break and become less than human, which would be dangerous for someone with my . . . gifts."

"There you go," she said. "You like the *uisge*?"

"You're getting the hang of it," he said. "Smokier."

"That's just the peat," she said. "It's not just us. It's getting older too. Now come on, bring a blanket. I like to watch the sunsets."

They found their way back out into the light and sat against each other, wrapped in blankets and leaning against the wall of the black house. The flock of ravens had moved discreetly further away, as if they had decided to allow them some privacy.

"So," she said. "To business. What message must the ravens carry?"

"The Iron Prohibition is broken; the Sluagh are unbound and may look to settle old scores. And the Last Hand fails."

She stared at him in shock.

"The Sluagh are unbound? You didn't think to tell me that when you first arrived?"

He took a sip of the whisky.

"Well, that might well have changed the mood a little, might it not?" His eyes flicked behind him to the black house. "You're not the only one who can make a ploy."

He smiled down at her.

"It's good once in a while to forget for a brief instant the thing you are bound to. You told me that a long time ago."

"Did I?"

"You did."

He pulled her closer, and put his lips on her forehead.

"And I thank you for it."

"And how has it been, this thing you are bound to?" she said.

He shrugged and looked at the flat line of the horizon.

"Sometimes it is good. Sometimes it's bad. And then at the worst times, it feels like forever."

"Forever?" she said.

"Doesn't it feel like forever to you?"

"No."

She shook her hair loose and ran her fingers through to comb some kind of order into it.

"Mostly it feels like it's all gone by in a flash."

"I can't believe that."

"Well, it's true. There's so much to see and think on."

He looked around at the wild emptiness all around them—the heather at their back, the grey rocks and the expanse of green machair sweeping away to the tufted dunes and the long, empty white-sand beach beyond it, and then the unending immensity of the ocean.

"But there's nothing but this to see," he said.

"There's much to be said for simplicity," she said. "Though if you were to come here in spring, the machair there contains worlds within worlds, so many small wildflowers, all shapes and sizes and variations, you'll find all the wondrous complexity you could wish for . . . and then the sea, every day it throws something new on the shore as it comes and goes. Oh, there's plenty enough to keep your attention if you know how to see things."

"You don't mind being cut off from the world?" he said.

"Cut off?" she laughed. "Is it cut off you think I am?"

She pointed at the ravens.

"It's not just their eyes I share. It's all ravens and their kin. Do you truly not see how it is after all these years of knowing me, knowing I'm here, always here and nowhere else?"

"The black house at the end of the world," he said.

"It has to be simple," she said. "With all that I see when I'm in their eyes, it has to be simple when I'm back in my own head. Just sky, sea, land and the weather moving across the gulf of air between them. If it wasn't simple, I'd go mad. Like you."

"You think I've gone mad?" he said.

"No," she said. "I think you've always been mad. You've always thought you could keep things in balance. You've always believed the darkness can be kept at bay."

"It can," he said.

"Not all the darkness," she said. "And not all the time. And isn't hope a kind of madness, like faith? I didn't say it was a bad kind of mad. It's the kind of madness that you need to have in order to keep walking forwards, I think."

"It's time to send the ravens," he said.

"Ah," she said after a pause. "It's that bad again."

"Yes," he said, finishing the glass and grimacing as the spirit burned gently down his throat. "Actually, it's worse."

"Worse than sending the ravens?"

"Yes. You're going to have to give me my blood back."

She exhaled in a low whistle.

"You're worried about the Wildfire," she said.

"I'm always worried about the damned Wildfire," he said. "I'm just even more worried about it when things are falling apart like this."

"Something else," she said. "There's something else, Wayland—what is it?"

"I'm not sure," he scowled. "The Wildfire always wants out. That's what makes it so . . . volatile. It's like it has a mind of its own."

"It's got a hunger of its own," she said. "I don't know if it has to have a mind as we think of a mind for it to have a hunger."

"Its hunger is bad enough, and we know how to keep it safe from that," he said, "but this is something new. When we've lost control, in the past, it has been because of accidents, more than anything. This time I think there's a different hunger at play. I think whatever is moving against us is after the fire itself. And that is new. And that is why—"

He paused and grimaced as if a chill had just shuddered through him.

"Well, that is why I need my blood back."

She smiled at him and put her hand on his shoulder.

"Are you hesitating because you know in one of the old stories they tell about us, this is where I trap you by my feminine wiles and leave you penned in a secret cavern, and kingdoms fall and fellowships are broken as a result?"

He reached his hand up and she let him pull her face down to meet his, she kissed his forehead, as if returning the previous one he had given her.

"Old stories," he snorted. "Stories are a good way to spoil perfectly fine truths by trying to explain them."

"If you say so," she said. "You of all people would know about that. Well, if you're to have your blood back once more, it's definitely something we'd be better doing at night. Wouldn't do to be seen lifting rocks in the daylight."

"No," he said. "Though in truth I wish I could forego the day and night it will take, for even twenty-four hours seems like a luxury we can ill afford, and good though our time together has been, I must be on my way south as soon as I can. The steamer will take me from Skye to Glasgow the day after tomorrow, and the railway will have me home by midnight on that day."

"So fast, the modern world," she said with a sigh. "You'll have time for another dram before we go to the hill. It'll warm your old bones."

She reached for the stone bottle.

"And then I'll put some broth on the fire for us both. It won't be fell dark for another hour, and it gets cold out there."

CHAPTER 25

THE ADMONITORY FLOORBOARD

Issachar Templebane did not particularly enjoy his enforced exile deep in the countryside, but it was not an uncomfortable one, the old house being sufficiently large to keep his sons close enough to ensure his safety, yet far enough away to diminish the irritation their company engendered.

He sat by the fire in the study that adjoined his bedroom, at a desk covered in neat piles of paper, the biggest of which was held in place by a significantly large pistol. He was reading the cream of the day's crop of letters and notes brought to him from the extensive network of lookouts and casual informers the house of Templebane had long cultivated and relied on. The one in question contained the very interesting information that a certain Ruby who plied her trade on Neptune Street had seen Mr. Sharp returned to London on the day previous, when he had been skulking about on the riverbank at Irongate Steps between St. Katherine's Dock and the Tower. He read it twice and made a corresponding entry in the crabbed and tiny handwriting that filled his daybook and was in its way part of a long-running, seemingly random and hidden history of London itself.

Ruby was a useful pair of eyes to him, and was even on occasion a useful pair of hands and lips, in that he used her to carry messages, verbal or written, to other intermediaries whom his sons might draw attention to themselves by meeting. It was Ruby who had heard from a friend of a friend that Coram Templebane still lived, a fact he had not shared with his other sons. Issachar had no interest in claiming the crippled man, especially since he was thought a lunatic now, and was held in the Bedlam Hospital, but he did, through other watchers, keep an eye on him, and through this was aware that The Oversight, the hated Oversight, visited him regularly and asked questions that he was apparently unwilling to answer. Issachar looked on life as a long transaction, a game in which every piece, however unimportant, might one day be useful. And so he monitored Coram in case he said something he shouldn't, and also because one day Issachar might want to use him to spread a little misleading information to his enemies. He had a girl who pumped a reformed drunk called Bill Ketch for news of Coram, and every fortnight or so her report arrived among the myriad other missives which flowed from the city to land on this desk.

Those missives reached him every day via a purposely circuitous route of errand boys, go-betweens, cut-outs and carriers, an untraceable journey designed to confound any enemies who might try and follow a note all the way from London to his anonymous ancestral bolthole. Locally he was not even known by his real name, nor had any of his forebears: here in the rarely travelled bucolic backwater, they were known as Fenman, a pseudonym chosen by one of his ancestors to refer to the flat watery landscape the family hailed from in the old witch-finding days.

The general air of anonymity was carried on in the décor of the house which, unlike other such old manors, had no family portraits on the walls. But instead, in his study at least, there was a mirror. And it was from that looking-glass, hung on the wall behind him, that a figure stepped without a word, the carefully placed foot landing on a floorboard that creaked alarmingly.

Issachar turned with surprising speed, the pistol already in his hand.

"That's new," said Dee, calmly looking down at the offending floor-board.

Templebane breathed again and returned the firearm to its former duty as a paperweight.

"I had them all loosened specially," he said. "I do not like being crept up on."

"You could just shroud the mirror," said Dee. "Hang something over it. That would stop it working."

"But then how would I avail myself of your valuable and instructive company, Doctor Dee?" said Templebane. "Will you take some brandy?"

Dee stood with his back to the fire and accepted a glass, which Issachar filled liberally. He sipped and nodded.

"Good," he said.

"My fathers built a cold house, but laid in a good cellar," said Issachar. "But you didn't come to sample my liquor, doctor. Please proceed."

He sat back in his chair and looked up into the goat-bearded man in front of the fire.

"You took it upon yourself to move against The Oversight?" said Dee, disapproval dripping from his words.

"I did."

Templebane answered frankly, as if it was nothing. Dee scowled.

"Your success was only partial."

"It was."

"You did not think to tell me of your plans?"

"I did not."

"You did not?"

"The matter was personal. They killed my brother Zebulon. It was a matter of great distress to me." Issachar looked profoundly, almost insolently undistressed as he said this.

"And Mountfellon knew nothing of it either?"

"Indeed not," said Issachar. "He would have objected strongly, obsessed as he was about stealing what was within the house and the library. I think he wished to take the whole library itself, all the esoteric incunabula and the various arcane objects stored there into the bargain. He is a very greedy man. One momentary keek at their strange cabinet of curiosities and he must have it for his own . . ."

"And he knows nothing of our connection?"

"Not from me," snorted Templebane, as if the suggestion was faintly shocking. "The house of Templebane prides itself on its discretion, as you know."

"I have known the Templebanes since they were burning old women and simple young girls for three ha'pence apiece," said Dee. "So don't come it with me, cunning man."

Issachar let a small smile tiptoe swiftly across his lips and then disappear.

"Mountfellon imagines himself the prime mover in all he does, such is the conceit of all great titled men."

"Good," said Dee. "Lucky for you that your success was only partial."

Issachar tasted more brandy, swirling it around the inside of his great pouchy cheeks before he swallowed it.

"It was partial in the heroic sense," he said, "in that though a failure, it was considerable in its impact: the house is destroyed and all the contents burned . . ."

"No," said Dee. "Not *all* the contents."

"Are you sure?" said Issachar. "My eyes and ears on the streets tell me it is no more than a rubble-strewn midden . . ."

"I assure you," said Dee. "If the item I have in mind had been touched by your pyromaniac efforts, considerably more than one house would now be ruined. It is, as I said, greatly to your advantage that it was not."

"Is that so?" said Issachar, hiding his interest by reaching for the brandy bottle and offering it to his guest.

"I would not say it if it were not so," said Dee, holding his glass steady as it was refilled. "They will have saved it and put it somewhere for safekeeping, most likely beneath running water as before."

Issachar's eyes flickered, and as he turned to replace the brandy bottle, he made sure to slide the note containing the rentable Ruby's information about Sharp and his interest in Irongate Steps back under the day-book.

"And," he said, "if I was to have an idea of its likely whereabouts?"

"You would be rewarded greatly. More in fact than we have ever paid you or your fathers. And even more so if you also found a way to retrieve it, or perhaps even better to persuade Mountfellon to use his considerable resources to do so," said Dee. "His riches and his hunger are—"

"—something for us to work with. Of course," said Issachar as he leant back in his chair and stared at the reflection of the fire playing across the simple plasterwork overhead. A slow smile flowered as he thought.

"You have a plan, cunning man?" said Dee, who had missed none of this, hiding his own satisfaction at having planted the seed about Mountfellon in the other's brain in such a way that Templebane was clearly in the process of making the whole stratagem his own. Issachar sat forward, suddenly all business.

"I am a simple man before I am a cunning one, Doctor Dee," he said. "I have three fears: I fear penury, like anyone else in this world. I fear The Oversight, for they would revenge themselves most pitilessly upon me if they knew, as I believe they do, that it was my hand that moved against them, and I have a similar but slightly lesser apprehension about our friend the noble lord, who would be most unsympathetic and I dare say spitefully vindictive if he knew I had destroyed the plunder he hoped to have off them."

"These are reasonable anxieties," said Dee. "And yet you smile."

"And yet I smile," said Issachar. "For I think I can see a way to kill all three birds with one stone."

"Can you?" said Dee, leaning forward with interest sparkling in his eyes.

Issachar reached for the bottle again.

"Yes, doctor, with a little bluff and some good planning, I think I can see a way to have the noble lord use his resources to get what you want, and then to have the Sluagh relieve him of it and give it to us. Brandy?"

CHAPTER 26

THE UNKINDNESS OF RAVENS

At midnight they made their way from the warmth of the fireside in the blackhouse to a point further up on the hillside. The moon was silvering the rocks and the sea below as they pushed through the unkempt heather towards a scrabble of larger rocks indistinguishable from several other groups around them. The Smith carried his long bag with the hammer in it in one hand, and a driftwood ladder over the other shoulder. Beira had a bale of dry heather-bedding on her back.

She stopped next to a rock seemingly picked at random, dropped the heather beside it and rolled the stone to one side with surprising ease, revealing a carefully made stone-lined hole leading down into the darkness below. He lay on his stomach and fed the ladder down into the shaft. It was an eight-foot ladder and he had to lean far into the hole to get its feet down on the floor of the chamber.

He pulled a candle from his pocket and snapped it alight, dropping it onto the rough slabs that had been laid on the floor of the underground cell. The walls were made of small flat rocks, laid like a dry-stone wall, making a rough beehive shape around a central pillar, itself made from stones similarly stacked one on top of the other. Just visible at the far edge of the souterrain a low tunnel led away, angled upwards with the slope of the hill, barely broad enough for a man to fit in, and tapering as it disappeared in the gloom beyond the throw of the candle flame.

"You know. I was thinking on what you said about how this feels like forever to you," she said. "And I think that's because you can't let go."

"I have let go of her," he replied, rolling around and dropping his legs into the hole, finding a rung on the ladder and pulling his bag closer, looping the handles over his arm.

"Not of her. I don't mean her," she said. "Though since you mention it, I don't believe you have let go of her either, and I'd be the very last to blame you—I mean you can't let go of an idea. Maybe it can't let go of you."

"An idea?"

"A belief then," she said. "The belief that you can change things."

"I do change things," he said. "We have changed things."

"And yet here you are. Once more," she said, looking down at him. "In this hole. Asking for your own blood again."

She could see the moon reflected in his eyes as he looked up at her silhouetted against the clear night sky.

"If you don't get up when you're knocked down, the fight is over," he said. "It's not more complicated than that."

"Exactly," she said.

"You agree?"

"No. I didn't say that. I said exactly. That's the precise cleft you're stuck in. That you've always been in. Maybe it's simply to do with being a man."

"That's all I've ever been. A simple man trying to do a simple thing."

"No. That's who you were before all this began," she sighed. "Neither of us have been simple since then, have we?"

"You're not so complicated, Beira," he said.

"If you believe that you're a fool, and I know you're not a fool, so don't go dirtying up a perfectly clean night with a lie like that," she said, voice sharp. Then she exhaled heavily and knelt on the lip of the shaft.

"I'm not fighting anything, Wayland. I'm just watching and being. Being and watching. That's why time does not chafe me as it does you, who try and swim against its current. And it is a flow, time, just like a tide in the sea; if you just be, if you just watch, you float with it, and its passage doesn't irk you at all."

"You know what I think?" said The Smith.

"Yes," she said. "After all the long years, I think I probably do."

"I think that just watching and being what you are is how you choose to fight."

"Do you?" she said.

"I do."

"Well," she said, rising and dusting nonexistent dirt from the front of her skirt. "Maybe you aren't as simple as you pretend to be. Make a hole there—"

She threw the bale of cut heather down the hole beside him.

"Everything you need is where you left it. No reason you should lie on the stones. Heather makes a good enough mattress, as you well know."

"I may take a full day," he said.

"How bad are you?" she asked, her hand reaching down and touching his arm. He shrugged.

"The Raven flew with me all the way in case I did not get to you. I knew it wasn't necessary, but Hodge insisted."

"The present Terrier Man."

"He's a good one."

"I know. He keeps a good guard on my ravens, and he has a young apprentice with a new dog."

"You do watch everything, don't you?"

"No one can watch everything. But like The Raven herself, I do keep an eye on those I am bound to. I think it's good that the Hodge man has a replacement in training."

Smith's head came up. Like a dog on point.

"What do you mean?"

"You well know what I mean," she said. There was something in his face that said part of him did not want to go down the ladder.

"I'll see you soon," he said.

"You will," she grinned.

She watched him go down the hole with a smile on her face. And then she dragged and rolled the big slab back on top of the hole, lost the smile and walked back down the hill towards her house, brow furrowed in thought.

She didn't see The Raven flap into position on top of the rock, like a guard.

But she knew it was there.

She got halfway to the house before she shook her head and walked wearily back up the hill. She snapped her finger and The Raven jumped off the boulder and floated onto her wrist. She bowed her head and whispered to it. It was a long conversation. And when it was done she put two fingers in her mouth and split the night with a shrill whistle, and all the other ravens flapped into the sky and came to wheel around her in the silver moonlight, like a slow black whirlpool in the air, until she lofted the Raven on her wrist towards the moon. It circled once, twice and then thrice for the luck of it, as if bidding a farewell to the others who were already flapping slowly southwards, and then dropped again and took up its former position on the boulder.

She slumped against the rock and sat with her back to it. Her eyes were wet. She picked up a smaller rock and tapped the bigger one.

Inside the souterrain The Smith was sitting in the dark. He looked up at the noise.

"Beira?"

She bent down and spoke through a thin crack in the rock.

"I've sent the ravens."

"Good."

She took a deep breath.

"But The Raven will stay. You will need an overwatch."

He tried to stand in shock, but was horrified to find his legs didn't work, and staggered back, steadying himself with a hand against the rough edges of the stone-stacked wall.

"What have you done?" he shouted hoarsely. "I can't . . ."

"It wasn't just the peat in the whisky, Wayland," she whispered. "I'm sorry."

"Beira!"

"Sleep," she whispered into the crack. "I know it's hard, but it's done. So take it soft. You sleep now. It will feel like sleep if you let it."

She wiped the tears from her eye.

"They need me!" he shouted, trying to claw himself to his feet. "The Oversight needs me!"

"They must stand or fall on their own now," she said. "In your heart you know this. In your head you know there are greater things at stake than this Last Hand. In your heart you know the game is much, much longer than that."

"You trapped me," he breathed hoarsely, his eyes fluttering in the dark.

"But I sent the ravens," she said. "I did do that."

"You trapped me," he repeated, hands falling limply to his side.

"And you forgot, Wayland," she said, her eyes watching the last of the ravens flap over the brow of the hill. "Everything is a circle, and not all the old stories come from the past. Some were born in the future. Now settle yourself on the heather before you fall, for the dark is coming and the floor is hard beneath you."

THIRD PART

BREAKING AND ENTERING

Malum quidem nullum esse sine aliquo bono.

There is, to be sure, no evil without something good.

Pliny the Elder

ON THE AMERICAS

Of the Americas I have less to say—knowing little and wishing to learn more . . . but I will say that though some believe America to be Aravot . . . as described in the Zohar, viz. Seventh Heaven and location of the Garden of Eden: "for there are the treasures of good life, blessing and peace" . . . I can as yet see no proof of it, nor can I believe the claims made by Thomas Thorowgood in his "Jews in America or Probabilities that The Americans are of That Race" holding the likely antecedents of the native American to be the ten lost tribes . . . the contrary view posited in the answering tract by Sir Hamone Lestrange refutes this spurious pamphleteer better than I . . .

(Handwritten addendum to the above, in the rabbi's hand:

The Great and Hidden History of the World is a living work, and in time I hope I or those that follow will correct the present lacuna, since the New World may yet vastly surprise the Old, if Old Mistakes are not re-visited.)

From *The Great and Hidden History of the World* by the Rabbi Dr. Hayyim Samuel Falk (also known as the Ba'al Shem of London)

CHAPTER 27

THE CUNNING MAN CASTS A FLY

Issachar Templebane had had himself driven at great speed and almost greater discomfort from his anonymous hiding place in the countryside to the much more ostentatious bolthole that was Gallstaine Hall, ancient family seat of the Blackdyke family. He endured the awkward cross-country journey, jolting from turnpike to high road to cart track and back again, by telling himself that he was going a-fishing, possibly for the biggest catch of his lifetime, and that if he was to land his prey, he would need all his faculties about him, and there was thus no benefit in wasting any valuable energy in venting his frustration at the discomfort of the journey. It was a bone-shaking passage, and the only good thing that could be said of it, he thought as the carriage swept along the underground tunnel from the estate gates to the house itself, was that he finally arrived.

There was nothing in his demeanour as he strode up the ironstone steps to Gallstaine that betrayed this, or his intentions of using Mountfellon—who he had long secretly discounted as being useless to his own ambitions—as a stalking horse to draw out the last of the hated Oversight, in order that he might ambush them and finish the destruction he had previously seen so badly and perilously bungled. Nothing betrayed the inner glee that he felt at the thought that once this final stratagem was executed (and it was, in his mind, a simple enough one and very hard to bungle if he played it right) London would be his.

He was also not surprised by the thunderously discourteous way he was greeted once inside the echoing cavern of the inner hall. Mountfellon came hurtling down the wide marble staircase like an avalanche of ill will, one fist clenching the thigh bone of the ape that he had taken to carrying with him wherever he went like a comforting bludgeon, enjoying the destructive heft of it in his hand.

"What the devil do you want?" he snarled.

"An explanation," said Issachar, holding his ground with remarkable equanimity.

Mountfellon skidded to a halt right in front of him and leant in offensively close.

"An explanation?" he roared, spittle flecking the collar of Templebane's travelling cloak and the saggy wattles of the chin above it. "The devil you do, damn your impudence!"

Issachar produced a handkerchief and calmly wiped his neck.

"I would simply like to know if it was your Lordship who undertook the spectacularly ill-advised attempt to blow up the house on Wellclose Square belonging to The Oversight," he said.

"Why the deuce would I blow it up, you cretin?" bellowed Mountfellon. "Blowing it up has deprived me of valuable items! Things that might help me in my present, intolerable position? I should have you thrashed and pitched back out into the high road for your damned insolence! I received note of this catastrophic fire from that wretched little magistrate you involved in your first woefully unsuccessful scheme, Bigwell or Bedwet . . ."

"Bidgood," said Issachar calmly.

"I do not choose to know his exact name," said Mountfellon. "He is a man clearly trying to curry favour with his betters by keeping me informed of a 'property in which I had shown such a close interest.' As if I should be pleased to hear of all those irreplaceable treasures gone up in smoke? And you know what, tradesman? I don't see why you coming here now is a whit different from his damned presumption."

"Then you would be a fool, Lord Mountfellon," said Issachar. "And we both know you are not. So I repeat: do I have your word that it was not by your hand that the house of The Oversight was attacked?"

"Why the hell should I deign to give my word?" said Mountfellon, shaking the bone club in his face. "What the blazes is it to you?"

Issachar, a lifelong wheeler and dealer, knew that the old axiom to the effect that more was got by honey than vinegar was not an infallible truth. He was canny enough to know that on occasion—and this was one of them—only vinegar will turn the trick. And with this in mind, he ignored the bone cudgel and appeared to lose his own temper.

"What is it to me, my lord?" he hissed in a fine simulacrum of cold fury. "What is it to me and my whole enterprise to have been discovered to have attacked The Oversight? To have had to curtail my business and remove myself physically from London itself, as you have done?"

He shook his head, appearing to get himself under better control with great difficulty.

"It is a great deal, sir, and I will not leave, or say more about a certain opportunity, until you tell me if I am bearing the punishment consequent on your ill-advised activities!"

Mountfellon stared at him with the stunned inability to recalibrate the current interpersonal equation common to all bullies who are unexpectedly stood up to.

"It was none of my doing," he said curtly, and then noticed the bait Templebane had dangled, doing so in order to move quickly on from a moment that was, to his noble self, uncomfortably close to a capitulation.

"What opportunity to remedy things?" he said.

Issachar stared at him. The fly was in the mouth of the fish. All that remained was to time the strike and embed the barbed hook.

"No, sir," he said. "I see my presence is an irritant to you, and that we have clearly reached a point of mutual disharmony that would render the retrieval . . . well, that is to say, sir, that I do not think our interests any longer . . . coincide."

He bowed slightly and turned.

Mountfellon grabbed his arm.

"Retrieval, sir?" he said. "Retrieval of what?"

Templebane's face was smoothly impassive as he turned back to look at Mountfellon. It gave no hint that the fisherman within felt any satisfaction that the hook was now set.

"They salvaged enough of value from the fire to have had to sink it again as a means of hiding it from us," he said.

Mountfellon's face went very still.

"The devil you say!"

"The devil I do," said Templebane. "And I know where. And all it will take this time is grappling hooks thrown from the shore and a long day or night to work in."

Mountfellon's face worked visibly, and he looked down at the bone cudgel in his hand. He straightened and held it discreetly behind his back.

"Mr. Templebane," he said, his voice measured and soft. "Mr. Templebane, you will excuse my intemperance, I hope, but the nightwalking gentlemen have subjected me to the most heinous and destructive depredations, and that has undoubtedly put me on edge. If I have been overly defensive, I apologise. Their new freedom from any fear of iron has forced me as you see, to live protected by running water, and to shun going abroad at night."

He took a pace back and indicated the stairs behind him with the bone club.

"Will you step upstairs to my salon and take some refreshment after your long journey while we discuss the import of your news?"

Templebane the fisherman relaxed inwardly. Now all that remained was for the fish to land itself. He waited a beat, for effect, and then visibly swallowed his justified affront and permitted himself a not ungracious smile.

"As your Lordship wishes," he said, and followed him up the great staircase.

Nothing on his urbane exterior betrayed the fact that as he climbed he was inwardly repeating five words in a cockerel crow of celebration.

"Three birds with one stone! Three birds with one stone!"

★   ★   ★

He would perhaps have been in less of a celebratory mood, and Mountfellon less composed than he was endeavouring to be had they both been aware that the Herne was sitting in a dense thicket of blackthorn on the slope facing Gallstaine Hall, where he and his dogs had been lying up and watching for days now as the Herne waited for Mountfellon to cross the safe cordon of running water with which he had surrounded himself. The Herne was patient, but he was also a pragmatist. The prey was clearly too protected to be taken head-on. It might simply be that the fat man who had just arrived in the mud-spattered coach could be used as bait to lure that prey into the open. And there was something strangely familiar about him. He put his hand on the bones running down the spines of each of the dogs lying patiently at his side, and nodded at the dew-pond behind them.

"Drink, dogs," he said, "for we may have a long run ahead of us this night."

CHAPTER 28

PLANS AND DECISIONS

A sound two days and two nights' sleep—and whatever Cook had put in Sara Falk's drink—had undoubtedly done a miraculous power of good. Charlie and Ida were sitting at the table in The Folley's kitchen having breakfast when the door swung open with a bang and she strode in like a small and barely controlled tornado. She was also barely dressed, bar her underclothes, a situation she paid no attention to, a feat Charlie was less successful in achieving. Until now, having only seen her very ill or dropping with exhaustion, he had thought of her as being the same age as his mother, more or less. Now her natural fire was re-kindled, he couldn't help realising she was perhaps closer to his age than Rose Pyefinch, and this, her surprisingly well-muscled arm and the flash of leg beneath her petticoat made him inexplicably self-conscious.

"Good morning," she said, neatly taking the newly buttered slab of bread which Charlie was holding halfway to his mouth. "May I?"

He watched her carry on towards the fire where, chewing happily, she poured herself a large cup of tea which she drained in alternating gulps as she devoured the bread. She looked up at the drying rack hanging from pulleys over the range from which hung her meticulously washed and ironed clothes, which Cook had put up to air the night before.

"Good bread," she said. "I'm ravenous. Would you do me the kindness of buttering me another slice please, Charlie Pyefinch?"

She reached up and pulled her oiled silk dress from the airing rack. As she did so, her camisole and corset parted from the waistband of her petticoat, exposing a scandalous view of the finely curved small of her back.

Ida kicked Charlie under the table. He tore his eyes away from the naked flesh and saw she was raising a very knowing eyebrow at him.

"Er yes," he said. "Um, of course."

Sara dressed herself with speed and a complete lack of self-consciousness that Ida, herself a workmanlike dresser, wholly approved of. In fact, she thought that Sara looked as if she was buckling on armour or donning a uniform. Sara found her newly polished boots standing in front of the warming oven and put her foot on the chair as she bent to cinch the laces tight, exposing another glimpse of her legs which Charlie tried not to see.

"You polished my boots?" said Sara, catching his eye before he could shift it.

"Er," he said.

"I mean Emmet normally does boots, so someone must have," she said.

"It was Hodge," he said, wondering why his voice felt so unaccountably thick in his throat.

"Must remember to thank him," she said. "Now, that bread . . ."

He handed her a second slice which she proceeded to devour with just as much alacrity as its predecessor. Archie appeared from under the table and licked his hand. He ruffled the young dog's fur with a gesture that was clearly so familiar now as to be automatic.

"You seem rested," said Ida.

"I'm angry," said Sara, and Charlie thought he'd never seen such a dangerous smile as the one that flashed across her face. "Gives you a lot of energy, being this angry. I intend to use it. Where are the others?"

"Sharp went to where his, er, friend is," said Ida. "The golem."

"Emmet," said Charlie. "He saw him yesterday too. While you were sleeping off Cook's draught. He's going to come back with Hodge, he said. Cook said you'd be up this morning."

"I suppose Emmet is his friend," said Sara, taking the third piece of bread and butter. "Never thought about it like that. Emmet's just Emmet. Well, we've no time for visiting. Be so kind as to go and hurry them back. We have things to do—"

"Not before you've had eggs and a nice piece of beef steak," said Cook, bustling in from the yard where The Smith, among other things, kept his chickens. She was carrying fresh eggs in a bowl which she brandished at Sara.

"I don't need eggs and steak," said Sara. "I need new weapons and the others brought here now. Please go and fetch them, Charlie."

"There's blades in The Smith's cabinet, back of the forge, you know that, and you may as well eat because it'll take some time for Charlie and Ida to go and hurry the others along," said Cook. She looked at Charlie and Ida and jerked her head in the smallest but most freighted of gestures.

They took the hint and evaporated out of the door.

As soon as they were out of earshot, Ida dug a sharp elbow into Charlie's ribs.

"Ouch," he said. "What?"

"You," she said. "Blushing like a choirboy because a lady walks past in her undermentionables."

"I wasn't—" he began, but she just grinned and set off at a jog, efficiently re-tying one of her pigtails as she ran. She had a quality when in motion that he had begun to notice and admire, which was a kind of efficient physical dexterousness, a bodily grace which made it hard not to watch her, and in watching he forgot all thoughts of Sara Falk.

Sara had gone into the smithy and had unlocked the cabinet behind the Holtzapffel Rose Engine with the key Cook had given her.

The cabinet was of age-darkened oak, and quite some age at that, given the fact that the wood, once a pleasing yellow was now black as a freshly japanned deed-box. Inside there were drawers protected by further locks, but the inner face of the doors were each fitted with racks of knives of different shapes and sizes in a startling variety of designs. The effect, with the doors swung wide, was of a triptych, and she stood in front of it for a long moment quite as still as any devotee in a church. But she was not making a prayer. She was making a choice, and once it was made she moved briskly, taking three knives, a long thin *misericorde*, an ivory-handled seaman's dirk and a brutal-looking push dagger with a T-shaped handle and a short stub-like blade.

She returned to the kitchen and proceeded to strap the weapons to herself beneath her skirt and jacket as she watched Cook making her breakfast with equal briskness.

"Why did you want them both to go?" she said, nodding towards the door Ida and Charlie had left by.

"Because you and I need a chat, and it's best not to discourage the young ones," said Cook, turning and sliding a plate onto the table in front of Sara. "Now you stop talking and eat."

"What's in it?" said Sara.

"Eggs, beef steak and a slight seasoning of don't-ask-questions," said Cook, her eyes flicking to the well-worn box of Chinese medicines which she evidently had salvaged from the ruin of the Safe House. "It'll do you good."

"If it was in the drink you gave me before I slept, it's already done me good," said Sara, "but I know your powders. They do you good, but take too much of them and you have to pay on the other side of the coin sooner or later."

"This is later, Sara," said Cook, sitting in front of her. "Right now, right here is later. It's nigh on as 'later' as later can get by my reckoning. That's why you may as well take all the help the powders can give you, because the devil knows we need it, and there's plenty of time to—"

She stopped herself, and then found one of the giant spotted handkerchiefs that had been jammed up her sleeve and proceeded to blow her nose. Sara, who had been raised by this sturdy block of a woman knew she only blew her nose if she had a genuine cold or she was hiding some treacherous emotion behind the theatrically loud nasal honking she was muffling in the billowing red cotton which hid her face.

"—plenty of time to rest when we're dead?" said Sara. "That bad?"

"So bad you can't hardly smell good, let alone see it from where we are," said Cook. "Now eat your breakfast."

Sara sat and cut into the strip steak. It was, she noted, nice and bloody. She couldn't help but feel that was going to be appropriate for what lay ahead.

"Go on," she said, round a mouthful of meat and egg yolk. "Talk."

Cook settled forward into the chair opposite which gave an alarming creak of protest as she leaned in across the table.

"Smith's gone north on some of his ancient business, and what with one thing and another he should have been back long ago. Either things are worse than he feared, or something's gone awry. Now we were lucky that young Trousers agreed to stay with us, because that gave us the numbers for a Hand when Lucy Harker took off with the Irish girl. Now Smith's gone absent, well, it's a good job you and Sharp came back when you did, because Hodge and I have been talking about how the sum don't add up to five if Smith stays gone."

"You think The Smith can die?" said Sara. "Really?"

"Don't know," said Cook. "But I do know he can stay gone for a long, long time. At least, that's something I heard a long, long while ago, in passing, from one of the ones that went missing in the Disaster. And I was too young or busy to ask her what she meant. Suppose I thought there'd be time enough to find out later on. Except there wasn't, of course . . ."

"You never asked him?"

"Seemed rude," said Cook. "It's not something that comes up in normal conversation, is it?"

"We're The Oversight," said Sara. "We're expected to have abnormal conversations."

"What do you mean?"

"Means I'm wondering if we've been stupid. If we've been so busy clinging on to the idea of surviving, no matter how few we are that we . . . I don't know. But I do wonder if we've got lost somehow."

"I'm lost most of the time," said Cook. "Life isn't a map you can navigate. It's a journey. You make your trail by walking it. We've done the best we could with what we came across . . ."

"And with what's come across us," said Sara. "We're not just stumbling on bad things. Bad things are moving against us. Now we know The Citizen is the one moving against us, for I saw him in the catacombs in Paris when I glinted the past. There is no guarantee he is dead, and indeed the gory ritual with the darkness that I saw seemed designed to ensure that he exceeded a natural span. So we must assume he has been moving against us for a generation and we've been so busy clinging on by our fingertips, trying to preserve the Last Hand that we forgot to go find him and destroy him."

"We didn't know it was him—"

Sara smacked her hand down on the table and smacked it so hard the plates jumped.

"We should have known!" she said. "We were weak!"

"We were surviving," said Cook.

"No," said Sara. "You and Hodge and Smith stayed when others who survived the Disaster left us, others like Charlie Pyefinch's parents. And we thought they had betrayed us, but now I think they were just realists. I think they saw what we . . . what you were doing was wrong, that The Oversight was too weak to protect anyone. And that because it gave the illusion of protection, it was actually worse than no protection at all. They saw the way to survive was to spread out and live as normally as they could. Because protection that is illusory is as dangerous as a pasteboard shield."

"We maintained the Last Hand," said Cook, "because we had to."

"But history tells us we don't have to," said Sara. "We know The Oversight has failed and dispersed in the past! Smith has told us. It disbands and scatters until there are enough strong new members found to gather new Hands. That is what The Smith does. That is why it endures."

"What are you saying?" said Cook. "That we shouldn't have tried?"

"You stayed together, the three of you, because I was a child and so was Sharp. You stayed as parents to me who had lost mine and him who never had them. If you had not had the care and raising of us, I think you would have dispersed."

"You had to be raised somewhere," grunted Cook. "Made sense to do it in your own home."

"No," said Sara. "It only made sense in terms of kindness, for which you have my life's gratitude. In terms of our duty, it was folly or pride, or both. And The Smith, if no one else, should have known better. It made us sitting ducks for our enemies. We should have dispersed to rise again."

"When we disperse, things happen that we're sworn to stop," said Cook.

"Even you can't make an omelette without breaking eggs," said Sara.

"Like the Dark Ages," said Cook. "They weren't worth any bloody omelette, were they?"

"After London burned in the Great Fire of 1661, there wasn't another Dark Age," said Sara. "There was the Age of Reason and Wonders. Natural philosophers. Drains. Steam engines. An industrial revolution. That's no Dark Age."

"Isn't it?" sniffed Cook. "Well, I'm sure you think you know best. But you don't."

"Have I told you that I love you?" said Sara.

Cook looked at her in shock, like a great square-rigged galleon in full sail which has suddenly been taken aback by a sudden change in the wind.

"Well, I do, and always have," said Sara. "You have been a mother to me since I was orphaned. I don't think I have ever said it before, because that's not how we talk, but I have always assumed you knew it. Same as me and Sharp. And I told him I love him too, while you're looking so shocked."

"I'm not shocked," said Cook, betraying herself by blowing her nose again.

"But love isn't the point," said Sara. "It's *a* point but it's not *the* point. It makes us weak. We cannot truly afford to let it cloud our judgement.

And that's what any new Oversight will have to make clear to those who swear to join it."

"What do you mean?" said Cook.

"I mean Jack Sharp went into the mirrors to save me. Not The Oversight, not those we protect, not those we are sworn to preserve from the predations of the supranatural: he foolhardily and irresponsibly went into harm's way to save just me! He loved me and he went into the direst peril to find my severed hand and my heart-stone ring. And you know what? By every possible criterion, he failed! That boy who just left, he and Lucy Harker returned my hand, they saved me. They brought back my hand. Not Sharp. And I was just as foolish as he was: I went into the same damned maze of mirrors thinking to rescue him in my turn. Out of love. And through the weakness of love, through a judgement clouded by . . . an indulgent sentimental affection, the Last Hand would have been broken anyway, had not sheer luck provided this trouser-wearing Laemmel girl from the top of who knows what bloody mountain in the middle of Austria!"

"Do you want another steak?" said Cook.

"No, I do not want another steak!" said Sara.

"Then stop flailing around with that fork in your fist or you'll put your own eye out," said Cook. "What did you mean by 'any new Oversight'?"

"The one that comes after we fail," said Sara.

There was a moment of silence.

"Have you decided we must fail then?" said Cook.

"No," said Sara. "Others have made that decision. The Citizen and his creatures have made that decision. Since I do not know how powerful the forces he has manoeuvred into action against us are, I cannot say we can survive. And I suspect we will not. But I do say we go down, if we go down, doing our damnedest to take him with us. This is life. This is reality. This is no fairy story. It has no happy ending. The great truth, the truth I am afraid you all forgot when you cobbled together a Last Hand consisting of the three of you and two children is that we are sworn to protect! Not to survive. The ones that follow us will carry on. The Smith endures. He will find the next Hands. The Oversight will survive without us. Our job is to protect what we can for as long as we can. And in this case, this Hand of The Oversight can protect the next one by removing this present enemy so that our successors can grow strong, free from his shadow."

"You're wrong," said a voice from the door.

She turned to see Hodge standing in the light, Jed sitting patiently at his feet as his friend fussed at his cutty pipe, trying to light a wad of damp tobacco. Behind him Sharp leaned on the opposite doorpost. Sara decided not to be embarrassed or wonder exactly how long they had been standing there.

"You're right about what we must do but you are wrong about love," said Hodge, drawing on the pipe and nodding in satisfaction. "You're wrong about something else too: you didn't fail when you went into the mirrors. You saved Sharp. You brought him home."

"Nothing truer than that," said Sharp. "I'd be dead, done and drowned in the dark if it wasn't for you."

Hodge sucked another lungful of tobacco smoke and then breathed it back out with a hacking cough.

"You're wrong about love too," he said with a rueful grin. "Don't look at me like that, Sara Falk: I know plenty about love. Damn sight more about it than you know about me, I reckon, but that's by the by and the way I've chosen to live, private like."

He pointed at the terrier sitting patiently at his feet. Jed looked back and thumped the lintel with his tail.

"But look at Jed then: he loves me same as I love him. Loves you all in his way, he does. Being a dog, he can't help seeing you all as his pack, I reckon. But love don't soften him, does it? And he fights without an ounce of back-off in him. You can fight for love. Doesn't have to be in spite of love. Damn sure doesn't have to be instead of love. And it doesn't have to be weakened by love. In fact, if you're not fighting for something you love, you're doing it wrong."

Sara stared at him, preparing her response and studiously avoiding looking at Sharp. And then the spell was broken as Ida and Charlie appeared at the other door, preceded by Archie who bounced in front of his father and barked excitedly. Jed, in no mood to play, growled back at him. Archie barked again and then retreated to sit between Charlie's legs, his tail thudding on the floorboards.

"Right," said Sara, standing decisively. "I didn't get up this morning intending to have a debate. I intend to act, and to act with purpose and despatch: I suggest you, Hodge, take Mr. Sharp to interview this Coram Templebane again at the Bedlam Hospital, and I will go and see precisely how abandoned the Templebane's wretched nest actually is. And if it is as abandoned as you say, I will search it and see if there is a clear connection to The Citizen."

"Search it?" said Sharp. "You mean—"

"I will take my glove off and touch every brick in the damned building if I have to," she said. "If that French bastard has been there, he will have left a foulness in the stones that I can glint the memory of."

"You are too . . . your energies are overly depleted to glint much," said Sharp.

"True," said Cook. "My powders just help you ignore how low your defences and your reserves of stamina actually are. You still need to take care of your energy."

"Plenty of time for taking care of my energy when I'm dead," said Sara. "You said it. Till then I intend to spend what I have. Like a drunk sailor if need be. Come on, Charlie Pyefinch, and you too, Ida Laemmel. They're not going to make more daylight just because we're sitting here wasting it."

She looked at Hodge.

"Can we use your lodgings at the Tower as a meeting place later?" He nodded.

"Then let us meet there at sunset. And if we have no more information at that point, we will take the next step as one."

"What is the next step?" said Sharp.

"We will go and find the noble lord who was so keen to see what was in our library. This Mountfellon. He seemed to be Templebane's partner or perhaps his sponsor. Let's see what's in *his* damned library."

CHAPTER 29

THE VIGIL

And so it was, after the death of his hopes in Wellclose Square, that Amos had joined the Ghost in haunting the environs of Chandos Place. On the first night, they had slept in the lowered area of a shuttered house opposite and listened to the subterranean gurgling of the municipal drains as they attempted to deal with the unprecedented volume of water the storm had tipped into the city during the day. They watched Mountfellon's house with its strangely regular but unsymmetrical façade. There was no sign of life within it, no lights, no noise, no toing or froing from either the front or the side. Neither he nor the Ghost could hear any human thoughts, though he at least thought he could hear some animal in pain which seemed to be beneath the house.

"A cat or a dog, swept into the sewers, like as not," sniffed the Ghost, who professed to be unable to hear it. "One of the thousand little tragedies that beset the city every day. Is it a human mind?"

He shook his head. It was just a voiceless panic. And he couldn't be sure if it came from the house or the one behind it anyway.

No

"Then it isn't Mountfellon," she said, and jammed herself into a corner of the area, looking through the railings, blanket over her head, only her eye peering out at pavement level, locked on the house opposite. "And if it isn't him, who cares? Not, I said, the fly . . ."

Amos wondered if she would give him one of the two blankets she was wrapped in. She didn't. He was too numb to mind much.

"We will watch," said the Ghost. "Turnabout: one sleeps while the other keeps an eye on the house."

Amos knew that a day before he would have baulked at this, but was too taken aback by the revelation of The Oversight's demise and the extinction of his last coherent hope that he agreed. He kept just enough of his own kernel of selfhood to be sure that he would not kill for her, no matter what. But watching gave him some purpose, and without purpose he knew he would drift rudderless into even deeper shoals of despair.

On the first night and the first day, he was mechanical and dazed, but as time passed he began to think about the implications of the end of The Oversight. He had not realised how strongly he had clung to the idea that there was a group who might be able to parse the perils of the unknown, and protect him from it.

He had only really come into contact with the supranatural proper when he had been sent to deliver the letter to Mountfellon and been pursued by the Sluagh. They had not caught him but they had chased him into a dark world from which there seemed to be no escape: he could not undo what he had done, or un-see the things he had witnessed. Innocence cannot be un-lost. He could not un-know that the night in fact held worse things in its shadows than his city-bound imagination could have possibly conjured up. He had heard all the stories told by his adopted brothers about the recondite aspects of his fathers' business, and had put them down as stories of ghouls and boggarts told to frighten small children in general and himself in particular, being the youngest child. And now he knew it was all true and worse, he felt naked and unprotected in a wilderness of darkness and thorns.

The Oversight had seemed like the possibility of more than protection. Even the simple idea of it alone had been a kind of armour against the malignity of this newly revealed occult world: it implied order could be imposed on the chaos of real terror lurking just beyond the lintels of his rational mind.

So he watched, he slept, he went out into the city and stole food and brought it back to share. And apart from that he tried to be no more, for a while, than an unthinking pair of eyes. The day was long and boring, and they were moved on from the area several times, but returned to it after dark. Sleep was almost as absent as Mountfellon, and when what came did grudgingly arrive, it was not restful.

Abchurch Templebane haunted his dreams, standing over him and conversing nastily with the partially headless overseer of the Andover Workhouse, M'Gregor. And when Amos turned from their grisly tête-à-half-tête, knowing he was asleep but hoping the Ghost would tell him it was a dream, he found not the Ghost but Mrs. M'Gregor, rattling her empty safe-box accusingly at him, her broken-necked head lolling and bobbling hideously aslant on her shoulder as she did so. And then he found the bed he lay on was not a bed but a pool, and the pool was not water but blood, and when he dipped his hand in it, he saw it was not red blood but black blood and the figures around him were not his victims but Sluagh and then he woke with the Ghost's hand over his mouth and a warning finger in his face.

You were moaning. Don't moan. It draws attention.

And of course the only rule of his newly curtailed existence, the alpha and the omega of the vigil was that any attention there was should be their own, wholly focused on the building opposite.

Privately, as his mind healed, he realised that Mountfellon was probably never going to come. But he didn't mind that. It wasn't his vengeance. It was hers. And no harm could come of just sitting out of sight, hidden among the flotsam and jetsam of the city, unremarked, unnoticeable, not even part of the background, just lost in the cracks. There was a comforting routine to their pointless lookout.

No harm could come of it.

CHAPTER 30

HUNTER'S MOON

The Herne was moving fast across the rolling landscape, heading broadly south again. He had the hunter's lope, a steady long-legged pace which he could maintain effortlessly for whole nights at a time. The bone dogs flowed over the rolling fields ahead of him, silent and determined. In a pursuit like this, where the Nose led, the Sight Hound ran alongside, half a body length off the lead, adjusting his speed to the slower pace of the other dog. In this way, if the Nose brought them on to a prey and flushed it, the Sight Hound could explode into action and accelerate to killing speed in less than a heartbeat. They were well-practised as a team, and did not need to bay or bark to communicate with each other, or the Herne. They also ran off the line of scent, parallel with it, keeping station but always nose to the drift of scent being pushed towards them by the prevailing breeze.

They were following the strangely familiar fat man's carriage as it sped back from Mountfellon and Gallstaine Hall to wherever he had come from.

Since it was dark, the Herne knew they would meet few if any people on the road, so he whistled the dogs in and ran them down the road itself, right on the scent line. And as he ran, he wondered, as he always did when tracking as yet unseen prey, whether he was doing the right thing in following this fat man back to his lair. It had been Badger Skull's suggestion that the way to get to Mountfellon might be through his confederates which had made him break cover and follow the carriage, but there was also a familiarity to him. Though the Herne had never seen him, he looked and smelled like a Templebane, and that was a family which Hernes and Sluagh had been dealing with for generations. Why he had been meeting Mountfellon was something that Badger Skull might well be interested in finding out. And from his surveillance of Mountfellon's moated retreat, it was going to take something unusual to get to him. So he ignored the stitch in his side and just ran through it, determined not to let the coach escape.

CHAPTER 31

SILENCE IN BEDLAM

Coram Templebane was greatly reduced, and not merely due to the amputation of his leg. He had been abandoned by his adoptive father at the very moment he most needed rescuing, and had been pitched into the hard stone kerb with his knee agonisingly shattered by a crossbow bolt, staring in disbelief at the senior Templebane's carriage racing away while the blood pooled around him and drained into the gutter. He'd tried to escape, dragging himself into the protective dark of the sewers, and then his memory blanked and the next thing he remembered was waking in the Bedlam ward with a horrible, unbelievable absence where his leg should be. He still felt violated by the surgery, which he registered as a brutal theft, and more than that he could feel that his vital force had been severely diminished by the traumas he had undergone. In the dark of the wards at night, he still cried, mourning the lost limb quite as much as if it had been a beloved person. Coram had not loved anything or anyone in his life with which this love could be fairly compared, raised as he had been as an orphan and then pitched into the venal and competitive adoptive family of the Templebanes. But, too late, he found he had very much loved being a whole man, something he never could be again. He could see the physical evidence of his decline every time he swung himself on his crutches past a reflective surface: his appetite had disappeared, which, given the standard of the food offered to the inmates of the Bedlam Hospital was no great loss to one who had previously prided himself on his epicurean tastes, and he had lost a great deal of weight in consequence. His hair, once thick, had been shorn so close to the head that, given the permanent hollows beneath his eyes and the gaunt cheeks below, he thought he now resembled nothing more than the skull that comprised the central part of the Templebane's family seal, the one which sat above the cheering motto "As I am, you will be." If Coram had been disposed to speak, he would have said the motto now seemed more like a prophecy, and one whose truth he was painfully beginning to incorporate.

But Coram did not speak. The doctors said it was shock. Coram felt more as if speech was an island he kept swimming towards, but never quite reached due to an insurmountable rip tide keeping him adrift in a sea of silence.

He was unaware that The Oversight, in the person of Hodge, had worked on his mind so that the idea of escaping the confines of the hospital would never occur to him, despite the fact that in almost every other way bar speech he had control of his faculties and memories. In fact, it might have been a mercy had Hodge worked on him more and deadened his capacity to recollect his past or reflect on what his future might hold, for the conjunction of these two streams of thought created a mighty river of dread which threatened to drown him at every hour of the day or night: he was jumpy and distracted when waking, and when what sleep might come did come to him with its illusory promise of rest in the long and lonely marches of the night, it was a sleep laced with nightmares through which he was pursued by things so terrifying that even nightmares proved too fragile to hold them, so that he repeatedly woke sweating and shaking in the darkness, and often met the morning even more exhausted than he had been at bedtime.

The only respite he had, and it was a strange kind of relief, was in the friendship and attentions of one of the porters, a kind of supernumerary nurse's aide called Bill Ketch. Coram was unaware that Ketch too had had his mind worked on, in this case by Mr. Sharp, as a consequence of his attempt to sell a girl—Lucy Harker, in fact—to The Oversight. Because of this, Hodge had set Ketch to watch over Coram, but he did so in an attentive and disarmingly kind way. It was disarming because Ketch looked like what he had been, which was a drunk and a bruiser, so that his acts of kindness were unexpected and somehow all the more poignant. His broken face was so at odds with his placid and serviceable demeanour that Coram did not get the full benefit of his kind actions, since he had been raised to mistrust everyone, and could never rid himself of the fear that Ketch was playing a game with him.

Ketch, on his part, was not playing any game he was aware of. He had not had an alcoholic drink since Sharp had raised the bloodstone ring to his forehead and worked his punishment on him. His brain, rendered "wet" by the previous three decades of almost constant inebriation, worked slowly but it worked true. He was not—freed from the curse of the gin that had ruined his life—a bad man. And because the drinking life had taken place in a cloud of forgetfulness in which even those memories that did remain were distanced and blurred, he was not haunted by his past. Sharp had enjoined him to find happiness helping others, and this he did. He had been rendered temporarily mute by Sharp as a further punishment for sticking Lucy Harker's mouth shut with a plaster made from tar and sacking, but now the period of enforced silence had passed, he was as amiably garrulous as he was helpful.

"Mr. 'Odge," he said, opening the wicket gate to let Hodge and his companion into the courtyard of the hospital. "Werry nice to see you and Mr, er, I'm sorry, sir, I seem to know you but have forgot your—"

"Sharp," said Mr. Sharp. "I believe we met during your earlier career as an inebriate."

Ketch took no offence at Sharp's referring to his past; indeed as he looked into Sharp's eyes and was struck by how many warm shades of brown seemed to tumble in them like the golden leaves of autumn, and he remembered how very, very much he liked this gentleman.

"Mr. Sharp," he said. "Yes, indeed, my memory's leaky as a sieve, but

I have the sense you done me a kindness, so I thank you for it. 'Ave you come to see our peg-leg pal then?"

He addressed the last part of this to Hodge, who nodded.

There was an understanding, though nobody could quite remember who had authorised it, that when Mr. Hodge or his associates wished to speak to Coram, a private room would be made available to them. In this case, it was a clean storeroom with a high window lined with racks neatly stacked with blankets and sheets on one side and dark wicker-bound carboys of various mysterious but presumably, from the smell, disinfectant liquids on the other. A deal table stood between the racks, and a single stool.

Sharp and Hodge waited on one side of the table, leaning on the shelves as Coram was shown in by Ketch.

"Here we go, me old mate, here's Mr. Hodge and Mr. Sharp come to inquire after your progress," he said, helping Coram negotiate the narrow gap between shelves and table, pulling the stool so he could sit on it, and helping him lean the crutches neatly to one side.

Coram's guts had turned to water when he saw the two members of The Oversight waiting for him. Hodge was bad enough, not as terrifying as The Smith, but bad enough in the way he tore at Coram's silence, trying to shake it apart, like a terrier worrying a rat. Coram knew his inability to speak protected him, as if his body automatically doing things that his mind was too broken to accomplish. He recognised Mr. Sharp from the many times he had seen him during the long surveillances of the Safe House which Issachar and Zebulon Templebane had ordered their sons to undertake. He carried an air of cold danger about him that was quite different to Hodge's ferocity or the walking thundercloud that was The Smith. Coram knew he had come to make him talk, to explain why he had rolled the grenadoes into the sugar factory, to atone for the crime of destroying the Safe House, Sharp's home. He did not know how many members of The Oversight had died in the conflagration, and indeed had assumed the fact he had only seen The Smith and Hodge meant that the fat Cook and the white-haired girl and all the others were dead and that their deaths lay heavy on his charge sheet.

Saying nothing seemed to be the only thing that had kept him alive so far, and so he let the rip tide grip him once more and sat mutely, ears open, mind racing, but tongue still as the questions began.

Sharp began without ceremony, giving the interrogation a chilling intimacy, as of an ongoing conversation between intimates being abruptly resumed without any need for formality.

The questions rained in on him like an artillery barrage: the fact he did not and could not answer them did not mean that he did not have the corresponding answers exploding in his head as each question landed. The only way he could escape the bombardment was to let the rip tide take him and pull him deeper and deeper into the sea of protective silence. He had done this before, and it had worked, the pain of detonating memories provoked by the questions being not much different to the waking nightmares he was constantly assailed by.

But this time he felt less safe, because as the questions continued to pound at him he was aware that a different assault was simultaneously in progress. The sea of silence was less warm and protective than he had become accustomed to; in fact some part of him became aware he was colder and more uncomfortable than he usually was. The chill had a lot to do with the fear he was trying to ignore. Sharp's questions were much like those he had been posed by The Smith and Hodge, except for a new line which seemed concerned with a personage Coram genuinely had no knowledge of, a Frenchman called The Citizen. Sharp was clearly obsessed by this character, and distracted by the new line of interrogation, it took Coram some time to realise that, while Sharp held his attention with words, other non-verbal questions were present in his head. It was as if he was being whispered to, and though the sound of the whispers was all but drowned by the onslaught of Sharp's words, they seemed to be lessening the protective pull of that rip tide and making it more and more likely that Coram would finally find a way to speak.

And then, blessed relief, Sharp leant back and looked at Hodge and the pressure relented.

"He knows something," said Sharp. "But damned if I can get at it. You?"

Hodge shook his head.

"Maybe he doesn't know anything."

"He knows enough to be terrified of us," said Sharp. He crossed to the door and opened it.

"Mr. Ketch. You will need a mop and pail: Mr. Templebane has pissed himself."

Coram looked down. There was a pool of urine surrounding his one foot. He realised the cold he had felt was the wetness in his groin cooling against his skin. He had been pulled so deep into the sea of silence that he had not known what fear had made his body do.

He looked down at the tabletop, not willing to meet either of the pairs of eyes boring into him.

"We may need a sturdier blade than either of us to shuck this particular oyster," said Sharp resignedly.

The mention of oysters brought a flash of memory to Coram, of his father Issachar sitting in his carriage casually eating oysters and dropping the shells out of the window into the very gutter that months later would be soaked with Coram's blood. He choked involuntarily, the first noise he had made since entering the room.

"Did you get that?" said Sharp, looking at Hodge.

Hodge shook his head.

"Just a shape," he said. Ketch bustled in and looked at Coram.

"Ho dear," he said. "We've had a little accident, have we? No worries, matey, we'll have you cleaned up and in dry drawers afore you know it. No shame in an accident when you're an invalid, is there, gents?"

And he looked at Sharp and Hodge for confirmation.

"None at all," murmured Sharp.

He smiled at Coram, who made the mistake of looking up at that moment and meeting his eye.

"We will return."

The thought of this and the promise in Sharp's eyes caused a new spasm in Coram's guts.

Back in the street and walking briskly towards the distant Tower, Sharp and Hodge discussed the failed interrogation as Jed bounded ahead of them, dodging handcarts and carriages and milling pedestrians.

"I hoped you'd get into the back of his mind while I stood pounding at the front door," said Sharp.

Hodge hawked and spat into the gutter.

"Wishful thinking, as it turns out. Worth a shot, but I can ride an animal's mind, not a man's," he said.

Sharp nodded.

"Yes. And we can both bend a man's mind, but not read it, more's the pity."

"Once upon a day, we had them as could talk without speaking within The Oversight. But now we barely got an Oversight, let alone a full complement of skills," said Hodge. "Reading men's minds, hearing their thoughts—why, that requires a horse of quite a different colour."

CHAPTER 32

BLOOD CRIES OUT

There is a silence to an empty house that is quite different to the quiet of a house with people trying to keep silent within it. Ida, as a born hunter, was especially tuned to the noise silence made when it was tenanted. She could hear people and animals keeping still like a disturbance in the air itself. It wasn't quite a vibration, more of a thickening of the atmosphere: the air in the Templebanes' counting-house was thin with abandonment.

It also smelled of decay. The front door had been closed but, on testing, it was found to be unlocked.

"Funny," said Charlie. "We tried that when we first came for a look-see, and it was locked."

"Let us take care then," said Sara.

They had entered without knocking and listened very carefully.

Ida shook her head, and pointed at the stairs. Sara nodded. Archie had trotted ahead of them into the counting-house. Ida had drawn her crossbow from under her loden cloak and swarmed silently up the steps.

As they walked towards the high double doors to the counting-house, Charlie stopped and put his hand on Sara's shoulder. She turned.

"Sorry," he whispered. "But there's a man in there."

She realised he was seeing through Archie's eyes. His nose wrinkled.

Sight was not the only sense he could share with the young dog. She noted with professional approval that he held a long knife in his hand.

"He's dead," he said, relaxing.

"How dead?"

"Ripe and not pretty," he replied. He in turn noticed she had the boarding dirk in her fist, something he had not seen her draw, nor could imagine where she had been carrying it.

"Archie says there's nothing bigger than a rat alive in the house, bar us."

They edged into the barn-like space of the counting-house and stood beneath the towering reefs of dusty papers reaching to the ceiling. The first thing she noticed was a bullet hole which had starred the glass in a store-cupboard opposite and clearly smashed a large ink bottle, from the star-shaped splatter of green on the white wall behind it. And then she saw the dog.

Archie was standing by the pot-bellied stove, wagging his tail.

The body was next to him, lying half on its back, head cocked at an awkward angle. It wasn't freshly dead, and there had, as Archie had communicated to Charlie, been rats.

"That's . . . hard to look at," gulped Charlie, shifting his gaze to the skylights.

Sara crouched over the body, concentrating on not inhaling anything through her nose.

"Ever see him before?" she said.

"Don't know," said Charlie. "Though if I had, he'd have looked different. With a nose and eyes and all, I expect."

The rats had been hungry.

"Think this is why the place is deserted?"

Sara went quickly through his pockets and found nothing except a couple of percussion caps and a bullet. She looked at the bullet hole in the store-cupboard glass, then down at his hands, and then around the surrounding floor, wondering if he had dropped a gun, but none was to be seen.

She was about to ask Charlie what he made of it when Ida came into the room from the far end, evidently having found another staircase which led back via the half-glassed supervisor's office.

"There is no one here," she said. "But there's a strong smell of someth—"

And then she saw the body.

"Ah," she said. "Well, I was right first time. No one home."

"Yes and no," said Sara, peeling the tight leather glove from her left hand. "There is no one in the rooms. But in a house this old, there are multitudes hiding in the walls."

"What are you doing?" said Charlie.

"Glinting," said Sara, handing him the glove. "We can start by finding out what happened here."

She walked to the side of the room and splayed her hand, then took a breath, a deep one, barely having time to notice she'd forgotten about not using her nose and starting to gag at the smell of the corpse when

Time jolted

as she felt the past smack into her.

She saw a dark-skinned young man, a boy sleeping at one of the sloped desks—head down on his arms, face pressed on a sheet of paper.

She saw a woman sprawled on a bench in front of the pot-bellied stove, grey hair hanging off the edge like a ragged banner, rose-tinted by the fire in the grate.

And then time jerked and a taller man was standing behind the sleeping one and jabbing a horse-pistol into the back of his neck.

She heard him speak

"Quiet now, young Amos Templebane, we don't want to wake your lady friend, do we?"

The dark-skinned man called Amos turned.

Sara now saw he was younger than she'd thought, but before she could examine his face more closely time jagged again

and the sleeping woman was on her feet, pointing a finger at the chin-less man with the gun, then time sliced straight to the impact as he smacked her back into the bench and from where she bounced onto the floor, landing in a tangle of limbs and hair like a broken doll

"You can mash that noise, you old bitch, or you shall have another—"

And then the time jags went slow as the true violence hit and Amos
was reaching behind him

Without looking

Hand closing around a steel-nibbed pen

Twisting away from the gun barrel as the man turned it on him

Moving strangely sluggishly compared to Amos

As if he was already dying

And everything became curves and lines

As fatal geometry took over

Amos blurred

She saw the sharp nib track a silver-blue semicircle like a scratch in the
air as the steel pen arced into the gunman's neck

The gun fired

Gout of flame, a bright straightness stabbing in the gloom

Bullet splintering the store-cupboard window

Shattering a pint bottle into a circular starburst of green ink

Amos pirouetted, reaching for another pen

Ready to attack again

But the gunman was already falling, corkscrewing as his legs twisted
and collapsed in shock

Blood spraying in a curiously elegant fan

Settling around him like a matador's cape

And then the clean geometry of lines and curves collapsed into something broken and choppier and brutal as he scrabbled desperately at the
three inches of blood-slick pen-shaft sticking out of his carotid artery

Fingertips slipping and sliding

Until he landed

Awkwardly

pen first

the force of the impact driving it through his slippery grasp

punching it deeper.

Even as she watched horror-struck, unable to close her eyes or look
away, Sara realised that the steel nib must have found the gap between

two vertebrae and severed the spinal cord, because the man's hands stopped working instantly and everything below the neck went limp.

She watched two more slices of time as the horrified face fish-mouthed and the bulbous eyes rolled right and left in shock and terror, the head arching against the floorboards as if he was trying to inch-worm his slack body away from something terrible

And then mercifully the something came and took him and the eyes settled and rolled back and he was still.

The one called Amos stood shaking over the ruin of his assailant, eyes bright with unshed tears.

The woman got off the ground and then—and this almost the worst thing in the whole brutal scene—threw back her head and laughed.

"'And he said, "What hast thou done?"'" she cackled gleefully. "'"What hast thou done?" the voice of thy brother's blood crieth unto me from the ground.' Book of Genesis, Bloody Boy, Book of Genesis"

Amos gripped the second pen. He looked at the still body on the floor one last time. And then he walked out of the room without a second glance.

"Where are you going?" she shouted. "Don't go there. The Oversight can't help you. I told you . . ."

The woman bent and rifled the dead man's pockets, taking coins and a jack-knife, laughing as she did so.

And then time sliced and the woman was coming back into the room from the door to the back corridor carrying a pair of man's boots

Still laughing as she jogged towards the front door

"Blood cries out, Amos Templebane, blood cries out!"

She followed the line of his exit, eyes bright, seeming to stumble so close to where Sara was transfixed, watching it all, that she could see right into the gleeful eyes.

And she saw they were quite mad.

And then the past let go of Sara and she slumped and sat on the floor, her legs unsteady, breathing hard, aware Charlie and Ida were watching her.

"You saw what happened?" said Ida.

Sara nodded.

"I always see what happened," she said. "And it's never good."

Ida reached a hand down and Sara took it, strangely touched by the matter-of-fact way the girl offered it, and grateful for the strength with which she pulled her to her feet.

"Must be a burden," said Ida. "I'm glad it is not my gift."

Sara took her glove back from Charlie, and as she put it back on she told them what she had seen of the death of Abchurch Templebane.

"He's looking for us," she said. "The one called Amos Templebane."

"We know the Templebanes are after us," said Charlie.

"No," said Sara. "He's different. I think he's looking for us for . . . help."

"Why would we help a Templebane?" said Charlie.

"We wouldn't help him because he's a Templebane," said Sara. "We'd help him because he asked. And more than that . . ."

"What?" said Ida.

"More than that, I think he's one of us. But I don't think he knows it. Like Lucy Harker didn't. Because no one had told her." She shook herself. "Right. Go to Wellclose Square and look for him. He's your age, and he's at least half black."

"Black?" said Charlie. "Like he's from Africa?"

Sara nodded.

"Like he's from Africa. Him or at least one of his parents, at a guess. But he has green eyes, which I do not think occur naturally in those of pure African blood, though I may be wrong. I do not have much experience of that. But they are striking eyes. You will know him if he still watches the ruins of our house. As you will know him if he still travels with the madwoman. If you find him, leave Archie watching him and come get us at the Tower. Don't approach him, but don't lose him."

"Fair enough," said Charlie. "What are you going to do?"

"Ida and I will search the rest of the house, not for people but for clues as to where they may have relocated to and what they have been involving themselves with," said Sara. "Now get going. He sat on that chair, and that's his coat."

Charlie led Archie to the stool by the desk, let him have a good sniff and then allowed him to bury his nose in the coat.

"He's got it," he said. "If he's skulking around the old place, we'll find him."

And he left Ida and Sara to search.

"What do we do now?" said Ida.

"All this paper," said Sara, looking around at the towering shelves crammed with files. "If we had time enough to read it, maybe we would discover a web of connections. But I doubt it. I think that safe held anything important, and it's empty. I think Issachar Templebane is a cunning man and has not left anything that would help us find him."

"We could burn it," said Ida. "It would make a nice fire. Same as he did to your house. There's lamp oil in that storeroom by the stairs and we could warn the neighbours so no one got hurt . . ."

"You've a tough and ingenious mind, Ida Laemmel. With a good instinct for practical vengeance," said Sara. "I like that in a girl."

"Well," said Ida. "Nothing wrong with a little pyromania if you keep it under control."

Sara grinned regretfully and shook her head.

"Warning the neighbours would save them, but fires in this city have a bad habit of jumping from building to building. We'd save lives but be responsible for them losing their homes and businesses and livelihoods."

"Then . . . we could just leave by the front doors and leave them open?" said Ida. "I mean, I am just a simple country girl from the mountains, but I hear cities are places full of thieves and those who cannot be trusted. There may be nothing in here of interest to us, but I'm sure it would not be too terrible to leave the Templebanes open to a little mischief."

"There's the body," said Sara.

"I know," said Ida. "That would be part of the mischief, no?"

"Well, it would certainly not bring credit to the house of Templebane," said Sara. "And it might bring the magistrates and the constables sniffing about, which would do us no harm. Very good. We will leave the doors wide open and let what mischief may come, come. I can see why Cook likes you. You've got just the right kind of nasty streak running through you, same as she does."

"I don't like the Templebanes," said Ida.

"It's good of you to take our enemies on as your own," said Sara.

"It's not that," said Ida. "I mean, you can do your duty, but I'm not sure you can hate just because of duty. I don't like them because I was raised a hunter: to kill what you need and do it clean and fast. You don't kill for fun, or carelessly. When the Templebanes set their trap, they parked the wagon of oil outside your house. They left the horse harnessed to it. They could have unhitched it, *ja*? They want to murder you, that's one thing. That's personal. That's the game we are born to. But when the oil caught fire, so did the horse. It wasn't born to be part of our struggle. Even in the kitchen as the house was falling on top of us I heard the horse screaming. There was no need for that. It was just a horse."

Sara looked at her.

"As I said. Just like Cook. Hard as nails yet soft in all the right places."

"I'm not so soft, Sara Falk," said Ida. "You Britishers are much too sentimental."

CHAPTER 33

THIEVES IN THE NIGHT

Amos and the Ghost no longer haunted the hitherto deserted area from which they had initially kept watch on the house on Chandos Place opposite. The owners of the building had returned inconveniently, preceded by a flurry of servants and baggage. The harassed servants had shooed the unwanted tenants from where they had become ensconced in the sunken area between the basement door and the pavement and had then proceeded to open the house with much clattering of shutters, throwing open of sashes and energetic beating of rugs hung from the windows. For a frenetic couple of hours, the previously blank-faced house became a hive of activity more akin to a Turkish bazaar as a procession of tradesmen made deliveries to both the front and back doors while the increasingly harried staff tried to clean and polish around them.

Finally the owners arrived in a smart phaeton that bore the tell-tale mud spray which strongly hinted of a journey made from the depths of the countryside, and a closed carriage drew up in convoy, from which a sickly child with a whey-coloured pallor was helped by a nurse and a footman up the steps, and then the front door closed behind them and the house resumed its stone-faced impassivity.

Amos and the Ghost found new lodgings in a nearby alley which had the advantage of being subject to ongoing but neglected repairs to a sinkhole which had alarmingly dropped a section of pavement into the drains beneath: a three-foot crater had been covered by a ragged tarpaulin and surrounded by a protective wicket to stop unwary pedestrians from inadvertently dropping into the noxious hollow below, but there the protective maintenance seemed to have stalled. With only minor adjustments to the tarpaulin, this fenced-off area made a reasonably weatherproof hide, though he felt it would be cold enough if the weather turned to snow again, and though the improvised shelter had no straight line of sight along which to view Mountfellon's home, if one of them loitered in the gloom at the mouth of the alley, it was possible to keep a good watch while the other slept or foraged.

Amos began the new regime by alternately loitering in the alley mouth and sauntering innocently past Mountfellon's house, circling its boundary in a kind of dismal patrol, but as time progressed he lost the impulse to keep doing it, partly because he was aware that the whey-faced child was always leaning against the upper bedroom window, face pressed against the glass, observing the area with a hungry look that told of her desire to be out and about and healthy. It was like having a watchman keeping tabs on whatever passed in the street, and it unnerved Amos, especially when she started tapping on the window and waving at him with a tentative, friendly smile. He found this heartbreaking for reasons he could not understand, but more than that, he found it dangerous. He didn't want anyone, even the whey-faced invalid child, taking notice of him and his comings and goings or thinking of him as a "regular." So he stopped walking past her vantage point and spent most of the time in an increasingly glazed stupor, propped in the shadows, watching the house and trying to ignore the mephitic odour emerging from the hole in the ground behind him. He didn't find it too hard to ignore, but this was due to the fact he didn't seem to mind much about anything any more. He was becoming deadened to everything around him, and the vigil had become a necessary routine upon which he could at least hang his continuing existence. Without the demand it put on him, he knew he would crawl into the depression beneath the tarpaulin one night and not bother to get out again. And in the few clear moments of thought his traumatised state allowed him, he did know that he was at the bottom of something he should climb out of. "Later," said a weasel voice, "tomorrow, maybe." And the weasel voice drowned out the other voice quietly pointing out that tomorrow was a comforting illusion which kept him stuck in the unending gloom of today, since tomorrow was always moving beyond his reach, always full of a promise of relief which remained ungraspable. He was now eating even less then the Ghost, and since she ate barely anything, he was getting weaker and thinner too.

He was sitting in the shadows in the mouth of the alley at about midnight, hunched over himself as he pulled his belt tighter, trying to see where he should make a new hole to stop his trousers hanging off his hips, which they had begun to do in a way that threatened his ability to walk properly, when the tail off his eye caught something he had almost forgot he was looking for.

Movement outside Mountfellon's opaque-eyed house. Movement like shadows made visible.

He kept very, very still and watched.

The last time he had seen darkness used as camouflage like this it had been with the Sluagh. He had no desire to be found by them again. And because he was suddenly so busy not moving and wondering why everyone in the sleeping street could not hear the pounding of his heart, he did not step back and wake the Ghost, who was fast asleep, tucked snug beneath her blankets and the tarpaulin.

Charlie's heart nearly stopped beating at least three times as he watched Ida attempt the sheer façade of Mountfellon's house.

It had been decided that if the building was to be breached it was likely to be easiest to do so from the top floor, but that getting there was nigh on impossible, the house being detached from adjacent properties by a chasm too wide to jump or bridge.

Ida had volunteered to scale the smooth cliff of grey stone as nonchalantly as if she had been proposing to climb a stair.

"What you going to use?" Charlie had said with a derisory tone he now, watching her, regretted. "A ladder?"

She'd asked if he had a ladder that tall and, when he replied in the negative, she had shrugged and said she'd better just climb it then.

At this point, all the others had piled into the discussion, explaining the lack of handholds, the height of the building and the sharp and lethally unforgiving railings below. Ida had listened patiently, tightening and re-tying her pigtails in a business-like fashion as she did so, and then she thanked them for their advice and politely pointed out that they were city-folk and she was, among other things they were not, a mountaineer.

"I promise you I can climb it," she said. "I climbed the Hochkönig from the hard side when I was a child. This is what I do."

"What's the Hochkönig when it's at home?" Hodge had asked.

"Tallest mountain in the Berchtesgaden," she said. "Means the High King. And I took his crown when I was twelve."

"Watch yourself, Trousers. Pride goes before a fall," Cook said.

"No," said Ida with a grin. "Losing your grip goes before a fall. And I never lose my grip. And I never try to climb something I can't."

And she certainly could climb. Charlie and Sara had walked with her to the front of the house on Chandos Place and then Charlie had taken her loden cape, which she had worn through the streets to hide the crossbow slung around her shoulders. She had tightened the strap, clamping it tightly to her back so it wouldn't slide around, and nodded.

"*Sehr gut*," she grinned. "See you in a minute."

"Good luck," Charlie said, immediately feeling a fool for saying something so clunky and pedestrian.

"Ida," said Sara, reaching out a hand. "Take your time."

"This is my time," said Ida, and then she spun and ran straight at the front of the house. Charlie's heart nearly stopped for the first time as she leaped up onto the railings and surefootedly sprang up onto the side of the pillared portico, almost seeming to fly as her outstretched fingertips found a handhold he thought far out of her reach. Without pausing, she swung herself up onto the roof of the portico and ran to the wall of the house. The first floor was particularly high-ceilinged as befitted the formal rooms to be found on that level; the windows were correspondingly tall, and there was no way a normal person could reach the top lintel and swing any higher, even if they could safely jump for it, which was not possible at this height. Ida climbed the stone face instead. She seemed to stick to the wall like a fly as she found hand- and toeholds which allowed her to reach the seemingly inaccessible strip of protruding sandstone between the first and second floors. She hoisted herself up on it as if her body weighed nothing, and from there reached higher and swung up into the window recess above and stood for a moment, motionless on the relatively secure window ledge. She rummaged inside her short leather hunting jacket and seemed for a terrible instant to fumble and drop something.

Charlie's heart almost stopped for the second time as she appeared to reach out into the void to try and catch it, and then he breathed again as he saw she was paying out a thin rope from which dangled a small grapple, swaddled in some kind of cloth.

She steadied herself in the window embrasure, her feet firmly braced against the counter-pressure of her free hand pressing upwards against the top of the recess, and then she leaned even further out over the now certainly fatal drop and swung the grapple.

It looped up and over the overhanging parapet above her and landed with a muted thump.

She immediately pulled the rope tight and tugged it, making sure the grapple was holding against the inner wall of the parapet.

Charlie was suddenly acutely aware of how easy it might be for the grapple to slip, or for the treacherous sandstone of the parapet to crumble, or even—and this he was just noticing—how thin the rope was, scarcely thick enough to be used as sash cord, more string than rope in fact . . .

He wanted to shout, to warn her, but instead just forgot to breathe as she swung herself sideways out of the window embrasure and leant back, walking up the side of the building, pulling herself hand over hand up towards the vertiginously high lip of the wall—a lip Charlie now realised was sharply cut, and likely sawing through the perilously insubstantial rope. And then she seemed to take an extra forceful tug on the rope and use it to somehow spring herself up in the air as she let go with both hands—here Charlie's heart bumped alarmingly for the third time—and reached out to grab a double hold of the top of the parapet. He heard the slap of flesh on stone, and then saw Ida hoist herself nimbly up and out of sight onto the roof beyond.

"Blimey," said Charlie, allowing himself to breath.

"Blimey indeed," murmured Sara. "I do see what you see in her, Charlie Pyefinch."

"I don't . . ." blurted Charlie, glad the darkness was hiding the treacherous blush he could feel colouring his cheeks.

"Yes, you do," said Sharp who had materialised out of nowhere and was now standing beside Sara. "And I don't blame you one bit."

"Hodge?" said Sara.

"At the back of the building, all quiet. Though Jed's on edge about something he can't quite get a hold on."

Sara swept her eyes around the surrounding street. A late-night hackney carriage was debouching two tipsy gentlemen onto the corner, but apart from that it was quiet and no one seemed to be noticing them in the shadows.

"Keep an eye on the door," she said.

"And a hand on your knife," murmured Sharp.

Archie stood up and started to whine, low and insistent, his back legs quivering.

"What?" said Sara.

Charlie drew the knife from the scabbard he had taken to wearing in the small of his back and held the long blade low at his side.

"I don't know," he said reaching for the dog's mind with his own. "And neither does he . . ."

"He's a terrier," said Sharp. "They're always either asleep or on edge about something."

"Well, he's not asleep now," said Charlie.

Up on the roof, Ida worked fast, using the burglar's kit Cook had provided her with: a circular glass cutter, a small bottle of dark treacle and a square of stout brown paper. She centred the cutter on a pane of the opaque glass and in two precise movements cut a perfect circle. She poured the thick treacle onto the paper and pressed it against the pane. She then tapped the glass sharply and pulled the paper back with the broken-out circle of glass held by the stickiness. She had practised this deceptively simple-looking feat back at The Folley to the point where the midden behind the yard was now full of glass shards as a permanent memorial to her many failures to achieve the present neatly turned trick.

The milky opacity of the window now had a perfect round of black-ness in it. Ida reached in the hole she had made and found the window latch, which she undid, and carefully slid the sash open.

She stepped into what had obviously been a servant's room, and a servant who had left the premises with some despatch, from the untidy state it was in. She climbed over the bed and stood in the dark, letting her eyes adjust. Her night vision was more than good, its unnatural acuity being one of the qualities that made her such an effective huntress. And as she stood, letting her pupils dilate, she listened. The house was silent, and she sensed no human presence, at least not close.

She loosened the strap on her crossbow, primed and nocked a bolt in it, then walked quietly through the warren of rooms in the attic, checking they were as empty as her senses told her. She did this because painful experience had taught her there were some things, some unusual and dangerous beings, which could mask their presence from even her heightened senses until they got much too close for comfort.

The attic floor was empty, and she flowed down the stairs like a shadow made flesh. The next floor was easier to check, the rooms being grander and thus bigger and fewer, and then the floor below was even quicker, being made up of the public rooms, a ballroom and dining room respect-ively. The ground floor was empty and she debated whether to check the basement was similarly safe, and decided it would be sensible to open the front door and proceed to the lower, darker levels with reinforcements.

There was something nagging at the back of her mind now, a rising tingle which had grown as she descended the stairs.

She unlocked the front door and stood back as Sharp, Sara and Charlie flitted out of the shadows across the street and wraithed inside the house to stand with her in the tall marbled hallway. Archie immediately ran to the top of the stairs down to the basement and stopped, fur bristling.

Charlie closed the door behind them. He looked at Ida. She nodded.

"What do you think?" said Sharp.

"There's no one here," said Ida. She looked at the ruff of fur standing up on Archie's back. "But there's something."

"What?" said Sara.

"I don't know," said Ida. "It got worse as I came downstairs. I haven't checked down there yet. If there's something, it's down there."

"That's what Archie thinks," said Charlie. "He doesn't know what it is either, but he doesn't like it."

Sharp took out a candle from his waistcoat.

"No," said Ida. "No lights until I say."

Sharp and Sara exchanged a look. Charlie could see they were adjusting to the fact this girl of his age considered herself to be in charge.

"I can see in the dark well enough," she explained. "Make a light, all you do is let whatever's down there see us."

Sharp nodded and slid the candle back in his coat.

"Lead on," he said. "But take care."

She nodded and soft-footed slowly down the half-spiral of stone stairs which led below. Unlike the restrained but still palatial decoration of the rooms above, the stair was suddenly austerely and characteristically spartan in the true Georgian style, just unadorned sandstone steps and an iron railing, as if leading to a completely different world from the one above. The ceiling of the long corridor that led from the bottom of the steps was low and seemed to press down on them as they followed Ida going from door to door, checking.

She came to a door that wouldn't open and stopped, raising a warning hand.

Charlie was feeling both what he could sense and what Archie's impressions were. The young dog was quivering at his side, eyes locked on Ida and the door beyond.

Ida pressed her ear against the door and listened. She grimaced and beckoned Sharp closer to stand ready as she carefully tried the door. It was definitely locked. She eased up on the handle, returning it to its original position slowly so as not to let it give a tell-tale click.

Sharp stepped back. Looked at Sara.

"We'll need Hodge and his lock-picks . . ."

"I can do it," said Charlie quietly.

He reached into his waistcoat and slid the wallet of picks from the inner pocket as he knelt at the keyhole. Ida bent and spoke into his ear, so close he felt the warmth of her breath raising the hairs on his neck.

"If something comes through the door in a hurry, don't stand up," she murmured, and then stepped back and shouldered her crossbow, aiming it at a point at chest height just above where he was crouched.

He listened, trying to make sense of the quiet animal noises which were just barely audible on the other side of the door. Then he eased the thinnest probe into the lock. And found it already occupied. Locks can all be picked, unless the key is still in them. He moved the tip of the pick gently, getting a feel for whether the offending key was aligned up and down, or at an angle that would need jiggling for his plan to have a chance of working. The bit was slightly offset, by less than ten degrees. He reached in another pick and held his breath as he eased it into what he thought of as the six o'clock position. Then he reached down and felt the gap at the bottom of the door. And then he held up a hand to warn Ida he was going to stand, and stepped back towards the others.

"The key's still in the other side," he said.

"So?" said Ida.

"So if there was no one in there, I could slide a paper under the door, poke the key out so it landed on the paper and pull it back under," he said. "But the room isn't empty, and the noise will alert whatever's in there. So it might be all we can do to try it . . . and it might work if we can move fast . . ."

Ida dropped to the floor and put an eye to the crack. She held up three fingers.

"You're pretty fast," said Sara, nudging Sharp and starting to unbutton her jacket.

"What are you doing?" he said, a little shocked.

She stripped the oiled silk jacket off and handed it to Ida.

"Use this instead of paper."

Ida nodded and fed the semi-stiff material under the door, directly beneath the keyhole. Sharp looked at Charlie.

"On three then," he said, "and no butterfingers please, Miss Laemmel."

He transferred the knife to his teeth and flexed his fingers like a concert pianist preparing for a performance.

"What is butterfingers?" whispered Ida.

"Don't drop it," said Charlie.

"Told you: my grip is good," she said.

Sharp nodded. Charlie took a breath, looked at Ida and mouthed "1, 2, 3" and then slid the lock pick deeper into the keyhole, finding the blunt end of the pin and pushing smoothly against it to force the key out.

Ida whipped Sara's coat back out so quickly that it fooled Charlie's senses into thinking she'd done it too soon, before the key had landed, but then he saw her snatch it from the folds of the jacket and hold it up.

Sharp seemed to blur, and there was click and a squeal and then Charlie was knocked aside as Sharp and Sara sprang past him into the dimly lit room.

Something pale moved very fast, snarling in from the right, but even as Sharp's blade was slicing air towards it, something else punched over Charlie's head, catching the assailant in the throat and knocking it clear of the slash. Ida's crossbow bolt pinned it to the wall where it hung with spasming fingers reaching in surprise for the feathered end sticking out below its chin.

It was a man from whom all colour seemed to have been leeched, the blood ribboning a dark strip from the arrow in his neck to the floor, except for the clenched teeth which were as black and shiny as jet. His uniformly dirty white clothes were ragged, though once homespun, and his long hair and spade-like beard were bleached with something other than age to the same hue as his clothes. His eyes rolled back in his head and his hand opened, dropping the heavy axe he had been gripping onto the bare floorboards against which his heels kicked convulsively and then were still.

"I had it," said Sharp tightly, without looking around.

"Yeah," said Charlie, staring at the pale thing dying on the wall. "But what is it?"

"Mirror Wights," said Sara facing the archway beyond, in the shadows of which stood three more monochrome figures, frozen in shock around something which looked like an animal cage . . .

Charlie couldn't see what was in the cage and, as he stepped sideways to get a clearer look, one of the Wights shifted to block his view.

"Be still," snapped Ida, stepping into the room with her crossbow reloaded and aimed at them.

The one closest to Sara shook his head. He was a bent, bow-legged figure, perhaps once a seagoing man from the look of his flat-brimmed oilskin hat, long pigtail and short jacket. He tipped the hat back on his forehead and sighed.

"Ach, there was no need for that now," he said, showing a mouth full of black teeth in his floury white face. "He was just surprised . . ."

"He was about to surprise my damned head off," said Sara, poking the axe with her foot.

"Well, you should have knocked, dolly," said the sailor.

"Don't call her dolly," growled Sharp. "And put your hands in the air where I can see them, all of you . . ."

Their hands stayed down. The two other Mirror Wights appeared to be twins, or at least to have entered the mirrors at the same point in history, from the look of it somewhere around the time of the Civil War,

for though what they wore was bleached out and colourless it was clearly
the uniform of Cromwell's New Model Army. Both wore metal breastplates over leather jerkins and high boots, and each had a sword belt hung
sash-like over one shoulder. The one closest to them had a metal helmet
with a faceguard, and the other was bareheaded and broken-nosed.

"Now don't be like that," smiled the sailor, tipping the hat even further
back on his head. "I'm just trying to calm this—"

And then he flung the hat at Sara, hard and flat, diving to the left as
Ida fired on reflex, the bolt catching him in the chest . . .

Sharp's hand snaked out and caught the spinning hat before it hit Sara.

"Damn," he said, wincing. He dropped it and looked at his fingers,
badly gashed and pumping blood. "Razors in the brim."

"We want no trouble," said the helmeted one, who was standing by
the cage.

"Then put your damned hands in the air," said Sara.

"They're just animals," said the other, raising his hands. "It's just like
you'd milk a cow."

"It's true," said the first, his hands hovering at shoulder height, as if
they couldn't decide to go all the way up. "They don't mind it so much,
and we never take too much neither."

Sharp had made a tight fist to try and close the wound in his hand.
He held it out, showing his ring, holding it steady as blood dripped to
the floor below.

"Step aside, or by Law and Lore we will end you now," he gritted.

"Ah well, we don't end so easy," said the Wight by the cage. "Just let
us return to the mirrors and no harm done. They're just animals really,
like I said."

Charlie didn't know what they were talking about, but the way they
spoke of it was tainted, their half-smiles curdled and wheedling and
somehow ashamed. There was palpable sense that something very bad
had been done in this room, was still being done in fact, right at the
moment they had burst in. Ida stepped up to his shoulder with a new
quarrel loaded in her crossbow. She grunted without taking her eye off

the Wights and, though there were no words, he could tell she was saying she too felt the taint of something very wrong here.

"Just milking 'em," said the other. "You let us go now. We'll be nice as nuns' hens, and everyone happy, eh? Them two you killed were soft boys, pusser's mate and a woodcutter, no great loss and no special friends of ours. You make us fight, you'll find we're tougher'n 'em, and trained to it too."

"Step away from that cage," said Sara, voice cracking like a whip. "Do it now."

"Your wish, milady," said the helmeted one and stepped sideways.

As soon as he did so, it became apparent that the cage door was unlocked and he had been keeping it shut with his leg, for it immediately sprang open and smashed back against the bars with a loud clang of iron on iron, and a green-faced thing charged out, keening horribly as it jumped at Sara.

There was a thunk as Ida fired. The bolt would have hit the attacker had not the roundhead's arm been chopping down in front of it as he went for his sword. His forearm was protected by an armoured bracer and the bolt spanged off it, ricocheting into the floor.

Charlie was already in motion, working on reflex, fist already bunched and inbound before his mind caught up with his body as he jumped forward, and he stopped the attacker dead in its tracks with a solid hook to the face. The impact jarred him to his boot-heels, but the punch poleaxed the assailant and dropped it unconscious to the floor. He had time to register it was a normal-looking man in a breechclout, normal, except for the fact his hair and skin were green. There was something wrong with his mouth and blood was dripping from a thin pipe sticking out of his forearm.

He saw all this in a fraction of a second, just enough time to also begin to wonder if he'd broken something in his fist—and then there was no time to wonder at anything because the roundheads attacked, trying to cut their way to the mirrored box on the wall with disciplined slashes of their heavy dragoon's swords.

He saw a thick blade cutting towards his midriff and then someone grabbed his collar and pulled him sharply out of the way of the blow, and as he tumbled backwards he saw a streak of midnight blue go past him which must have been Sharp, and then he was falling and saw mostly ceiling and Sara hurdling his body as she sprang into the attack, and then he banged his head and saw ceiling and stars and then blackness as unconsciousness took him.

Sharp parried the blow that had nearly cut Charlie in two, sending the blade high and holding it there for a short second as Sara, as if she knew without a word what his intention was, darted beneath his outstretched arm and sunk her blade into the now vulnerably exposed armpit of the dragoon, just above the curve of the armoured breastplate.

She stabbed twice, fierce and fast, and then spun out of the way as Sharp stepped back and kicked the dying body into the path of its twin, who was snarling and swinging at him. The surviving Wight was a quick thinker and an even faster mover because he leapt sideways, avoiding getting tangled in the corpse, and turned his blow into a sudden backhanded slash at Sara who was already moving to get behind him.

She parried the blow, but the force of it knocked her spinning backwards. She checked herself from falling by reaching behind her and bracing on the downthrust blade of her other knife. The Wight immediately turned fast, hacking a brutal upwards slash at Sharp, who caught the gutting blow in the fork made by his two crossed knives, keeping the sword just below waist level, inches from splitting him in half.

Sara had not stopped spinning, but used the momentum to pivot on the knifepoint, which cut a small spiral curl of wood-shaving from the floorboard as she slashed around with the other blade, held at full length, cutting across the exposed back of the snarling Wight's knees, hamstringing him.

He grunted in surprise as his legs began to collapse, and in the instant of realisation, Sharp pushed his blade aside with one knife while with the other he stabbed a single devastatingly surgical lunge through the helmet's face guard, jabbing in and out of the Wight's eye so fast that Ida, who saw it, almost missed it.

And as the Wight crumpled and fell backwards, Sara used the last of her gyratory momentum to unfold upwards through his collapse so she seemed to shrug his boot-heels over her shoulder as she stood.

And then it was suddenly over as his heavy, helmeted head hit the floor behind her with a final thump.

"You are unhurt?" said Sharp.

"Never better," she said. And Ida again was unsure whether she saw a smile go between them, so fast was its passing.

Charlie lurched out of unconsciousness, his eyes opening to see that the white ceiling now had a spray of dark liquid slashed across it, liquid that was dripping back onto the ground. Some of it splashed into his face and he wiped at it groggily and looked at the blood smeared on his hand. And then Ida swung into view overhead, reaching a hand down.

"Don't worry," she said. "It's not yours."

She pulled him to his feet and he saw the Mirror Wights—one was awkwardly sprawled on the floor of the cage, his eye welling blood out of a brutal wound which made Charlie want to be sick, so he looked away and saw the other sitting against the wall by the mirror-box, his legs splayed wide with his hand clamped impotently over the blood spilling out of the ruined armpit above his armoured breastplate.

Sharp and Sara were crouched in front of him, talking urgently.

"What?" grunted Charlie.

Ida shook her head.

"I've never seen anyone move as fast as he did: he just sort of flowed around them, under the blades, moved like water; she got behind them before they knew she was there; he lunged and blocked and she attacked in the gaps he made. It was very, very swift," she whispered. "I mean, I work in a team, and we are also very good, but . . . they are something else, those two."

"Wish I'd seen it," said Charlie, rubbing the knot on the back of his head and wincing.

"Wish I could do it," snorted Ida. "Perhaps he can teach me."

Sara and Sharp were knelt close together, simultaneously questioning the Wight while binding the gash in Sharp's hand.

"Mountfellon," said Sara. "Did he bring you here?"

"Mount-who?" said the Wight.

"He owns this house," said Sara.

"What was the deal? What did you do for him?" said Sharp.

"Dunno whose house this is," choked the Wight, blood welling over his lower teeth. "Just a place we lucked on. Place to take a Blood Toll, somewhere we . . ."

He coughed the shiny blood onto the dull white breastplate.

"Thought all our Christmases come at once, we did."

"Who invited you?" said Sara. "Was it Mountfellon or The Citizen? Was it a man called Robespierre?"

"Don't . . . know these names," said the Wight.

"What did he want from you in return?" said Sharp.

"Don't know who . . . No one invited us," said the Wight. "By the blood I swear; we only found it because we saw 'em coming out. We saw them passing, two old men, one looked like death himself . . ."

He spat more blood and looked into a distance further away than the walls of the room.

"Well. Well. Well. Think I'm taking the short road home now . . ."

"The men," said Sharp, shaking him gently.

The eyes returned to the room for a moment.

"The men? Oh . . . we tracked back to see where they come from . . . we just looked through the mirror . . . found these things just left and caged . . . we just milked . . . we just milked . . . we just milk—" and he stopped with a shudder.

And then he just left himself.

He didn't slump; his eyes didn't roll back: he just wheezed and halted, mouth half open, waterfall of blood stilled at his teeth, chin and breast-plate streaked with its outflow, eyes now vacant and lifeless.

"I think he was telling the truth," said Sharp.

"Hold still," said Sara, who was finishing tying the neckerchief around his wounded hand. "Yes. He was telling the truth. They found this mirror by accident."

"Not by accident. By watching," said Sharp. "If it was The Citizen who went into the mirrors, he could be anywhere. He could even be back in France."

"Wherever he is, we'll find him," she said. "Now we will hold until Cook can sew you up."

"If it was The Citizen they saw," said Sharp, "who was the companion?"

The Green Man suddenly came awake, scrabbling to his knees in a panicked, vicious frenzy that took them all by surprise, lashing out and giving a terrible noise that was part shrieking moan and part growl. One hand snatched Sara Falk's skirt.

She looked down and saw the green face and the wild eyes and suddenly in a treacherous instant, like glinting-but-not-glinting, she wasn't Sara Falk of The Oversight, she was young Sara, Sara the child, being chased by a snarling green-skinned madman through the upper floor of the Safe House; she was black-haired Sara the moment before her hair went white with pure terror; she was the little girl tumbling down the unforgiving stone backstairs in her desperate attempt to escape the nightmare made real, and she ripped herself out of the grip of the thing scrabbling at her leg and fell, dropping her knife, forgetting she knew how to use it in the primal panic that had ambushed her, crabbing back until she got tangled in Ida's legs and they both fell, feet slipping in the blood still dripping from the ceiling.

"Kill it!" Sara yelled. "Kill it!"

Charlie was closest and he lunged and got his hand on the keening thing's throat even as it tried to buck against the floorboards and jerk to its feet. He bulled it backwards and they hit the desk hard, toppling it over and landing in an avalanche of blood-spattered papers and parchment. Charlie put a knee on its chest and felt the nails of its flailing hand cut painful tracks across his cheek.

He heard Sharp say, "Sara."

And then the Green Man writhed and lashed out again, slippery with cold sweat. Charlie struggled to keep a grip with his one hand and knee as he fumbled for the knife in the sheath at the small of his back. He found it and drew it fast, gripping it tight—

The white eyes in the green face were wild and desperate, and then they stuttered suddenly and focused on something just over his shoulder.

Don't kill it!

The voice seemed to come from deep inside his own head, loud and urgent.

A hand slapped onto his wrist and grabbed it, stopping the knife.

Charlie yanked against the grip and twisted his head to find he was looking into the dark-skinned face of a young man of his own age, a face shaking its head in an emphatic "No," a face with eyes that were somehow trying to speak as urgently as the voice now echoing shouting in his head.

Don't kill it! Please! Enough blood!

Behind him, Sharp pulled Sara to her feet as Ida untangled herself and cocked her crossbow warningly.

"Ida," said Sara, gasping for breath, sounding like herself, her adult self again. "If he doesn't let go of Charlie right now, shoot him. He's a Templebane; I saw him when I glinted in their counting-house. He's a killer and he's dangerous."

No. Enough blood. Too much blood.

Amos let go of Charlie's wrist and held out his badge like a shield.

No. No. Read. Not a killer. Not a Bloody Boy!

"Amos Templebane. Mute but Intelligent," said Sharp, exhaling calmly. "Please don't do anything stupid. Hands where we can see them."

He stared into Amos's eyes. Amos blinked and shook his head.

Don't. That won't work on me. Sorry.

Sharp looked at Sara.

"Well. Can you hear him?"

She nodded.

"Anyone else?"

"I can," said Ida and Charlie simultaneously.

Amos seemed to sway a little in relief.

Please don't hurt the Green Man. He's not dangerous. He's scared. And a bit mad. They sewed up his lips so he couldn't scream and took his blood. He's been screaming inside ever since . . .

He pointed. Charlie saw that this was what had been wrong with the Green Man's mouth. It had been stitched shut to mute him.

He heard Amos's voice change as he tried to go into the Green Man's head.

Don't struggle. They won't hurt you if you don't struggle. They're meant to protect you. They're not bad. They're not like the others. Look at the rings they wear. They are The Oversight.

Sara's eyes dropped to her hand, and for a moment she felt something like a twinge of guilt.

"Amos Templebane, Mute," said Sharp. "You've told us who you are. But . . ."

". . . but *what* are you?" said Sara.

Amos looked at them all.

Lost.

He tried to smile, and was suddenly too weak to mind about the tears which seemed to be rolling freely out of his eyes.

Lost. And very, very tired.

CHAPTER 34

A SHORTCUT FROM MARBLEHEAD

Once the decision to allow Cait and Lucy to proceed had been made, the Circle had broken up and they were left alone to make their plan with the two "visitors" from the Western Remnant, as the Guardian called them. She had gone too, under the pretext of fetching them some coffee, but Lucy had the strongest feeling the Guardian had absented herself in order to soothe the ruffled feathers of those among the Circle who objected to the outcome of the meeting. Mrs. Tittensor, perhaps the most discomposed, had left immediately for Boston in order to fetch the dog she had reluctantly agreed to allow to go with them on their search. This errand, they were told, would take a couple of hours.

Any relief that Lucy felt on being freed from the general scrutiny of such a large group of mildly hostile people was severely offset by the fact that, as soon as they were gone, the specific hostility which her actions had triggered in Cait was all the more unavoidable. And to make the atmosphere even worse, Armbruster had pulled out a villainous-looking pipe which he proceeded to fire up and puff happily, producing a pall of acrid tobacco smoke which hung around them in the still air of the meeting room like swamp gas.

Lucy herself was torn between a feeling of anger at Cait's stubborn inability to recognise that she had broken the impasse with the Remnant for no other reason than to help Cait's quest for the stolen child, and a growing despair that their friendship seemed to have curdled irrevocably.

"I don't know why you're so angry about this," she said quietly.

"And I'm no longer under any obligation to continue your instruction in the ways of the world," said Cait. "So you'll maybe have to untangle that for yourself."

"I've untangled why everyone seems to have a problem with *fiagaí*," said Lucy.

Cait raised an eyebrow at her. Lucy held her breath.

"Well, you're going to spit out your little bit of poison eventually, so crack on," Cait said.

"You're monomaniacs," said Lucy, using a word she had learned from Cook. The thought of Cook made her eyes suddenly prick, which was annoying because she didn't want Cait to think she was tearing up because of her. "You've got one-track minds which makes you just as annoying as anybody who's obsessed with just one thing. It makes you hard to be around. It's . . ."

"And there was you wanting to learn to be one," said Cait. "And now I'm thinking you don't."

"Well, at least you taught me that," said Lucy, feeling spiteful even as the words left her mouth.

Magill exchanged a look with Armbruster, and then pulled a leather satchel from under the chair he had been sitting on and proceeded to unfold a large and well-used map which he spread on the floor between them.

"If it's untangling you want, maybe it'd be as well you see what you're asking us to do," he said. "And this map here will give you an idea of the great wilderness in which you're hoping to find this baby."

He unsheathed the largest knife Lucy had ever seen, nearly a foot long with a thick brass cross-guard more appropriate to a cutlass, and crouched over the map, using the distinctive concave tip as a pointer.

"That's a fine blade," said Cait appreciatively, "for all that it doesn't seem to quite know if it's going to grow up to be a knife or a sword."

"One of Black's original bowie-knives," said Magill. "Won it in a poker game."

"Poker, is it?" said Cait, still eyeing the blade. "And would I be right in thinking that the poker is a sort of game of hazard played with the cards and that?"

If Lucy had not seen Cait quietly draining the sailors of their savings over many hands of poker on their voyage over, she would have imagined from her innocent tone that she had never once held a pack of playing cards in her life. As it was, she knew Cait could manipulate cards quite as dexterously as she could people, and had decided to have the impressive knife for her own. And then she saw Magill's smile and realised he was not taken in any more than she was.

"Miss ná Gaolaire," he said. "I wouldn't dream of attempting to teach you the fine and manly art of poker: firstly since your evident innocence in the ways of the world should not be besmirched by one as crude as I; and secondly because I got this knife such a long while back that I'm kinda used to the feel of the thing on my belt and wouldn't feel dressed without it . . ."

"Well then, there'd be no fun in the game," said Cait. "For you're clearly not a man to be bluffed."

"No," said Armbruster. "Though Jon being Jon, flirting'll probably get you there in the end."

"Fred thinks I'm too romantic," said Magill.

"And are you not one for the romance?" said Cait, trying out a very convincing look of dewy-eyed disappointment.

"No, ma'am," said Magill. "Out where we range, it's real and practical as gets the job done; romantic just gets you killed."

"Jon," said Armbruster. "The matter in hand?"

Magill grinned at Cait and looked back down at the map.

"This is Boston here." He reached out and indicated a spot on the other side of the continent. "That's the Willamette Valley. More than three thousand miles off. That's as far as you came by sea, more or less. It's only in the last couple of years that there's been a route you can take a wagon on. Some call it the Medicine Road, some the Oregon Trail. Either way, it's a hell of a journey to take at the pace of an ox-wagon."

"And here's the thing," said Armbruster, around the stem of his reeking pipe. "And when I say thing I mean things, plural, because we got good news and bad news."

"Mainly bad, Fred," said Magill. "Don't shine 'em on. Close, but no cigar won't put a smile on their faces."

"Why don't you just tell us and let us make our own minds up?" said Cait.

"The good news is that closet over there," said Armbruster. "Though I'll bet you can't tell us what that is . . ."

"I'll take the bet," said Lucy. "And if I'm right, you put the pipe out. It's making my eyes sting."

"And if you're wrong?" said Armbruster. "What do I get?"

"Nothing. I'm not wrong," said Lucy. "It's a Murano Cabinet. Mirrored inside and out."

Armbruster raised his eyebrows in surprise. Then he nodded ruefully and crossed to the fire, where he tapped out his pipe.

"These are reckoned rarer than hen's teeth," said Magill, looking genuinely impressed. "Now where'd you see one before?"

"There's one in the Safe House in London," said Lucy.

"Is that so?" said Armbruster, looking sceptical. "I never heard of that . . ."

"Know what it does?" said Magill.

"It's used for taking shortcuts between looking-glasses," said Lucy. "So you don't always have to walk in the mirrored passages to get between places."

"You know a lot," said Armbruster, looking at Magill.

"I should do. I fell into one and ended up somewhere completely different," said Lucy. "They're dangerous things, and so is the mirror'd world, by all accounts."

"She's right about that too," said Magill.

"So let me guess," said Cait. "You've been using it to pop back and forth between here and wherever you are in the west. For a shortcut."

"And why'd you think that?" said Armbruster.

"Because you're dressed for travelling in colder climes than this," said Cait. "Not like the rest of the folk here. And you smell of woodsmoke, not the coal that's in the grate over there. So that says camp-fire to me. And the mud on your boots, Mr. Magill, is loamy and red, and the soil round here from what I've seen of it is black or sandy."

"Don't play poker with her, Jon," said Armbruster, "not if you really want to keep hold of that knife of yours."

"Wasn't going to," said Magill.

"So I'm right then?" said Cait.

"Yes and no," said Magill. "We don't much like the mirrors and what's behind them. But we can get you to St. Louis or even Fort John up on the North Platte a damn sight quicker than if you went any other way. You could take the train from Boston to Springfield, but then it's post roads and stages all the way west which'd take you the best part of ten days, or we can step into that cabinet and just step out in a house in St. Louis on the banks of the wide Missouri more than a thousand miles away. But . . ."

He shrugged.

"But what?" said Cait, an edge to her voice.

"But even then it'd be too late," said Armbruster. "This Graves see, the fisherman with your baby, he's heading for the Willamette Valley, fixing to be a farmer like they all do. He left in the spring. Takes time to travel the Oregon Trail, and you can't leave it too late. So, from what they tell us he jumped off early with the first wagon trains of the year, and if he made—and that's a big old if, by the by—and if he made it, he's unreachable until winter's passed and the snows have opened the great Stoney Mountains again."

"It's not full winter yet," said Cait, looking out of the window.

"Not here, ma'am," said Magill. "But out there in the west, where the weather'll kill you soon as spit in your eye, the mountain passes are already getting snowed in. There'll be no more western passage along the Medicine Road until the thaw."

"That," said Cait, "is unacceptable."

"Likely so," said Magill. "Don't mean it's not true."

"What do you expect me to do?" said Cait.

"Sit out the winter in St. Louis. That way you can get a jump on next year's damn migration," said Magill.

"Or you could go home," said Armbruster. "Though note that I'm not recommending that seriously, because I can see it's an idea that's poison to you and I don't want you popping me one in the nose again."

"I can't just sit in St. Louis," said Cait. "Why can't you use your mirrors to take us further, to this Fort John or beyond?"

"Fort John's no place for a young single woman to overwinter," said Magill.

"And we can't take you beyond that now," said Armbruster. "Certainly not further than the Devil's Gate this late in the year."

The look he gave Magill had something in it that Lucy noticed before they both hid it.

"Why?" Cait said.

"Mirrors don't go everywhere, and the mirror'd world ain't safe, and it only works where there are other mirrors," said Magill. "There's passages made of looking-glass, but they don't go everywhere, and in some places they just don't work. The Murano Cabinets, well, sure they can sometimes be set to take you from somewhere you know to somewhere else if you've the knack of setting them right, without having to walk the passages, kinda like a shortcut inside a shortcut I guess, but out beyond all this civilisation here, beyond Independence, say?"

He waved his hand.

"Precious few mirrors out there, in the unsettled territory."

"So I have a different question for you," said Cait. "Why are you here?"

"Sorry?" said Magill.

"Why do you happen to be paying a visit to this circle as you call it, so conveniently, seeing as how you don't belong to it," said Cait. "I mean. Just at the same time we happen to be here?"

"We're not here because of you," said Armbruster. "That's just luck."

"Yes, well, I never got very far with just trusting luck," said Cait. "I don't trust it, nor strangers being unexpectedly helpful."

"Suspicious, ain't you?" said Armbruster.

"Always," she said.

Armbruster again looked at Magill, who nodded.

"We're not exactly helping you. We're helping her because she's a member of The Oversight," he said, pointing at Lucy. "Because we been helped by them."

"In the past," said Cait. "So this is just a sentimental thing?"

"No, ma'am," said Magill. "It wasn't in the past. It's now. We're being helped by one of her colleagues right now."

"Jon and I are about as sentimental as you are trusting, which is to say, not a bit," said Armbruster.

Magill reached into his satchel and pulled out a dull grey rectangle of lead, about six by eight inches. Lucy could see it was incised with writing and symbols on both sides.

"If you're from London, you'll have seen one of these," said Magill, looking at Lucy. "I know you're as worried about them as we are, which is why he's been out here. We're the ones been helping him track 'em down."

"Who?" said Lucy.

"Mr. Sharp."

Cait's head came up.

"You've seen Sharp?" said Lucy.

"Jack Sharp?" said Cait.

"The very one," said Armbruster.

"But . . . he doesn't know we found it," said Lucy, staring at Cait.

"Found what?" said Armbruster.

"Sara Falk's hand," said Lucy. "He got lost in the mirrors looking for it, but . . ."

She stopped, trying to work out how to explain it and figure out why Cait was stepping on her foot again.

"Well, he ain't lost now," said Magill. "He knows his way round the mirrors better than anyone could. That's why he's looking for more of these, that's how come we're here, reporting on what we found so the First Circle here is up to speed."

"And what have you found?" said Cait.

"Closest way I can tell it is this," said Magill, "and this is Sharp's view, really: the French, you know the Paladin? They been working against The Oversight and The Remnant ever since never was ever. And they found out about the mirrors, and they didn't like the way the Spanish and the British were carving out new colonies on this side of the Ocean."

"So they decided to cheat," said Armbruster. "They paid woodsmen from Upper Canada, that is fur traders and *coureurs des bois*, French and Scots mainly, to move fast and deep into uncharted territory. They didn't survey and they didn't leave settlements as they went. They just upped and headed west, travelling light except for two things."

"Mirrors and these tablets," said Magill. "It was a genius scheme, except for it broke the prime law we're all sworn to uphold."

"Which is that the supranatural is not to predate upon the natural," said Cait.

"Yep," said Magill. "And vice versa. Except they was sent by kings, and kings cheat and lie as easy as other folks breathe air. Which is why The Remnant and The Oversight never had kings in their number. The French though, the Paladin? They ran things different. And this one French king got so obsessed by mirrors I heard tell he built a vast hall of them in his palace at Versailles, hoping to use it as a place to go anywhere in the world he wished to, once they'd mapped the trails beyond the glass."

"See, the plan was to plant new mirrors as far into uncharted territory as they could, then head back, resupply, and then leapfrog by jumping to the last mirror placed without having to trek on foot, and continue pushing on west," said Armbruster. "These tablets, they put them on the closest, highest point in the surrounding area to where they'd cached the mirrors, in case they got lost. They're always hidden in a cavern or a crack in a mountain or some such. The writing gives precise directions to the mirror."

"Was mainly a family of trappers called de la Vérendrye done it, but it wasn't just *coureurs des bois*," said Magill. "They got one tough little Scottish kid called Mackenzie to walk all the way to the damn Pacific, years before Lewis and Clark done it."

"Anyway," said Armbruster, "it was a scheme as would have given the French control of everything, once they'd started putting settlers and soldiers through the mirrors. But they had them a revolution and cut that king's head off, and something broke the mirrors, so the passages don't quite seem to line up like they did, and they never finished their plan."

"And this is what Jack Sharp has you helping him with?" said Cait. "Why would he need your help?"

"Because we're mountain men," said Armbruster. "The chain of mirrors the de la Vérendryes strung out across the uncharted territory is broken. And that's a good thing. But we don't know where they all are, and we don't want those who were behind the plan thinking to repair it and use it again. So what Sharp can't scout through what remains of the mirror'd world, we been scouting in the real world."

"A two-pronged attack," said Magill.

He pointed at the tablet.

"We didn't find that one. It was brought to us by a Dakotay from up in the Black Hills," said Armbruster. "But this is all by the by. Point is we're engaged to help Sharp map the hidden mirrors and neutralise them, and because of that we can give you a shortcut of sorts."

"We can have you in St. Louis in a minute," said Magill. "Murano Cabinets mean you don't even have to walk the mirror'd world. You could outfit yourselves for the territories, if you had cash money and we got another pair of mirrors set up where the Laramie meets the Platte at Fort John but like Fred said, I wouldn't recommend two young ladies getting themselves snowed in with the kind of lowlifes that hang around the fort until spring. You should stay in St. Louis and overwinter there in comfort."

"Where is Sharp?" said Lucy.

"Sharp's in the mirrors," said Magill. "But we got a rendezvous planned to see him."

"In London?" said Lucy.

"No," said Armbruster. "That takes days, from what I hear. No, there are no shortcuts to London. Maybe there was once, mirror to mirror, but there aren't any more. You have to walk the long passages of glass to get there and though it's faster than a sea passage, it's likely a brutal walk. No. We'll meet on this continent, and we're engaged to report on what the Guardian here does, whether or not she agrees with the plan."

"Is that so?" said Cait. Lucy wondered if the momentary smile on her lips was to do with the prospect of seeing Sharp, for whom she had expressed admiration on several occasions. Admiration and something a little baser, something that curdled in Lucy's heart and stung like jealousy.

"What plan?" she said, hoping to move the subject on. Magill pulled his ear thoughtfully before speaking.

"Ever since things went real bad real fast with the first settlers and the Indians, there's been an agreement not to interfere with them, not to have their gifted work with ours. Our two ways of seeing the world don't match up, see. So we don't deal with them, they don't mess with us. We stay separate, and funnily enough, that's how we stay friends. But Sharp thinks we should ask them to look for the tablets, so he can deal with the mirrors and stop unscrupulous leftovers of the Paladin reviving it. Those who'd put king and country or gold before keeping the balance between the natural and the supranatural. There's a damn sight more of them than us, and they know the land a thousand times better than we do. It's in both our interests."

"We don't have the power to make that decision," said Magill.

"And Jon's leery of it," said Armbruster.

"Just a lick," said Magill. "Seems good on the surface, but I don't know if it's a good thing to start pulling the Indians into our doings. Not like they ever come well out of it when that happens. Still, it's the devil and the deep blue sea, so I'm happy for older and wiser heads to have a say on whether we should jump with Sharp's plan."

"And what has the Circle decided?" said Cait.

"Guardian is minded to agree with Sharp," said Armbruster. "Just this once. That's what we're telling Sharp when we see him."

"You got more questions, you can ask him yourself," said Magill, looking at Lucy. "If you'd like to take us up on our invitation?"

"We'll come with you," said Cait. "Once we've got Mrs. Tittensor's dog, that is. If that's all right with you, Miss Harker?"

Lucy nodded. The "Miss Harker" stung, as was intended.

"It will be good to see Sharp," she said. And in her head she thought the best thing about it would be his advice on whether to spend a winter in this St. Louis or not. Perhaps as a member of The Oversight he could take responsibility for Cait, if that was what The Remnant required, and Lucy might be able to be, finally, free to start a fresh life of her own in this new country.

Magill and Armbruster excused themselves and said they would go and communicate the decision to the Guardian who seemed to have got waylaid in her stated plan to bring them coffee.

Lucy looked at Cait.

"I was trying to help," she said. "And I have helped. And you're behaving like I'm suddenly your enemy."

Cait said nothing.

"Do you trust them?" said Lucy.

"Trust is a romantic notion," said Cait, not turning to look at her as she spoke. "And you heard the gentlemen say what romanticism gets you out here in this brave new world you think so much of . . ."

"And Sharp being here," said Lucy. "That's good, isn't it?"

"Maybe," said Cait.

"Maybe?"

Lucy was filled with a very strong urge to hit Cait, just to get a reaction from her. She bunched her fists and jammed them in the pocket of her coat, sitting hunched and miserable in front of the fire.

"A lot of things could have happened in London while we were on the voyage over," said Cait. "But as to this plan, once the Tittensor woman's dog is here, if it gets me west, we go with it. And if we see Jack Sharp, no one'll be more please than I."

Lucy waited for her to thank her for enabling it, but Cait just walked over to the Murano Cabinet and examined it as if Lucy was no longer in the room.

As they closed the door to the meeting room behind them—and discreetly bolted it—Magill spoke softly to his taller partner.

"She didn't know about the lead tablets," said Magill. "The Harker girl."

"Saw that," said Armbruster.

"Trouble you?" said Magill.

"Her ring's real. I looked close," said Armbruster leading the way up the stairs.

"But she doesn't seem to know about Sharp's mission over here."

"She's a young one, Jon. Maybe they don't share everything," said Armbruster.

"Well. They're not going anywhere. I like 'em. Both feisty in their ways," said Magill. "Younger one's troubled by something, wears it like a cloud, but who isn't troubled by something? 'Cept you. You're troubled by everything."

"I'll be less troubled by them when Sharp gets a look at them and confirms they're both who they say they are," said Armbruster.

"Well, it won't be long. We said we'd step through tomorrow, didn't we?"

"We did."

"Well, how much trouble can they get into in one night?" said Magill. "We'll take them to meet Sharp when we make the rendezvous. You keep an eye on the Lucy girl, I'll keep mine on the redhead. Now let's go tell the Guardian we'll take 'em off her hands."

"Why do you get to watch the redhead?" said Armbruster.

"I'm just guarding her, Fred, not taking her to a damn cotillion . . ."

CHAPTER 35

A SCOWLE BY MOONLIGHT

The Herne had found the Sluagh at the rendezvous that had been set deep within a certain scowle in a wild and largely untravelled area of woodland in the Forest of Dean, "scowles" being the local name for the peculiar rock formations which the entanglement of ancient trees grew out of, a moss-covered maze of pits, hollows and shake-holes, some of which led to secret caverns formed by erosion of the natural underground cave networks that interlaced their way through the limestone beneath.

"Mountfellon is at Gallstaine," he told Badger Skull.

"Good," said Badger Skull. "We will do what we must do here for the fallen Woodcock Crown he violated, and then we shall go north and violate him in the same manner."

"No," said the Herne. "He is unreachable."

The Sluagh band growled in disappointment. The Herne held up his hand.

"He has a stream of running water circling the house, and I have watched long enough to see he will not cross it. He only moves by the bright light of noon, and I suspect if he travels it will be by fast coach and by daylight."

A rumble of protest grew, again waved down by the Herne, whose bone dogs stood on either side of him—tense as bowstrings—like guards.

"There is another who came to meet him. By sight and by smell, I think him to be an old family of daywalkers known to us. I think he is a Templebane."

"Issachar Templebane is known to us, but he is gone from London and we do not know where to find him," said Badger Skull.

"Or whether to trust him," said the Woodcock Crown. "Or just skin him too."

There was another low rumble of agreement.

"Whichever," said the Herne. "I marked your words about mayhap getting to Mountfellon through his friends, and so I followed him and have found where he and his sons are hiding."

"Then we should go and visit him when we are done here," said Badger Skull, quieting the murmur of the band with a sharp gesture of his hand. "Maybe we should ask him what this business is that takes him to Mountfellon's lair."

There was a general murmur of approval and then, all of a sudden, a woman's voice cut through it like a clear bell and stilled it instantly.

"Well met, the Sluagh."

It was a deep voice for a woman, and Badger Skull turned from the Herne, who took the opportunity to twitch his head at the bone hounds and fade into the night before the Sluagh and the band at his back were able to take their attention away from the indistinct forms flowing out of the scrabble of darkness in front of them.

"And well met, the Shee, for here you are," said Badger Skull. "As and where you always are."

And he bowed his head in greeting as a tall woman stepped into a slash of moonlight. One side of her head was clean-shaven, and on the other her hair was long, thick and braided with the bones of small animals. A thick tracery of tattoos circled her head in a band running sideways between her eyebrow and her cheekbones, so it looked as if she was wearing a mask of coarse black lace. The eyes that held Badger Skull's were steady, blue and unusually pale.

"We are Shee. You are Sluagh," she said with a ghost of a shrug. "You choose to troop abroad. We choose to remain."

Behind her, a large band of women coalesced out of the tenebrous landscape, all dressed in variations of the theme she set. Her clothes were a long patched leather tunic worn beneath a black and white cloak of magpies' feathers, the tunic fastened with a wide belt, slit at both sides to reveal doeskin leggings tucked into high, well-worn boots. The whole was decorated with animal bones, like the Sluagh, and around her long neck she wore a thick necklace made from barnacled limpets with a single hawk skull hanging at the centre of it, the beak plated with beaten silver which caught the moonlight as she moved.

His lips peeled back in a smile as he reached for her.

"Shee and Sluagh are but two sides of the same leaf, wife."

She shook her head and stepped away from his hand.

"You and I are no mere leaf, husband. Leafs wither, fall, die."

"And what are we then?" he said, conscious that the band of Sluagh behind him had seen his overture if not rejected, neatly sidestepped.

"We are an endless war, broken by truces," she said. Behind her, the other Shee laughed in quiet approval. He hoisted one side of his mouth higher, turning the smile into a vulpine leer.

"I like the truces."

The Sluagh at his back laughed now, a low ribald sound compared to the more controlled laughter of the women. He reached for her again, and once more she neatly stepped out of his reach.

"And I the absences," she said. "In your absence things can grow."

A tic of irritation jerked the tattooed lines on his face.

"You do not just mean bellies and children."

"I mean lives. And thinking. And plans."

"You have plans," he said, dropping to sit on the ground with a sigh. "And we have actions. Did you not marvel at how we broke the Iron Prohibition?"

"It was marvellous," she said, looking down at him. "But only of real interest to you, who like to go among the daywalkers. To us, who have no interest in their doings, it is less so."

"Were you always so hard to impress?" he said with more bitterness than good humour.

"I hope so," she said, almost smiling for the first time.

"But the Iron Prohibition," he said.

"It was a great deed," she said and neatly sat herself against the mound opposite him. "But too late. It was a deed for the old days, for the time when our forefathers made legends of themselves. Now the time for such things has been overtaken by the daywalkers and the Hungry World. You have broken the chain of iron, but they will still come. It will not stop them. The quiet places and the lonely retreats will be probed and broken and lost."

"So they win?" he spat.

"Yes," she said. "Maybe they do, if you see everything as a battle. But they do not win because they are right, or more virtuous, or braver or more cunning, husband. They just win because there are more of them, and they have found a way to move faster and dig deeper than we ever can."

"I thought we came to bury the Woodcock Crown," he scowled, "not our hopes."

"I did not say we should bury our hopes," she said. "I said we should make new plans."

"New plans for a new world," he hissed, shaking his head. "You've started to sound like one of them."

"And you say that as if it's a bad thing," she said, cocking her head on one side, giving him a long look.

"Change is weakness," he said. "We are Pure because we do not change. Change is betrayal."

"And those are just words," she said. "But if you stay still and watch things grow—from a seed to a tree, from a cub to a fox, from the fleshly pleasure of a . . . truce, to the laughter of the child that comes from it and on to the strength of the woman or man that child grows into—you cannot see change as a bad thing: you see it as life itself."

"You would have us betray our history?" he said. "Our long past?"

"No," she said. "I would have you think. But maybe if you stopped holding onto that past by running away from the present, maybe if you stayed still and thought sometimes instead of always being moving and doing, you might come to see things as we have come to see them. And we might have a future."

She rose fluidly to her feet. The rest of the Shee rose with her as one.

"Now let us go and bury this crown. And if you are congenial afterwards, maybe I will tell you what news came to me by a raven from the northern isles."

"A raven from the north?" he said, shock and disbelief writhing across the inked lines on his face. "From her? But . . . I thought she was long gone under the hill . . ."

"Oh no," smiled the Shee, nimbly ducking under an overhanging branch. "Beira was just silent. And watching. And it is not her who is gone under the hill . . ."

CHAPTER 36

THE OLD ENEMY AND A NEW RECRUIT

"This is a grotesquery," said Sharp, looking around The Citizen's rooms. "Saving your graces, Sara, but you don't have to be a Glint to know that very bad things have happened here."

Now the fighting and the adrenalin that went with it was over, he had lit candles and they'd been able to take a proper survey of the place. And when he looked closer, it was clear that the dead Wights and the blood sprayed on the ceiling and pooling treacherously on the floors was not the most horrific thing about it. The second tiled chamber was the worst thing, with the cages and the dissecting slab and the rows of shiny medical instruments and things that looked as if they would be more at home in a butcher's shop.

"They have been experimenting on these creatures, and maybe worse," said Hodge, who had been admitted by the back door. Archie and Jed had been sent to search the house and see if their noses could sense anything that might have been missed.

Hodge, perhaps because of his affinity with animals and the self-taught healer's expertise gained by patching Jed up over the years, had immediately examined the Sluagh—whom he confirmed was insensible, possibly permanently—and then, very carefully and gently, had been trying unsuccessfully to look at the Green Man's mouth. Amos stood by him, endeavouring to help by calming the terrified patient.

He just wants to see your mouth to free it.

Hodge smiled encouragingly and drew a small knife from his pocket, pointed at his mouth and used it to pantomime cutting the stitches.

The Green Man hunched his chin into his chest and shook his head wildly. Amos looked at Hodge.

He hurts. He wants to be in the open air. Away from all the buildings.

"I know fine what he wants and what he needs: he can find the wildwood and the deep green again, easy as pie," said Hodge. "But with a mind shot like his, and his mouth sewn shut, he'll starve in a week. I just want to cut the stitches for him."

He just sees the blade.

Amos's eyes travelled to the rack of surgical instruments.

I think he has seen too much of what blades do.

"It's for his own good, and who are you exactly?" said Hodge, frustrated. Amos held out his badge.

"Templebane?" said Hodge. "What . . .?"

"Oh for goodness' sake, we do not have time," said Sara, who had regained control of herself and was compensating for having uncharacteristically lost that iron restraint by being brisker than usual. "The four of you take the Sluagh and the Green Man back to The Folley. Cook can care for them with Hodge, we can see if they have any information that would help us and you, Amos Templebane, can explain yourself later."

She stepped across to the Green Man, took a deep breath and knelt by him, forcing herself to crouch closer and look in his eyes.

"I can do it," said Sharp.

"Yes," said Sara. "But I must."

She held out her ring. By an act of sheer willpower, her hand no longer shook.

"By oak, ash and thorn, I ask this: you will look in my face. You will look in my face so that we can help you."

Slowly, the head came up and their eyes locked. The Green Man's seemed to fizz with tension. He flinched as Sara reached forward and placed the stamp of the seal firmly on his forehead, and then the eyes smoothed out as if going somewhere else for a while.

"And now by Lore and Law, you will sleep, and when you wake, you will be in a place of safety away from the city close by the free-flowing river and the woods. You will let yourself be helped and healed, if healing is possible. But now you will be calm and you will sleep and dream of the Greenwood."

The Green Man nodded and kept nodding, slower each time, and then the wide staring eyes fluttered like moths, and his head dropped and he slept. Sara stepped back and looked at the others.

"I owe you all an apology," she said. "The Green Man, this . . . being, this tortured creature, he surprised me and . . . well, if I had been born the boy my grandfather wanted so badly, I would say he unmanned me for a moment: I don't know if you can be unwomanned, but the effect is the same, and I became what I was once. A child. When I was that child, my grandfather inadvertently let a Green Man who had run mad loose in the house. It chased me, and I have never, ever been so scared. And I shamefully panicked and I . . ."

She shrugged and took a deep breath.

"I think that after that event I decided to become what I am so I would never be that frightened little girl again. I thought if I looked into the shadows and faced what was lurking there, I would be able to stare down my fears. It turns out that I am not quite the woman I thought I'd become . . ."

"Nonsense," said Sharp.

"It's not nonsense, Jack," said Sara. "And if I have an Achilles heel, at least I know where it is. Maybe that's a little like facing down those things in the shadows. Anyway. I am ashamed to have shown that weakness, but I'm sure tomorrow, in the cold light of day . . ." She grinned and let Sharp pull her to her feet, squeezing his hand as she did so. He returned the pressure before releasing it. ". . . I'll be twice as embarrassed about it." She looked at Hodge, who pretended that he and Jed hadn't noticed the unaccustomedly intimate gesture at all.

"Can you take them back in the dog cart?"

"I don't think the Sluagh'd normally let us take him over flowing water, but he's out of it, so shouldn't be a problem," said Hodge.

"We could give him to the Sluagh waiting at the Gut," said Sharp.

"You think that's a good idea?" she said.

"An act of goodwill," said Sharp. "Unless they take it the wrong way."

"They're Sluagh," said Charlie. "The wrong way is how they do things."

Sara nodded at Sharp.

"Just make it clear we did not do this, that we rescued . . . whatever is left of him."

"I don't know if there's much left except a pulse," said Hodge, pointing at the silver cannula in the tattooed arm. "Whatever the bastard who was keeping him in here was doing was bad enough, and then these blood thieves must have drained whatever was left. Don't know how his heart's still pumping, because there's damn all blood in him. He's dry as a stick of kindling."

Sara beckoned Amos. He was looking almost as white-faced and drained as the Sluagh had been beneath the pale tattoos.

"You know. I cannot trust you."

I know.

"What do you want from us?"

Sanctuary.

"We do not offer sanctuary," said Sharp.

"But you acted selflessly in saving the Green Man," said Sara. "It would be unbalanced if we were not to match that . . . kindness."

"Sara—" said Sharp.

"Go with the others. We will give you food for the night and a safe place to sleep. And if you behave, we may talk in the cold light of day, when things are calmer," she said, and nodded at Charlie.

Thank you.

Amos felt his eyes growing hot and moist again.

Thank you.

Sharp swallowed what he was clearly wanting to say, and he and Sara stood back as Hodge carried the Sluagh from the room. Charlie and Amos took the shoulders and feet of the snoring Green Man and followed him. Sara's hand snaked out and stopped Ida, who had moved to follow them. They waited in silence until they heard the back door creak, and then Sara spoke.

"Tell Cook all he did, and that I glinted him killing another Templebane in their house. He's capable of very fast violence, and I'm not sure if he can control it. But he takes no pleasure in it. Please ask her if she senses what I do in him."

"Which is?" said Sharp.

"Which is that the Templebanes may have been raising a cuckoo in their nest," she said. "He may just be on the right side of things."

"Or he may be a wonderfully gifted dissembler," said Sharp.

"He may be," said Sara. "But I cannot see why he'd risk his life to try and save a creature like that."

"To make us think he was on your 'right side of things' perhaps," said Sharp.

"I think he's damaged. But not bad," said Ida with a shrug.

"Tell Cook to feed and water him and see what comes next," said Sara. "And you and Charlie keep clear of the kitchen while she does it. She'll work better undisturbed."

"Work?" said Ida.

"Cook can tease things out in a way no one else can," said Sara. "She can quiz people without them even noticing they're being drained of all their secrets. She'll get a measure of this youngster better than any of us."

Ida nodded and flitted away.

Sharp and Sara went to work searching the chambers.

"It's like a surgeon's dissecting room back here," said Sharp from the depths of the back room, eyeing the dissecting table and the cages as he ran his hand over the white tiled walls. He opened the door to a large incinerating stove set into the wall.

"Or a charnel house. I'd advise against touching these tiles with your bare hand. I think you'd see a lot of pain and blood."

Sara nodded. She was crouched in front of the door to the mirrored cabinet, working the hinge, trying to see if the looking-glass back wall also opened, which it didn't.

"So this is how the Wights got in," she said. "It still makes me shudder to think of the world beyond this glass."

Sharp joined her.

"Knowing what's there does make me mistrust every mirror I pass these days," he admitted. "Now I understand that they truly are looking-glasses, not because we look into them, but because all manner of malignity might be behind them, looking out at us." He scowled at his own reflection. "For all we know, there's another of those murderous black-toothed blood-stealers staring at us right now."

"I know," she said. "If we had time, it'd make your skin crawl to think of it, but we don't have time. Look at how this thing is constructed: it's like a Murano. Smaller, plainer, but the same principle: mirrored inside, glass held parallel when the door is closed, a sconce here for a light to preserve a reflection and a connection. I don't know what the little bell on the spring is for, nor this clip . . ."

"Let us just be very clear and agreed on this one thing, Sara: we are absolutely not going in the mirrors again," said Sharp. "Not without a get-you-home."

"No," she agreed, peeling off her glove. "No more mirrors."

"Good," he said, and before she could stop him, he had taken a knife from his belt and used the butt of the handle to smash the glass, clearly taking pleasure in the release the momentary violence gave him as he comprehensively disabled the cabinet. He stepped back and looked at the shards on the floor with a nod of satisfaction.

"Better?" she said.

"No," he said, sheathing the weapon. "But if Mountfellon or the damned Citizen has been using this cabinet to come and go, as the Wights said, they can damn well stay gone."

"I hope we don't regret that," she said, looking at the pieces of glass scattered on the floor.

"Well, we certainly do not have enough of us to just sit here, waiting to trap him as or if he comes back," said Sharp. "So I'll settle for disrupting him where we can, and if he stays lost in the mirrors as a result, well, I could not think of a more fitting end."

Sara shrugged.

"Well. It is done. But I am still going to see what's been happening in this house."

He reached out and gently took her hand. The look she gave him was anything but gentle, but he kept his soft grip on her gloveless palm.

"I would not presume to tell you what to do, but I would point out you are exhausted, have not fully recovered from your previous ordeals, that glinting is a great drain on your vitality at the best of times and that, perilously reduced as our numbers are, we cannot afford another . . . indisposition."

"We cannot afford not to know what's been happening here," she said.

"You yourself think you may collapse," he replied, reaching for her arm. "It's why you sent the others away. You didn't want them to see you if that happened."

"Well," she said after a pause. "I let you stay."

"Sara. You don't have to do penance because the shock of the Green Man caught you at a low ebb and brought back the great distress of your childhood."

"I am not doing penance," she said, taking a step away from him. He kept his grip on her arm. "I am doing my job. I am going to touch the walls. You know I have trained myself to moderate my glinting and, to an extent, control it and direct it in search of memories trapped in the stones that are connected with my concerns. It is not an exact thing, but I can—if you will allow me to stay calm and focused and undisturbed— direct the inflow of the past and use it as an interrogatory tool."

"That takes a great deal out of you," he said. "That is—"

"That is why I would like to get this done while I still feel energetic.

I will glint to see who has been here and what clues it may give us as to what is going on. I hope most strongly that the glinting spares me any flashes of what has been going on in that torture chamber behind us, but if not, it is most likely from past experience that I may reacquaint us with what I ate for supper," she said. "So I apologise in advance for the indelicacy you may be about to witness, and would advise you to stand behind me while I do this, to spare your boots a spattering."

"Sara—" he said quietly. She shook him off with a curt jerk of the head.

"If I fall, you may catch me," she said. "But until then, be so kind as to unhand me and let me get to it."

CHAPTER 37

THE TWIG AND THE RILL

Issachar Templebane walked in the moonlit orchard and listened to the distant church clock almost chime thirteen, it being a quirk of the mechanism that the striking train was poorly aligned and had a habit of letting the hammer come to rest just kissing the bells lightly at the end of each series of chimes, instead of being held clear, which meant there was always the ghost of an extra chime. It was a local quirk which everyone had ceased to notice, but Issachar always waited for it. In his mind the almost-sound was like the shadow of midnight. For him, it symbolised the added part of things, the dimension beyond the normal, the aspects of the world that others could not see or give credence to, but which he and his had always studied and traded upon.

"You're not afraid," said a patch of darkness by a gnarled tree trunk.

"Of course I'm afraid," said Issachar, stopping. "So what? Only a fool would not be afraid of the dark."

"And the things in it," said the voice.

"Indeed," said Issachar.

"And yet you have stopped walking with one or other of your sons keeping watch over you with a loaded gun," said the Sluagh, detaching from the tree he had been leaning on. "You do not carry iron."

"I do not wish my sons to know all my business, and I am aware you no longer feel the repulsive quality of cold iron. So why would I carry a protectant that no longer worked?"

"What business?" said the Sluagh. "We have no need of your business any more. The flag you tried to bargain with us for is gone. We are freed. We do not need you except for one thing—"

"Everyone needs an honest broker," said Issachar. "I did not cheat you or mislead you."

"You did not get us the flag," said the Sluagh.

"That you took your own way to take it is not a fault of mine," said Issachar. "I would have got it for you. I congratulate you on your success, but the truth remains the truth: I did not fail you, and in fact you prevented me from making good on our deal by jumping the gun."

"Jumping the gun?" said the Sluagh. "We took what was ours!"

"And do you have Mountfellon?" said Issachar.

There was a short interlude of almost complete silence, then another patch of shadow stepped out and resolved itself into a Sluagh wearing a badger skull on its forehead.

"That is the one thing. What do you know of Mountfellon?"

"I know you destroyed his collection. That displayed a great rage. I saw the damage. I felt your anger."

"He skinned one of us and hung his bone cage like an ornament," spat Badger Skull. "We will be revenged on him."

"Not if you can't get to him," said Issachar. "And you can't."

"He cannot hide behind iron bars any more," said Badger Skull with a snarl.

"No," said Issachar, stepping across the rill and snapping a twig from the apple tree. "Do you know what this is?"

"A twig."

"What kind of twig?"

"A twig from an apple tree."

"What else?"

"What else does it need to be?" said Badger Skull. "A twig is a twig."

"The tree is Braddick's Nonpareil. My brother Zebulon liked the apples;

he used to say they were like biting into Old England itself," said Issachar, twirling the twig between his fingers. "But then that was the kind of fanciful thing he would say occasionally, being the whimsical one of the family. They are certainly strong-tasting, sharp and a little like honey that has gone sour: not as bad a taste as you might think."

"What do I care?" said Badger Skull tightly.

"You don't," said Issachar. "I'm just demonstrating that I know things that you do not."

"Useless things that would only interest a light-grubbing bug like yourself," said Badger Skull.

"Ah. But no knowledge is useless," said Templebane. "All knowledge has value to someone, somewhere. And trading knowledge is what I do. What we always have done. Light-grubbing bugs we may be to your eyes, but the Templebanes have always traded with the Sluagh, knowledge for knowledge, aid for aid."

Badger Skull and the other Sluagh stood looking at him in the moonlight. The night was hushed and scarcely a leaf moved in the still air. There was something in Templebane's demeanour that prevented Badger Skull from asking him for help, though that was what he had come for. It wasn't that he didn't trust him—which he didn't—it was that every transaction with a Templebane left him feeling toyed with. Maybe, he thought, he should just kill him and be done. Maybe the Herne's plan was a bad one. He remembered the Shee, however, and rather than leaping at the fat man with his blade, he stopped to think. The only sound was the light babble of the rill and something small shrieking in the woods at the bottom of the drive. Issachar waited and did not blanch beneath the weight of their scrutiny.

"You are scared," said Badger Skull after a while. "You would not be justifying yourself if you were not trying to persuade me of your friendship."

"Of course I'm afraid, but I am not unmanned by it, and nor am I your friend," said Issachar, voice blunt as a hammer. "I am something much more useful and reliable to you: I am your go-between."

"Go-between?"

"Go-between, jobber, broker, middle-man—call it what you will. I get what you cannot get for yourself," said Issachar. "Sometimes even things you don't yet know you need."

"And what do you sell that we could possibly now need?" said Badger Skull.

"Intelligence," said Issachar. "Knowledge. Offered, as I have said, by an honest broker."

"A 'broker,' you say," rasped Badger Skull, and he spat contemptuously on the moon-silvered grass. "I broke the Iron Prohibition. I do not need you."

"Then break this twig," said Issachar, holding it out. "If you broke the Iron Prohibition and think that means you don't need me and what I can do for you all, just break this twig."

The Sluagh snorted.

"I'm not here to play games."

"Then break the twig and prove it," said Issachar.

"Why don't I break it and then stab both jaggy ends in your ears?" said Badger Skull. "I could do that, you know. Just for being a friend to Mountfellon."

"I am no friend of his. Our relationship was purely professional. But if you think you can, be my guest: here is the twig and here are my ears at your disposal."

Badger Skull stepped forward, hand outstretched, and then stopped with a jerk. He tried to walk forward, but his body rebelled. He exhaled in a tight grunt of frustration.

He looked down at the thin rill which ran between them.

"Iron no longer confounds you, but you cannot cross running water," said Issachar.

"You are not telling me anything yet that I do not know," growled Badger Skull.

"And yet you thought you could break this twig," said Issachar.

"You think it is clever or wise to make sport of us?" said Badger Skull, and held up his hand.

Shadows moved and rippled and resolved into a host of Sluagh standing in a rough perimeter of the portion of the orchard on his side of the rill.

Issachar quelled the cold fear that ran up his spine at the sight of so many nightwalkers so close to him. He knew that he was only safe on his side of the rill for a while, and that the Sluagh had their convoluted ancient paths through the countryside, one of which would inevitably lead them to his side sooner or later. In fact, for all he knew, other Sluagh were in the darkness behind him. It was not beyond the Sluagh to have already planned a pincer movement and sent others along that tangled path ahead of this meeting. And with that in mind, and acutely conscious that the fortunes of the house of Templebane were at a perilously low ebb, he did what a normally cautious broker never does, except when it is absolutely necessary and unavoidable. He did it knowing that if he did not adjust to the realignment of powers consequent on both his failed attempt on The Oversight and the eradication of the Iron Prohibition he was lost anyway.

He stepped back across the rill and put the twig in Badger Skull's hand.

"Why?" said Badger Skull. "Why do you think I will not do what I said I would do?"

"Because you are no fool," said Issachar. "You just forgot to notice something for a moment. We all make those small mistakes; the secret is to adjust and correct ourselves when we do."

"I could be no fool and still kill you," said Badger Skull, looking at the twig.

"You are not going to kill me," said Issachar. "You are going to let me give you a present. And then we are going to make a deal. Just like old times."

"I need no present," said Badger Skull.

"It is just a piece of information," said Issachar. "My stock in trade, as it were. It is the present whereabouts of Francis Blackdyke, Viscount Mountfellon."

"He is at Gallstaine Hall, protected by running water which we cannot cross," rasped Badger Skull, throwing the twig and grabbing Issachar by the throat. "Tell me something I do not know, and you may live."

"You do not need get to him at Gallstaine," said Issachar, his voice beginning to strangle. "Your b—broker has the means by which he can be lured into the open, away from his place of safety and put at your mercy."

There was a pause as his eyes bugged with the pressure around his throat and Badger Skull stared into them, his grip unshakeable.

"You can do this?" he hissed, releasing his grip on Templebane's throat.

Templebane gasped for air, and then straightened and held out a hand, rubbing his neck with the other.

"The old deal. Like for like, aid for aid, and my word is, as ever, my bond," he said.

"And yet you betray Mountfellon," said Badger Skull.

"No," said Issachar. "He betrayed me. I am merely retaliating, as I said, like for like—"

"Mountfellon wants power," interrupted the Sluagh. "What do you want?"

"I want protection from The Oversight," said Issachar. "They think I tried to destroy them. I do not think they know where I am, nor that they can, in their reduced state, operate far outside London. But they will be coming for me."

"And did you try to destroy them?" said Badger Skull.

"Of course," said Issachar. "They were becoming an obstacle to my honest trade."

Badger Skull grinned.

"Well. I cannot fault you for that. But what else do you want, broker-man? What do you want to survive *for*?"

"I want to let the great men and fools scrabble for what they think is power, while I make a profit by going between them," said Templebane. "For if my family's history proves anything, it is that the great and the deluded come and go, as their power and wealth waxes and wanes, but the brokers remain. And people always want information."

The Sluagh reached out and gripped his hand.

"The old alliance," he said. "Like for like, aid for aid, if you bring us to Mountfellon."

"We get to Mountfellon by giving him what he thinks he wants," said Issachar, shaking the cold hand of the Sluagh. "And it may be that in doing that we deliver a fatal blow to The Oversight into the bargain."

CHAPTER 38

THE VIOLATION

Sara had walked through the house, her hand trailing the stone and the plasterwork, pausing as she sifted through the fragments of the past recorded in the walls. It was a draining process, trying to keep calm enough to trace a single path through a three-dimensional maze full of nasty surprises that could jump out and bite you just when you least expected it.

It had taken her no time to ascertain that The Citizen had been a guest here for a considerable while, news which had led to Sharp reacting to the news with an oath, the only time she had ever heard him swear. She had been similarly appalled that their greatest enemy, the man who had been responsible for the death of her parents and eighty-three of their companions, had been quietly ensconced in their city without them even having a hint of it, but the business of controlled glinting required a smooth mind to succeed so she put this thought away to unpack and examine later, and continued.

On the first floor there was a small salon leading off the main room: it was a well-proportioned space, with high ceilings, a bookcase on one side, tall windows glazed with the opaque milk-glass with which Mountfellon secured his privacy, a hard parquet floor on which stood an elegant chaise-longue upholstered in faded rose silk and, on the wall at right angles to it, a large painting or mirror hung with a sombre dust-cloth like a shroud.

"Well, this is a more pleasant room," said Sharp.

"No," said Sara, teeth gritting as she trailed her hand along the plaster-work. "No. It isn't."

Time jagged and bit into her as she found the most pungent strand of the room's history hiding in the warp and weft of the varied pasts recorded in the walls.

Sara went rigid as she glinted an earlier night lit by candles.

A young woman sat on the chaise-longue—which was disconcertingly in quite another part of the salon, beneath a large giltwood pier-glass which reflected the flames of the many candles lining the room.

Her blonde hair was neatly put up in a style more than two decades out of fashion, and she wore a pale blue dress which looked well on the faded rose of the chaise-longue.

She was reading.

And then time jumped and a man was in the room, tall, young, dark-haired, smiling and sliding onto the seat next to her, carefully taking the book from her hand and replacing it with a glass of champagne.

Sara gasped as she saw the profile and recognised it.

It was the young Mountfellon.

And then the two of them were sitting comfortably together, and the candles were lower, and he was opening a second bottle of champagne.

They both laughed as the cork popped, bouncing off the plasterwork and hitting the door with a loud smacking noise.

"The servants!" she said, laughing.

"I have locked the door," he smiled. "No one will surprise us."

He filled her glass and then his own.

"Do you love me?" he whispered.

Sara felt unclean, watching the intimacy, this private moment of love, for that was what she saw glowing in the young woman's eyes, that and a kind of mischievous sparkle.

"Why, Lord Mountfellon!" she said. "You know I hold you in the highest affection, to be sure."

"Don't joke," he said. "Do you?"

"Francis," she said, and the warmth was still in her eyes.

"Do you?" he said, more urgent now. And Sara sees his eyes have their own warmth, but a very different one, one that surrounds them and makes them seem hot and uncomfortable.

He turns and fills her glass.

Unseen by her, he pours a powder into it.

Then time jolts.

And the young woman has moved away. Not far, just a hand's breadth, and she is laughing and leaning back on the arm of the chaise-longue and he is not laughing but he is leaning forward.

Time slices again

and he is touching her.

And she is not laughing.

She is blinking too much and not quite right. Her face is flushed.

She is pressed against the arm of the divan. But she is talking, and trying to make light.

"No," she says. "Francis. It is the wine. I feel a little—"

His smile is no longer young or happy or kind.

"It is these new friends," he says. "This group, this sect you have joined, whose damned ring you wear."

"You know nothing of them," she laughs, trying to cajole him back to a sunnier place. "And you a Man of Science, judging without observation, surely that is poor practice—"

"Do not mock me," he says, his lip curling. "I do not apologise for being an open, rational man who seeks to understand the physical world. If the Royal Society was good enough for Newton, it is good enough for me. It is not some damned secret sect of charlatans."

He lifts her hand. Twists it cruelly to show her the ring.

"Francis," she says, trying to laugh. "You hurt. It is not a sect. It is a Free Company."

"How can it be free when you are not at liberty to tell me about—?"

"I cannot," she laughs, but now the sound is forced and something close to fear has taken the place of warmth.

"I want you," he says, reaching for her.

A small explosion of crystal at her feet.

Her champagne glass, dropped to the parquet.

"No, Francis!" she says.

She looks down at her smashed glass and then her hand, as if surprised it should have let the thing slip.

"What have you done?"

His smile is a travesty.

"It is not only you who can have secrets."

She shakes her head fast three times, as if trying to loosen the grip of whatever has her fumbling at things.

Time slices. Sara gasps.

The woman says,

"NO, Francis."

Material rips.

"No . . . don't . . . please! this is not right . . .!"

"It is right," he snarls. "It is MY right!"

Buttons ping across the parquet floor.

And she fights.

Kicks at him.

Squirms an arm free of his grip.

Throws a punch. Hard.

He jerks his head back.

Sara sees the fist hit the giltwood on the frame of the chaise—hears the crack as the stone in the ring breaks.

Sees the gouge in the wood.

Mountfellon laughs now.

Then gasps as her second punch smashes into his cheek.

A glancing blow.

Leaves a red furrow.

Broken ring scoring a blood trail into the side of his nose.

He snarls.

Time slices again.

Weight and strength have prevailed.

Sara cannot shut her eyes, however hard she tries. Caught in the inexorable grip of the glinted moment.

And of all the bad things she has been forced to witness through her gift, this is one of the worst.

Not the physical violation alone.

The girl's eyes.

The initial disbelief, the innocence destroyed, the love dying as he—

And then time slices

Mercifully, for once

And now the candles have guttered and only a few cast a much dimmer light over the aftermath.

He sits on a chair at a distance. Wiping blood from himself.

Coldly watching her make herself outwardly whole again. Fumbled fingers trying to match torn buttonholes with absent buttons.

She is in pain.

She is scared.

But she is something else too, and whatever this new hard thing is, she is becoming it in front of Sara's eyes.

"Please open the door," she says calmly.

"I think you have all but broken my nose," he says, equally calmly.

She looks down at her ring. It is broken. Half the bloodstone is missing.

"And you have broken my ring," she said.

She does not care.

"What did you put in my drink to muffle me so?"

"It does not matter," he said.

"No. I suppose it does not. Please open the door, Milord."

He reaches for her hand. In the circumstances, the smile on his face is grotesque.

"Not until you call me Francis again. Come. It was not so bad . . ."

She steps away.

"I will call you Francis," she says, rationally, calmly, "but only when I return and stop your heart as you have killed mine."

She walks straight towards the chaise-longue and then, without pausing, steps up on it and takes a further step

into the mirror

and passes right through it.

Mountfellon spasms off his chair, which falls back with a crash as he stands there frozen in disbelieving shock.

"How?" he chokes as he stumbles across the floor and puts his hand to the surface of the mirror, which stops it dead.

"But . . . how?"

Sara can see every detail of his face, clearly reflected in the mirror.

It is a rare thing to see the moment of transmutation, the moment a life steps from one state to another and she has seen two in these painful shards of the past.

She has seen an innocence violated and lost, and its replacement by a blunt resolve towards vengeance.

And now she is seeing the violator's eyes as the steely and self-proclaimed Man of Science is presented with irrefutable evidence that there is another set of rules which disproves the very system by which he had held the world works.

His eyes stutter as he comes to understand that the rational mechanism which he thought underpinned things was no more than a first layer hiding a second and more arcane clockwork by which the universe is really governed.

Sara is witnessing a mind convulsing and deciding not to judge itself mad. She is seeing the birth of obsession.

The shock has changed the young Mountfellon.

He no longer looks stunned and disbelieving. He looks hungry, and fiercely so.

He looks made anew and now wholly consumed by the need to control the supranatural world and all of its hidden clockwork.

And then glinting ended and the past stopped jolting into her and Sara felt Sharp catch her shoulders and she leant there for a moment, allowing herself the luxury of being held up.

And then she nodded and turned to look into his worried face.

"What?" he said.

She needed time to absorb what she'd seen, and the implications of it. She walked to the chaise-longue, now—disorientatingly—at right angles to where it had just been in her mind. She bent and looked at its giltwood back, running her gloved hand along it, finding the dint where the woman had broken her ring.

She pointed at the shrouded frame on the wall.

"Do you know what that is?" she said.

"A painting?"

"It's a pier-glass," she said.

He crossed and twitched the material hanging over it, revealing the reflective surface. He let the material fall back.

"Just as well to leave i—" he began.

"Jack," she said. "I think I know who Lucy Harker is."

And he came and stood with her, his hand on her arm as she told him.

And when she had, he shook his head in incredulity.

"So then . . . Mountfellon is her father?"

"I think he might be. He raped the young woman, and she was wearing the ring, the ring that was broken, the one Lucy showed us and said was the only thing she had of her mother . . ."

"Do you think Lucy knows?"

"No," she said. "No. I don't think so."

"Let us go home," he said. "We can come back whenever we wish. But you are exhausted."

"Yes," she said. "I think I am. And I want to see what Cook has made of that Amos Templebane."

"You think we can use him?"

"I want to know if she thinks we can trust him. Because if we can, maybe he can help us get inside Coram Templebane's head, as you and Hodge were unable to do."

"That's a risk," said Sharp.

"At this stage, it's all risk," she said. "That's why we need good judgement. And no one's a better judge than Cook."

They left by the front door.

"Leave it unlocked," said Sara, thinking of Ida. "If Mountfellon gets burgled, so much the better, but in truth I do not think anyone would try the front door on such a public street, and we can get back in without trouble on the morrow, if we need to."

They stepped onto the pavement and moved fast into the side streets, heading east.

They did not notice the Ghost.

But she had been watching the door, alarmed at having woken to find Amos gone from his post. And as soon as they were out of sight, she flitted across the cobbles and proved Sara's judgement to be entirely wrong, as she opened the front door and slipped inside, almost without anyone seeing her at all.

High in the face of the house opposite, the whey-faced child who could not sleep was at her customary position, nose pressed against the pane of her bedroom window. If anyone else in her house was awake, she might have told them what she saw, but they weren't, and she yawned and watched on.

The Ghost stood in the middle of the high-ceilinged hallway and listened, and for a very long time the building was silent as the grave. And then she began to search the house like a silent wraith, moving from the basement to the attic. She armed herself with a brutal dissecting knife from The Citizen's study. And when she came downstairs, she faced the one door she had yet to try.

She carefully eased open the door to the salon with the shrouded pierglass and stood in the doorway, knife at her side.

CHAPTER 39

NIGHT AND THE DREADNOUGHT PORTER

The dog cart slowed as they approached the narrow bridge spanning the water that flowed through The Gut, the thin steep-sided channel separating the Isle of Dogs from the rest of London. Hodge loosened the knife in his belt and noticed, from the sudden lightening of the springs, that Ida had dropped silently off the back. At the edge of his vision he caught a flicker as she ran wide of them, taking up a covering position in the shadows, with a good line of sight towards the spot where the three Sluagh had taken up their semi-permanent residence.

A second creak of the springs told him Charlie had dismounted and was now walking alongside.

"Easy now," muttered Hodge. "Keep your blades out of sight. Don't want to set them off. This is going to be ticklish enough as it is."

He wasn't entirely comfortable with the idea of presenting the Sluagh with a severely damaged and abused member of their tribe. It was a situation ripe with potential for things to tumble into violence before explanations could be given or heard. However, he knew the Sluagh would be able to minister to him better than they could, and he had severe reservations about whether the thing would survive transit across the running water. It was the nature of the prohibition that they were unable to voluntarily cross, but that if they were either invited or carried across the flow by one with authority they felt considerable discomfort but survived. Hodge was a Terrier Man, as ruthless towards his natural enemies as Jed was to rats, but he also had the gentleness of a man who spent his life with animals, hating unnecessary cruelty or suffering. He too had arrived at the destruction of the Safe House in time to hear the burning horse screaming, and part of the liking he had quickly developed for Ida was her matching fury at the inhumanity of it. The Sluagh was an historic enemy, but this one had also clearly been cruelly and painfully mistreated. Jed hated rats, but he killed them clean. There was nothing clean about what had happened to this Sluagh.

So he drew on the reins, applied the brake and stood and looked down at the place where the three Sluagh had taken up their sentry post. He held his hands wide.

Jed whined on the seat next to him. He heard an answering noise from Archie, who he was pleased to see was now disciplined enough to have remained close to Charlie's legs. The terrier might still be close to a puppy, but he was learning.

"We need to talk," he told the darkness. "No harm meant, and good may come of it for you and yours. Let's have a parley, like."

The darkness held its tongue. Somewhere in the distance, a locomotive clanked along the Blackwall Railway, approaching West India Docks, but apart from that the night was as still as it got on that eastern edge of the city.

"Hello?" he said, peering blindly into the shadows, as if his ruined eyes could see, when in fact he was riding in his dog's head, seeing with Jed's eyes. "Anyone home? We've a hurt one of your own here in the cart, not hurt by us, but needing what succour you can give better than we can."

No one came forward. The shadows remained shadows.

"No tricks here," he said. "He needs help, and sharpish too, I reckon."

"Archie can't smell them," said Charlie quietly.

"Mmm," said Hodge. "Nor Jed. Go on, dogs. Seek 'em."

Jed bounded off the box-seat and scrabbled into the darkness. Archie followed close on his tail.

Ida came up to the cart, crossbow lowered.

"They're not there. I'd see them if they were."

The dogs barrelled back out of the darkness and leapt back on the cart.

Amos was sitting between the unconscious figures of the Green Man and the Sluagh, his eyes locked on the same darkness all the others were focused on.

You're sure?

Hodge turned and looked at him.

"That's the Sluagh for you, always turning up where you least expect them, never there when you need them. Now, you and Charlie keep a hold of that one you've got there, because crossing the water's likely to make him buck and thrash like a whirligig."

Charlie and Ida got back on the cart, and the Sluagh did not buck or thrash as the cart took the bridge with all the speed Hodge could muster as he tried to minimise the pain the creature would feel: it just flinched and gagged out a noise halfway between a whimper and a croak, and then was still.

"How'd he do?" said Hodge, looking back.

Ida held two fingers to the tattooed neck.

"Still alive but he's got a pulse like a baby bird. I think he'll be leaving us soon."

Amos stared at the drawn face, arced and stippled with the hated tattoos, and tried to feel the sympathy they all clearly felt. He just felt a thin drizzle of fear and a strong wish to get out of the cart and away from it.

Five minutes later, he had his wish. The dog cart stopped outside The Folley and Cook emerged to meet them carrying a shuttered lantern. As Hodge brought her up to speed with the night's adventures, Amos helped Charlie and Ida carry the Sluagh into a clean wood-panelled room behind the forge. It was warm and there were four bunk-beds, two on either side, and one box-bed across the end of the room, built in with sliding wooden doors. They laid the Sluagh on one of the lower bunks.

Ida then took Amos through to the kitchen and sat with him by the welcome heat of the range while Cook went to look at the injured Sluagh. Ida didn't talk as they waited and watched Cook bustle back in and get her medicine box with much tutting and a brow like thunder, but her presence was companionable. As soon as Cook left for the second time, she darted across the room and cut a wedge from a thick truckle of cheese on the sideboard. She broke it in half and gave one to Amos.

"Cheshire Cheese," she said. "It's crumbly but good."

He took it and watched her sit back with her chair tipped against the range as she ate it. He bit into the piece she had given him, and realised how hungry he was.

It is good.

"Told you," she said with a wink. "Just don't tell Cook. She's very strict about us taking food behind her back."

Thank you.

She nodded and smiled and for the next ten minutes said no more, but managed not to look at all like she was guarding him. Which of course they both knew she was. And then Cook returned, muttering and angry, and scrubbed her hands in the sink as Ida was called away by Charlie to help Hodge with the Green Man who, according to the dictates of his nature, was to be quartered in the open air.

Cook clattered about with pots and pans and plates and spoons, murderously engaged in some species of diversionary culinary warfare to dissipate the anger she had felt at the sight of the tortured creature in the bunkroom. Amos was content to just sit and watch and bask in the warmth of the fire, and consider the fact that The Oversight was not—if these were representative examples of its membership—at all what he'd imagined. It seemed much more like a chaotic family than a disciplined order of supranatural guardians. And he also wondered if all this noise and bustle might possibly result in some more cheese. The piece Ida had shared with him seemed to have loosened the juices in his mouth and he was, shamefully, almost drooling at the smells coming from the direction of the range.

Cook suddenly turned and pointed a wooden spoon.

"So," she said. "You can't talk?"

Amos shook his head. It was just a spoon, but it felt like a pistol was being aimed at him.

No.

"Have you ever talked?" she said.

No.

"Can you hear our thoughts?" she said.

He concentrated. His brow crinkled slightly.

No.

"Would you tell me if you could?"

He met her eyes. A long beat passed.

Probably not. But I can't anyway.

"It's the rings," said Cook, showing the bloodstone on her finger. "They're not just badges. They're wards."

What are wards?

"Shields. They're protection."

She turned to the range and clattered something into a plate.

Against people like me?

"Against people like you," she said, turning and now sliding a heaped plate across the table towards him. "Now eat this, if that cheese hasn't spoiled your appetite."

He noted that those pale eyes clearly missed nothing, and put the thought away for future perusal.

Sorry.

She grunted.

"That young Trousers thinks I can't see through her. Not like you. Eat up, because I can almost see the blessed gas lamp right through you, you're so sharp-set."

He stared at the plate.

"Go on," she said. "It won't bite you."

Eel pie?

"You don't like eels?" she said. "What kind of Londoner are you?"

No. I like eel pie. I mean, I did. Once.

The memory hit him of the first time he met the Ghost: he'd been drawn to the thrilling yet unsettling novelty of a voice in his head addressing him directly, the first time he had ever had someone talk back to him without words. He'd crossed the moonlit water meadow and opened the bolted door to the little brick-built shed straddling the chalk stream, and there she'd been, up to her thighs in the water, her cracked smile visible in the moonlight, eyes reaching for him as hundreds of pale elvers writhed and roiled around her legs.

He became aware that Cook was staring at him.

"Well, Amos Templebane, I'd give you a penny for them, but I haven't got a penny on me right now. But tell you what . . ."

She picked a pewter tankard off the hooks along the ceiling and then went into the room behind the forge. Amos watched until she came back and pushed it across the table to him. It was now full and had a thick head of foam on it.

". . . give you a pint for them instead. The Smith's Dreadnought Porter. How about that?" she said.

He reached for the tankard and took a sip. It was cool, dark and mild, not at all as bitter as he'd been expecting: it tasted rich but not thick, with definite overtones of chocolate and toffee contrasting with a delicately bitter bite of liquorice and maybe even coffee on the aftertaste.

Good. It's good. Thank you.

"Thank The Smith. Brews it himself. He's had longer than anyone to get his brewing right, and you can taste it in every drop. You sup that and tell me why a good London boy like you doesn't like my pie."

Maybe it was the warmth of the fire, or the quality of the porter, or perhaps the steady eyes of the square-built woman sitting opposite him, but Amos found he was doing something he had not done in a very, very long time.

He relaxed.

He relaxed and he told her about the Eel House, and the Ghost, and he even told her about the fate of the M'Gregors and his part in it, and then one thing led to another, and somewhere in the midst of it all, as he meandered back and forth from that moment, telling the middle of the story before the beginning and then jumping round to sketch the end and bring things up to the present, he found he'd eaten the pie and drunk more of the delicious porter and was now facing a wedge of steamed pudding studded with currants and swimming in a lake of custard.

I think I'll burst.

"Nonsense," she said. "But don't eat it if you don't want to. The others'll be in soon and that Charlie scoffs anything he can lay his hands on and if he doesn't get it, young Trousers has a healthy lack of shame about leftovers. But just tell me what happened at that dew pond again."

Hodge took the Green Man to the small copse of trees that grew close by The Folley on the windward side, facing the marshes on the other bank of the river. Although the trees had been planted for protection, it was not only from the wind: there was oak, ash and thorn, and there were two cavernous holly bushes and the old English quickbeam, also known as rowan. This late in the year, only the holly and the ivy-cloaked ruin of an ancient beech retained any leaf cover against the elements, and it was here that Hodge waited with the Green Man until Charlie re-appeared with a bail of straw, a tarpaulin and a pair of thick blankets.

Hodge sat with one comforting arm around the Green Man's shoulders while Charlie, brought up on the road as a showman's son and thus no stranger to the swift erection of temporary shelters, lashed off the tarpaulin and made a dry bed beneath it. The Green Man had stopped shivering by the time he finished it, calmed and perhaps warmed by Hodge on one side and Jed who leaned companionably against his legs on the other.

"You get him any food?" said Hodge.

"Here," said Ida, appearing with a couple of bowls and a jug. "Cook said the beer is good for him, and there are nuts and dried fruits from her baking supplies. I brought apples as well."

"Just put them in the shelter," said Hodge. "He likely don't want to be watched while he's eating. They're skittish at the best of times and I reckon his poor mouth's going to smart some from that damned stitching."

He helped the Green Man onto the impromptu straw mattress and looked straight at him, as if his own ruined eyes could see him clearly.

"The food is for you, as is the shelter. You are free to take it, or not take it as you will, just as you're free to stay or go. This is the closest we can get you to the deep green for now, but the air is fresh, these trees are old and sacred and their roots go deep. And you can smell the tang of the wildness coming off the marshland. So, as a friend—and we are friends—I suggest you lie up with us for a while until you get over what them bastards done to you and get your strength back. But it's your choice."

He stood up and stepped away from the Green Man, who sat there looking at him mutely as he took the knife from his belt and crossed to the trees. He cut a leafless twig from an oak sapling, and similarly bare branchlets from the ash tree beside it and the blackthorn that overshadowed them both. He returned to the Green Man and put them in his hand, closing his fingers for him until he gripped them firmly. The Green Man nodded but said nothing.

"Best I can do for now," Hodge said. "Come rap at the door if there is anything you need. Cook in there has got a powerful lot of physick if you're ailing, and if it gets too cold there is always a place by the fire."

He looked at the terrier who lay down next to the Green Man.

"Dog's called Jed. He reckons he'll stay close by, if that's fine with you. For warmth and company."

The Green Man blinked at him. He said nothing but nodded infinitesimally. As they walked back into The Folley, Ida nudged Hodge.

"Jed likes him?"

"Dog's always had a connection with the wild, and Green Men like nature breathing round them as they sleep. And you don't get more natural than Jed."

In the warmth of the forge, Amos carried on talking and Cook carried on listening and prompting him and refilling the tankard until he yawned and let his head drop onto the table and began to snore.

She looked at him for a long moment, as if making up her mind about something. Then she took the tankard and emptied the remaining beer into the sink.

"You heard that," she said without turning.

"Yes," said Hodge, who had been leaning in the doorway behind Amos. "And I'll tell you what . . ."

"You don't trust him?" said Cook.

"Trust him fine, I reckon," said Hodge. "What I was going to say was: give me that spotted dick I can smell, if there's any left, before either of those young 'uns get their pie-hooks into it."

She slid the plate across to him. He pulled up a chair and dug in.

"Ah," he said, round a mouthful of pie. "Thing of beauty."

"Me or the pudding?" she said.

"Well, both of course," he said, and nodded at Amos. "Sure he's asleep?"

"He had something to loosen his tongue in the first pint, and something to make him sleep in the last two," she said. "He'll be out until after midday I'd say. Looks like he could do with a long sleep."

"I'll put him snug in the room at the back alongside the Sluagh," he said. "Poor bugger. You think of his life. Foundling, raised in the orphanage at Cat Cree—that's a hard place to have landed, with no time for kindness or soft edges, I can tell you, and he'll have been singled out because he's got more'n a touch of the tar-brush in him. Anything makes you a whit different gets you marked out for blows in a brutish sty like that place. Then he gets adopted, and thinks he's out of the frying pan, but then it's the Templebanes and he's up to his chin in that nest of snakes."

"And all the while he doesn't tell anyone he can hear their thoughts," she said thoughtfully, looking at Amos's head on the table. "So he's not an idiot either."

"Got a lot of blood on his hands," said Hodge.

"Well, who the hell hasn't?" said Cook. "We're no angels."

"Yeah, but we're on their side," said Hodge.

"He's never killed anyone out of spite or badness," said Cook. "He's done it out of self-preservation or saving someone else. Just like us. He's got more of a hum of power about him than I've ever felt in one so young, too."

"Well yeah, he has powers and don't know that they are powers," said Hodge. "Like that Lucy Harker."

"He doesn't feel like Lucy did," said Cook. "His troubles came on him unbidden, as it were. She had a different thing."

"She carried a flaw in her," agreed Hodge. "Her flaw went back to her beginning, I'd say. He's just lost. Looking for somewhere to be. She was the other kind of lost, always wanting not to be where she found herself, always running towards someplace else."

"I liked her," said Cook. "Still do."

"Me and all," said Hodge. "She's a sparky one, right enough. Maybe one day she'll run so far she'll catch up with herself. Then perhaps we'll see her again."

"No," said Cook, shaking herself as if a chill had run through her. "My gut tells me I've seen the last of Lucy Harker."

She nodded at Amos, snoring on the tabletop.

"Why don't you carry him to the bedroom? And then we need to talk about what he told us, about Mountfellon and the Sluagh."

"And the eel lady," said Hodge.

"The Ghost of the Itch Ward," said Cook, nodding. "Yes. Her, and her saying she was one of us once upon a time . . ."

"Smith'd know," said Hodge, "if it was true. I can't think who she might have been. And I reckon you've as good a tally in your head of who's been and who's gone as I do."

"Yes," said Cook. "It's got me foxed too. I miss the old days when we were more numerous. I miss being part of a crowd. Felt safer. And a sight more convivial, somehow."

"Nothing unconvivial about your pudding," said Hodge hopefully, nudging the now empty plate towards her.

"Put him to bed and I'll cut you another slice," she said. Hodge grinned and stood up.

"And what d'you think she is, this Ghost?" he said, lifting Amos out of his chair as easily as if he weighed nothing at all.

"A torment and a tribulation," said Cook. "The only question is for whom."

CHAPTER 40

THE *MONARCH* ENGAGED

John Rogers Watkins was a shrewd man, proud of his vision and enterprise. He was as healthily eager to make money as any enterprising man who plied his trade on the Thames, but it was his vision that set him apart from the crowd of speculators and opportunists elbowing each other to claim their piece of the rapidly expanding pie afforded by the growth the Port of London was enjoying. It was a phenomenon driven both by the explosion of manufacturing at home and imperial expansion abroad, and its result was ships, ships and more ships crowding into the narrow and twisting gut of the river, where they became less and less able to manoeuvre themselves amid the jam of other vessels. Watkins saw this, and realised the opportunity that small vessels with powerful paddle wheels powered by steam might avail themselves of in being paid to tow the increasingly ungainly cargo ships against tide and wind. Watkins was the king of the London steam tug trade, and the fact he named his business after his young son William was proof that this was a man who thought in dynastic rather than short terms.

He also prided himself on being something of an inventor, having devised something called a chain-box which was essentially a small wagon on rails which ran across the deck of his prize tug, the *Monarch*, between the two paddle wheels. It was loaded with heavy chain, so that by pushing it from side to side of the boat, the equilibrium was altered, lifting one or the other paddle wheels out of the water while the other dug deep. This, he was explaining to the noble lord who had so flatteringly attended him at his offices at St. Katherine's dock, made the tug as responsive as if he had a pair of engines enabling him to run each wheel separately, a design his new tug, presently under construction at a boatbuilders just up the river at Limehouse, was going to have.

"That," said Mountfellon, "is precisely the kind of mechanical ingenuity that my fellow members of the Royal Society admire. Why, sir, you may decry your innovation as merely practical, but it takes a keen mind to apply the laws of physics without excessive complication, and simplicity, as Occam's razor reminds us, is the straightest path to the greater truths."

Watkins flushed, his face pinked with pleasure at the liberal application of Mountfellon's flattery.

"Most kind of you to say so, my lord," he said.

"I would be delighted, once our business is concluded, to encourage my colleagues to invite you to expatiate on your mechanical innovations," said Mountfellon. "Indeed I would. The damned chemical gentlemen and the confounded bug-hunters get too much of our time at meetings, I always say, when it is the earnest extension and application of the Newtonian certainties afforded by mechanics or—as I term it—applied physics, that really pushes our society forward and raises us beyond the apes."

The "business" to which he referred was still fresh in Watkins' mind: Mountfellon had explained that he wished to engage William Watkins Ltd's most powerful tug, the *Monarch*, a sturdy sixty-five by fourteen-foot wooden boat, to drag the river. In order to do this, he had given Watkins a sketch of a simple rig he wished to be towed behind the boat, essentially a long spar from which was to be hung a series of chains with grappling hooks, each chain being independently winchable back up, if it hooked anything on the bed of the river.

When Watkins had ventured—with the utmost deference—to inquire what the object of the fishing exercise was, Mountfellon had been most pleasingly willing to condescend and explain that the object was "some leaden caskets unfortunately dropped in the river in the past by a now departed fellow of the Royal Society, caskets whose whereabouts had only recently come to light . . ." He had gone on to confide that the contents were a matter of extreme secrecy, and that Mr. Watkins, by helping in their recovery, would be making a very good—nay, an irreproachably attractive—name for himself among some of the most influential gentlemen in Britain, the membership of the Royal Society being of course the *ne plus ultra* of clubs and associations.

Watkins was almost as attracted to the job by that hint of future preferment as he was by the price he was offered for his discretion and ingenuity in putting the noble lord's plans into speedy action. He was not a snob in the social sense, but he was as eager as any man who thought himself a practical innovator to be seen as such by his peers, and a Royal Society whose members had included his personal heroes Stephenson and Brunel was one whose approval he craved almost as much as the bag of gold sitting so satisfactorily on the leather surface of the desk separating him from his new benefactor.

"So, Mr. Watkins," said Mountfellon, on whom the strain of appearing to be pleasant was beginning to tell. "When might you be ready to begin? Speed is, as I intimated, of the essence."

Watkins looked at the sketch of the rig in front of him: a sturdy spar, any length of chain and as many grapples as he wished for could be acquired from any of the nearby chandleries, and knowing that Mountfellon knew that, he put aside his usual practice (which was to think of a reasonable time and then double it in case of the unexpected) and allowed he could have the thing rigged and assembled by the end of the day.

"So we could start tomorrow," said Mountfellon, his eyes brightening.

"Indeed, my lord," said Watkins. "If that would suit."

Mountfellon looked out of the window at the stubby vessel moored below them. Two semicircular cowlings covered the paddle wheels, which added to the broad-beamed look of the craft, an ungainly stockiness offset by a tall, thin smokestack topped with a spiked crown like a metal thistle.

"That will suit," said Mountfellon. "That will suit me very well indeed."

CHAPTER 41

THE DOG DIGGER AND THE BAD STEP

The young dog named Digger was the one brought back from Boston by Prudence Tittensor to be entrusted to Lucy and Cait to aid them in their search for the Factor's baby. He was a little shorter than his mother, the bitch Shay, but he shared the same broken grey coat, and had some of her wolfhound profile but on a slightly more compact body. He looked tough and scrappy, and his eye was clear and remarkably alert.

While they had waited for her to return with the dog, various things had been agreed, plans sketched and timetables revised. Chief among these had been that the agreement to help Lucy, and thus Cait, was dependent on Armbruster and Magill confirming it with Sharp himself, since he was clearly the senior member of The Oversight presently authorised to work on this side of the Atlantic. Cait visibly seethed with frustration—not at being made to see Sharp, whom she clearly liked, but on the more general principle of rebellion against being told what to do. She was by inclination and choice a free agent: The Remnant had, as far as she was concerned—and as she had even more unfortunately told them—"clearly spent more time setting up miminy-piminy rules and regulations than doing anything remotely useful with this fine new world they had trespassed upon in the first place." When the Guardian, always calm and reasonable, had said she didn't understand and was being a little intemperate and might indeed benefit from "regulation" if she wished to volunteer for it, as it would perhaps correct her view of things, Cait had demurred. She had instead doubled down on her intransigency, saying that as far as she could see, the "sainted" forefathers of The Remnant— and indeed all these fine new "Americans"—had arrived on these shores like "rogues, ruffians and thimble riggers," and had immediately set themselves up as a bunch of jack-in-offices to frame laws and regulations to stack the deck and hide the fact that in stealing the land from the original owners they were, for all their fine words, the biggest parcel of rogues and thieves in a nation that she'd ever seen.

The Guardian had taken this onslaught with an infuriatingly calm smile of politeness, but Lucy had seen Magill trying to hide a grin of a very different nature.

"You know, Miss ná Gaolaire," Armbruster had said as the Guardian left to make sure rooms were prepared for them to spend the night before setting out, not for St. Louis as previously planned, but for an earlier rendezvous with Sharp. "When you're trying to steal the honey, it doesn't do to be stirring up the bees like that."

"I don't want any damn honey," Cait had said. "I just want the baby and a fast ship home to freer air."

"Oh, there's plenty of freedom where we're going," said Magill. "Out beyond the states, in the territories, you'll see all the freedom in the world."

"And most of it'll kill you if you don't treat it with a sight more respect than you've been showing the old woman," said Magill. "She's more on your side than you know, and a thank you rather than a damn you might answer better, but you're free to do as you please. Just a suggestion."

And then, as the thought of the promised beds was getting more and more alluring, and Lucy was stifling a yawn for the fifth or sixth time, Prudence Tittensor had arrived back with the dog Digger and an ill grace to match Cait's truculence.

"You'll care for the dog," she said.

"Well, I won't be giving him away to the first Tom, Dick or who the hell I feel sorry for, if that's what you mean," said Cait. "Not like you and the Factor's baby. I will look after him a sight better than that."

"That's not fair," said Mrs. Tittensor.

"No, but it's true and it's real," said Cait. "And real life's not a bit fair, from what I see of it."

She did, however, drop to her knees, look in the dog's eyes and hold her hand out to be sniffed. Digger's nose took stock of her, and then his tail thumped once, which Mrs. Tittensor clearly thought an unconscionable act of betrayal, made worse by the fact he then bowed his head and allowed himself to be scratched behind the ears.

"I'm lending Digger to The Oversight," said Mrs. Tittensor, looking at Lucy. "Not to a common venatrix."

"I have no pretensions as to being anything other than I am, common or no," said Cait. "But it's my word you'd be wisest to rely on: if I tell you the dog will be brought back safe, that's what will happen, and on that I do give you my word."

"None the less, I'll trust The Oversight," said Mrs. Tittensor. And with that, she turned from Cait and gave Lucy the long leash she was carrying. "You'll need this if you're to take him through the mirrors, most likely. He'll do anything else, but I don't know if he'll do that without encouragement, never having done it before. No dog, as far as I know, having done it."

She looked at Magill and Armbruster.

"This is on your heads too, gentlemen."

"How does the dog let us know when we find the fisherman Graves and the baby?" said Lucy.

"I've told him he's to come to you and—" began Mrs. Tittensor.

"Don't you worry about that," said Cait. "I can hear him well enough, though I can't see through his eyes or ride along in his mind."

Prudence Tittensor looked as if this was the last insult she could bear. Cait might as well have slapped her.

"I don't have your gifts, Mrs. T," she said, standing and unconsciously ruffling the dog's fur. "But my father did. I can hear the shape of what Digger here is thinking to me. He'll do."

The dog yipped once and wagged his tail. Mrs. Tittensor turned to Lucy.

"The dog's young and reckless. I want your word that you or the men will take him through the mirrors. The venatrix is not to be trusted."

"The devil she isn't," said Cait. "But I'll not argue. I'm not one for leashing a dog any more than I'd like to be leashed myself, so if it's to be done, Lucy Harker may do it as well as anyone else."

And so it was agreed, and Mrs. Tittensor took her leave with a bilious ill grace, and Lucy and Cait were shown to a comfortable room for the night, with an understanding that they would make the step through the mirrors to meet Sharp on the morrow. The door wasn't locked behind them, but when Cait opened the door to check it was so, they found Armbruster unpacking a bedroll across the threshold in the passage beyond, while Magill was already sitting in a chair a little further down the way, reading a book by the light of a candle.

"Sure and aren't there other beds for you in this great well-appointed house?" she said. "This looks awful uncomfortable, and I'd hate to think we were discommoding you."

Magill grinned.

"Happy to be discommoded by you whenever you wish, Miss ná Gaolaire," he said.

"Jon," said Armbruster, shaking his head. He looked up at Cait.

"See, he's usually the shy one. Whatever you're doing to him, you'd as well stop it, 'cause it ain't going to get you anywhere we aren't going to take you anyway. You got our word on that already, and our word don't break any more than yours."

"I'm not doing anything to him, Mr. Armbruster," she said.

"Fred," he said. "And yes, you are. Only question is are you doing it on purpose?"

When the door was shut and the candles extinguished, Lucy lay on the bed and looked at the sliver of moonlit water she could see through a crack in the curtains. She heard Cait get into the bed beside her, and was immediately conscious of the silence and the narrow gap of unoccupied linen that lay between them.

She listened to the dog Digger settling himself on the floor at the end of the bed.

"I was just trying to help," she said after a while. "And I did."

The silence remained unbroken, and every second it continued she felt that six-inch cordon of crisp, cool bedsheet that lay between them widen until it became a heartbreakingly unbridgeable chasm.

"I know," said Cait, just at the point Lucy had become convinced she had fallen asleep. "I know. And if you give me enough time to swallow my pride, no doubt I'll thank you for it by and by. Now go to sleep and don't fret. Things are square enough between us. Just different than they were."

The bed moved as she turned away, and Lucy lay alone in the dark, not sure if she felt better or worse, and then she slept.

When she woke, Cait was gone, and so was the dog Digger. She tumbled out of bed and threw open the door. Armbruster's bedroll was gone too, as was Magill, but Armbruster himself was there, leaning against the casement of an open window, smoking his pipe and watching the smoke disappear into the crisp daylight.

"Morning," he said. "They're having coffee downstairs. I'm just sparing them my pipe smoke."

Lucy knew this was a lie and that he'd been standing some kind of guard on her, but it seemed an amiable enough untruth not to bridle at. And then he tapped out his pipe, closed the window and walked off down the stairs, as if to prove her wrong.

"Come on down when you're ready," he said. "Get a bite to eat for the road, and then we'd best be on our way."

She watched him disappear and then listened to the quiet house. She wondered if she might just get out of that window and climb down and run away and be shot of all this, and then she looked down at the ring The Smith had made her.

She couldn't decide if it was the ring, or not being quite ready to say goodbye to Cait that stopped her, but she didn't run. She washed and tidied herself, laced her boots tight, and went downstairs to see what this new day would bring.

CHAPTER 42

A DEAD DAY AFTER

Amos slept for most of the day following his long night under Cook's scrutiny. The Green Man slept all of it, and the injured Sluagh hovered between life and death like a guttering flame that would not see tomorrow.

Ida was sent to check the Templebanes' counting-house to see if it remained undisturbed and untenanted, and Charlie was sent to the Tower. No matter how bad things were, it had to be ratted and the ravens protected, and Hodge had a council of war to sit at with Sharp, Sara and Cook. He knew he and Ida were being sent away so the elder members could go over what they had found out at Chandos Place, and he didn't particularly mind. He was more excited by Hodge's instructions which were to bring back the oldest of the remaining ravens, since he was now convinced that the Raven was as unlikely to return any time soon as The Smith was, and so wanted Charlie to begin training an understudy. Charlie had ridden inside a raven's head before, watching as it swooped and circled around the Tower, and he found the aerial perspective especially exhilarating. He didn't enjoy talking to the birds as much as he did to his dog since they were less communicative and somehow scratchy in his mind where Archie was a warm and comfortable fit, but he still thrilled at the experience. Hodge told him it was time to "bring on the understudy" and have the new raven start to watch the city with them as the Raven had done.

Charlie asked if this new bird would one day become "the" Raven, and Hodge had snorted and shook his head, assuring his apprentice that the Raven was at least as old as The Smith and hopefully as unkillable. The new bird would merely be a poor substitute. But with things as they were, beggars couldn't be choosers and it was time for all hands to man the pumps . . .

Charlie's spark of enthusiasm for the new job with the substitute raven was the only bright spot in what was otherwise, for all of them, a sad, lost day, as if they were all mourning something they could not or would not name.

Ida checked the door to Templebane's chambers and found it was still unlocked. She cracked it open and didn't bother to enter, as her nose told her clearly that Abchurch's body was undisturbed and thus undiscovered.

She jogged off towards Chandos Place, unaware that she was right in the first instance, but wrong in the second. Abchurch had been found by Vintry and Shadwell Templebane only an hour and a half earlier. They had filtered back into the city with the rest of the brothers, who were billeted discreetly elsewhere as Issachar was moving his pieces into position for his great final stratagem, and he did not want to risk its success by alerting any watchers to the fact the house of Templebane had returned.

Vintry and Shadwell had been horrified by what they had found, and left very quickly, making sure they were neither seen nor followed. They had debated whether this was a sufficiently important bit of news for them to abort their next errand and report back to Issachar. After some thought and several pints in a dingy corner tavern in Half Nichols Street they decided telling him they had not gone on to Bedlam and planted information with their diminished brother Coram was perhaps the only thing that could make sharing the news about Abchurch worse. So, their sinews stiffened by the hops and ale, they headed for the hospital.

Shown into the day-room by Bill Ketch, they were horrified by what had become of Coram, not through any residual affection, but as a more general reminder of the vulnerability that all flesh is heir to.

"You been being asked questions by The Oversight," said Vintry.

"From what we hear," said Shadwell, eyes darting around the room. "And you know old Issachar, he's got eyes and ears all over the shop where you least expect it."

Coram had sat quietly, trying not to look at them, trying not to hear them, waiting for the moment they would leave; he didn't want to talk to them. He wanted to bite their faces off. He wanted to scream. He wanted to burst out of the room and run and run and run until he met the horizon. However, he had but the one leg, and so he just waited for them to be gone.

Vintry leant in.

"Thing is, old son, Issachar's been looking for you high and low. And now he's found you, he wants you to come home so you can be looked after as you deserve, you being a loyal son. He wants you out of Bedlam and back in the bosom, but before that, there's a bit of business he'd like you to do for us."

"'E knows you been silent as a nun's fart so far, and he loves you for it, but 'e does wish you'd decide start flapping your trap and pass on one little bit of tittle-tattle, like it's something you got off us, your loving brothers," said Shadwell.

Coram had nodded, knowing they'd go away if he did so, and also knowing that it'd be a cold day in hell before he did a favour for Issachar Templebane, who had left him crippled when he might have saved him.

"Lovely grubbly," said Shadwell. "We'll tell that Ketch feller you told us you wanted to speak to those chaps what have been speaking to you, shall we?"

When Charlie returned after dark, he told Ida, out of the hearing of the others, of his sense they were all grieving something they wouldn't talk about.

"Maybe they're mourning something that hasn't happened yet," she said.

"You're a ray of sunshine and all," he said.

"I know," she said. "Cook's making the steak and kidney pudding again, and I shall have to pretend I like the kidneys in case she gets all offended like last time."

"Give them to Archie under the table. He'll be happy to destroy the evidence."

But even the pudding failed Cook, collapsing as she carefully turned it out of the steaming bowl.

"It'll taste just the same," said Hodge.

But it didn't. And whatever the council of war had discussed, it was clear to the younger members that nothing had been decided and that things were, if anything, gloomier than they had been before the secrets of the house at Chandos Place had been revealed, for reasons they could not quite fathom.

"We don't know enough," said Sharp, clearly continuing a line of earlier conversation as he watched Cook tutting as she spooned a glutinous mess of meat, gravy and tattered suet pastry onto a plate.

"I think maybe we don't know enough to know we should give up," said Hodge.

"Knowing we shouldn't ever give up is all I *do* know," said Sara.

Of all the suppers they had shared, each felt that this—though none said it—was the gloomiest, as if an ominous and ill-starred future was, impossibly, casting its shadow back into the present.

No one slept well that night.

FOURTH PART

THE LOWEST TIDE

vulnerant omnes,
ultima necat

Every hour wounds,
the last kills.

On the Golem

On the making of a golem, in which enterprise I have the honour of being the only man in Britain to have succeeded, I will say no more than that if you follow the directions used by Rabbi Eliyahu, Ba'al Shem of Chelm, informed by a close reading of the Sefer Yetzirah, success may be yours . . . the only additions I myself made were in the matter of materials, not process . . . concerning myself with how to stop the clay from which the golem is made from drying out over time and prolonged exposure to the sun, I came across a passage reproduced by Wm. Caxton in 1481: "This Salemandre berithe wulle, of which is made cloth and gyrdles that may not brenne in the fyre." Pliny, Augustine and Isidore of Seville all attest to the salamander's ability to quench heat, and so I dried salamander skin, powdered and added it to the four clays from which I formed the golem. It has yet to dry out and is as limber as the day it was formed . . . and in this way I hope the unpleasantness that occurred latterly in Prague can be avoided . . .

From *The Great and Hidden History of the World* by the Rabbi Dr. Hayyim Samuel Falk (also known as the Ba'al Shem of London)

(In the margin of the page bearing the above, the rabbi has left a handwritten addendum beside which a different hand, possibly a much later reader, has left their own comment. The rabbi's hand-writing is as follows:

The snake is not a snake but a dragon, and the dragon not a dragon but a salamander. The key is not a key but a holder. And the holder holds not a key but the fire.

The second hand—possibly a woman's—writes:

Stuff and nonsense!)

CHAPTER 43

THE EXCHANGE

He wakes looking up at the first light of dawn as it filters through the small canopy of leaves which tickles his face in the light breeze coming off the Thames from the marshy land beyond. He inhales deeply. It smells of the deep green.

He has slept for two nights, and has healed faster than they knew was possible, because although they know much, they do not know everything. They do not know as much as their fathers and mothers once did either. They are lesser than they were, this Oversight, he sees this; he saw this even as they carried him here to heal.

But the dog man knew enough to put twigs of oak, ash and thorn in his hand and to leave him in the open, and what is better, under a rowan tree. And, from the neat pile of jacket, shirt and trousers resting on a pair of boots at his side, someone was kind enough to believe he would heal eventually. He puts the foliage still gripped in his fist to one side, removing the small canopy of leaves, for it is the once bare twigs that have budded and sprouted in his grasp as he slept, a whole lush spring in two nights.

There is a gentle ripping noise when he sits up and gets to his feet as the grass that has grown and woven itself over him like a blanket against the chill gives way.

He looks down at the clothes as he feels the scars on his lips. They have scabbed over and, though they smart a little, he knows they will soon be gone. He strips off the rags he was wearing and walks naked to the river's edge, crossing the towpath and lowering his body into the flowing water without flinching. For him, the water is never cold nor warm. It is always as it should be for the season. He ducks his head beneath the flow and for a long moment there is no sign that this green-skinned man was ever on the face of the earth.

And then he emerges, long hair slicked back like a raven's wing with an emerald sheen on it. He smiles, white eyes and teeth, and then laughs, a short chop of delight, and if there had been anyone to see this, they would have seen the startling flash of red made by the inside of his mouth and the tongue behind the teeth. But no one sees him as he pulls himself out of the water and strides back towards the copse.

He does not get dressed immediately. Instead he stands looking at The Folley and the wisp of smoke emerging from the smoored-up fire beneath the forge's ancient chimney. Finally, when the wind has dried his bare flesh, he gets quickly dressed in the worn white shirt, the brown jacket and the buff stovepipe trousers that Hodge left for him and sits on the ground, his bare feet plunged deep into the thick grass which slowly begins to twine around his toes in a tickling way that makes him smile once again.

He begins neatly stripping the fine young twigs from the unseasonably leafy boughs he discarded earlier, and then quickly and methodically sets about plaiting them into triple-wood bracelets. When he has made nine, he puts one on his own wrist and then retrieves his feet from the gentle embrace of the grass, and puts on his boots. He nods in satisfaction. The dog man judged his size well.

He stands and looks down at his clothes. Buff, white and brown have been banished by the colour that has leached itself from the grass into his body and garments. He is, once again, a truly Green Man.

He bends and picks up the blanket they brought for him. He folds it neatly and then walks towards The Folley, blanket in one hand, triple-wood bracelets in the other.

He will be gone before they wake, but he will leave his thanks.

CHAPTER 44

OUT OF THE GLASS CLOSET

In the end, the leaving of Marblehead was a swift and business-like thing. Breakfast eaten, their bags hefted—bags which had been returned to them by the Proctor who had disconcertingly found their hotel room without having been told where they had left them—they lined up in front of the cabinet.

Cait had made to take the dog Digger's leash, but Lucy had got there first. It was a mulish thing to do, since Mrs. Tittensor was not there to witness it, but she had given her word, and told Cait so.

"Oh, and now you're all for keeping your word," said Cait, roiling her eyes. "Well, it's a little late to be playing Little Goody-Two-Shoes, but crack on then."

Lucy looked at the cabinet and grimaced, trying not to remember the time she had fallen out of the Safe House and into the showman's tent, taking Sara Falk's hand with her.

"Now you'll be arriving in a dark closet," said Armbruster, eager to get on. "He ain't expecting us so soon, but there'll be a bell if the door's locked on the side wall. Just rattle it and he'll come running . . . or I can go first if you like."

Because there was something kind in his voice, as if he knew she was scared, Lucy shook her head and made herself go stony inside.

"I'm fine," she said and, without looking back at Cait, she gripped the dog's lead and stepped through the mirror. She felt a familiar light popping sensation, as though piercing the skin of a bubble. The doors of the cabinet were indeed closed, letting in just a pencil-width of dim candle-light, so she stopped and blinked for a moment as her pupils adjusted from the brighter light of the room she had just left. The dog too went very still, but for entirely different reasons. It froze at her feet, hackles raised, bristling with tension.

Had she not had the dog with her, she might well have just pushed the door open and stumbled into the room beyond, but the dog saved her.

Back in the room she had just left, Cait turned and blocked Armbruster and Magill from following.

"One word," she said. "The girl Lucy. If my quest is as full of peril out there in the west, I do not want her coming with me. I do not want to put her into unnecessary danger, and she is reckless enough to insist. So give me your word that if Jack Sharp vouches for me, as he will, we then leave her behind. She'll bridle and hate me for it, but I like her and would rather leave her safe."

Armbruster and Magill exchanged a look.

"Deal," said Magill.

"If Sharp vouches for you," said Armbruster. "Now let's go."

"He will," said Cait, turning to face the mirror. "He owes me a favour . . ."

Lucy stood in the dark closet holding her breath, listening to two voices that were and were not strangely familiar to her. She could put no name to them, yet they rankled in her mind like the fragments of an almost remembered melody she could not quite piece together.

"Everything in London is arranged," said the first voice. "Mountfellon will be dragging the Thames at Irongate Steps today, I believe. Once he hooks the Wildfire out of the depths, the broker Templebane has arranged a surprise for him, and we shall have it delivered into our hands."

"And The Oversight?" said the other.

"If The Oversight interfere, there is not one but two ambushes laid on. They will walk into a killing ground but they will not walk out. The Oversight is finished, once and for all."

Although she didn't know who the voices were, she did know neither of them were Sharp. The dog at her side also knew something was wrong.

In the room beyond the closet in which Lucy was hidden listening, Dee and The Citizen were sitting opposite one another across the fireplace.

"God rot the damned Oversight," said The Citizen. "They have been a festering thorn in my side for too long now."

"The Wildfire will cauterise all old wounds," said Dee.

"And then we shall purge the mirrors, and all will be ours, and none to stop us," smiled The Citizen, finishing loading the pistol with a snap as he closed the mechanism.

"This is a thing of true beauty, this American gun. Truly we are living in an age of machines now, when we put our powers together with the fruits of new industry."

Dee was about to reply when he stopped dead, sure that he had heard a creak from across the room, from the Murano Cabinet. He held a hand out to silence The Citizen.

He grabbed the candlestick and drew a long knife as he rose from his chair and moved slowly towards the cabinet.

As he moved, he came into view for Lucy, framed in the narrow slit of the imperfectly closed doors.

And that is when she should have run. Because the tall figure with the blade in one hand and the light in the other was one she had seen before, a long time ago in a sad county town when she was travelling with showmen, and it had been walking towards her as it was now, only then it was a vision glimpsed in the mirrored doorway of a shop in which she was crouching, recovering from another horror, that of glinting the centuries-old death by fire of a young witch. She had had the sense to run from the reflection of the nemesis walking through the mirrors then, but now that the reality of what had clearly been a presentiment was made flesh, it was paralysing her.

The horror of it robbed her of the ability to do the one thing she knew she should do, which was turn and leap back into the mirror out of which she had just come. But she couldn't. And then it was too late.

He hooked open the door just at the moment Magill and Armbruster stepped out of the mirror, followed by Cait. They knocked Lucy forward towards Dee whose arm lashed out and pinned her inside the cabinet, with her back against the mirror facing the one she had just come out of.

Before anyone could react, he switched hands, and had his knife at her neck.

Cait and the men had no time to respond before The Citizen had scrambled towards the cabinet with his new pistol pointed at them. He moved so fast that his chair crashed backwards and made a rattling thump on the floor. They instinctively backed up against the mirror facing Lucy, all trapped in the glazed cell of the cabinet, facing each other in a way that would have been ridiculous had it not been so fraught with impending peril.

"Be very still," hissed Dee.

"I have five bullets," said The Citizen. "More than enough for all of you."

"Mr. Sharp," said Armbruster. "What is th—"

There was a banging on the door which stopped them in their tracks as a hesitant man's voice came through it, evidently alerted by the noise of the falling chair.

"*Monsieur! Monsieur! Est-ce qu'il y a un problème?*"

"*Non! Allez vous en, et n'espionnez pas vos supérieurs!*" barked The Citizen.

"*Nous sommes à Paris?*" said Lucy, further jolted by the familiar sound of the language of her childhood in these unfamiliar surroundings. "You said we were staying in North America . . . Are we . . . in France?"

"No," said Magill uneasily. "Montreal. Canada. Mr. Sharp, why—?"

"You think that's Sharp?" said Cait. "That's not Jack Sharp."

"She's right. He isn't—" said Lucy, who then stopped as Dee jabbed the knife, pricking her skin and drawing a bead of blood.

"Silence," The Citizen hissed.

"Lucy Harker," snarled Dee. "Another word and your head parts company with your neck."

The fact this man she had never consciously met knew her name froze Lucy.

"Lucy Harker?" said The Citizen. "Well, well, and so it is. You see, Dee, nothing is wasted. For this is indeed Lucy Harker, though what she is doing here, so far from London, is a great mystery . . ."

He moved with unrelenting deliberation towards Cait and Armbruster and Magill, the gun unwavering enough to stop Cait's hand in its almost imperceptible attempt to shuck the razor from her sleeve.

"Good," he said. "If you'd carried on doing that, your gentlemen friends would have been wearing the inside of your head."

"No harm meant," said Cait.

"And none done," he said, as he came close enough to rest the muzzle of the gun on her chest. "But you are uninvited, whoever you are, and if there are more of you about to step through the mirror, you will be the first to die."

"There's just us, friend," said Armbruster. "Mr. Sharp there knows us fine."

"He may know you, but he's not Sharp," said Cait.

"What do you want to do?" said Dee, looking at The Citizen.

The Citizen smiled and stepped into the cabinet, between Lucy and Dee on one side, and the others facing them. He reached up and into the cabinet, where he touched the design, which Lucy saw was an inlaid mosaic or marquetry of some type, like a compass rose made from different shades of brown and white marble that glistered like mutton fat in the light of the candles. Something clicked and he leant forward. Pushing Armbruster with the barrel of his gun so he in turn reversed into Cait, backing her against the mirror.

"Steady now, mister," she said. "Just tell us what you want."

Lucy, behind him, could not see his face, but she heard the chilly smile in his voice.

"I just wish you to leave the way you came."

Magill's eyes were still locked on the ceiling of the cabinet.

"What did you do?"

"Just asked you. Politely. To leave," said The Citizen, shifting the gun to Cait, prodding her. Armbruster grabbed her arm, steadying her so she wouldn't fall into the mirror.

"Hold on. You did something to the cabinet," he said.

The Citizen swung the gun off Cait and pointed it at Armbruster.

"Just shoot them," said Dee. "I don't know why you—"

Lucy found the one thing that she could do. Now the gun was off Cait, she opened her hand and let go of Digger's leash.

The dog sprang forward.

Armbruster moved with shocking speed. His hand batted the gun out of his face and up towards the roof of the cabinet.

The Citizen pulled the trigger.

The gun detonated with the sound of a cannon in the confines of the room.

The bullet powdered the thin ceiling of glass and marble above him, but before gravity had a chance to shower him with the dropping fragments, the dog had hit him in the small of the back, powering him forward into Cait with enough velocity that they tangled and took the others with them as they fell away out of the room, through the mirror, leaving Dee and Lucy staring at themselves in the now unobstructed glass.

Lucy saw the horror-struck disbelief in Dee's eyes, felt the knife waver.

"What have you done?" he gasped.

The unaccustomed quiver in his voice was matched by a slackening of the knife pressure on her neck. She threw herself backwards as fast as she could, away from the wavering blade at her throat, right into the other mirror.

Dee might have been stupefied, but he was still almost fast enough to stop her.

She fell into an endless mirrored passage and was nearly on her feet before he tumbled out of the glass she had fallen through and grabbed her by the hair, yanking her head backwards and putting the blade to her neck.

"You stupid little bitch," he snarled. "I should open your neck right now."

She stayed very still. Everything she wanted to say was stuck in her throat.

"You have killed him," said Dee, his voice shaking with disbelief. "Do you know that? You killed him."

He stood staring at her, matching her stillness, stunned into gaping immobility by the enormity of what had just happened. And then he spasmed into action as though remembering himself, one hand keeping the blade crooked around her throat, the other sliding over her body like a questing eel as he searched her for her hidden weapons, all of which he found and pocketed.

He stood back and was silent for another unnervingly long period, calming his breathing, not so blank this time, the cogs of his mind now visibly turning as he adjusted to the new reality.

"Right," he said. "Right."

He found a length of silk rope in his coat and looped it around her neck. Only then did he step back and look at her. His voice was not so much angry as tired.

"You killed him," he repeated, as if trying to convince his mind of what his eyes had just seen. "The Citizen. A stupid little girl killed a great man like that, almost by accident, as if it was nothing."

"I just sent him after the others," she said, regaining a little spirit. "I didn't kill anyone."

"It was a trap," said Dee, looking as exhausted as he sounded. "One he'd used before. Designed to deal with meddlers like you. You killed your friends too, by the way. There would be irony in it if it were not such a bleak, bloody tragedy."

Cait and the Americans were dead.

Lucy felt the truth of it like a sudden aching hollow had opened up behind her sternum. She gulped but it didn't go away. She felt her eyes go treacherously hot. She took a deep breath. Then another.

"Pretty stupid to get caught in his own snare then," she said, deciding not to cry in front of this terrifying goat-like man.

"He was more intelligent than any man you will ever meet," hissed Dee. "Do you know who he was, what he did, how he cheated death . . .?"

"Ah," said Lucy.

"Ah what?" said Dee.

"A cheat was he?" said Lucy. "Cheats never prosper."

He yanked the rope hard, cinching the slipknot, making her stumble and choke.

"I should pull this tighter," he snarled. "Watch you strangle and die. Because that's what he's doing right now. That's what your friends and that damn dog are doing. Dying, drowning, most likely, without oxygen at the bottom of a very deep lake in the middle of nowhere."

She clawed the loop loose enough to breathe again.

"What?" she said.

"The trap. That's where they went. A pair of mirrors dropped by accident from a canoe while one of the damn *coureurs de bois* was crossing a lake in the wilderness. Nearly killed me when I looked through and found it, and that was summer. He liked the idea of it as a trap. His insurance, he called it."

He shook his head.

"Our plan was the finest stratagem in the world. And you—a nothing, a witless little girl, not even a man—you broke it."

He pulled the Coburg Ivory from within his long coat and held it in front of him, rotating it in his hand and slowly sweeping it in a wide arc until he heard the first tell-tale click. He stopped still and faced the direction it was pointing.

"I break things a lot," said Lucy, hearing the dull pain in her own voice. "It's my special skill."

"Well," he said, waving her forward. "Now you walk. You walk home to London with me."

"Why didn't you just kill me?" she said. "You wanted to. I saw it in your eyes."

"Because you're a hostage. And sometimes hostages have value."

"There's no one in London would pay for me," she said. "You could just let me go."

"There's no one in London that you know would pay for you," he said, pointing the ivory balls at her. "But what you do not know could fill an ocean. Walk on and keep silent. I don't want to miss a click from the get-you-home."

So Lucy walked ahead of him down the sterile uniformity of the mirrored passage, fighting the sense of vertigo triggered by the unchanging vista opening up in front of her, and thinking that wherever he was taking her it wasn't home for her. Because she had no home, not now, not ever.

Cait was dead. And she'd killed her.

CHAPTER 45

EXCHANGE OF GIFTS

Sara found the neatly folded blanket and the bracelets on a stool just inside the door of The Folley when she went to open the door. It was being pummelled by a very thin and energetic message boy who had clearly run all the way from the Bedlam Hospital, whence he had brought a badly penned message from Ketch, written just this morning and referring to the previous day's visitors to Coram.

She had given him a small coin and a tin cup of water, and Cook had given him a day-old iced bun to see him on his way, and then Sara had read the note.

"What?" said Cook.

"It appears Coram Templebane has spoken. Ketch thinks he wants to speak again. To us."

"Well, that's good," said Cook. "I'm making coffee."

"Maybe," said Sara, looking at the note.

"What are those?" said Sharp, coming in behind her. She looked at the triple-wood bracelets.

"The Green Man is gone. He left these . . ."

"What are they?" said Charlie who entered from the other door with Ida close behind him, both looking flushed with running.

"Oak, ash, thorn," said Sharp, taking the proffered note from Sara's hand, brow rucking as he read it.

"Put them on," said Sara, holding them out, then sliding one onto her own wrist.

"For luck?" said Ida, taking one.

"For protection. We looked after him; he's returning the favour the only way he can," said Hodge, who'd been sitting by the fire with Jed at his feet, so still no one had noticed him. "Pass me one of them."

Charlie handed one to him.

"What are you two looking so hot and bothered about?" said Sharp, giving the note back to Sara.

"The Sluagh are back at The Gut," said Ida.

"Right," said Cook. She jerked her thumb over her shoulder at the room where the injured Sluagh lay. "Well, he's definitely dying in there. What do we do?"

Sara and Sharp followed her back and looked into the room. The Sluagh lay on the bed, so still they had to watch for a moment to see if he was still breathing.

"Look," said Sharp, pointing at the twist of twigs circling the Sluagh's thin wrist. "The Green Man looked in here too before he left."

"Yes," said Sara, looking down at the fresh bracelet circling her own wrist. "And I think he told us what to do."

She squared her shoulders and looked up.

"We'll get it done and then see what this is that Coram Templebane wants to tell us."

"He's mad," said Hodge. "Like as not, we'll schlep over there and find he's clammed up again."

"We'll deal with that if it happens," said Sharp. "Let's go and see our tattooed friends."

The Sluagh stayed in the deep shadow of the warehouse, watching Sharp walk across the bridge towards them.

"Is The Smith returned?" said the taller Sluagh with a nasty smile. He wore a Woodcock Crown.

"No," said Sharp. "I am."

"Oh well," said the Sluagh. "I'm sure he'll be along directly. But if you want to match blades, I'd be happy to show you your insides to pass the time."

"I haven't come to fight," said Sharp. "And unless I see you harming anyone, I will keep my blades sheathed."

"Scared are you?" grunted the other Sluagh, stepping forward from behind Woodcock Crown. It was Badger Skull.

"Of many things," said Sharp. "For I am not a fool or a braggart like you."

Woodcock Crown hissed and began to draw his blade.

Sharp didn't look at him; he kept his gaze locked on the eyes of the other one.

"But we are not on the list of things you are scared of," said Badger Skull, putting his hand on the arm of his companion, stilling him. He looked behind Sharp.

"The one with the arrow gun is watching, isn't she?"

"Yes," said Sharp.

"But that is not why you are not frightened of us," said Badger Skull. "Why is that, then?"

"Because I know my capabilities," said Sharp. "And I also know why I have come to talk to you."

"Why would we talk to you, mongrel blood?" said Woodcock Crown. "Why would the Pure consort with crossbred cur like you?"

"Because I come to ask your help," said Sharp.

There was a shocked silence. The two Sluagh looked at one another.

"Our help?" said Woodcock Crown. "What kind of trick are you hoping to play—?"

"No trick," said Sharp. "I need your help."

"Well, you can whistle for it like the spavined whelp you—"

"Enough," said Badger Skull, putting a hand out again and planting it on the chest of his companion, pushing him back a pace.

"What would make The Oversight ask for our help, we who are sworn enemies?" he said.

"Only sworn on your side," said Sara, stepping out of the gloom behind them. The Sluagh spun, blades instantly drawn, clearly thinking they had been encircled and were about to be ambushed. Sara didn't flinch, but just kept walking towards them, arms raised to waist level, palms forward, open and empty.

"I'm not armed," she said, "but I would give you my hand."

"Why would I take it?" said Woodcock Crown, bristling with fury, straining against his elder's firm grip.

"Because if I invite you and lead you by the hand, you are able to cross running water, are you not?" said Sara.

Both Sluagh gaped at her.

"And why would you do that?" said Badger Skull.

"If not to trap us?" said the other.

"Because we rescued one of you from a laboratory where a man was experimenting on him. Taking his blood. And he is very close to death, and we do not have the knowledge of how to help him recover," said Sara.

Again the Sluagh gaped at her.

"Please come quickly," she said.

"Why would you do this?" said the older Sluagh. She held up her fist and showed him her bloodstone ring.

"Because Law and Lore command us," she said, and then she turned her fist and opened it into a beckoning hand. "Bring three men to carry him, because he cannot walk."

Badger Skull paused, then reached out and took her hand and let her lead him across the narrow bridge.

Cook had warned Amos that Sluagh were coming. He had blanched and looked panicked, but she told him why, and though he tried to tell her the Sluagh were not to be trusted, in the end he allowed himself to be shooed upstairs until they were gone. Even so, he felt the vibration of them as they entered, and did everything he could do not to listen to their thoughts and conversation by retreating behind the carefully erected buttress in his mind.

When Badger Skull and Woodcock Crown were shown the injured Sluagh, there was a moment when their shock could have turned to violent fury. Amos, despite himself, heard their thoughts begin to come to a bloody boil. But they hadn't spilled over into ugly recrimination, mainly because Cook bustled in with a blanket and showed how four of them could take a corner each and carry him more comfortably. And then, after a close examination, Badger Skull had tersely instructed the Sluagh who had accompanied them to pick up the wounded one and get him, with all speed, out of London and up to the Scowle as fast as they could.

They had followed his orders, and Woodcock Crown, who seemed to be a kind of second in command, led them at a fast pace back to the bridge, escorted by Sara and Sharp and Cook and Charlie.

"We will send him to the Shee," said Badger Skull as they re-crossed the bridge.

"Will he survive the journey?" said Cook.

"If he does not, he will die among his own," said Woodcock Crown.

"And if he survives," said Badger Skull, "the Shee can heal better than we."

"We wish him well," said Sara.

Woodcock Crown halted the carrying detail and turned back.

"You? The Oversight? Wish him well?"

He spat on the ground.

"Why else would we have brought you to him?" said Sara.

Badger Skull waved Woodcock Crown on ahead. He watched the Sluagh jog off into the shadows, carrying the limp form between them, then turned to look at Sara.

"He does not like to think we now owe you something," he said.

"You don't."

He shrugged.

"That is true. Your past treachery outweighs this small gesture like a mountain outweighs a mouse."

"How very gracious of you," said Cook. "Don't let us keep you."

He smiled.

"I will give you something to balance what you have done. Something you do not have."

"You could just say thank you and jog after your friends," said Cook. "That'd be fine by us."

"Cook," said Sara.

"My gift is my thanks," he said. "But I fear you may not like it."

"I'd say that's a certainty," said Cook.

"He's not coming back," said Badger Skull.

Cook and Sara and Sharp went very still.

"This is 'intelligence,' I think you call it," said Badger Skull, a thin smile breaking the mask of his tattoos. "At least that's what the cunning man Templebane calls it. He places high value on 'intelligence.' So. There it is. My gift. You did not know. You lived in false hope. Now you know."

"What do we know?" said Charlie.

"He's talking about The Smith," snapped Sharp. "Though how he knows . . ."

"The Shee," said Badger Skull. "They know what the ravens see. And they have seen that Wayland Smith is gone, gone under the hill, and that's the truth of it."

And with that he bowed slightly, turned and left.

Badger Skull caught up with Woodcock Crown as he waved off the four Sluagh charged with carrying the injured one all the way to the Scowle. As they watched them disappear, Woodcock Crown turned back and glowered at the older Sluagh.

"We could have killed them," he said. "We were on their cursed island."

"And they could have let him die," said Badger Skull.

"He will die."

"Maybe. Maybe not. But if not, the credit is theirs."

"And if he dies?" spat Woodcock Crown.

"Then the credit is still theirs."

"So we owe them a life?"

Badger Skull took out his blade. Looked at it for a long time, as if remembering how it had got every ancient scratch and nick on the savagely recurved blade. Woodcock Crown and the others in the war band watched him.

"I don't say we owe them anything," he said. "I'm just pointing out that they have done something they have not done for a very long time."

"Made a mistake?" said Woodcock Crown.

"No," snorted Badger Skull. "No, this Oversight, this Last Hand, they have made plenty of mistakes."

He stifled a laugh and re-sheathed his blade.

"So what is this thing they did that they have not done for a very long time?" said Woodcock Crown.

Badger Skull looked up into his eyes.

"They did their duty. To us. To the Sluagh. Not just to the light-grubbing people of the Hungry World."

"What does that mean?" said another Sluagh in the group behind Woodcock Crown.

"I don't know," said Badger Skull. "Maybe it means nothing. Or maybe it means the Shee are right."

"No," hissed Woodcock Crown. "We do not have to change."

"Maybe not. But we do have to think," said Badger Skull, looking up at the sun with a grimace of distaste. "All this light is making me sick. Time enough to talk on this after we venge ourselves on Mountfellon. The lowest tide is coming. Let us get to Irongate Steps. If Templebane's word is true, there is blood to be spilled before the moon rises."

CHAPTER 46

THE INBOUND CHILL

Once the hated Sluagh had left, Amos had come down into the forge to find the others sitting around the table too stunned to be talking. Even Cook was looking into her empty teacup with no thought of refilling it or anyone else's.

"Smith's not coming back," said Hodge flatly. "Someone's got to say it. We're done. We're on our own."

"No," said Sara. "We still have a Hand."

Hodge dragged himself to his feet again and stood, supporting himself on his fists on the tabletop.

"No, Sara Falk. This is the time for you to disperse until more members can be found to make The Oversight anew. I stay and guard the ravens in the Tower. As happened before. As The Smith told us has happened at least three times earlier in our history."

Cook cleared her throat.

"Ah. Well, as to that, he never quite told us exactly how that happened though, did he?"

"What d'you mean?" said Hodge, looking a little betrayed by her interjection.

"I mean, maybe him striding off and not coming back without warning isn't a part of it," she said.

"He would never have left us on purpose without explaining," said

Sharp. "We don't know how we communicate when we disperse to the four winds, how we search, how we persuade those we do find to join us without him, without—"

"When my parents died, I was alone, as we are alone," said Sara. She stood away from Sharp's hand and looked around at them all.

"I didn't give up just because they hadn't told me what to do exactly: I grew up."

"But you still had The Smith," said Sharp.

"And we have each other," said Sara, turning slowly as she counted them off. "Cook. Hodge. Charlie Pyefinch . . . Ida?"

Ida nodded.

"Of course," she said. "It is not the moment to go home, is it?"

"Thank you," said Sara. "Five. That's a Hand."

And you have my help too, if it will serve.

They all turned to look at Amos who was standing in the doorway, looking hesitant.

"Thank you," said Sara. "Maybe so. We have a Hand. And maybe the way we renew ourselves at the lowest point in our fortunes is by growing up and helping each other. And maybe if the eighty-five had not been killed in the Disaster, we would have been taught this is the way The Oversight rises like a phoenix from the ashes, again and again. Who knows? Maybe if they'd lived there would have been time for more lessons about our history, but there wasn't. They died. The Citizen killed them. And since then there has only been time to try and keep afloat, a single Hand to save a city, five to guard the Wildfire.

"Six," said Sharp. "There were always six. Emmet is one of us. You know I have always felt that. Maybe even the steadiest of us."

"So we grow up," said Sara. "We stand alone. We try and grow our strength again. We reduce our enemies and we guard—above all, we guard the Wildfire until The Smith returns."

"And if he doesn't?" said Cook.

"Then maybe, once present danger is past—if it passes—we go and find him."

She looked around at them all.

"But not until then."

"Don't know what the world's coming to when someone you've dandled on your knee as a baby tells you to grow up," said Cook, sniffing.

"Its senses?" said Sara. She turned to Amos.

"I don't know if we can trust you. And I don't know how to test you. So I'm going to take a leap of faith . . ."

"No, Sara—" said Sharp.

"Enough," she snapped, hating the edge in her voice even as she heard it. "You will stop worrying about me; you will stop caring for me; you will above all stop telling me I am wrong. Someone must make the decisions even if they are the wrong ones, because the only thing that is certain is that if we spend our time debating what to do but do nothing, we will certainly fail, and The Citizen will win."

Sharp opened his mouth to protest, but bit it shut upon catching Cook's warning look.

"Good," said Sara. "All that matters is the job in hand. You will take Amos Templebane and see if he is the knife that can unshuck the oyster of his brother's silence. We must know how far the cancer of this conspiracy has spread if we are to burn it out."

"Yes, Miss Falk," said Sharp, bowing very stiffly. "As you wish."

She watched him beckon Amos and leave without a backward glance. She was grateful for that. If he had looked back, she might have been tempted to unbend and apologise for upbraiding him in public for his loyalty to her. And the time for sentiment was gone.

She could feel the inbound chill of it on the wind. She hoped it was The Citizen who would be doing the departing, but one thing was certain.

There was dying to be done.

CHAPTER 47

UNDER THE KILLING FLOOR

Cait had fallen backwards out of the mirror, and several things had happened at once, none of them good.

She fell out of light into pitch dark.

She fell out of warm air into icy water.

She fell into water so cold it burned her eyes.

Her eardrums stabbed with sharp pain, as though they were bursting.

The shock of it clenched her so tight she didn't breathe a lungful of water, but she did exhale half the air inside her before choking the reflex off.

Armbruster and Magill got tangled up with her as they tumbled after her, which made her lose track of where up and down were.

She took a thrashing elbow in the eye, and a knee in the ribs, and then something desperate and furry scrabbled past her, claws raking her cheek as it headed in panic for the surface, and she realised it was the dog Digger.

She kicked after the dog, too desperate to notice that her boot connected with what might have been Magill or Armbruster's head.

As she rose, she felt the screaming pressure on her ears ease, and though she felt the ache in her lungs beginning to bite she ignored it and clamped her teeth together so she would not take a fatal breath of water before breaking the surface.

She clawed upwards through the darkness, aware that the surface above was becoming clearer, a rosy glow, treacherously warm-looking.

She saw the dog's silhouette just ahead of her, a dark rangy shape scrabbling against the ruddy backlight.

She kicked harder, furiously determined to use all her energy before the bone-crack pain of the freezing lake-water sapped the vitality from her limbs and fuddled her mind.

She kicked for her life, and hit the surface.

Hard.

Hard enough to hurt. Hard enough to knock stars into her eyes.

She steadied herself with a splayed hand against an immoveable ceiling.

The surface wasn't air.

It was thick ice.

She felt Armbruster and Magill arrive on either side of her, but her vision was too blurry to make out their faces with any clarity. They hit and punched at the ice roof, and it didn't buckle or flex one bit.

Cait fought panic and scrabbled inside her coat and fumbled one of The Oversight's candles from her inner pocket. Her fingers were not her own. They were numb rubber sausages that seemed to work on a delay. The candle slipped from her grip, and she snatched clumsily at it to catch it before it tumbled out of reach.

She caught it, but the movement of her hand broke it against her leg, so that she had only a stub left in her hand. She gripped hard, and snapped her wrist.

The candle ignited and showed her a strobing vision of hell.

The harsh flickering light of the Wildfire turned Magill and Armbruster into macabre, dancing marionettes, each of them treading water, faces desperate, eyes popped wide, cheeks bulging and mouths clamped shut as they hacked at the thick and unyielding ice using their knives like picks.

Their assault had no effect.

The desperate urgency in her lungs went from an ache to a shrieking pain.

Armbruster wrestled his gun free from its holster but then dropped it.

It somersaulted away into the darkness below.

The dog Digger died in front of her eyes.

It stopped scrabbling and opened its jaws as reflex made it breathe the lake, and immediately lost buoyancy, dropping past her.

No, she thought.

No.

She caught the dog's tail with her left hand as she punched the fist holding the candle and the Wildfire flame into the unyielding ice-floor above her. She felt the fire blaze and burn, heating the water around her hand as she kept churning her legs, trying to power upwards against the unmoveable roof.

Magill swam over to her and began chunking his bowie into the ice closer to the light.

It was futile. It was doomed. It was over.

All she had was the energy for one last furious blow as she bunched her fist and slammed it into the ice in a final act of defiance, not just punching the adamantine barrier between her and the air, and not punching with any hope now, but just punching everything, everything that had brought her to this sudden, grotesque and irreversible end, punching the whole damned world with all the power and anger left in her dying body. She punched without caring whether she broke her bones because in a short mouthful of water from now all pain would be gone . . .

And above her was no stone to mark her grave, just a flat plane of ice, a lonely frozen lake surrounded by steep mountain slopes covered with ancient pine trees heavy with snow; and above all that, an immensity of mountains whose jagged peaks soared heroically into a bloody sunset that painted everything with its ruddy light, even the incoming face of the dark storm-clouds rolling in from the north.

All this, and nothing moving in the crisp, cold moment before the sun drops behind the peaks and leaves the world to darkness and the next fall of snow.

Nothing moving except the small fist that punched out of the killing floor, the fist carrying the fire, the fist followed by the tall red-haired woman who drags herself and the dog out and onto the ice and just lies there as the two mountain men follow her, Magill using his bowie like an ice axe to get enough of a purchase on the slick surface to help Armbruster choke and splutter out of the hole.

Cait rolled over and reached for the dog.

"Got it," hacked Magill, dropping the bowie and staggering to his feet, grabbing the dog by its back legs and holding it upside down, swinging it lightly.

The dog choked and made a raw gagging noise as lake-water left its lungs, and then it convulsed and he half put it down, half dropped it as he too fell back and lay on the ice, getting his breath as the dog coughed and gacked and shook itself back to life.

"Goddamn," said Armbruster. "Hell was that . . .?"

Magill shook his head. Lost for words.

"Damned if I know," he said. "But we're alive."

"Get me out of here or that will change," said The Citizen's voice, punctuated by the unmistakable click of a revolver hammer being cocked.

Cait rolled over and saw the back of the old man's head sticking out of the hole, his arm pointing the long-barrelled pistol at Armbruster.

"Your gun is wet," said Magill.

"But my cartridges are sealed," said The Citizen. "If you want me to demonstrate, I will blow his head off to show you. Get m-me out of here."

His white face was going blue at the lips but his eyes were alive with an unquenchable fury of will-power.

Armbruster looked at Magill.

"Chances are it won't fire," he said. "And he's shaking like a—"

Cait didn't have to do much. She didn't even have to get off the ground. She just reached out and gripped the handle of Magill's discarded bowie-knife and scythed it across the ice in a fast powerful arc, letting the weight of the heavy blade power the razor-sharp cutting edge cleanly through The Citizen's neck, scarcely snagging at all as it clove the vertebrae and passed on and out the other side.

The force of the blow and the jetting pulse of The Citizen's heart bobbled the severed head around so she saw the shocked eyes seem to widen as he saw her, and then it tumbled sideways on the ice as the body it had been separated from sent a final dark fountain into the sky before it dropped back into the water and sunk.

Cait staggered to her feet and looked down at the head and then at Magill and Armbruster, whose faces were stuck somewhere between shock and something a little closer to awe.

"What?" she said, beginning to shake, either from the extreme cold or the hot flush of adrenalin.

"Nothing," said Magill.

"Good," she said. "There was too much talking going on, and I've no mind to die of cold after all that."

She looked down at The Citizen's head, and then flipped it with her boot, sending it back into the hole in the ice, where it bobbed, bubbled and sank without trace.

She handed the bowie-knife to Magill.

"Fine blade," she said.

Magill took it automatically, his hands trembling with the cold, his eyes still locked on the hole in the ice.

"Who the hell was that guy?" said Magill.

"That ain't the question, Jon," said Armbruster, looking around at the icy peaks and the wilderness of pines. "Question is: where the hell are we?"

"Well, that's easy," said Cait, teeth chattering as she slipped and stumbled past them, heading across the ice towards the tree-lined shore. "We're where we're going to die if we don't get warm and dry before it starts snowing again."

She began to jog towards the snow-laden pines.

"Why are you heading that way?" said Magill.

"I'm just following the dog," said Cait. "He's heading for the trees."

She reached a shaking hand into her jacket and held the last candle up over her shoulder without looking around.

"And trees burn."

Magill and Armbruster shared a look, and then began to trot unsteadily after her.

"It upset you that she's now probably saved us twice?" said Armbruster.

"Not a bit," said Magill. "Think we make a good team."

"We're not a team," gritted Cait, teeth now chattering like castanets. "We're just three d-d-damned idiots following a half-drowned dog."

"Upsets me," said Armbruster, "almost as much as not knowing who that fellow pretending to be Sharp was."

"You worry too much," said Magill.

"Upsets me because we owe her now. And that means we got to help her find that baby she keeps talking about."

Magill grimaced at Armbruster through chattering teeth.

"Let's just try and stay alive until morning," he said. "Finding stolen babies is a whole other story."

CHAPTER 48

A BLADE TO SHUCK AN OYSTER

Coram Templebane sat perched unsteadily on the tall three-legged stool in the narrow storeroom in which he had previously been interviewed by Sharp and Hodge. He leant back, feeling the rough texture of the protective wickerwork bound around the carboys on the shelf behind him. He rubbed himself back and forth on it, scratching the persistent itch he had been tormented by for the last couple of days. It had coincided with the message that had shaken him badly, in that it came from his past life, the one beyond the relative safety of the hospital, the one containing his Day Father. He still felt betrayed by Issachar, but more than that, he felt scared of him. He hadn't known how scared until the message had been delivered by his brothers. It had been a simple message, informing him that all would be forgiven if he would just tell Ketch he wanted to say something to The Oversight. He had been told what that something was, and assured that if he did not do it, then Issachar would send someone else to inquire why this was. "Sending someone else" was always a mortal threat in Templebane's business jargon, and Coram was unmanned by the thought. And yet the spark of resistance was there in his breast, and he had, for a day so far, kept his mouth shut. But it had left him with this damnable itch.

He felt like he was falling apart, and this new affliction of the skin was beginning to erode his already limited ability to think straight about anything other than his growing compendium of ailments.

He'd been left by Ketch propped in a most inconvenient attitude, and the normally helpful attendant had made things even more awkward by taking his crutches. With only one leg, this made his present position somewhat precarious. He carefully craned around to look at the door.

He's worried about you. He knows he's here for more questioning. He's worried you're going to hurt him.

"We didn't hurt him last time," said Sharp.

The two of them were leaning against the wall of the corridor outside the storeroom, where Amos was eavesdropping on his adopted brother's thoughts.

He's got a kind of . . . drift in his mind.

"What's that?" said Sharp. Amos shrugged.

Can't really explain. You'd have to feel it. It's like he's floating inside himself and not really holding on to the outside.

"The outside?"

Where we are.

"Is he unhinged then? Run mad . . . ?"

He's terrified.

"Of us?"

Amos hunched his shoulders, as if straining at the great weight of trying to explain the impossible. He gestured with hands, pointing all around them.

Of everything.

Sharp pushed off the wall and turned to the door.

"Let's put him out of his misery. I'll ask; you listen to what he's not saying—there'll be clues there . . ."

Can I ask? It would be better if I asked.

Sharp stopped, hand poised on the door-handle.

You told me what you want to know. If I ask, then I think I will be more connected to him if he tries to drift.

"Explain?"

I can't. If you can't feel it, it won't make sense. Like telling a blind man what blue is.

Sharp looked at him very closely. His scrutiny was distinctly uncomfortable. Amos swallowed and tried not to blink too much.

"You want me to trust you?"

Yes.

The deep brown eyes held him. Then Sharp nodded.

"Very well. Remember: first, we must know where Issachar Templebane is hiding; and secondly, why did he cause the loss of the Safe House when it was quite clear Mountfellon wanted to take the contents of the Red Library? Why did that impulse to theft turn to the fact of destruction? What changed? You must find that out. He must tell us."

Yes. If he knows. But the Day and Night Fathers kept their cards close to their chests. So Coram may indeed not know the answers.

"I may not know what he knows, Amos Templebane, but I have looked in enough guilty pairs of eyes to be assured that he absolutely knows something."

Coram turned as the door opened, steadying himself with a fumbling hand on the shelf behind. He was expecting to see the two members of The Oversight he met last time. His mouth fell open when not Hodge, but Amos followed Sharp into the room. Sharp leaned against the wall and gave Amos the seat in front of his erstwhile sibling.

"Coram, you remember your brother—"

Amos stared at Coram, equally shocked, eyes and mind trying to find the thick-haired, well-fed bully he had always been so scared of in this cropped, pale, one-legged skeleton in front of him. Coram of the sharp tongue and ready fist had turned into something almost fragile and birdlike.

Coram in turn stared at Amos, then at Sharp, then back at Amos and felt the old panic rising like a tide and decided once more not to fight it but to let go of everything and let it float him away into the safety of silence and insensibility.

Coram. It is me. Amos. This is my voice.

Coram flinched as if he had been stung. The voice was loud, but Amos's lips had not moved. Yet Coram could hear it clear as a bell, as if it was echoing around inside his skull. The presence of the words, the voice, the very idea that the blasted darkie was inside his head felt like a grotesque violation which made him want to vomit. He decided he must be imagining it. Possibly he had a fever. Perhaps the intolerable itching had been a harbinger of a new illness that came with its own delusional state. He closed his eyes and concentrated harder on dumbly not being a part of whatever was happening in the room.

Coram. Answer me.

The mute's words were like grappling hooks, sharp barbs cutting into him, stopping his escape on the swelling flood and tugging him.

I did not recognise you. They did not tell me you had lost a leg. Or that you looked so very . . . diminished in yourself.

Coram screwed his eyes even more tightly shut and began to moan. This intrusion into his head was a violation, a defilement, an outrage—

Open your eyes, Coram. We have questions for you.

"We?" The word burst out of Coram unbidden. He opened his mouth in shock.

We.

Coram flattened himself against the shelf as if trying to squirm back in among the carboys to distance himself from the word he had let escape. And yet more were bubbling behind his clenched teeth, and his jaw spasmed and he heard the incredulity in his own ragged voice.

"You? You are with The Oversight?"

"Yes, he is," said Sharp. "And now you have decided to talk, we would like you to tell us about the attack on our home . . ."

Coram shut his eyes again and shook his head.

Coram. You have one leg. You cannot escape. And even if you could, you cannot escape me now. Do you know what they call me?

Coram was outraged. Issachar had ordered him to do something as if he was just a puppet. The Oversight, on the other side, was ordering him to do something else. And in the middle, turning the thumbscrews, was the hateful younger brother Amos.

Something unlatched in his head.

"Traitor? Because you are, you fucking little pickaninny!"

The last word spat itself out like a vile bullet in an explosion of spittle. Amos calmly wiped his face. The name the brothers had branded him with, always preceded by the other two words, the casual obscenity twinned with the specific diminutive, brought back the full fury and the bitterness that had fuelled his decision to try and run from the house of Templebane. The fury was still there, banked up and ready to burst out. But because he felt it and because he both now knew what he was capable of doing and how fast he could do it, he kept it latched behind a cold smile. There were other ways to attack.

The Bloody Boy. They call me the Bloody Boy, Coram. And if you like, I will tell you why they call me that, and then you will answer the questions we have, because you will understand how very different I have become, and what I am capable of since you last saw me.

The panicked squirming sent the stool toppling to the ground with a sharp crash, and Coram found himself kept upright only by his shaking grip on the shelf behind. Sharp calmly righted the stool and slid it back beneath him.

"Now," he said, with a cold smile. "Amos will start again. And you will answer his questions."

Amos's smile was just as cold as Sharp's. In fact, a fragment of Coram's rational mind realised the tightness in both their smiles was the same: it was the tension of a great mainspring kept in check, a spring that if unleashed would release some hideous destructive power.

Amos leant forward slightly.

You will answer my questions, Coram Templebane. Because you know as well as I do that men have more to lose than legs or life. They can lose their minds and be trapped in a living hell that seems endless. Lie to us? Thwart us? . . . And this fucking little pickaninny will put you right there. For ever.

Coram whimpered.

Behind the buttress in his own mind, Amos smiled. He had no idea how to make the threat he had just issued actually happen. But Coram didn't know that.

Where is the Day Father?

And then warmth flooded into Coram's mind, because there was a way out of the cold hell he had found himself in. All he had to do was answer the question with the information Issachar had been so keen he should plant anyway. Everybody would be happy, and he could go back to his safe, silent routine.

"Irongate Steps," he said. "He's going to be at Irongate Steps, with Mountfellon. They're dragging the river at the lowest tide of the month, see? Now leave me alone . . ."

How do you know that?

"He got word I was here. He's been looking for me. He ain't one to betray 'is family, not like you. Shadwell and Vintry, they came by and said hello, see how I was. Yesterday."

Amos looked at Sharp.

"Irongate Steps then . . ."

"Irongate Steps at the lowest tide, which is this afternoon—and not a moment later," corrected Sharp.

CHAPTER 49

MOTHERS AND DAUGHTERS

Walking through the mirror'd world was nothing like using a Murano Cabinet. There was no immediate transport from Point A to Point B; rather a long and gruelling walk made all the more taxing by the unchanging vista of infinite reflections stretching away on all sides.

Lucy lost her sense of time as she trudged ahead, goaded forward by Dee's knife whenever she faltered. She walked into a blur of repetition which blunted her senses as exhaustion began to unmoor her from her sense of self. She may have stopped and they may even have dozed for a while, but then again she might have hallucinated this. All she really could be sure of was the ache in her feet and the pain in her heart, because no matter what the other numbing and disorientating effect of the long walk back to London was, the cruel truth was that it never allowed her to forget that Cait was dead, and that it had been by her hand.

And then, when she had given up all thought of ever arriving and had come to believe her future would just be this endless walk, Dee yanked the cord around her neck as the Coburg Ivory gave one last click.

They had arrived.

It happened fast.

Dee turned Lucy to the mirror to her left, and pushed her ahead of him into her own dead-eyed reflection, through the glass.

She stumbled out of the mirror'd world and fell forward as her foot

found there was no floor but an eighteen-inch drop onto the soft upholstery of the chaise-longue.

The Ghost, who had been sitting half asleep, sprang forward, a coiled
spring finally freed to strike, knocking her sideways with a sharp blow
that seemed to punch all the air out of her.

Dee stopped, face horror-struck, half in, half out of the mirror.

Lucy, spun by the blow and not yet aware of any real damage, saw
him hesitate and she punched on reflex, open-handed, the heel of her
palm catching him under the chin, snapping his open mouth shut with
a sharp crack of broken teeth, sending him staggering back into the
mirror. In the same moment the Ghost saw him and instantly struck
again.

Her blow only hit the glass and smashed it into a crazed star pattern.
Dee had disappeared back into the mirror'd world. The broken mirror
cut the connection and also severed the thing Dee had been holding in
his hand, slicing the handle of the Coburg Ivory so that the interlinked
balls fell unheeded on the chaise and rolled onto the floor.

The Ghost twisted and looked down at Lucy in a kind of hushed
confusion.

"You. You. But . . . you are not Francis," she said, a tone of mild
accusation colouring her words, as if this fact were Lucy's fault, as if she
had purposely chosen not to be Mountfellon out of some kind of wilful
impulse.

Lucy's reflexive elation at having finally escaped from Dee had passed
almost instantaneously as her body caught up with the seriousness of the
blow she had been dealt. She wondered if she had cracked a rib, the pain
was so suddenly sharp and intense.

She slumped down, despite herself, and lay awkwardly against the arm
of the chaise, staring at this crazed woman with the wild grey hair who
had punched her as she stepped out of the mirror. She had punched her
so hard that Lucy was too winded to speak clearly, too winded to get a
proper breath.

"Who is . . .?" she coughed. "Who is Francis?"

The Ghost looked around the room, distracted by some new music in her head.

"Mountfellon. I thought you were Mountfellon. He must die." She looked down at Lucy as though seeing her properly for the first time. "Mountfellon must die. Everybody knows this . . ."

"Mountfellon is not here," coughed Lucy. "Why'd you hit me?"

"You were supposed to be him," said the Ghost.

"Mountfellon's at Irongate Steps," Lucy wheezed, remembering the fragment of conversation she had overheard before exiting the closet in the fateful bedroom in Montreal where everything had come undone. Maybe this woman would go away and find him and leave her alone to catch her breath. "By the Tower."

"By the Tower," repeated the Ghost. "Yes. Hard by Traitor's Gate. That's better. That's a better place for Mountfellon to die."

"Why don't you go there?" said Lucy, wincing as she moved. "I'm not Mountfellon . . ."

Talking was hard.

"You're not," said the old woman.

Lucy looked up at the mirror she had stepped through and was relieved to see the second punch had clearly shattered it and that Dee was trapped on the other side. That was something.

If only she could get her breath.

". . . I'm Lucy Harker," she gritted.

If only she could stand up and look her attacker in the eye.

The old woman was staring at her, and something strange, something almost painful to see was happening to her face. Her expression twisted as though her face was trying to unpeel itself from her skull; only her wide staring eyes seemed to be holding it in place. And the eyes were filling with some kind of awful realisation.

"He is," said the madwoman. "Oh, my dear. He is your father."

Lucy decided she must get to her feet before the crazy woman decided to punch her again. She squirmed away and put her hand on the silk upholstery in order to push herself upright.

The silk was warm and wet. And then she looked down and saw the faded rose colour was dark now, and the darkness was hers. The chaise was covered in blood. And then she realised the dull pain from the punch was not a punch at all, but that the ghost had stabbed her in the side, stabbed her with the cruel-looking surgeon's knife she held slackly as her face writhed in its own circle of hell.

Lucy got to her feet.

"Please," she coughed, meaning to ask the woman not to stab her again.

And then she fell down and lay on the floor, looking at the ornate gilt plasterwork on the ceiling.

"You weren't meant to be you," said the old woman. "You were meant to be him."

"Help me," said Lucy, holding her hand over the warm spring bubbling out of her side. "Help . . ."

"Of course I will help," said the madwoman. "Why would I not help, my darling, my dear one?"

She knelt beside her and her writhing face paused for one moment and was still and sane and full of love and gentleness. It was a look Lucy had been waiting for her whole life, and in that look she saw through the dirt and the wild white hair and the lines the years had left and saw her mother.

She opened her mouth, but could not speak.

And then the Ghost stood up and nodded and strode purposefully to the door, as if she had never harmed a fly in her whole long life.

"Just stay, my love, just never leave, and I will go and kill your father and then you shall inherit this beautiful house and we shall live here happily ever after."

CHAPTER 50

THE FINAL CUT

Irongate Steps was the same dank cut sliced at right angles into the bank of the Thames between St. Katherine's Dock and the Tower where Sharp had gone to find Emmet, the place where they had then sat together and communed silently as they watched the river grind past.

Stuck between two significant landmarks and with its one-time utility as a landing place superseded by the easier access afforded by the neighbouring dock, it was an overlooked, forgotten place, haunted by the deep shadows thrown by its steep sides, and visited only infrequently by mudlarks, gutter-snipes and other riparian scavengers. There was a small fan of gravelly beach and the ruin of a wooden jetty at the wider, river end of the wedge, and at the narrow point of the cut where the shadows were darkest there was the ancient iron grating from which it got its name and out of which flowed that combination of underground stream and sewer which made London's waterway such a sure and constant source of noxiousness and disease.

The high sides of the gulley were gravel and clay, held back by a villainous patchwork of greasy pilings and tie-beams wedged in place by buttresses made from great baulks of timber, blackened with age and filth where they were not greened with slime and mossy waterweed. The tapering defile had an air of being a shunned, forgotten place, its forlorn atmosphere heightened by the largely blank rear elevations of the ramshackle warehouses and dwelling houses that overhung it on either side, as if the buildings had entered into a silent conspiracy to turn their backs on the narrow space that was, both physically and in terms of civic respectability, far beneath them.

It was also, thought Issachar Templebane as he peered down at it from one of the few garret windows that overlooked it, a perfect killing ground and a capital place for an ambush.

He checked his pocket-watch. The tide was almost at its lowest, and it was at this point that he had advised Mountfellon to come to the beach with his team of labourers and grapples to start the laborious process of dragging the river. Whether or not the noble lord succeeded in finding whatever chests The Oversight had notionally hidden beneath the water was of secondary importance to Issachar. It was simply the bait to a trap. He had offered to provide Mountfellon with a gang of workers but, given the failure of their last adventure on the river, Mountfellon had told him that he would provide his own men this time. Issachar didn't care much about this in either way. All that mattered was that he draw Mountfellon out into the open and deliver him to the ambushers who lurked in the shadows. He could not see them, but he knew that by prior conspiracy the vengeful Sluagh were hidden beneath him in the many convenient shadows thrown by the buttresses and bulwarks of the stygian cut below. Delivering their hated enemy to them would mend his relations with the nightwalkers and restore their former profitable association.

Below Issachar, but above the hidden Sluagh, was the second layer of the ambush, his sons and their guns. They were not there for Mountfellon. Nor were they there for the Sluagh whom they had been most severely admonished to leave unmolested. They were there for the more significant eradication.

They were there for The Oversight.

Issachar was not a bloodthirsty man, and if it was possible to conduct his business without the need for killing he would always prefer that course of action: death made ripples in the smooth pool of commerce, and the secret of the Templebanes' long success was that it was best achieved unobtrusively, beneath a calm surface of respectability. But The

Oversight had been an obstacle to his family's free trade for too long now, and since circumstance had reduced them to a conveniently erad-icable size, he was committed to blot them from the ledger, once and for all.

It was for this that he had armed and trained his sons. It was for this that he now stood beside Garlickhythe Templebane and his rifle, the best shot of them all.

It was for the insurance of this that he had two of Coram's explosive iron grenadoes laid on the windowsill, with a lit candle for their fuses standing by on a shelf, just in case bullets alone were not enough.

A very distant third item on his list was the retrieval of the object Dee had told him to tell Mountfellon about. If the day's events ended with him able to hand them over to the goat-bearded mirror-walker, so much the better, but it was—for Issachar—only a secondary thing. Dee would always have a use for the Templebanes' services, as he did not like to spend any time in London for reasons that were unclear. If the river had to be revisited, *post* the several *mortems* that were imminent, so much the better for Templebane, for he could extract further payment in kind, specie or favours. And he did like—as all businessmen do—to be able to dip twice into the same pocket if he could get away with it.

But the fact was that his pocket-watch told him Mountfellon should be on the beach with a gang of burly watermen, hurling grapples into the middle of the river and dragging them out, and his eyes told him this was not happening. Punctuality might be the courtesy of kings, but in this case it was clearly not the virtue of the viscount in question: and yet Templebane knew Mountfellon, though haughty and proud as any aristocrat he had ever met, prided himself most of all on being a man of scientific training and habit, and a man of that sort would not do other than respect the non-negotiable strictures of time and tide. Templebane's watch told him that low tide had arrived without the attendant Mountfellon. He sucked his teeth in irritation. And then he saw the steam tug and the man at the stern, and with a sickening jolt realised the day was not, perhaps, going to go strictly according to plan.

Mountfellon strode back and forth on the deck of the *Monarch*, his eyes glued to the trawling rig being towed behind as it churned manfully against the turbid seaward current. The sound of the steam engine and the threshing of the paddle wheels obscured the noise of the city around them, and so most communication was yelled from close quarters or indicated by simple sign language, but the small crew was well used to each other, and things were progressing well.

The rig he had designed was proving to be an excellent device. Twice already the array of grapples had snagged and pulled up treasures from the deep bed of the river, and though those had only amounted to a broken cartwheel with part of a snapped axle still attached, and a stone anchor with a chain rusted fast in the hole through its middle, both were early proofs of concept and pointers towards eventual success. Mountfellon, for a change, was feeling distinctly bucked.

Every now and then, he looked up and took a rough bearing relative to the significant landmarks on the riverside, checking that the steersman provided by Mr. Watkins was following his instructions. He had been ordered to methodically quarter the section of river opposite Irongate Steps, going back and forth so as to leave no section of its bed unharrowed by the trailing grappling hooks.

Mountfellon squinted at the narrow gravel strand debouching from the cut and Irongate Steps, and thought how poor Templebane's suggestion had been, the plan that he should attempt to drag the river by lobbing grapples from such an unpromising launching point: even the strongest sailor, well-practised at casting a line into the severest winds, would not have got a grapple even a quarter of the way across the width of the river. His own appliance of scientific principles to the problem was infinitely superior. Templebane's suggestion was in fact so patently impractical that it made him doubt the man's much vaunted intelligence. Perhaps the cunning man was more unnerved by the failure to eradicate The Oversight than Mountfellon had imagined.

Back in the deep shadows of the cut, the Sluagh too had finally seen and recognised Mountfellon on his steam tug.

"We cannot touch him out there on the flowing water," snarled Badger Skull. "We have wended our way through this maze of a city for naught."

"We are betrayed," said Woodcock Crown.

Badger Skull shook his head.

"To what end?" he said. "It makes no sense."

"The cunning man has been outfoxed then," spat Woodcock Crown.

"Or maybe Mountfellon intends to land here," volunteered a stocky Sluagh with a bull tattooed across his back.

"No, brother," said Badger Skull. "Mountfellon is a walking vileness but he knows well that we hunt him. I left a clear enough message at his damned house."

"Then maybe we can follow his progress along the river and waylay him when he lands . . ."

"A good thought, but a futile one. There are too many streams that cross any path along the river's edge. We would lose track of him before he landed and he would be able to lose himself in this ant's nest of a city before we came upon him."

Bull Tattoo shook his head angrily and shared a look with Woodcock Crown.

"We did not sharpen our blades by the light of the new moon to leave them unslaked," he growled. "If we cannot hack Mountfellon into the long darkness, maybe there are other reckonings to be had?"

Woodcock Crown was about to agree when his eye caught movement in the watery sunlight high above them on the edge of the cut, and he splayed his hand on Bull Tattoo's broad chest and pressed himself and his murderous companion back into the shadows as all the Sluagh band followed the direction of his gaze.

★   ★   ★

Up on the outer edge of St. Katherine's Dock, Sharp and Sara leapt from the dog cart only a step ahead of Hodge and Ida. Charlie swiftly looped the reins over the horse's head and told it to stay where it was, and then ran after them with Amos at his side. Jed and Archie flowed down the slippery steps which led down the side of the cut ahead of them.

They all overtook the sightless Hodge who had to take the slippery steps slower, though he too was moving at quite a clip.

"Jed!" he said. "Slow up!"

The dog turned and waited, letting the Terrier Man use his eyes, though he was quivering to get into the coming mischief his every instinct told him was about to begin.

"I must warn Emmet," said Sharp, drawing his knife as he ran across the beach to the old chain he had once rapped on to summon the patient golem from the depths of the river.

High above them in the garret window, Issachar put his hand gently on Garlickhythe's shoulder.

"Wait for it, my boy," he breathed. "Your brothers will not shoot until you do, and we must be sure all The Oversight is within their view."

Amos, on the steps below, heard the voice of his father like a distant whisper in the back of his head. The shock of it made him slip and almost fall on the treacherous footing. He grabbed at Charlie and shouted words into his brain.

Stop them! It's a trap!

Charlie looked at him in momentary incomprehension.

"Wh—?"

Jed barked a warning, and Hodge stopped and flattened against the wall, ten steps from the bottom.

"Where?" he shouted.

Amos pushed Charlie aside and ran towards Sara, waving mutely, his arms windmilling a warning he could not voice and she—at a greater distance than Charlie—could not quite catch. The metal plate around his neck bounced wildly as he ran, smacking an edge into his silently yelling mouth.

Stop! It's an ambush. There are guns! Templebane is here!

He was oblivious to the pain in his now bleeding mouth. He sprinted past Ida, who was halfway between him and Sara. She had heard him and was already turning, eyes scanning the embankment above for sign of their enemies as she unslung the crossbow from beneath her cloak.

"Where?" she said.

Everywhere! Up there!

He could hear his brothers' voices in his head. He could hear the shock in Issachar's voice as he pointed down at him.

"By Christ's bloody stripes, if it isn't the damned mute!"

Amos felt the scream of rage and frustration that had been building inside him for a whole lifetime swell to such an immensity that he knew he was going to burst like an overripe fruit if he could not let it out. He pointed upwards for Ida, and went fast-but-slow as he leaped towards Sara who only now was turning as she heard the intensity of his silent shouts in her own head.

Mr. Sharp! Mr. Sharp! Come back!

Sara spun away, yelling at Sharp who was now crouched over the chain, tapping it urgently with the haft of his knife.

"Jack!" she shouted. "It's a trap!"

From his godlike vantage point high among the overhanging rooftops, Issachar could see all The Oversight was fully exposed and in the open.

"Now," he snarled. "Kill them all."

Sharp's instinct on hearing Sara Falk's warning was of course not to save himself, but to run towards her in order to get her to a place of greater safety.

A bullet from the first volley unleashed by the hidden sons of Issachar sent him sprawling sideways, smacked untidily off his feet into the shallows.

Sara shouted his name in horror and lurched forward, trying to run towards him, but Amos grabbed her with one hand and slammed her into an angle of the broken jetty, putting himself between her and the guns.

Stay!

He held his other arm out and waved furiously, pointing at the badge around his neck, willing his brothers to recognise him.

They won't shoot me. You're safe—

A bullet had missed Jed by less than an inch, but sent a spray of sandy grit into his eyes. He yelped and stumbled blindly around the foot of the steps, pawing at his eyes, trying to clear them.

"Jed. Come! Come here!" Hodge shouted urgently, reaching sightlessly towards the animal. "Come. Let me."

The dog loped towards him, navigating blurrily by the sound of his voice more than sight.

Cook had been the last but one of The Oversight to come down the steps, leaving Hodge and Jed just behind her, but she had been the first to fall. She dropped to her knees and then sat back, a surprised look on her face.

Ida turned and saw her.

"Cook!" she shouted.

Cook smiled and tried to wave her away. She appeared not to notice that her hand had been blasted away by a blast of buckshot and was lying behind her on the gravel, beside the shredded triple-wood bracelet. She also seemed unaware of the pumping wound on her chest.

"Just winded myself," she said. "Don't you worry about me. Just give me a help getting up—"

"No," shouted Ida. "Stay down."

She ran and slid in next to Cook in a spray of mud and gravel.

"Oh," said Cook, looking down at her front and coughing. "I see. Bugger."

She looked at her wrist.

"I could have had a hook," she said. "If not for this other . . ."

She coughed red and grimaced. She looked more irritated than scared or in pain.

"Well," she said. "Anyway, there it is. Stupid way to go. Tell them I loved them, eh, Trousers?"

"No," said Ida, trying to drag her to her feet. "No, you're not—"

Cook shook her head.

"I am. I'm not scared of this. Getting old and losing my wits and my faculties . . . having to be looked after. That's what I was scared of. This is . . . I've seen the wide world and I've had my fill of all that took my fancy. No complaints," she said, and coughed another gout of blood, which she wiped off her chin, trying to find a grin and almost getting there. "One of you'll have to turn cook now . . . there's a plum pudding I made in the back pantry. Been feeding it brandy for Christmas . . . Don't let it go dry, eh?"

Ida tried to say something but the words got snagged in her throat.

"Don't start blubbing, you fool." Cook coughed more blood, finally smiling through it, and squeezed Ida's hand. "Blub later. After you've killed the bastards."

She coughed again, tried to reach for Ida's face, but her hand missed and dropped and she was still.

Ida didn't waste time wiping her eyes. She just turned and sprinted for the sheer wall of the cut beneath Issachar's warehouse and leapt at it, reaching for a high handhold with a wild, animal roar of grief.

Sharp staggered to his feet, face white with shock, the hand clamped to his side wet with something darker and thicker than water. Sara shouted at him:

"Jack! No. Stay!"

She tried to wrench herself free again. Amos had tears in his eyes as he jammed himself back, keeping her trapped and safe by brute force alone.

No, please; you're safe—

"Kill the Jewess; shoot the mute. I've no more use for him," spat Issachar.

Garlickhythe was the sharpshooter among the brothers, the one Abchurch had been most jealous of. He was also the most cold-blooded of them, which might have been a contributing factor to his prowess as a marksman.

"I'll blow his treacherous black heart right out the back of his spine," he grinned, and pulled the trigger.

In the instant before the hammer fell, he thought he heard a voice screaming his name inside his own head, but by then it was too late.

Garlickhythe, no—!

The bullet flew true, the lethal lead rifling through the air at more than eight hundred feet per second, hitting Amos square in the chest, front and centre, the force of it sledgehammering him off his feet and knocking his body into Sara, who saw his mouth gaping wide, bloodied teeth gasping for a breath that wouldn't come—

Aah—

He spasmed against her.

Aah—

"Amos!" she cried.

Ah . . .

The world went away from him, just like that: no fanfare, no goodbye, just a heavy black cleaver brutally cutting him off from the light and the noise.

"Amos, come. Push with your legs!"

Sara, unaware that he had gone, was trying to drag him back to the scanty cover of the ruined jetty, but her eyes were on Sharp. He was moving now. He was alive. She didn't hear another ragged volley from the ramparts above them, but she felt a dull blow in her leg which knocked her away from Amos's unmoving body and tumbled her into the water.

A glimpse, before her head went under, of Sharp.

Snarling.

Blades in both hands.

Going fast-but-slow.

Charging straight towards the guns, fury moving him so fast that his wound left a thin ribbon of blood-spray hanging smeared across the air as he went.

Her ears were full of water, so the sound of the next volley was muffled. She saw gravel and mud kick up all around Sharp, who stopped abruptly as if punched by a giant invisible hand, arms wide, blades flying left and right from his lifeless hands, flashing as they spun in the thin evening sunlight—

—and then another streak of movement as Charlie Pyefinch blistered across the width of the cut, small stones spitting from beneath his feet, tearing in to try and rescue the fallen Sharp, slowing as he slid to a halt and bent to lift the body.

A single shot cracked out from the high warehouse window and again an invisible fist seemed to just cuff the boy sideways into the filth beside Sharp's unmoving body, now lying next to him face down in the ooze.

"A lovely shot, my beauty," said Issachar, an exultant laugh in his voice. Garlickhythe smiled

and then slammed backwards, his head smacking into Issachar's side with enough force to wind him, and then, horribly, to stick there.

"Wh—?" said Issachar, looking down in shock.

Garlickhythe stared back at him with one lifeless eye, the other one having been replaced by the feathered end of a crossbow bolt. He shoved the body away and yelped as the arrowhead, which had pinned it to his side, wrenched out of his flesh. It was not a mortal injury, just a flesh wound, but Templebane had a lot of flesh and it bled copiously as he stood gaping down at it in disbelief.

Sara was gasping in the water, having been dragged out by the current, weakened by the bullet in her leg. Something hit her hard in the ribs, and she scrabbled hold of it. It was the last remnant of the ruined jetty, a tilted piling that canted crazily off its original vertical, now pointing downstream about a foot below the waterline. It held her steady against the relentless pressure of water.

Hodge was crouched on the steps, protected by the corner in the wall, hurriedly trying to clear Jed's eyes, the dog quivering with tension but allowing his friend to dab at him with his handkerchief soaked in water from the puddle he was sitting in.

He shook his head and barked. One eye was clear, the other foggy but clearing. Hodge saw the devastation in front of him for the first time, through the dog's eyes.

"No!" he breathed. "It's a bloody massacre."

He pushed himself to his feet and pulled the knives from his belt.

"Come on boy. Stay close. Let's go among 'em."

He kept close to the wall and began to edge around the corner.

In the shadows by the Irongate, Badger Skull pointed at the fallen members of The Oversight splayed on the gravel.

"We must help them."

"Are you run mad? Why would we?" snarled Woodcock Crown, grabbing Badger Skull's arm. "Just because they saved one of ours? Their debt is far from paid. No, brother, we should finish them while they're down."

Badger Skull snarled back at him.

"If we start keeping close tally on our debts, we are no better than the Hungry World. And if we are no better than the Hungry World, who are we?"

He spat on the ground between them.

"If you wish to fight, fight me—or get out of my way. The Shee was right. Change does not mean surrender."

Charlie pushed himself to his feet once more, his face now streaked with blood, which he wiped from his eyes as he reached for Sharp and tried to drag him to some kind of safety behind one of the thick wooden buttresses.

Sara's heart leapt. If Charlie was risking his life again to pull the dead-weight of Sharp's unresponsive body, it must mean he could see he was still alive.

A wave thrown by the churning progress of the paddle-tug swamped her from behind, and she lost sight of the shore, and then as she coughed and spat back into the air and shook the water from her eyes she saw Charlie still on his feet, but now he was twisting away from the river to face something new, something which killed that treacherous leap of hope in her heart stone dead.

A compact swarm of unmistakably tattooed men came boiling out of the deeper shadows, fierce-faced men with bronze blades like broken-backed sickles in their hands. In an instant, the Sluagh engulfed Charlie and Sharp like an angry wave, and then more bow wash from the tug dunked her beneath the water and when she fought clear again the cut was now empty and Charlie was gone and Sharp was gone, and she knew with absolute certainty that any opportunity to unsay the things she had said was gone too, and gone for ever, as was the chance to say new, kinder, truer things to make up for the past words, because even if she survived this, she would never see him again, not alive.

She would, if spared, make herself see whatever butcher's shambles the Sluagh had hacked him into, but only to fire her resolve to now burn them out of the world once and for all.

And hanging on half-drowned in the Thames, she realised the true horror of her love, that in this moment she would burn a world to avenge him, two worlds if it would bring him back even for an hour. But of course it wouldn't. Natural or supranatural, one thing was constant and irrevocable: death was death, and though everyone's last door was different and passed through alone, all those doors opened only once and slammed shut for ever as soon as that final threshold had been crossed.

No one came back.

And worse than that was the thought that this moment would pass.

This was the split curse of the clear mind Sara Falk bore, a mind always in the moment but always watching herself in the moment too: even as she hung in the water, clinging to the mooring ring, seeing everything she loved die, she was outside herself, knowing worse truths than the ones unfolding in front of her eyes.

This moment would pass.

Time would move on.

She would burn no worlds, for no good would come of it.

She would mourn this instant of clear elemental fury too, as she would grieve the death of Sharp and the others. She would feel perpetual sorrow for the loss of everything she cared for, and she would be left alone to lament the one thing that lasted, the cold obdurate unloved thing which would now fill the shockingly painful gulf in her heart: duty.

Duty was the last remnant of what she had once had, the thing that would banish any treacherous warmth and softness in her for ever. She would deplore the fact that this thankless duty was all that was left her in place of solace.

But she would do it, precisely because it was all that remained.

And because, of course, that was what he would have done in her place.

She wrenched her eyes from the killing ground of the cut and turned towards the steam tug.

Mountfellon was dragging the river.

Mountfellon was trying to steal the Wildfire.

There was no more last Hand. There was only her.

She was The Oversight.

Her duty was to protect the city.

There was only one way to make sure of that.

The thought came into her head in a different voice, like a scream from a distant shore.

Mountfellon must die.

CHAPTER 51

A FACE AT THE WINDOW

The Ghost was gone, the house was empty and Lucy, still sprawled on the chaise-longue, knew if she matched its stillness, she would die. She needed to save herself, because no one was coming to do it for her. She had wadded one of her gloves into a pad she held tightly against the wound in her side to try and staunch the blood flow, but every time she moved it felt as though she was being stabbed again, though this time the sensation was not the dull, winding impact she had mistaken for a mere punch, but an increasingly sharp and disabling pain.

But pain or no pain, she had to move. If she just stayed on the chaise, she would eventually bleed the rest of her life out onto the already sodden silk upholstery. If she moved, she would probably bleed faster, but it was only in movement that there was any chance of success. Somewhere in the shocked core of herself she was proud she was able to think clearly, and that spark of pride got her off the seat and gave her enough power to stagger on disconcertingly heavy legs across the parquet floor to the windows. The opaque milk-glass hid the street from her and prevented any bystander from seeing her waving for help. So the glass would have to go. She looked around for something with which to break it: there was a candlestick on the table by the bloodied chaise, but she did not have the energy to stumble back and pick it up. Instead she reached for the heavy damask curtains, wrapped them around her fist and punched the nearest pane of glass.

The fragments fell on top of the portico, and did not land on the street below where they might have caught the attention of any of the several pedestrians nearby. As it was, the noise of the breaking glass was lost in the sound of the city beyond, and no one looked up at the pale face in the broken astragal.

She tried to shout, but her voice had been taken by the blow. She only heard a thin rasping wheeze, more like a whisper.

"Help . . ."

She pushed her head and her arm out of the window and waved weakly.

"Help, please . . ."

No one looked up and saw her face, or the bloody hand waving at them. The city drowned her weakening voice.

But someone looked down and saw her.

She heard a rapping noise, and raised her head to see a whey-faced child banging at the glass of a closed window in the house opposite. The child was shouting something excitedly and pointing at her. Another face, and adult, swung into view over the child's shoulder, looked at Lucy in horror, and then dragged the child away from the window.

Lucy waved one last time and then laid her head on the cool stone of the windowsill. She would just close her eyes for a moment. She would regain her strength with a little rest. Then she would try and shout louder. Surely someone would hear. When she wasn't so tired.

Her eyes closed and the city went away.

CHAPTER 52

THE BLOODIEST BOY

It was on one of the moments when Mountfellon was checking the thus far exemplary station-keeping of the steersman that he saw figures running out into the cut at Irongate, and then heard what seemed, over the clank of the steam engine and the sound of the paddle wheels, to be a series of light cracks and popping noises, at which some of the figures appeared unaccountably to topple over . . .

The nasty jolt of recognition he felt at the sight of Sara Falk's unmistakable white plait was too brief for him to parse the oddity of the apparent situation, because at the very moment he saw it, the chain men at his side whooped and cheered and began winding in one of the grapples.

"We got something, my lord!" the closest one shouted into his ear. The elation in their voices and the alacrity of their actions was a direct consequence of the lavish bonus payment Mountfellon had offered if they found the desired lead caskets.

Immediately, he lost interest in the strange tableau being enacted in the cut, parking it for later analysis, and focused on what evidently heavy item the chain men were pulling in from the bed of the river.

This was what his life had been moving towards ever since that fateful moment when he had seen the girl walk through the mirror and reveal the true hidden clockwork behind the world. This was the moment when he would grasp the key to that great and secret mechanism. And with that in his grasp, he would have power, more power than one man had perhaps ever had over his fellow man, the power to move where he would, see what he wished, overhear what he needed, and the ability to take, to influence, to steer, to suborn and manipulate any and everything that came within his ambit. He had never had any doubt of his greatness, either of intellect or station, and the power he was about to acquire seemed, in this moment, to be no more than his due, his birthright. The anticipation he felt was violent and sexual: he was to embark on a destiny whose ends and greatness even he, with his fine mind, could not yet envision. He had a heady sensation, as if he had miraculously grown two feet taller in this moment, and his whole body felt vibrant and engorged with anticipation of the now inevitable.

Beneath the water, not one but two grapples had hooked on two things.

The first was caught on the massive ancient chain that stretched from the shore, the one Sharp had tried to use to alert Emmet about the imminent danger churning overhead.

The second caught Emmet himself, and the casket he had so doggedly attached himself to. The hook trapped his arm against the side of the chest and yanked him off the riverbed with it. It was on this grapple that the excited men on the boat were pulling.

The first grapple, as the tug continued to power downstream, lifted the submerged chain off the bottom, pulling it tight, bringing it ever closer to the surface, until it went tight as a bar and held suddenly, slewing the paddle boat to one side.

Closer to the water's edge, it swung across Sara, knocking her from her handhold on the submerged piling. She had just enough time to see it coming but not enough to realise what it was, though she did manage to grab it with one hand before her grasp on the mooring bolt was torn free and she was dragged out further into the river.

Mountfellon went sprawling, steadying himself on the iron track that crossed the deck carrying the heavy counterweight chain-box Watkins had been so proud to demonstrate: he nearly lost a hand as the wheels on the carriage jerked forward, just managing to snatch it out of the way on reflex.

The men hauling on the grapple also lost their footing for an instant, and in that moment the line from the grapple which had trapped Emmet's arm loosened and he broke free in the water. A second or so later and the steersman and the engineer had stopped the wheels and corrected the rudder and the tug hung in the river, no longer tilting crazily, but moored by the grapple on the old chain which acted like an impromptu anchor.

"Hold steady!" shouted the men on the grapples, and by the time Mountfellon had pulled himself to his feet they were using a boathook to help drag a dripping wet grey metal casket inboard, a heavy coffin-sized object which smashed to the deck boards as it came over the bow rail.

Mountfellon grabbed a sledgehammer and a chisel and fell upon it in a frenzy of excitement, his heart leaping as he bludgeoned first the lock shackle and then hammered away at the lead solder rendering the thing waterproof. He was oblivious to the difficulty the steersman was having coordinating movements with the engineer as they tried to free the tug from its impromptu anchoring spot. It was only when they tried to take the sledgehammer in order to knock out the pin that held the trawling rig in place that he took any notice, and that was just to tell them to hang off and wait, because the rig was not to be abandoned until they were sure all the caskets were off the damned river bed.

Then he went back to jimmying the casket open. The first thin crack he made in the seal made him chuckle in satisfaction: a stripe of light was clearly visible from within. He put his hand on the lid. It was warm.

He laughed exultantly, louder this time. He had it. And in a few more blows he would get the lid open enough to get his hand inside and grasp the Wildfire for himself.

Issachar had steadied himself, lit the grenadoe and hurled it into the cut below. The fizzing iron ball fell out of the sky and thumped on the mud next to Hodge. Jed ran towards it. Hodge ran for the dog and grabbed blindly at it, his hands flailing so that his mind tried to compensate for the fact he was seeing himself through the dog's eyes.

"No, Jed, get away from it!" he yelled hoarsely.

The terrier stopped. The pause gave Hodge enough time to grab the dog by the scruff of its neck and fling it clear.

The fuse stopped fizzing. Hodge threw himself away from it too, starting to sprint after his dog, but he ran blindly, straight into the angled beam of one of the buttresses and fell senseless to the ground, tumbling into the gravel on the other side of the selfsame wooden spar that Sharp and Emmet had sat on to watch the Thames.

The grenade exploded with a short, brutal concussion. Mud flew everywhere, flung savagely away from the epicentre of the blast. Had it not been buried in the ooze before it detonated, no doubt the damage would have been more immediate, but as it was, the detonation blew a ragged hole in the pilings holding back the side of the cut. For a moment, as the mud spray hung in the air in a fine brown mist, nothing happened— and then with an initially slow, and then gut-wrenchingly sudden movement, the gravel slumped out as the bank collapsed on top of Hodge, burying him completely.

Issachar stood with his back to the wall beside the window, terrified that another bolt would follow its predecessor through the opening if he was to show himself.

"Go down and finish them off!" he screamed. "Fifty gold guineas for whoever brings me the damned crossbow!"

Fifty gold guineas was a fortune none of the sons of Issachar had dreamed of possessing, and their blood was up, fired by the rush of adrenalin and the strong sense of mortal power the bucking of the guns in their hands had transmitted, a sense as palpable as the smell of black powder hanging in the air around them. As one they rose from their shooting positions and ran towards the steps leading down into the cut, jostling each other, cursing, fumbling and stumbling as they tried to run and reload at the same time.

The Sluagh had been far enough away from the blast to avoid lethal wounds, backed up as they were against the iron gate at the narrow blade-end of the cut, but they had been knocked off their feet and bloodied by pieces of gravel and wood shards. They had also been deafened by the bang.

Badger Skull levered himself to his feet and looked at the splinter of ancient wood sticking out of his calf like a rough-hewn tent peg. He bent and jerked it out with a tight grunt of irritation.

He caught Charlie's eye.

"Stay still," he said, pointing. "Keep pressure on the bullet hole or you will bleed out."

Charlie could not hear what he was saying as his ears were still ringing, but he understood the gruff gesture. He understood it more than he understood what had happened to him and Sharp. He understood it more than the death of Cook, a death he had seen but which was so impossible, so wrong, that he didn't yet believe it. Sharp was behind him, closer to the gate, so he would have been protected from the worst of the blast by the phalanx of Sluagh between him and it, the band of men getting to their feet and cursing the bloody marks left on them by the grenadoe.

Charlie had known that he and Sharp were dead the moment the snarling crew had burst from the shadows and surrounded them. He had thought there might have been a chance for him to drag Sharp and himself back into cover, and perhaps to staunch their wounds long enough for some help to arrive, but help had not arrived and the Sluagh had come in their place.

He had grabbed for his knife and had it immediately cuffed from his hand as other hands had reached for him. Not blades, but hands, hands that grabbed and lifted and dragged both him and Sharp to safety. And when he looked up, the grotesque, terrifying whorl of tattoos looking back down at him had smiled and he recognised Woodcock Crown and Badger Skull, who had leant in and growled:

"A favour for a favour, boy, just as you said."

★   ★   ★

The brothers formed a rough line across the cut and walked towards the narrow end, guns raised.

When their eyes adjusted and they were close enough to see the knot of Sluagh bunched against the iron gate, they stopped and raised their weapons.

"Christ," said one. "These are ugly bastards and no mistake."

"They're on our side," said Vintry. "Dark allies of the Day Father. 'E ain't after them. 'E just wants The Oversight done."

"Them on the ground is Oversight," said one of his brothers excitedly.

"True," said Vintry.

He raised his gun and pointed it at Badger Skull.

"You step aside, matey, and let us have a crack at them two," he said. "We got no argument with you; we're on the same side. Oversight no friends of yours, are they?"

Badger Skull rocked his head from side to side as if unkinking a particularly persistent knot in his neck.

"No," he said. "No, they aren't."

"So step away, and keep them blades at your sides, and we'll just take over from here," said Vintry.

"Or . . . what?" said Badger Skull.

Poultry Templebane had a hair trigger on the blunderbuss he favoured as a weapon. He waved it towards the Sluagh.

"I'd kill me own mum for 'arf a gold guinea if I 'ad one," he snarled. "So you just fuck off out the way right now, you nasty-looking buggers, or I'll pulp you to fucking mincemeat, you see if I don't, you just see if—"

He did. By mistake. Jerk the trigger.

And blasted the nearest Sluagh off his feet, dead before his shoulderblades hit the ground.

There was a stunned silence.

Then the Sluagh looked up from the dead body and growled as one.

"Fuck it," said Vintry. "Now we got to kill them all."

Charlie saw that no matter how fast the Sluagh attacked, the bullets would be faster.

"Suits me," said another brother, cocking his gun and aiming it at Woodcock Crown. "Fifty guineas is fifty guineas, even if we 'as to split it. Night-night, ugly boys."

NO.

The voice in their heads was so loud and so powerful that they all winced.

NO MORE BLOOD.

Vintry turned and saw who was roaring in his head.

Amos walked towards them, stumbling as he came. The metal plate he wore around his neck was no longer flat, but dished in by the lead bullet that had hit it. He winced as he walked, the force of the impact having broken his sternum so that each step felt like a hot knife jagging into his chest, but despite that his progress had an unstoppable momentum to it.

NO MORE KILLING.

"How's he doing that?" said the brother who had just spoken.

"Dunno," said Vintry. "Don't care none neither."

He aimed his gun at Amos.

Vintry. Please. Please don't make me stop you.

"Fuck off, you black bastard."

Or what?

The brothers laughed.

"Just shoot him and let's get on with—"

No.

"I warned you," said Vintry. And he spun on his heels and squeezed the trigger.

All the brothers jerked at the same time, brother suddenly facing brother as if they were marionettes unable to control their own movements as they fired their own weapons into one another, even one who had not yet reloaded his blunderbuss, impotently squeezing the trigger at the very instant Vintry's bullet blew the back of his head off.

Charlie blinked reflexively at the noise and then his eyes went wide at the sight of the brothers falling to the ground while Amos continued to walk towards them, through the blood mist, past their jerking bodies.

"How did you do that?" he breathed. "Howd'you make 'em shoot each other?!"

Badger Skull exhaled, face stuck somewhere between shocked and impressed.

"What are you?" he said.

Amos stopped and looked around at the fallen bodies.

I don't know.

He looked up at Charlie. This time his eyes were dry.

But I did warn them.

"He's one of us," said Sharp weakly, looking up from the gravel. "Now give me my candles, for I must cauterise these wounds before I bleed away, and so must you . . . Amos, please go and help those dogs . . ."

"No," said Charlie, looking down at the hand clamped over the bullet wound in his side. "No. You don't need flame for the wound . . ."

Sharp followed his eyes, then coughed in surprise before looking down at his own hands staunching the flow of blood from his chest. He tried to take his hand away but found he couldn't.

On both of their wrists, the triple-wood bracelets had sprouted, green tendrils twining over their hands and around their bodies as strands and threads of vegetation wound themselves into patches which began to look like bark scars over their wounds.

"What is this?" said Charlie, his voice a half-sob of pain and wonderment.

"I don't know," grimaced Sharp, allowing himself to lie back as a thick tendril of ash probed into a bullet hole and thickened, blocking the flow of blood. "It hurts like blazes . . ."

He pushed himself up on his elbow and looked at the river, eyes searching for a small head in the water.

"I recognise the pain though," he said.

"Me too," said Charlie, sitting up with a grimace as he tried to drag himself towards the fallen gravel bank and join the dogs' excavation with his one free hand.

"It's life."

CHAPTER 53

THE WILDFIRE UNBOUND

Issachar gaped at the window under the eaves, staring down in shock at the carnage his murderous sons had inexplicably unleashed on each other. He gaped, but not for long. He paused only to snatch the fallen rifle from Garlickhythe and a handful of bullets from the open box on the window ledge, and then he ran.

He pounded down the creaking wooden warehouse stairs like an unstoppable avalanche of wobbling flesh, his breath coming in short, panicked barks which turned to a higher-pitched wheezing as he reached ground level and hurled himself towards the door beyond which his carriage waited.

He wrenched the door open and burst into the street, smashing into a passing pedestrian with such velocity that they both sprawled into the road beyond. The rifle went flying one way and the bullets another, and he scrambled to his feet with so little concern for the old woman he had steamrollered that he put his knee on her stomach and launched himself upright with his flabby crablike hand pushing straight down on her heaving chest. He spared her not a look, let alone an apology as he ran towards his waiting carriage.

And then he stutter-stepped to a halt as he saw the young girl who rolled herself over the low wall at the lip of the cut. It was not her trousers that shocked him into stasis: it was the ease with which she swung the crossbow from her back and aimed it at him.

"No," he said. "No. You can't. You can't. I can make a deal. I can give you money. You can't."

"I know," she said.

Father?

The voice inside his head was the final straw. Issachar felt his bladder empty down his shaking leg.

She can.

Issachar screamed at Ida, spittle flying from his mouth as he did so.

"No! You can't."

"I know," she repeated.

And shot him.

"But I did."

She jogged over to him and put her foot on his chest, pulling the quarrel free with a workmanlike tug. She stared at his dimming eyes.

"You kill my friends; I kill you. That's my deal."

And she slung the crossbow and turned back to the wall over the edge of the cut. She paused a moment to take in the dogs digging furiously at the slump of gravel on the other side, and then she scrambled over the wall and began climbing down as fast as she could, to help them.

She hadn't spared more than a glance at the old woman Templebane had bowled over, more than to register that she was well enough to have got back onto her feet.

She was gone by the time the Ghost had got her breath back, wincing at the pain the fat man's knee had left as he knelt on her stomach. She did not see her pick up the rifle and a bullet and stumble to the edge of the parapet closest to the river.

The Ghost had no interest in the furious activity below her. Her eyes were only for the unmistakable figure of Mountfellon on the tilting deck of the chain-snared steam tug beyond.

"Francis," she said, and her eyes were bright with an inner sunlight.

"Francis. There you are. And here I am. And I am not as I was, and you are Mountfellon. And now I must act, and everyone knows what you must do, Francis . . ."

She giggled a little as she loaded the rifle with an efficiency that would have surprised any onlooker had the backstreet behind the warehouse been peopled by anyone other than herself and the still-twitching body of Issachar Templebane.

She rested the gun on the wall top, and squinted down the sights.

". . . everyone knows, Mountfellon must die."

Emmet's head broke the surface and stared around. He saw the tug. He saw the casket disappearing over the rail. And then he was hit in the back by the taut chain that had swept across the width of the river as the current took the tug on the end of it. He gripped it and looked around.

His hollow eyes fell on the figure at the end of the chain.

It was Sara, and she was hauling herself hand over hand towards him, her face a mask of pure determination, eyes locked on Mountfellon's back.

"The Wildfire," she shouted, waving at Emmet. He nodded and turned back to the boat, wrenching himself through the water.

The boatmen didn't see him come over the rail, and he had two in the air, cartwheeling overboard as he flung them clear, before the others noticed. He threw two more and then the steersman just jumped without a second thought, terrified by the drenched man-monster that appeared to have just risen from the deep river like a nightmare made flesh.

The engineer had a cooler head and, as Emmet stepped towards him, he kicked the brake-lever on the chain-box, which was on the higher port side of the sloping deck. Emmet lunged for him, but just as his fingertips brushed his collar the golem was slammed brutally sideways by more than a ton and a half of fast-sliding wagon that pounded him into the starboard buffer and pinned him there.

Sara hauled herself over the railing and pointed a dripping finger at the engineer.

"You, over the side, now," she said, and the force behind her look was enough to turn his mind and his body as he ran for the river and leapt for his life.

Sara shook water from her eyes and turned her attention to Mountfellon. "The Wildfire," she said. "Give it to me."

She moved towards him, her eyes locked on the candle in the box and the wreath around it. Even without knowing what it was, she would have recognised the flame anywhere, having spent a lifetime guarding it: it was just a tiny lick of fire held by the thin wick of a candle, but seen with the right eyes it was also huge, a peephole into a whole other dimension of roiling conflagration, a perpetual hunger bursting to escape and consume all that fell before it. The pure power and destructive danger of the thing was all the stronger for being pent up in the tiniest of candle flames.

As she moved towards it she worked the Green Man's bracelet off her wrist and held it at her side.

Mountfellon scrabbled in his jacket and fumbled a pair of smoked-lens spectacles over his eyes.

"You cannot make me," he said. "You're just a woman without a weapon. You can do nothing. Stay where you are."

"I am alone, that's true," she said, continuing to step towards him. "But I can do something. I can save London. Now be very careful and hand that candlestick to me."

He jerked back, away from her. The triple-wood wreath bobbled alarmingly. She stopped.

"Be careful, Mountfellon," she said. "You don't know what you have there."

"The key. The key to all the hidden clockwork," he grinned. "Pure power."

"You don't know how to control it, or why you must not ever try," she said, easing towards him again, her eyes locked on the protective wreath.

"I will find out. I am a man of science. I will experiment. I will master it," he said, stepping back until the chain-box dug into his shoulder-blades and stopped him. "This is my destiny. And if you come an inch closer to me, you pale-faced bitch, I will start by seeing if you burn."

"Emmet," she said calmly. "Gently now."

Mountfellon had no time to register what she had said before a shovel-sized hand had closed around the back of his neck and tightened like an immoveable vice.

"Emmet will snap your neck if I tell him to," said Sara. "Now you will hand me the candle very, very carefully, taking extreme care not to dislodge the small wreath. If you do let it fall clear of the flame, we will all die. If you hand it to me, we will all live. You have my word on both of those certainties."

Mountfellon tried to pull free. The wreath slipped alarmingly. The Wildfire flared with a hungry roar then died back to a small candle flame as the triple-wood band settled back into place.

Mountfellon's eyes went wide at the sight of it. Then he licked his lips as his mind began to sort through the options still open to him.

Sara's eyes bored into his, unwavering.

"Part of me would like you to do what you are considering. Part of me would welcome the oblivion you are thinking of bringing down on both of us. But you will give us the flame, and you will not be harmed if you do so."

"And why would I trust you?" he sneered.

"Because Lore and Law command me," she said. "I am the—"

And here she paused, her voice suddenly ragged as she looked at Emmet, who had pushed the wagon back with one hand while holding onto Mountfellon with the other. Or rather she looked towards him but she saw instead Cook's body lying on the gravel, unmoving. She saw Hodge's dogs digging desperately at the riverbank. She saw Charlie being swamped by a tide of angry Sluagh. She saw Sharp falling. Again and again she saw Sharp falling, as he would now be for ever falling. She shook her head and nodded at Emmet in a kind of mute acknowledgement that said more than words might have.

". . . We, Emmet and I, are The Oversight now. And we have given our word."

"And I should take the word of a monster and a Jew?" he said.

"Yes," said Sara. "You should."

Emmet stepped forward and let the chain-box thud back onto the buffers.

"I am going to give Emmet this bracelet," she said. "You will give him the candle. He will place the bracelet around it to make doubly sure of the Wildfire. And then we will think about how we are to get ashore."

"You are very certain I will agree," said Mountfellon.

"I am only certain you are not a fool," she said, reaching the bracelet to Emmet's outstretched hand. "And only a fool and a little man would do what you were thinking of a moment ago."

"And you can read my mind?"

"No. But you believe you are worthy of greatness. You want power; you want knowledge; you do not want to take the coward's way out because in the moment before we both died, I would know it was the vengeful act of a vain and petty man, and you would know I knew it, and that is not how you would want to be seen at the end."

The boat tremored under their feet. He shook his head.

"I want more," he said. "If I give this back, I want your word on something."

Sara relaxed. She took no real pleasure in it. This was just duty now, but she could see the Wildfire would now be safe again. Whatever followed that was sure. This was just a negotiation.

"Tell me," she said.

He licked his lips and bared teeth that were, she thought, much more like yellowing fangs as he leant towards her.

"I want your word that—"

The Ghost's bullet missed Mountfellon by a good two yards.

The superheated jet of steam from the boiler which the bullet did hit did not miss him. It hit him foursquare in the side of the head. If Emmet had not got such a tight grip on him he would have been blown overboard, his face a flayed, hideous mess, but maybe still alive. Instead, the steam jet punched into his face, lifting the skin, flensing the smile from his teeth as his neck snapped back and mercifully killed the scream in his throat as it broke and bought him more mercy than he deserved.

But his hands dropped the Wildfire.

Fast as she was, Sara couldn't catch it.

Obstructed by Mountfellon's body as he was, neither could Emmet.

The candle hit the deck and fell out of the protective ring of oak, ash and thorn.

And as simple as that, the fire was free. Free and wild and hungry. And of all the things the Wildfire hungered for, the first among them was more fire, because fire breeds fire, and the Wildfire has a world to burn.

The candle hit the planking and shot towards the steam engine and the glowing firebox beneath it.

Sara didn't think. She just leapt for it, even as it flared, even as she knew she was too late, too far, too hopeless—

Emmet flung Mountfellon's corpse aside like a rag and grabbed her, stopping her dead in the air.

"No, Emm—!" was all she had time to gasp before he hurled her clear, high into the air, as far from the tug as he could manage. As she flew helplessly away, in the few seconds she was airborne she saw him turn and step into the obliterating fireball that belched out of the exploding steam engine. And then she hit the cold hard surface of the Thames and all the breath was knocked out of her and she was kicking and sinking and trying to tear herself back to the surface, and when she did so she saw the tall black funnel of the tug toppling lazily end over end as it fell out of the sky in an accompanying shower of flaming debris, and she ducked under as it hailed down all around her, and when she surfaced again,

there was silence.

And she was in the water, but she could not see the city.

And in this moment there is nothing but the pain of the now: no past, no future.

And she can see nothing but flame.

And failure.

And her hand, reaching, trying to catch the sky, trying to hold onto the air, trying to stop the growling river swallowing her too.

She is the last of the Last Hand.

She does not wonder if there will be another.

She does not wonder if one day The Smith will return and build anew.

She only wonders why snow is falling again, this early in the year.

CHAPTER 54

FIRE ON FIRE

The Wildfire would burn the city.

The Wildfire would burn the world.

The Wildfire would burn everything but itself.

And Emmet knows this. And that is why he walks into the fireball.

That is why he can walk into the fireball. That is why he was made. That is why he is a hollowness.

That is why he ignores his clothes flamed to cinders as they burn off his powerful clay body.

That is why he ignores the pain of the conflagration as it wraps around him, for Emmet does indeed feel pain. He feels it as keenly as if he was made of flesh and blood.

That is why, as the explosion bellies a rapidly expanding circle of flame across the Thames as it searches for new things to burn, he is reaching for the still, small point that will now not move until the world has been put ablaze by the spreading ripple of fire.

And that is why he grabs the tiny brightest candle flame at the centre of the light.

And crams it in his mouth.

The candle tumbles into the void inside him and he breathes in, and as he breathes in he grips the Green Man's bracelet and feels the deeproot strength of the oak and the healing of the ash and the resolute protection of the thorn, and he keeps breathing in.

And the sound of his inbreath is low, an almost subsonic scream borne on a mighty wind.

And the scream is a scream and it is his scream but it is only part pain and the other part is defiance, because Emmet is now, at the end, everything Sharp felt him to be, and part of the reason that he is this—a feeling being, with a mind of his own beyond mere mulish obedience—is because Jack Sharp befriended him and loved him and in so doing showed him how to be more than the empty clay automaton his original creator had made him to be.

So the pain was part physical, as the Wildfire hardened him, firing the wet clay of his body from within, beginning to turn him into that unmoving statue he sometimes resembled, and it was a heart's pain too, a farewell to the freedom of motion, of life.

The part of the scream that was defiance was life's own shout, hurled into the destructive core of the fire he was swallowing.

He felt his hand beginning to stiffen as the Wildfire acted like an internal kiln. Before he dropped it, he jammed the Green Man's bracelet around his wrist. The woven twigs stretched and a couple sprang free, but the amulet stayed together, and as he looked around the featureless, roaring world of fire in the middle of which he now stood, he saw the city slowly fade in and reappear as the ball of flame was sucked back towards him by his screaming indrawn breath, and then he saw it clear again, with no flames between him and it as the Wildfire was all pulled back inside him and he clamped his mouth shut, clenching his jaw tight.

Sara, in the water, surfaced in time to see him swallow the last of the Wildfire.

"Emmet!" she shouted.

The clay man turned towards her, moving with great effort now, with an unusually creaky movement. And in the instant before he toppled stiffly over the side of the tilting deck and disappeared into the water below, she saw three things.

His empty eye sockets were now full of fire.

He looked down at the hand on the arm that bore the Green Man's bracelet.

And then he looked up at her.

And tried to force his hardening face into a smile.

It is Sara who is now hollow inside. Where her heart was is nothing but a great void, an inner emptiness to match the brutal loss of her friends, her companions, her one true love.

Maybe it is the hollowness that keeps her afloat, moving downriver, away from Traitor's Gate, away from the cut at Irongate Steps, towards the great curve of Blackwall Reach, hidden around the bend ahead of her. Maybe it is this hollowness that stops her sinking into the comforting oblivion beneath the cold river water.

Maybe it's just duty.

She decides to cry later, and starts swimming towards the passing riverbank.

It is dark under the gravel, and he cannot move.

If he could move, he would move his hand inside his jacket and then he could light a candle and then he would be able to see and then he remembers he could not because he is blind and he would laugh if he could get a full breath, but he can't. There is hard gravel and cold mud between his teeth. He tries to move again but, despite his great strength, the weight of debris has him clamped tight.

He feels a sharp pain in his legs as he tries to twist and realises that they are broken.

It does not matter. He stops twisting. He will be gone soon.

Something growls in protest and he realises Jed is in his head.

He grins but his mouth is half full of mud and stones.

He remembers he can see through Jed's eyes if he tries and so he does so.

All he can see is a blur of gravel and mud and paws, too many paws and then he realises Archie is digging next to his father, the young dog tearing at the landslide with equal fury.

Hodge is glad he got Jed across that red-haired bitch. At least the bloodline will continue.

At least he is now seeing the light, even if it is through his terrier's eyes and not his own. At least he will not die in the dark. And Jed too is telling him he will not die alone.

That's something.

It feels like his chest is being crushed from all sides. He can't expand his lungs any more.

It doesn't matter. The air in the narrow pocket between the beam of wood and the gravel is not enough to breathe much more of anyway.

He is beginning to fade now. Even what he can see through Jed's eyes is becoming faint and jumpy. He can feel his grip on what was and what is beginning to loosen, maybe because what will be is now nothing, nothing and more nothing, for ever.

It's not so bad.

There is comfort in knowing he is not alone and he drifts into the past, to when he was a boy, to the long brutal night he spent trying to dig Jig, his first terrier, out of a collapsed hole in a riverbank just like this. The night his heart first broke. He'd failed, but he hadn't stopped digging until he'd found the dog's body, hoping for a miracle right up until the very last.

He'd sworn he'd never lose another dog, and he never had.

That was something.

And he now knew that not giving up on Jig had given the long-departed dog some comfort as it died in the dark, alone but not alone.

That was something else.

And the last thing he saw, before he lost his connection with Jed, was that other hands were joining the dogs' paws, helping scoop away the gravel, but they were not hands that he recognised, not friends' hands, they were hands looped and whorled with dark tattoos, the hands of enemies, impossible hands, and so he knew his oxygen-starved mind was now giving him hallucinations, and so before he lost the ability, he told Jed that he was the best friend he'd ever had and that he loved him, but that he would have to go now and it was all right.

He told him that Charlie Pyefinch would look after him now, and that he in turn should look after Archie who was a fine young pup but needed some . . .

. . . and then he forgot what the younger dog needed and told Jed to stop digging, because he could feel the dog's great heart pounding to bursting point, and he knew that Jed, being a terrier, would literally work himself to death rather than give up any kind of fight.

He told him he was a good dog.

And then the next shallow breath wouldn't draw in and the nothing he had known was coming arrived and the world went away.

And outside in the air a high keening note cut through the sound of the digging and the Sluagh paused in their work and looked down at the inconsolable dog howling up at the failing light through which snow was beginning to fall.

CHAPTER 55

TIME PASSED

And now, weeks later, it is Christmas and London lies buried under a deep blanket of snow, which for a brief, unsullied moment makes everything look magical and clean.

Out on the Isle of Dogs, on the coldest curve of Blackwall Reach, The Folley is silent. No smoke comes from the chimney, the kitchen is empty and the forge is cold. There are two long mounds between the holly and the rowan behind the forge. They are dug close to each other, as if for companionship and shared warmth against the cold. There are no head-stones, but one has a huge and much-used copper cooking pot on top of it, and the other has a narrow-bladed ratcatcher's spade at its head. There is an old half-barrel on its side by the spade, and inside this improvised kennel is a well-worn dog blanket.

Of the dog there is no sign.

The vacant lot in Wellclose Square where the Safe House once stood is a flat expanse of white, and the congregation emerging from the Danish Church in the middle of the square is treated to an uninterrupted view of St. George Street, the London Docks and the glitter of the river beyond.

* * *

In Templebanes' counting-house the snow on the skylights has brought an unaccustomed gloom to the long main room. A figure stands listening to the silence, just beside the stove where Abchurch met his end. He shakes himself, pulls a coat from the stool at his side and walks to the main door. He locks it, for it is his house now and he values its contents if not its history, and limps out into the street, heading north.

"Merry Christmas, Mr. Self!" says the greengrocer's boy, who is sweeping the snow from the pavement opposite.

The figure nods and gives him a smile.

Despite himself he hears the boy's thoughts.

'E's not like the rest of them Templebanes as used to live there. Maybe that's why 'e changed 'is name to Self. Anyway. 'E's all right, that one, for all 'e's a mute.

Amos Self grins. The boy is correct. He is all right. And he changed his name because he didn't belong to any damn Templebane. He took the name of the one person he did belong to.

In the Bedlam Hospital, Coram Templebane, now the last to bear the name, sits and looks out at the snow-covered courtyard below, wondering if Bill Ketch will bring him something special to eat for his Christmas meal when he has finished gently escorting the grey-haired madwoman who is carefully walking round and round, well muffled against the cold as she happily looks into the sky and snatches at the air, trying to catch snowflakes as they fall.

He does not hear the Ghost tell Ketch that they are not snowflakes, but May blossoms, and that now all is well and spring has come and her daughter will be coming to see her soon, and will no doubt bring sugar-plums as she did yesterday.

The house on Chandos Place is no longer milk-eyed and blank-looking. The opaque window-panes have been replaced with clear glass, and through it can be seen candles and the warm glow of the fires banked up within.

The whey-faced girl watches from the bedroom window opposite as a man's hand reaches up to the front door and knocks on it, the blood-stone ring on his finger making a sharp rapping noise.

A slender young woman, newly elegant in a green oiled silk riding habit, opens the door. Her dark hair is pulled back and her gloved hand, which she extends in greeting, also bears a ring.

"Amos," she says with a smile. "Welcome."

Merry Christmas, Lucy Harker.

He looks at the thick garlands of evergreen boughs decorating the hall behind her.

Your house is looking very festive.

"That was Ida. She and Charlie are in the kitchen arguing about the pudding," she says, beckoning him in. "And it's not just my house, Amos. It's all of ours."

Sara Falk is walking down the stairs, leaning on Emmet's arm to hide her limp.

"That's why it's called the Safe House," Sara says. "Now come in. Jack has been making something called a wassail cup from Cook's book of receipts and whatever it is I think we should help him drink it before he tastes any more. There's a severe danger he might start singing if he keeps sampling, and though I'd follow him to the end of the world, the truth is he couldn't carry a tune in a bucket."

Emmet moves with unaccustomed stiffness, which makes him almost stately as he walks at Sara's side.

In the aftermath of the massacre at Irongate Steps, Sara engaged another tug for three weeks, fruitlessly scouring the riverbed for his body, reporting her failure to the recovering Sharp every night. It was actually Jed who found him early one morning when Charlie, still recuperating from his own wounds, limped to the riverside at Traitor's Gate to see what the old dog was barking so insistently at: low tide had revealed a familiar clay hand wound around a rusting chain shackled to one of the pilings, just below the waterline. Emmet had seemingly hardened into a statue, and the Wildfire was gone from within him. They had taken the unmoving figure straight to The Folley in the dog cart, convinced he was lost, intending to inter him next to Cook and Hodge, only to have Sharp notice that his arm still bore the triple-wood bracelet, and claim he felt living warmth in his hand.

Sharp had insisted on sitting with him, holding that hand and talking to him and sleeping on a palette beside him for almost a week, after which the golem had slowly sat up one morning and leant over and woken the sleeping Sharp with a slow smile.

It was at that point that things generally seemed to have taken a turn for the better, and Emmet was well on the road to regaining his former mobility.

Amos smiles at the golem.

You have a new coat.

Emmet looks at him and nods slowly.

Jack Sharp gave it to me. He made a joke.

Jack Sharp made a joke?

He pretended he wouldn't give it to me until I told him where I have hidden the Wildfire.

And did you?

Of course not. It's our job to protect it. And it's safer if no one else knows, because then no one can tell.

And then when nobody else was looking, he winked at Amos behind Sara's back.

And I can't talk, Amos Self.

Lucy Harker remains behind in the doorway with her back to the plain Georgian grandeur of the pillared hall, looking out at the snow-muffled street. She can't believe this is her house, that she has a home, but she is Mountfellon's only child, and though she did not appear on any will he made, she did appear on the one his lawyers immediately believed he had made following a visit from Sara and Sharp. Lucy asked them if using their powers on the unsuspecting normal attorney was not a violation of The Oversight's prime mission, to stop the natural and the supranatural from preying on each other.

Sara had snorted and Sharp had gripped her shoulders and told her very firmly that Law and Lore was one thing, but that natural justice was there before they were. And he, and all of them had a great debt to nature, due to the healing power of the Green Man's triple-wood bracelets. The hidden force of the deep green was perhaps the oldest and most normally benign of the supranatural powers that The Oversight came into contact with, and they did that so rarely that Sharp understood very little of it. But he and Charlie certainly owed their lives to it.

She closed the door and followed the noise to join the others in the kitchen below, not thinking about Law and Lore, or natural justice, just happy there were so many of them down there: Sharp, Sara, Charlie Pyefinch, Amos and Emmet made five. A full complement for a Last Hand, even if Ida went back to Austria as she was due to do at the turn of the year.

And then there was the tall woman presently fussing over the glistening bronze turkey, the strangely reassuring one who had recently taken over the cooking (on the strict understanding this was only a temporary measure, as she and her tough and cheerful husband overwintered their wagon in the mews behind the house instead of their more normal out of season billet with the other show-people in the yard behind the Old Harry Inn). Who was to say they might not relent their current refusal and be the basis of a new, second hand? It would certainly make their son very happy to have Rose and Barnaby Pyefinch close by, especially since he was now going to be much less likely to travel, due to his new duties as Terrier Man to the Tower of London.

He would need something cheering if Ida left, thought Lucy, seeing how he watched the girl carefully topping up the water in the boiling pan in which the knotted muslin ball that contained Cook's last plum pudding was steaming. She had refused to let anyone near it in the weeks leading up to the feast, keeping it topped up with brandy and making it quite clear that Rose's culinary duties stopped at the precise point where she, Ida, would be fulfilling Cook's final wish.

That wasn't why Charlie was unable to stop looking at her. She was—

scandalously—not wearing her normal soft leather hunting garb, but a previously unsuspected tight-fitting dress and low-cut under-blouse which revealed a trim-waisted curvaceousness that her usual more utilitarian garb failed to make apparent.

"Not a dress, idiot," Ida had said with a toss of her pigtails when he'd first sputtered his surprise on seeing her in the unaccustomed clothes. "This is a special occasion, no? Can't be Trousers all the time. It's a dirndl."

"That's not a dirndl," Sara had said under her breath, for Sharp's ears only. "That's a provocation. Charlie's gone redder than Cook's handkerchief."

And then she saw that Lucy had overheard, and stared at her. Lucy had felt embarrassed for a moment until Sara dropped an eyelid at her in what was, most disconcertingly, a friendly wink.

Lucy looked at them all cheerfully arranging themselves around the groaning table piled high with all manner of festive foodstuff.

She was hoping it would not spoil their midwinter feast when she told them she would be taking a boat to America and going west on the Medicine Trail as soon as it opened up in the spring. There was another stolen child to take home, and though finding it would not bring Cait back to life, it would pay a debt.

The whey-faced girl looks away from the window as the front door closes on the Last Hand, and smiles at her father who has come to take her downstairs for the festive feast that she has been smelling all morning.

She does not exactly know who all the interesting characters are who have taken over the house on Chandos Place, but she is friends with Lucy who visits her often and tells the girl, who she calls her Good Samaritan, most amusing stories about the streets of the great city that she, as an invalid, is forbidden to visit.

She does not know who they all are, these five oddities who Lucy Harker once accidentally called the Last Hand.

But she does feel safer that they are there.

EPILOGUE

At the beginning there is noise.

At the beginning he is underground but he can hear the world above.

At this beginning, at the end of a long chain of beginnings, buried under the peat and the carefully laid rocks, he can see nothing but darkness.

But some ancient part of him can hear the soft fall of midwinter snow on the wild heather on the hill above.

This is not a new sensation.

He has, he recalls, been here before.

He is the first of the First Hand, as he is sworn to be the last of the Last, if it comes to that.

If it has not already come to that.

He will sleep now, and when the snow that is softly falling on the slopes above has gone, maybe then he will rise with the spring, next spring or maybe one of the ones that will come after.

He has not gone.

He is healing under the hill and the world will see him when it needs him, or when the black stain of the darkness has fully gone from his back. He can feel the blight of it now, and he knows why the Mother of Ravens trapped him beneath the ground.

As ever, for his own good.

Maybe when he next wakes, the black stain will be less, be gone even.

The Smith turns and closes his eyes. He will sleep again. But now he knows he will wake one day and leave the darkness in the darkness and climb back into the light.

And then he shall see what he shall see . . .

ACKNOWLEDGEMENTS

I'm really grateful, as ever to my editors, Jenni Hill and Joanna Kramer at Orbit UK, and to Will Hinton in the U.S. Just the right combination of tough and indulgent. Again thanks to Lauren Panepinto for the work on the covers. Thanks too to my agents Karolina Sutton at Curtis Brown and Michael McCoy at Independent for helping me juggle my book and screenwriting lives. Much gratitude to Morag Stewart for keeping me straight with the Gaelic. And most importantly, thanks to my family—all three generations—for tolerating the grumpily ursine version of myself that seems to accompany the writing of books.

There's a very well hidden and extraordinarily well preserved souterrain on North Uist that precisely matches the one in which we left The Smith: I'm really grateful to Hugh Potter for being kind enough to allow me to climb down and explore it. My old friend the traveller and writer Barnaby Rogerson has been fascinated with these carefully made stone-lined galleries since we were students and passed on his enthusiasm to me. No one has much idea what they were built for—they appear to have no obvious ritual significance and weren't used for burials, or food storage (as proved by absence of bodies or food debris). They seem to have been built, in Scotland at least, by the same Iron Age people who built the brochs, one of which is indeed close by the one I visited. Perhaps now we've seen where The Smith sleeps, we know at least one use.

If you want to see a picture of the *Monarch*, the sturdy paddle-steamer tug which Mountfellon hired from Mr. Watkins, chances are you probably already have—Turner painted it towing in the dismasted hulk of the Temeraire in one of his loveliest and saddest paintings.

The Fairy Flag which The Smith was so disappointed in is still held in Dunvegan Castle, and if you ask the MacLeods they may show it to you. Don't tell them it's an imposter. The fabled MacCrimmons were indeed the MacLeod's hereditary pipers for generations, until they inexplicably just stopped. Now you know why. If you want to see the small island cemetery in the river where The Smith expected to find the true flag, take the road from Portree to Skeabost and you'll find it to the west of the high bridge that crosses the River Snizort. Go at dusk. Don't slip on the way down.

The lead plates which interest Armbruster and Magill are very likely twins to the one found buried near the town of Pierre, North Dakota, left by the de la Vérendrye brothers in 1742 to claim territory as they pushed west across the Great Plains from their base in Quebec to become the first Europeans to see the Rockies from the east. As to why this is of concern to Armbruster and Magill, well, that's a whole other story . . . Caitlin Sean ná Gaolaire may well now have to share it with them.

extras

orbit

meet the author

CHARLIE FLETCHER is a screenwriter and children's author living in Edinburgh. His Stoneheart trilogy has been translated into a dozen languages and the film rights have been sold to Paramount. The first volume, *Stoneheart,* was shortlisted for the Branford Boase award and longlisted for the Guardian Children's Fiction Prize. His standalone novel for children, *Far Rockaway,* was published last year to great critical acclaim and has been longlisted for the Carnegie Prize. As a screenwriter, Charlie is currently working on two series, one for the BBC, the other for HBO.

Find out more about Charlie Fletcher and other Orbit authors by registering for the free monthly newsletter at www.orbitbooks.net.

introducing

If you enjoyed
THE REMNANT,
look out for

BATTLEMAGE

by Stephen Aryan

"I can command storms, summon fire and unmake stone,"
Balfruss growled. "It's dangerous to meddle with things
you don't understand."

***Balfruss** is a battlemage, sworn to fight and die for*
a country that fears and despises his kind.

***Vargus** is a common soldier—while mages shoot lightning*
from the walls of the city, he's down in the front lines
getting blood on his blade.

***Talandra** is a princess and spymaster, but the war may force*
her to risk everything and make the greatest sacrifice of all.

Chapter 1

Another light snow shower fell from the bleak grey sky. Winter should have been over, yet ice crunched underfoot and the mud was hard as stone. Frost clung to almost everything, and a thick, choking fog lay low on the ground. Only those desperate or greedy travelled in such conditions.

Two nights of sleeping outdoors had leached all the warmth from Vargus's bones. The tips of his fingers were numb and he couldn't feel his toes any more. He hoped they were still attached when he took off his boots; he'd seen it happen to others in the cold. Whole toes had come off and turned black without them noticing, rolling around like marbles in the bottom of their boots.

Vargus led his horse by the reins. It would be suicide for them both to ride in this fog.

Up ahead something orange flickered amid the grey and white. The promise of a fire gave Vargus a boost of energy and he stamped his feet harder than necessary. Although the fog muffled the sound, it would carry to the sentry up ahead on his left.

The bowman must have been sitting in the same position for hours as the grey blanket over his head was almost completely white.

As Vargus drew closer his horse snorted, picking up the scent of other animals, men and cooking meat. Vargus pretended he hadn't seen the man and tried very hard not to stare at his longbow. After stringing the bow with one quick flex the sentry readied an arrow, but in order to loose it he would have to stand up.

"That's far enough."

That came from another sentry on Vargus's right who stepped out from between the skeletons of two shattered trees. He was a burly man dressed in dirty furs and mismatched leathers. Although chipped and worn the long sword he carried looked sharp.

"You a King's man?"

Vargus snorted. "No, not me."

"What do you want?"

He shrugged. "A spot by your fire is all I'm after."

Despite the fog the sound of their voices must have carried as two others came towards them from the camp. The newcomers were much like the others, desperate men with scarred faces and mean eyes.

"You got any coin?" asked one of the newcomers, a bald and bearded man in old-fashioned leather armour.

Vargus shook his head. "Not much, but I got this." Moving slowly he pulled two wine skins down from his saddle. "Shael rice wine."

The first sentry approached. Vargus could still feel the other pointing an arrow at his back. With almost military precision the man went through his saddlebags, but his eyes nervously flicked towards Vargus from time to time. A deserter then, afraid someone had been sent after him.

"What we got, Lin?" called Baldy.

"A bit of food. Some silver. Not much else," the sentry answered.

"Let him pass."

Lin didn't step back. "Are you sure, boss?"

The others were still on edge. They were right to be nervous if they were who Vargus suspected. The boss came forward and keenly looked Vargus up and down. He knew what the boss was seeing. A man past fifty summers, battle scarred and

423

grizzled with liver spots on the back of his big hands. A man with plenty of grey mixed in with the black stubble on his face and head.

"You going to give us any trouble with that?" asked Baldy, pointing at the bastard sword jutting up from Vargus's right shoulder.

"I don't want no trouble. Just a spot by the fire and I'll share the wine."

"Good enough for me. I'm Korr. These are my boys."

"Vargus."

He gestured for Vargus to follow him and the others eased hands away from weapons. "Cold enough for you?"

"Reminds me of a winter, must be twenty years ago, up north. Can't remember where."

"Travelled much?"

Vargus grunted. "All over. Too much."

"So, where's home?" asked Korr. The questions were asked casually, but Vargus had no doubt about it being an interrogation.

"Right now, here."

They passed through a line of trees where seven horses were tethered. Vargus tied his horse up with the others and walked into camp. It was a good sheltered spot, surrounded by trees on three sides and a hill with a wide cave mouth on the other. A large roaring fire crackled in the middle of camp and two men were busy cooking beside it. One was cutting up a hare and dropping pieces into a bubbling pot, while the other prodded some blackened potatoes next to the blaze. All of the men were armed and they carried an assortment of weapons that looked well used.

As Vargus approached the fire a massive figure stood up and came around from the other side. It was over six and a half feet tall, dressed in a bear skin and wide as two normal men. The man's face was severely deformed with a protruding forehead, small brown eyes that were almost black, and a jutting bottom jaw with jagged teeth.

"Easy Rak," said Korr. The giant relaxed the grip on his sword and Vargus let out a sigh of relief. "He brought us something to drink."

Rak's mouth widened, revealing a whole row of crooked yellow teeth. It took Vargus a few seconds to realise the big man was smiling. Rak moved back to the far side of the fire and sat down again. Only then did Vargus move his hand away from the dagger on his belt.

He settled close to the fire next to Korr and for a time no one spoke, which suited him fine. He closed his eyes and soaked up some of the warmth, wiggling his toes inside his boots. The heat began to take the chill from his hands and his fingers started to tingle.

"Bit dangerous to be travelling alone," said Korr, trying to sound friendly.

"Suppose so. But I can take care of myself."

"Where you headed?"

Vargus took a moment before answering. "Somewhere I'll get paid and fed. Times are hard and I've only got what I'm carrying."

Since he'd mentioned his belongings he opened the first skin and took a short pull. The rice wine burned the back of his throat, leaving a pleasant aftertaste. After a few seconds the warmth in his stomach began to spread.

Korr took the offered wineskin but passed it to the next man, who snatched it from his hand.

"Rak. It's your turn on lookout," said Lin. The giant ignored him and watched as the wine moved around the fire. When it reached him he took a long gulp and then another before walking into the trees. The archer came back and another took his place as sentry. Two men standing watch for a group of seven in such extreme weather was unusual. They weren't just being careful, they were scared.

"You ever been in the King's army?" asked Lin.

Vargus met his gaze then looked elsewhere. "Maybe."

"I reckon that's why you travelled all over, dragged from place to place. One bloody battlefield after another. Home was just a tent and a fire. Different sky, different enemy."

"Sounds like you know the life. Are you a King's man?"

"Not any more," Lin said with a hint of bitterness.

It didn't take them long to drain the first wineskin so Vargus opened the second and passed it around the fire. Everyone took a drink again except Korr.

"Bad gut," he said when Vargus raised an eyebrow. "Even a drop would give me the shits."

"More for us," said one man with a gap-toothed grin.

When the stew was ready one of the men broke up the potatoes and added them to the pot. The first two portions went to the sentries and Vargus was served last. His bowl was smaller than the others, but he didn't complain. He saw a few chunks of potato and even one bit of meat. Apart from a couple of wild onions and garlic the stew was pretty bland, but it was hot and filling. The food, combined with the wine and the fire, helped warm him all the way through. An itchy tingling starting to creep back into his toes. It felt as if they were all still attached.

When they'd all finished mopping up the stew with some flat bread, and the second wineskin was empty, a comfortable silence settled on the camp. It seemed a shame to spoil it.

"So why're you out here?" asked Vargus.

"Just travelling. Looking for work, like you," said Korr.

"You heard any news from the villages around here?"

426

One of the men shifted as if getting comfortable, but Vargus saw his hand move to the hilt of his axe. Their fear was palpable.

Korr shook his head. "Not been in any villages. We keep to ourselves." The lie would have been obvious to a blind and deaf man.

"I heard about a group of bandits causing trouble in some of the villages around here. First it was just a bit of thieving and starting a couple of fights. Then it got worse when they saw a bit of gold." Vargus shook his head sadly. "Last week one of them lost control. Killed four men, including the innkeeper."

"I wouldn't know," said Korr. He was sweating now and it had nothing to do with the blaze. On the other side of the fire a snoozing man was elbowed awake and he sat up with a snort. The others were gripping their weapons with sweaty hands, waiting for the signal.

"One of them beat the innkeeper's wife half to death when she wouldn't give him the money."

"What's it matter to you?" someone asked.

Vargus shrugged. "Doesn't matter to me. But the woman has two children and they saw who done it. Told the village Elder all about it."

"We're far from the cities out here. Something like that isn't big enough to bring the King's men. They only come around these parts to collect taxes twice a year," said Lin with confidence.

"Then why do you all look like you're about to shit your-selves?" asked Vargus.

An uncomfortable silence settled around the camp, broken only by the sound of Vargus scratching his stubbly cheek.

"Is the King sending men after us?" asked Korr, forgoing any pretence of their involvement.

"It isn't the King you should worry about. I heard the village

Elders banded together, decided to do something themselves. They hired the Gath."

"Oh shit."

"He ain't real! He's just a myth."

"Lord of Light shelter me," one of the men prayed. "Lady of Light protect me."

"Those are just stories," scoffed Lin. "My father told me about him when I was a boy, more than thirty years ago."

"Then you've got nothing to worry about," Vargus grinned.

But it was clear they were still scared, more than before now that he'd stirred things up. Their belief in the Gath was so strong he could almost taste it in the air. For a while he said nothing and each man was lost in his own thoughts. Fear of dying gripped them all, tight as iron shackles.

Silence covered the camp like a fresh layer of snow and he let it sit a while, soaking up the atmosphere, enjoying the calm before it was shattered.

One of the men reached for a wineskin then remembered they were empty.

"What do we do, Korr?" asked one of the men. The others were scanning the trees as if they expected someone to rush into camp.

"Shut up, I'm thinking."

Before Korr came up with a plan Vargus stabbed him in the ribs. It took everyone a few seconds to realise what had happened. It was only when he pulled the dagger free with a shower of gore that they reacted.

Vargus stood up and drew the bastard sword from over his shoulder. The others tried to stand, but none of them could manage it. One man fell backwards, another tripped over his feet, landing on his face. Lin managed to make it upright, but then stumbled around as if drunk.

Vargus kicked Lin out of the way, switched to a two-handed grip and stabbed the first man on the ground through the back of the neck. He didn't have time to scream. The archer was trying to draw his short sword, but couldn't manage it. He looked up as Vargus approached and a dark patch spread across the front of his breeches. The edge of Vargus's sword opened the archer's throat and a quick stab put two feet of steel into Lin's gut. He fell back, squealing like a pig being slaughtered. Vargus knew his cries would bring the others.

The second cook was on his feet, but Vargus sliced off the man's right arm before he could throw his axe. Warm arterial blood jetted across Vargus's face. He grinned and wiped it away as the man fell back, howling in agony. Vargus let him thrash about for a while before putting his sword through the man's face, pinning his head to the ground. The snow around the corpse turned red, then it began to steam and melt.

The greasy-haired sentry stumbled into camp with a dagger held low. He swayed a few steps one way and then the other; the tamweed Vargus had added to the wine was taking effect. Bypassing Vargus he tripped over his own feet and landed face first on the fire. The sentry was screaming and the muscles in his arms and legs lacked the strength to lift him up. His cries turned into a gurgle and then trailed off as the smoke turned greasy and black. Vargus heard fat bubbling in the blaze and the smell reminded him of roast pork.

As he anticipated, Rak wasn't as badly affected as the others. His bulk didn't make him immune to the tamweed in the wine, but the side effects would take longer to show. Vargus was just glad that Rak had drunk quite a lot before going on duty. The giant managed to walk into camp in a straight line, but his eyes were slightly unfocused. Down at one side he carried a six-foot pitted blade.

Instead of waiting for the big man to go on the offensive, Vargus charged. Raising his sword above his head he screamed a challenge, but dropped to his knees at the last second and swept it in a downward arc. The Seveldrom steel cut through the flesh of Rak's left thigh, but the big man stumbled back before Vargus could follow up. With a bellow of rage Rak lashed out, his massive boot catching Vargus on the hip. It spun him around, his sword went flying and he landed on hands and knees in the snow.

Vargus scrambled around on all fours until his fingers found the hilt of his sword. He could hear Rak's blade whistling through the air towards him and barely managed to roll away before it came down where his head had been. Back on his feet he needed both hands to deflect a lethal cut which jarred his arms. Before he could riposte something crunched into his face. Vargus stumbled back, spitting blood and swinging his sword wildly to keep Rak at bay.

The big man came on. With the others already dead and his senses impaired, part of him must have known he was on borrowed time. Vargus ducked and dodged, turned the long blade aside and made use of the space around him. When Rak overreached he lashed out quickly, scoring a deep gash along the giant's ribs, but it didn't slow him down. Vargus inflicted a dozen wounds before Rak finally noticed that the red stuff splashed on the snow belonged to him.

With a grunt of pain he fell back and stumbled to one knee. His laboured breathing was very loud in the still air. It seemed to be the only sound for miles in every direction.

"Korr was right," he said in a voice that was surprisingly soft. "He said you'd come for us."

Vargus nodded. Taking no chances he rushed forward. Rak tried to raise his sword but even his prodigious strength was finally at an end. His arm twitched and that was all. No mercy was asked for and none was given. Using both hands Vargus thrust the point of his sword deep into Rak's throat. He pulled it clear and stepped back as blood spurted from the gaping wound. The giant fell onto his face and was dead.

By the fire Lin was still alive, gasping and coughing up blood. The wound in his stomach was bad and likely to make him suffer for days before it eventually killed him. Just as Vargus intended.

He ignored Lin's pleas as he retrieved the gold and stolen goods from the cave. Hardly a fortune, but it was a lot of money to the villagers.

He tied the horses' reins together and even collected up all the weapons, bundling them together in an old blanket. The bodies he left to the scavengers.

It seemed a shame to waste the stew. Nevertheless Vargus stuck two fingers down his throat and vomited into the snow until his stomach was empty. Using fresh snow he cleaned off the bezoar and stored it in his saddlebags. It had turned slightly brown from absorbing the poison in the wine Vargus had drunk, but he didn't want to take any chances so made himself sick again. He filled his waterskin with melting snow and sipped it to ease his raw throat.

Vargus's bottom lip had finally stopped bleeding, but when he spat a lump of tooth landed on the snow in a clot of blood. He took a moment to check his teeth and found one of his upper canines was broken in half.

"Shit."

With both hands he scooped more snow onto the fire until it was extinguished. He left the blackened corpse of the man where it had fallen amid wet logs and soggy ash. A partly cooked meal for the carrion eaters.

"Kill me. Just kill me!" screamed Lin. "Why am I still alive?" He gasped and coughed up a wadge of blood onto the snow.

With nothing left to do in camp Vargus finally addressed him. "Because you're not just a killer, Torlin Ke Tarro. You were a King's man. You came home because you were sick of war. Nothing wrong with that, plenty of men turn a corner and go on in a different way. But you became what you used to hunt."

Vargus squatted down beside the dying man, holding him in place with his stare.

Lin's pain was momentarily forgotten. "How do you know me? Not even Korr knew my name is Tarro."

Vargus ignored the question. "You know the land around here, the villages and towns, and you know the law. You knew how to cause just enough trouble without it bringing the King's men. You killed and stole from your own people."

"They ain't my people."

Vargus smacked his hands together and stood. "Time for arguing is over, boy. Beg your ancestors for kindness on the Long Road to Nor."

"My ancestors? What road?"

Vargus spat into the snow with contempt. "Pray to your Lantern God and his fucking whore then, or whatever you say these days. The next person you speak to won't be on this side of the Veil."

Ignoring Lin's pleas he led the horses away from camp and didn't look back. Soon afterwards the chill crept back in his fingers but he wasn't too worried. The aches and pains from sleeping outdoors were already starting to recede. The fight had given him a small boost, although it wouldn't sustain him for very long. The legend of the Gath was dead, which meant time for a change. He'd been delaying the inevitable for too long.

Carla, the village Elder, was standing behind the bar when Vargus entered the Duck and Crown. She was a solid woman who'd

432

seen at least fifty summers and took no nonsense from anyone, be they King or goat herder. With a face only her mother could love it was amazing she'd given birth to four healthy children who now had children of their own. Beyond raising a healthy family the village had prospered these last twenty years under her guidance.

Without being asked she set a mug of ale on the bar as he sat down. The tavern was deserted, which wasn't surprising with everything that had happened. On days like this people tended to spend more time with their loved ones.

"Done?"

Vargus drained the mug in several long gulps and then nodded. He set the bag of gold on the bar and watched as Carla counted it, but didn't take offence. The bandits could have spent some of it and he didn't know how much had been stolen. When she was finished Carla tucked it away and poured him another drink. After a moment's pause she tapped herself a mug. They drank in comfortable silence until both mugs were dry.

"How is everyone?" asked Vargus.

"Shook up. Murder's one thing we've seen before, in anger or out of greed, but this was something else. The boy might get over it, being so young, but not the girl. That one will be marked for life."

"And their mother?"

Carla grunted. "Alive. Not sure if that's a blessing or a curse. When she's back on her feet she'll run this place with her brother. She'll do all right."

"I brought in a stash of weapons and their horses too. You'll see she gets money for it?"

"I will. And I'll make sure Tibs gives her a fair price for the animals."

The silence in the room took on a peculiar edge, making the hairs stand up on the back of his neck.

"You hear the news coming in?" asked Carla. There was an unusual tone to her voice, but Vargus couldn't place it. All he knew was it made him nervous.

"Some," he said, treading carefully and looking for the trap door. He knew it was there, somewhere in the dark, and he was probably walking straight towards it.

"Like what?" asked Carla.

"A farmer on the road in told me the King's called on everyone that can fight. Said that war was coming here to Seveldrom, but he didn't know why."

"The west has been sewn together by King Raeza's son, Taikon."

Vargus raised an eyebrow. "How'd he manage that?"

"Religion, mostly. You know what it's like in Zecorria and Morrinow, people praying all the time. One story has our King pissing on an idol of the Lord of Light and wiping his arse with a painting of the Blessed Mother."

"That's a lie."

Carla grunted. "So are all the other stories about him killing priests and burning down temples. Sounds to me like someone was just itching for a war. A chance to get rid of all us heathens," she said, gesturing at the idol of the Maker on a shelf behind her. Most in Seveldrom prayed to the Maker, but those that didn't were left alone, not killed or shunned for being different. Religion and law stayed separate, but it was different for the Morrin and Zecorrans.

"What about the others in the west? They aren't mad on religion, and no one can make the Vorga do anything they don't want to."

Carla shrugged. "All people are saying is that something bad happened down in Shael. A massacre, bodies piled tall as trees, cities turned to rubble because they wouldn't fight. After that it sounds like the others fell in line."

"So what happened to King Raeza then? Is he dead?"

"Looks like. People are saying Taikon killed his father, took the Zecorran throne and now he's got himself a magician called the Warlock. There's a dozen stories about that one," said Carla, wiping the bar with a cloth even though it was already clean. "I heard he can summon things from beyond the Veil."

"I didn't think you were one to believe gossip," scoffed Vargus.

Carla gave him a look that made men piss themselves, but it just slid off him. She shook her head, smiling for a moment and then it was gone.

"I don't, but I know how to listen and separate the shit from the real gold. Whatever the truth about this Warlock, and the union in the west, I know it means trouble. And lots of it."

"War then."

Carla nodded. "Maybe they think our King really is a heretic or maybe it's because they enjoy killing, like the Vorga. Most reckon they'll be here come spring. Trade routes to the west have dried up in the last few days. Merchants trying to sneak through were caught and hung. Whole trees full of the greedy buggers line the north and southern pass. The crows and magpies are fat as summer solstice pheasants from all their feasting."

"What will you do?"

Carla puffed out her cheeks. "Look after the village, same as always. Fight, if the war comes this far east. Although if it comes here, we've already lost. What about you? I suppose you'll be going to fight?"

There was that odd tone to her voice again. He just nodded,

not trusting himself to speak. One wrong word and he'd plummet into the dark.

"People like you around here. And not just for sorting out the bandits," said Carla scrubbing the same spot on the bar over and over. "You know I lost my Jintor five winters back from the damp lung. The house is quiet without him, especially now that the children are all grown up. Fourth grandchild will be along any day, but there's still a lot that needs doing. Looking after the village, working with the other Elders, easily enough work for two."

In all the years he'd known her it was the most Vargus had ever heard her say about her needs. The strain was starting to show on her face.

He settled her frantic hand by wrapping it in both of his. Her skin was rough from years of hard labour, but it was also warm and full of life. For the first time since he'd arrived she looked him in the eye. Her sharp blue eyes were uncertain.

"I can't," Vargus said gently. "It's not who I am."

Carla pulled her hand free and Vargus looked away first, not sure if he was sparing her or himself.

"What about the legend of the Gath?"

He dismissed it with a wave. "It was already fading, and me with it. There aren't many that believe, fewer still that are afraid. It's my own fault, I guess. I kept it too small for too long. It would only keep me for a few more years at best. This war is my best way."

Carla was the only one in the village who knew some of the truth about him. She didn't claim to understand, but she'd listened and accepted it because of who he was and what he could do. It seemed churlish to hide anything from her at this point. He waited, but to his surprise she didn't ask for the rest.

"So you'll fight?"

"I will," declared Vargus. "I'll travel to Charas to fight and bleed and kill. For the King, for the land and for those who can't defend themselves. I'll swear an oath, by the iron in my blood, to fight in the war until it's done. One way or the other."

Carla was quiet for a time. Eventually she shook her head and he thought he saw a tear in her eye, but maybe it was just his imagination.

"If anyone else said something like that, I'd tell them they were a bloody fool. But they're not just words with you, are they?"

"No. It's my vow. Once made it can't be broken. If I stay here, I'll be dead in a few years. At least this way, I have a chance."

Reaching under the counter Carla produced a dusty red bottle that was half empty. Taking down two small glasses she poured them each a generous measure of a syrupy blue spirit.

"Then I wish you luck," said Carla, raising her glass.

"I'll drink to that, and I hope if I ever come back, I'll still be welcome."

"Of course."

They tapped glasses and downed the spirit in one gulp. It burned all the way down Vargus's throat before lighting a pleasant fire in his belly. They talked a while longer, but the important words had been said and his course decided.

In the morning, Vargus would leave the village that had been his home for the last forty years, and go to war.

introducing

If you enjoyed
THE REMNANT,
look out for

A CROWN FOR COLD SILVER

by Alex Marshall

"It was all going so nicely, right up until the massacre."

*Twenty years ago, feared general Cobalt Zosia led her
five villainous captains and mercenary army into battle,
wrestling monsters and toppling an empire. When there
were no more titles to win and no more worlds to conquer,
she retired and gave up her legend to history.*

*Now, the peace she carved for herself has been shattered by the
unprovoked slaughter of her village. Seeking bloody vengeance,
Zosia heads for battle once more, but to find justice she must
confront grudge-bearing enemies, once-loyal allies, and an
unknown army that marches under a familiar banner.*

Five villains. One legendary general.
A final quest for vengeance.

Chapter 1

It was all going so nicely, right up until the massacre.

Sir Hjortt's cavalry of two hundred spears fanned out through the small village, taking up positions between half-timbered houses in the uneven lanes that only the most charitable of surveyors would refer to as "roads." The warhorses slowed and then stopped in a decent approximation of unison, their riders sitting as stiff and straight in their saddles as the lances they braced against their stirrups. It was an unseasonably warm afternoon in the autumn, and after their long approach up the steep valley, soldier and steed alike dripped sweat, yet not a one of them removed their brass skullcap. Weapons, armor, and tack glowing in the fierce alpine sunlight, the faded crimson of their cloaks covering up the inevitable stains, the cavalry appeared to have ridden straight out of a tale, or galloped down off one of the tapestries in the mayor's house.

So they must have seemed to the villagers who peeked through their shutters, anyway. To their colonel, Sir Hjortt, they looked like hired killers on horseback barely possessed of sense to do as they were told most of the time. Had the knight been able to train wardogs to ride he should have preferred them to the Fifteenth Cavalry, given the amount of faith he placed in this lot. Not much, in other words, not very much at all.

He didn't care for dogs, either, but a dog you could trust, even if it was only to lick his balls.

The hamlet sprawled across the last stretch of grassy meadow before the collision of two steep, bald-peaked mountains. Murky forest edged in on all sides, like a snare the wilderness had set for the unwary traveler. A typical mountain town here in the Kutumban range, then, with only a low reinforced stone wall to keep out the wolves and what piddling avalanches the encircling slopes must bowl down at the settlement when the snows melted.

Sir Hjortt had led his troops straight through the open gate in the wall and up the main track to the largest house in the village…which wasn't saying a whole lot for the building. Fenced in by shedding rosebushes and standing a scant two and a half stories tall, its windowless redbrick face was broken into a grid by the black timbers that supported it. The mossy thatched roof rose up into a witch's hat, and set squarely in the center like a mouth were a great pair of doors tall and wide enough for two riders to pass through abreast without removing their helmets. As he reached the break in the hedge at the front of the house, Sir Hjortt saw that one of these oaken doors was ajar, but just as he noticed this detail the door eased shut.

Sir Hjortt smiled to himself, and, reining his horse in front of the rosebushes, called out in his deepest baritone, "I am Sir Efrain Hjortt of Azgaroth, Fifteenth Colonel of the Crimson Empire, come to counsel with the mayor's wife. I have met your lord mayor upon the road, and while he reposes at my camp—"

Someone behind him snickered at that, but when Sir Hjortt turned in his saddle he could not locate which of his troops was the culprit. It might have even come from one of his two personal Chainite guards, who had stopped their horses at the border of the thorny hedge. He gave both his guards and the riders nearest them the sort of withering scowl his father was overly fond of doling out. This was no laughing matter, as should have been perfectly obvious from the way Sir Hjortt had dealt with the hillbilly mayor of this shitburg.

"Ahem." Sir Hjortt turned back to the building and tried

again. "Whilst your lord mayor reposes at my camp, I bring tidings of great import. I must speak with the mayor's wife at once."

Anything? Nothing. The whole town was silently, fearfully watching him from hiding, he could feel it in his aching thighs, but not a one braved the daylight either to confront or assist him. Peasants—what a sorry lot they were.

"I say again!" Sir Hjortt called, goading his stallion into the mayor's yard and advancing on the double doors. "As a colonel of the Crimson Empire and a knight of Azgaroth, I shall be welcomed by the family of your mayor, or—"

Both sets of doors burst open, and a wave of hulking, shaggy beasts flooded out into the sunlight—they were on top of the Azgarothian before he could wheel away or draw his sword. He heard muted bells, obviously to signal that the ambush was under way, and the hungry grunting of the pack, and—

The cattle milled about him, snuffling his horse with their broad, slimy noses, but now that they had escaped the confines of the building they betrayed no intention toward further excitement.

"Very sorry, sir," came a hillfolk-accented voice from somewhere nearby, and then a small, pale hand appeared amid the cattle, rising from between the bovine waves like the last, desperate attempt of a drowning man to catch a piece of driftwood. Then the hand seized a black coat and a blond boy of perhaps ten or twelve vaulted himself nimbly into sight, landing on the wide back of a mountain cow and twisting the creature around to face Sir Hjortt as effortlessly as the Azgarothian controlled his warhorse. Despite this manifest skill and agility at play before him, the knight remained unimpressed.

"The mayor's wife," said Sir Hjortt. "I am to meet with her. Now. Is she in?"

"I expect so," said the boy, glancing over his shoulder—checking the position of the sun against the lee of the mountains towering over the village, no doubt. "Sorry again 'bout my cows. They're feisty, sir; had to bring 'em down early on account of a horned wolf being seen a few vales over. And I, uh, didn't have the barn door locked as I should have."

"Spying on us, eh?" said Sir Hjortt. The boy grinned. "Perhaps I'll let it slide this once, if you go and fetch your mistress from inside."

"Mayoress is probably up in her house, sir, but I'm not allowed 'round there anymore, on account of my wretched behavior," said the boy with obvious pride.

"This isn't her home?" Hjortt eyed the building warily.

"No, sir. This is the barn."

Another chuckle from one of his faithless troops, but Sir Hjortt didn't give whoever it was the satisfaction of turning in his saddle a second time. He'd find the culprit after the day's business was done, and then they'd see what came of having a laugh at their commander's expense. Like the rest of the Fifteenth Regiment, the cavalry apparently thought their new colonel was green because he wasn't yet twenty, but he would soon show them that being young and being green weren't the same thing at all.

Now that their cowherd champion had engaged the invaders, gaily painted doors began to open and the braver citizenry slunk out onto their stoops, clearly awestruck at the Imperial soldiers in their midst. Sir Hjortt grunted in satisfaction—it had been so quiet in the hamlet that he had begun to wonder if the villagers had somehow been tipped off to his approach and scampered away into the mountains.

"Where's the mayor's house, then?" he said, reins squeaking in his gauntlets as he glared at the boy.

"See the trail there?" said the boy, pointing to the east. Following the lad's finger down a lane beside a longhouse, Sir Hjortt saw a small gate set in the village wall, and beyond that a faint trail leading up the grassy foot of the steepest peak in the valley.

"My glass, Portolés," said Sir Hjortt, and his bodyguard walked her horse over beside his. Sir Hjortt knew that if he carried the priceless item in his own saddlebag one of his thuggish soldiers would likely find a way of stealing it, but not a one of them would dare try that shit with the burly war nun. She handed it over and Sir Hjortt withdrew the heavy brass hawkglass from its sheath; it was the only gift his father had ever given him that wasn't a weapon of some sort, and he relished any excuse to use it. Finding the magnified trail through the instrument, he tracked it up the meadow to where the path entered the surrounding forest. A copse of yellowing aspen interrupted the pines and fir, and, scanning the hawkglass upward, he saw that this vein of gold continued up the otherwise evergreen-covered mountain.

"See it?" the cowherd said. "They live back up in there. Not far."

———

Sir Hjortt gained a false summit and leaned against one of the trees. The thin trunk bowed under his weight, its copper leaves hissing at his touch, its white bark leaving dust on his cape. The series of switchbacks carved into the increasingly sheer mountainside had become too treacherous for the horses, and so Sir Hjortt and his two guards, Brother Iqbal and Sister Portolés, had proceeded up the scarps of exposed granite on foot. The possibility of a trap had not left the knight, but nothing more hostile than a hummingbird had showed itself on the hike, and now that his eyes had adjusted to the strangely diffuse light of this latest grove, he saw a modest, freshly whitewashed house perched on the lip of the next rock shelf.

Several hundred feet above them. Brother Iqbal laughed and Sister Portolés cursed, yet her outburst carried more humor in it than his. Through the trees they went, and then made the final ascent.

"Why…" puffed Iqbal, the repurposed grain satchel slung over one meaty shoulder retarding his already sluggish pace, "in all the…devils of Emeritus…would a mayor…live…so far…from his town?"

"I can think of a reason or three," said Portolés, setting the head of her weighty maul in the path and resting against its long shaft. "Take a look behind us."

Sir Hjortt paused, amenable to a break himself—even with only his comparatively light riding armor on, it was a real asshole of a hike. Turning, he let out an appreciative whistle. They had climbed quickly, and spread out below them was the painting-perfect hamlet nestled at the base of the mountains. Beyond the thin line of its walls, the lush valley fell away into the distance, a meandering brook dividing east ridge from west. Sir Hjortt was hardly a single-minded, bloodthirsty brute, and he could certainly appreciate the allure of living high above one's vassals, surrounded by the breathtaking beauty of creation. Perhaps when this unfortunate errand was over he would convert the mayor's house into a hunting lodge, wiling away his summers with sport and relaxation in the clean highland air.

"Best vantage in the valley," said Portolés. "Gives the head-person plenty of time to decide how to greet any guests."

"Do you think she's put on a kettle for us?" said Iqbal hopefully. "I could do with a spot of hunter's tea."

"About this mission, Colonel…" Portolés was looking at Sir Hjortt but not meeting his eyes. She'd been poorly covering up her discomfort with phony bravado ever since he'd informed her what needed to be done here, and the knight could well imagine what would come next. "I wonder if the order—"

"And I wonder if your church superiors gave me the use of you two anathemas so that you might hem and haw and question me at every pass, instead of respecting my command as an Imperial colonel," said Sir Hjortt, which brought bruise-hued blushes to the big woman's cheeks. "Azgaroth has been a proud and faithful servant of the Kings and Queens of Samoth for near on a century, whereas your popes seem to revolt every other feast day, so remind me again, what use have I for your counsel?"

Portolés muttered an apology, and Iqbal fidgeted with the damp sack he carried.

"Do you think I relish what we have to do? Do you think I would put my soldiers through it, if I had a choice? Why would I give such a command, if it was at all avoidable? Why—" Sir Hjortt was just warming to his lecture when a fissure of pain opened up his skull. Intense and unpleasant as the sensation was, it fled in moments, leaving him to nervously consider the witchborn pair. Had one of them somehow brought on the headache with their devilish ways? Probably not; he'd had a touch of a headache for much of the ride up, come to think of it, and he hadn't even mentioned the plan to them then.

"Come on," he said, deciding it would be best to drop the matter without further pontification. Even if his bodyguards did have reservations, this mission would prove an object lesson that it is always better to rush through any necessary unpleasantness, rather than drag your feet and overanalyze every ugly detail. "Let's be done with this. I want to be down the valley by dark, bad as that road is."

They edged around a hairpin bend in the steep trail, and

then the track's crudely hewn stair delivered them to another plateau, and the mayor's house. It was similar in design to those in the hamlet, but with a porch overhanging the edge of the mild cliff and a low white fence. Pleasant enough, thought Sir Hjortt, except that the fence was made of bone, with each outwardly bowed moose-rib picket topped with the skull of a different animal. Owlbat skulls sat between those of marmot and hill fox, and above the door of the cabin rested an enormous one that had to be a horned wolf; when the cowherd had mentioned such a beast being spied in the area, Sir Hjortt had assumed the boy full of what his cows deposited, but maybe a few still prowled these lonely mountains. What a thrill it would be, to mount a hunting party for such rare game! Then the door beneath the skull creaked, and a figure stood framed in the doorway.

"Well met, friends, you've come a long way," the woman greeted them. She was brawny, though not so big as Portolés, with features as hard as the trek up to her house. She might have been fit enough once, in a country sort of way, when her long, silvery hair was blond or black or red and tied back in pigtails the way Hjortt liked... but now she was just an old woman, same as any other, fifty winters young at a minimum. Judging from the tangled bone fetishes hanging from the limbs of the sole tree that grew inside the fence's perimeter—a tall, black-barked aspen with leaves as hoary as her locks—she might be a sorceress, to boot.

Iqbal returned her welcome, calling, "Well met, Mum, well met indeed. I present to you Sir Hjortt of Azgaroth, Fifteenth Colonel of the Crimson Empire." The anathema glanced to his superior, but when Sir Hjortt didn't fall all over himself to charge ahead and meet a potential witch, Iqbal murmured, "She's just an old bird, sir, nothing to fret about."

"Old bird or fledgling, I wouldn't blindly stick my hand in an owlbat's nest," Portolés said, stepping past Sir Hjortt and Iqbal to address the old woman in the Crimson tongue. "In the names of the Pontiff of the West and the Queen of the Rest, I order you out here into the light, woman."

"Queen of the Rest?" The woman obliged Portolés, stepping down the creaking steps of her porch and approaching the fence. For a mayor's wife, her checked dirndl was as plain as any village girl's. "And Pontiff of the West, is it? Last peddler we had through here brought tidings that Pope Shanatu's war wasn't going so well, but I gather much has changed. Is this sovereign of the Rest, blessed whoever she be, still Queen Indsorith? And does this mean peace has once again been brokered?"

"This bird hears a lot from her tree," muttered Sir Hjortt, then asked the woman, "Are you indeed the mayor's wife?"

"I am Mayoress Vivi, wife of Leib," said she. "And I ask again, respectfully, to whom shall I direct my prayers when next I—"

"The righteous reign of Queen Indsorith continues, blessed be her name," said Sir Hjortt. "Pope Shanatu, blessed be *his* name, received word from on high that his time as Shepherd of Samoth has come to an end, and so the war is over. His niece Jirella, blessed be *her* name, has ascended to her rightful place behind the Onyx Pulpit, and taken on the title of Pope Y'Homa III, Mother of Midnight, Shepherdess of the Lost."

"I see," said the mayoress. "And in addition to accepting a rebel pope's resignation and the promotion of his kin to the same lofty post, our beloved Indsorith, long may her glory persist, has also swapped out her noble title? 'Queen of Samoth, Heart of the Star, Jewel of Diadem, Keeper of the Crimson Empire' for, ah, 'Queen of the Rest'?" The woman's faintly lined face wrinkled further as she smiled, and Portolés slyly returned it.

"Do not mistake my subordinate's peculiar sense of humor for a shift in policy—the queen's honorifics remain unchanged," said Sir Hjortt, thinking of how best to discipline Portolés. If she thought that sort of thing flew with her commanding colonel just because there were no higher-ranked clerical witnesses to her dishonorable talk, the witchborn freak had another thing coming. He almost wished she would refuse to carry out his command, so he'd have an excuse to get rid of her altogether. In High Azgarothian, he said, "Portolés, return to the village and give the order. In the time it will take you to make it down I'll have made myself clear enough."

Portolés stiffened and gave Sir Hjortt a pathetic frown that told him she'd been holding out hope that he would change his mind. Not bloody likely. Also in Azgarothian, the war nun said, "I'm...I'm just going to have a look inside before I do. Make sure it's safe, Colonel Hjortt."

"By all means, Sister Portolés, welcome, welcome," said the older woman, also in that ancient and honorable tongue of Sir Hjortt's ancestors. Unexpected, that, but then the Star had been a different place when this biddy was in her prime, and perhaps she had seen more of it than just her remote mountain. Now that she was closer he saw that her cheeks were more scarred than wrinkled, a rather gnarly one on her chin, and for the first time since their arrival, a shadow of worry played across the weathered landscape of her face. Good. "I have an old hound sleeping in the kitchen whom I should prefer you left to his dreams, but am otherwise alone. But, good Colonel, Leib was to have been at the crossroads this morning..."

Sir Hjortt ignored the mayor's wife, following Portolés through the gate onto the walkway of flat, colorful stones that crossed the yard. They were artlessly arranged; the first order of business would be to hire the mason who had done the bathrooms at his family estate in Cockspar, or maybe the woman's apprentice, if the hoity-toity artisan wasn't willing to journey a hundred leagues into the wilds to retile a walk. A mosaic of miniature animals would be nice, or maybe indigo shingles could be used to make it resemble a creek. But then they had forded a rill on their way up from the village, so why not have somebody trace it to its source and divert it this way, have an actual stream flow through the yard? It couldn't be that hard to have it come down through the trees there and then run over the cliff beside the deck, creating a miniature waterfall that—

"Empty," said Portolés, coming back outside. Sir Hjortt had lost track of himself—it had been a steep march up, and a long ride before that. Portolés silently moved behind the older woman, who stood on the walk between Sir Hjortt and her house. The matron looked nervous now, all right.

"My husband Leib, Colonel Hjortt. Did you meet him at the crossroads?" Her voice was weaker now, barely louder than the quaking aspens. That must be something to hear as one lay in bed after a hard day's hunt, the rustling of those golden leaves just outside your window.

"New plan," said Sir Hjortt, not bothering with the more formal Azgarothian, since she spoke it anyway. "Well, it's the same as the original, mostly, but instead of riding down before dark we'll bivouac here for the night." Smiling at the old woman, he said, "Do not fret, Missus Mayor, do not fret, I won't be garrisoning my soldiers in your town, I assure you. Camp them outside the wall, when they're done. We'll ride out at first"—the thought of sleeping in on a proper bed occurred to him—"noon. We ride at noon tomorrow. Report back to me when it's done."

"Whatever you're planning, sir, let us parley before you commit yourself," said the old woman, seeming to awaken from the anxious spell their presence had cast upon her. She had a stern bearing he wasn't at all sure he liked. "Your officer can surely tarry a few minutes before delivering your orders, especially if we are to have you as our guests for the night. Let us speak, you and I, and no matter what orders you may have, no matter how pressing your need, I shall make it worth your while to have listened."

Portolés's puppy-dog eyes from over the woman's shoulder turned Sir Hjortt's stomach. At least Iqbal had the decency to keep his smug gaze on the old woman.

"Whether or not she is capable of doing so, Sister Portolés will *not* wait," said Sir Hjortt shortly. "You and I are talking, and directly, make no mistake, but I see no reason to delay my subordinate."

The old woman looked back past Portolés, frowning at the open door of her cabin, and then shrugged. As if she had any say at all in how this would transpire. Flashing a patently false smile at Sir Hjortt, she said, "As you will, fine sir. I merely thought you might have use for the sister as we spoke, for we may be talking for some time."

Fallen Mother have mercy, did every single person have a better idea of how Sir Hjortt should conduct himself than he did? This would not stand.

"My good woman," he said, "it seems that we have even more to parley than I previously suspected. Sister Portolés's business is pressing, however, and so she must away before we embark on this long conversation you so desire. Fear not, however, for the terms of supplication your husband laid out to us at the crossroads shall be honored, reasonable as they undeniably are. Off with you, Portolés."

Portolés offered him one of her sardonic salutes from over the older woman's shoulder, and then stalked out of the yard, looking as petulant as he'd ever seen her. Iqbal whispered something to her as he moved out of her way by the gate, and wasn't fast enough in his retreat when she lashed out at him. The war nun flicked the malformed ear that emerged from Iqbal's pale tonsure like the outermost leaf of an overripe cabbage, rage rendering her face even less appealing, if such a thing was possible. Iqbal swung his heavy satchel at her in response, and although Portolés dodged the blow, the dark bottom of the sackcloth misted her with red droplets as it whizzed past her face. If the sister noticed the blood on her face, she didn't seem to care, dragging her feet down the precarious trail, her maul slung over one hunched shoulder.

"My husband," the matron whispered, and, turning back to her, Sir Hjortt saw that her wide eyes were fixed on Iqbal's dripping sack.

"Best if we talk inside," said Sir Hjortt, winking at Iqbal and ushering the woman toward her door. "Come, come, I have an absolutely brilliant idea about how you and your people might help with the war effort, and I'd rather discuss it over tea."

"You said the war was over," the woman said numbly, still staring at the satchel.

"So it is, so it is," said Sir Hjortt. "But the *effort* needs to be made to ensure it doesn't start up again, what? Now, what do you have to slake the thirst of servants of the Empire, home from the front?"

She balked, but there was nowhere to go, and so she led Sir Hjortt and Brother Iqbal inside. It was quiet in the yard, save for the trees and the clacking of the bone fetishes when the wind ran its palm down the mountain's stubbly cheek. The screaming didn't start until after Sister Portolés had returned to the village, and down there they were doing enough of their own to miss the echoes resonating from the mayor's house.